# The
# Armless
# Maiden

## Other Anthologies Edited by Terri Windling

*Elsewhere 1* (with Mark Alan Arnold)
*Elsewhere 2* (with Mark Alan Arnold)
*Elsewhere 3* (with Mark Alan Arnold)

*Faery*

*Borderland* (with Mark Alan Arnold)
*Bordertown* (with Mark Alan Arnold)
*Life on the Border*

*Snow White, Blood Red* (with Ellen Datlow)
*Black Thorn, White Rose* (with Ellen Datlow)
*Ruby Slippers, Golden Tears* (with Ellen Datlow)

*The Year's Best Fantasy, First Annual Collection* (with Ellen Datlow)
*The Year's Best Fantasy, Second Annual Collection* (with Ellen Datlow)
*The Year's Best Fantasy and Horror, Third Annual Collection* (with Ellen Datlow)
*The Year's Best Fantasy and Horror, Fourth Annual Collection* (with Ellen Datlow)
*The Year's Best Fantasy and Horror, Fifth Annual Collection* (with Ellen Datlow)
*The Year's Best Fantasy and Horror, Sixth Annual Collection* (with Ellen Datlow)
*The Year's Best Fantasy and Horror, Seventh Annual Collection* (with Ellen Datlow)

# The
# Armless
# Maiden

◆ ◆ ◆ ◆ ◆

## and Other Tales for Childhood's Survivors

EDITED BY

## TERRI WINDLING

A Tom Doherty Associates Book
New York

THE ARMLESS MAIDEN AND OTHER TALES FOR CHILDHOOD'S SURVIVORS

*This book would not exist without the faith of the good people at Tor Books (particularly Tom Doherty, Beth Meacham, and Patrick Nielsen Hayden); the work of Donald G. Keller and Teresa Nielsen Hayden; and the encouragement I received in Boston: from the Endicott Studio Women's Art Group, the old Sunday morning "art bar" crowd, and also Paul Plaskey, Joanna Volpe, and Dr. Laurel Rice at Massachusetts General Hospital. Thank you all for the help you've given so generously, and in so many ways.*

—T.W.

Design by Lynn Newmark

This book is printed on acid-free paper.

A Tor Book
Published by Tom Doherty Associates, Inc.
175 Fifth Avenue
New York, N.Y. 10010

Tor® is a registered trademark of Tom Doherty Associates, Inc.

Library of Congress Cataloging-in-Publication Data

The armless maiden and other tales of childhood's survivors  /  Terri
   Windling, editor.
        p.     cm.
      "A Tom Doherty Associates book."
      ISBN 0-312-85234-7
      1. Fantastic fiction, American. 2. Fantasy—Therapeutic use.
3. Children—Fiction. I. Windling, Terri.
PS648.F3A7 1995
813'.087660852054—dc20                                    94-47224
                                                              CIP

First edition: April 1995

Printed in the United States of America

0 9 8 7 6 5 4 3 2 1

# Copyright Acknowledgements

# Contents

# 8 ✦✦✦ Contents

"Deeper meaning resides
in the fairy tales told to me in my childhood
than in any truth
that is taught in life."

—Johann C. Friedrich von Schiller

"When a woman tells the truth, she makes
room for more truth around her."

—Adrienne Rich

"If you've got skeletons in the family
closet, then you might as well make them dance."

—George Bernard Shaw

# The
# Armless
# Maiden

# Introduction

*The Armless Maiden* is a theme anthology, that theme being childhood and its darker passages. Yet it was not created in the usual anthology fashion. It grew, over three years, out of conversations and correspondence, out of shared tales, artwork, memories, and dreams. Creating this book was less like compiling text for an anthology than like building a collage: a collage made of voices. The background voice is my own, the stories that have meant the most to me in twenty years of working with fairy tales. Arranged against that background are the answering voices of thirty-three other writers.

This is a book *about* childhood; but, even though it is full of fairy stories, it is not a book *for* children. The notion that fairy tales were exclusively meant for children's ears is one that came about largely in Victorian times, when the adult oral storytelling tradition was widely replaced by printed novels and a new fashion for stories of social realism. As the old oral tales were banished to the nursery, the more violent or sexual stories were changed, watered down to make them more suitable for "innocent ears." Even folklore enthusiasts like the Brothers Grimm used a heavy hand to edit the tales, changing, for instance, cruel mothers and fathers into wicked "stepparents" instead. These watered-down versions are the fairy tales most of us are familiar with to this day. The Victorians fancied a highly romanticized view of fairy stories, and of childhood itself. They clung to the notion of the Idyll of Childhood, a bucolic time of simplicity and innocence, despite the daily evidence of homeless, overworked, and prostituted children crowding their city streets.

Today, while we still hold the ideal of childhood as a time of joy, play, growth, and exploration, we know all too well that for many, many children this is hardly the case. In America, we have the highest proportional statistics of malnourished, undermedicated, undereducated children of any industrialized nation. Our statistics of child fatality are a disgrace. Child abuse (and the concurrent problem of violent domestic abuse, aptly redefined by U.S. Attorney General Janet Reno as "terrorism in the home") has entered public consciousness as a societal dilemma of numbing proportions. We are a society that has not made our nation's children a priority. We worship money instead, depending on it to build and secure our future, forgetting in the process that our children, all children, *are* the future of this country.

Bookstores shelves are full of advice books for the more literate adult survivors of childhood violence and molestation. But we can only hope that someday there will be an equal number of books devoted to promoting political and societal changes that will attack the problem by putting a *stop* to the abuse of children, rather than by funnelling those children into self-help groups years later when they reach adulthood.

In this current flood of attention to the subject, we do well to remember that less than a decade ago all these self-help books on the topic didn't exist, nor did the growing resources for both children and adults. The silence, denial, and tacit acceptance that has allowed child abuse to go on behind closed doors for so many centuries is a silence we must still beware of today. Our initial shock as the proportions of the current problem are exposed can easily change to boredom as the topic becomes "yesterday's news" in our media-saturated lives.

Questionable use of "memory retrieval" therapy techniques and overzealous abuse investigations have taken on aspects of witch-hunt hysteria, leading attention away from the immediate problem: the children who are arriving in hospital emergency rooms across the country every day, and the greater number of less-visibily damaged children who will never get even that amount of help. While some of the wilder claims from the fringes of the Adult Survivors movement may cause many people to believe the scope of the problem has been much overblown, the truth is in the evidence faced by physicians, police officers, and public prosecutors in their daily work, forcing us to confront a painful reality that we are still loathe to admit: Adults are capable of hurting children. They do it, and they do it often.

This is a reality that was not ignored or glossed over in the old traditional tales. Here we are not limited to a "Brady Bunch" version of family life; here are mothers capable of handing their daughters poisoned apples, fathers capable of selling them for bags of gold. Here are heroes armed with nothing but their wits, and heroines who do not wait passively for rescue (as the watered-down versions would have us believe) but who use their courage and intelligence in order to survive.

And yes, in general, they do survive—but what's important about these stories, from the point of view of any of us who have gone through the deep dark woods in childhood ourselves, is not the expectation of ending "Happily Ever After." Rather, it's the way that ending is achieved, through the process of transformation. It is all too easy to get lost in that wood, stuck in the mindset of victimization. These stories urge us to pass on through, to toss off the spells and the donkey-skins, to pick up the sword, the stone, the ring, to transform ourselves and our lives with the old-fashioned strengths of goodness, persistence, and *action*.

The fairy tale journey (as various writers have pointed out, from psychologists Carl Jung and Alice Miller to mythologist Joseph Campbell) can be seen as a metaphor for the therapeutic journey into the depths of the soul, or one's life journey from birth until death. The fairy tale journey reminds us (and teaches children) to beware of the dangers along the way. It reminds us the terrain can be rocky underfoot as we pass through the lands of childhood. Even those with the brightest passage through those lands are likely to remember a dark valley or two. Children can be cruel to other children (even lethal, as the recent rise of inner-city murders can attest), and adults can be downright treacherous. If we wish to see clearly, understand fully, the whole spectrum of life going on around us, we must not cling to the Victorians' sweetly romanticized version of childhood—or of old fairy tales.

While we are doing so, we must no longer pretend that only a few aberrant, wild-eyed adults hurt children: other adults, lurking on playground corners and in daycare centers, always the Other and not ourselves. We must stop focusing on sensationalistic tabloid stories of serial killers and Satanic rings, and notice instead the perfectly nice, secretly troubled people next door, whose child flinches when you touch her arm and whom you hear crying herself to sleep every night. It disturbs me that recent attention to the subject of child abuse largely focuses on "self" help (usually years after the fact) without a concurrent commitment to societal help, societal change, and a concerted political effort to address the root causes of the problem, to make violence against children, sexual or otherwise, completely unacceptable.

It is time to make our children a vital political concern. We must insure that the children of our wealthy nation do not live in conditions that would shock the Third World; that all children, rich and poor alike, have access to health care, education, and a safe bed to sleep in at night. Children are not property; they need legal rights of their own, and the societal support to enforce those rights. We must acknowledge the simple, difficult fact that currently our homes are danger zones for too many of our young people. Let's face that fact, not so we can get bogged down with blame and breast-beating cries of victimization; let's face it so we can change it.

All acts of political change must begin with an act of imagination. I want to re-imagine this country as a place in which no child is left hungry, sick, or cringing alone in terror. Impossible? But I'm a fantasist; I believe in the impossible. I believe in the strength of the imagination, clear sight, persistence, and a steadfast heart. These are the attributes of the heroes and heroines of the old fairy tales, the "magical" virtues with which they transformed themselves, and their perilous worlds.

The fairy tales in this book are both dark and bright, with pain and anger, wonder and hope. They are new tales spun from the threads of the old. Through the metaphoric language of fantasy, they look into the darkest shadows of the night, yet find by night's end the silver glimmer of dawn. The works contained herein have been woven together to form a journey in themselves, and while it is the usual anthology reader's practice to read stories in a random order, I hope you will consider letting this book lead you on a path from start to finish, into the woods and out again.

I remain grateful to the authors who have contributed the tales, essays, poems, and reminiscences in the following pages (as well as to the publishers who allowed reprinted work to be included). Many of them are well-known writers; yet there are also a few who are new to the printed page. Some write with the painful urgency that comes from working with personal childhood memories; others, who do not come from troubled backgrounds themselves, write with concern for what has happened to relatives or friends, or to children in society at large.

Readers of this book may be interested to know that most of the authors contributing to the volume have given up payment for their stories to agencies offering shelter, counseling, and medical care to abused children. A portion of the money you paid to buy *The Armless Maiden* will aid the work of an organization in Tucson, Arizona for troubled families and children at risk.

*The Armless Maiden* is dedicated to those children, and to the adults who used to be those children. And to the French fairy tale artist Adrienne Segur (illustrator of *The Golden Book of Fairy Tales*) who, although I've never met her, was my own bright fairy godmother.

—Terri Windling
The Endicott Studio
Tucson and Devon, U.K.

The European tale of "The Handless Maiden," or "The Girl With Silver Hands," is similar to tales told all over the world, including the "Armless Maiden" stories of Africa. In each case a young girl is maimed by a male figure—sometimes her father, sometimes her brother, and sometimes the Devil himself. There is generally a wicked female figure as well, a jealous mother- or sister-in-law. It is a story not only about the state of "woundedness," but about the subsequent healing process, which must be initiated by the Armless Maiden herself. Although she wins love and marriage halfway through the story, the tale is only complete when true healing has occurred.

# The Armless Maiden
### ✦ Midori Snyder ✦

There was once a husband and wife who lived beside a great forest. They were not royalty, but neither were they poor. Their house was built of fine white stone and they looked out upon their gardens and fields from windows of glass. There was much love between this couple, and in time, there were children as well. The first born was a son, called Richard, and he had his father's dark hair and night-black eyes. The second born was a daughter, Marion, born fair as her mother before her, with hair the color of the sun. The white stones of the house echoed with the sounds of the family; the husband rousing his hounds and servants to the hunt, the clattering of the wife's spinning wheel, and the bright sound of the children's laughter.

But time passed like clouds beneath the sun, first bright, then dark. And it happened one fall that the wife took ill, and with the first soft drifting of winter's snow, she died. They buried her at the garden's edge, and in the brittle soil the husband planted a rosebush, covering the tender roots with leaves to shelter it against the cold.

Day into night and night into day, the husband knew only the stab of grief. He sat by the hearth and stirred the fire, thinking of his sorrow. And so great was his grief that he forgot all else, even his children.

In the spring, the rose bush sent forth its first shoots. The children watched as branches lifted wearily from the soil, their thick gray boughs covered in black thorns. The summer came, and the rosebush spread, becoming a grove of thorns. There were no flowers, no green stems or leaves. And though the summer sun was bright and warm, in the shadow cast by their father's grief there could be only winter.

So Richard and Marion passed their childhood, each the only companion for the other, and all laughter and joy was shared in secret between them. They promised then never to marry and never to leave the other.

One spring came and their father, aged by his grief, died. Richard buried him in the far corner of the garden. The new sunlight was hot against the straining muscles of his back and sweat streaked his face. As he bent to brush the dirt from his hands, he looked up across the garden and stared in amazement.

There trapped amidst the grove of thorns was a young woman, struggling to free herself. She strained against the thorny claws and her brown hair was snarled in its fierce grip.

"Help me, please," she pleaded.

Richard dropped his shovel and with long, quick strides came to the woman. As he lifted the heavy boughs of thorns to free her, he stared into her green eyes and felt a longing he had not known before. She smiled at him, stepping lightly from the tangled web of thorns and gratefully placed her hands in his.

"Who are you?" Richard asked.

"Fiona," she replied and smiled again. Her green eyes sparkled and Richard was drawn into the cool gaze.

"But how did you get here?"

Fiona did not answer, but held tight to his hands.

Again Richard asked, and again Fiona refused to answer, but only laughed, a sweet sound like rushing water.

And with that sound, nothing else mattered to Richard. He wanted forever to hear Fiona laugh, and to gaze into her emerald-colored eyes.

Richard brought Fiona home to the stone house and introduced her to Marion.

"Sister, I met a woman by the grove. I mean to marry her."

"As you wish," Marion answered simply. But her gray eyes filled with the sadness she felt, for Fiona's smile was sharp as thorns and her green eyes were bright with jealousy.

Richard claimed he could not rest until he and Fiona were wed. So, in haste, they were married, and as they left the chapel, Marion's heart grew heavy with dread.

Time passed like a spinning coin, first bright and then dull. Marion did her best to welcome Fiona and to please her brother as before, but now Richard found only fault with her. The stitches on his shirt were clumsy, the meat she cooked was dry and tasteless, and the butter she churned curdled. Everything Marion put her hand to came undone. And always there was Fiona's cold green eyes following her, triumphant each time Marion failed.

One night in their bed, Fiona whispered into Richard's ear. "Send your sister away, she is a burden to us."

"Where would she go?" asked Richard.

"Why do you care?" Fiona said spitefully.

"No." Richard shook his head. "She is still my sister. Her faults are small."

The next morning Fiona rose from her bed crying. "Husband dear," she said, "I dreamed that Marion has emptied your barrels of wine."

"It was a dream," Richard replied sleepily, but Fiona shook him.

"Go and see for yourself."

Richard went to the cellar and there were the barrels of wine, their sides smashed open and red wine spilled over the cellar floor. Richard turned away from the sight, anger pricking his heart like a thorn, but he said nothing.

The next morning, Fiona rose again, crying out, "Husband, dear husband, I dreamed that your sister Marion has murdered your hounds and left their bodies by the hearth."

"It was a dream," Richard replied, wary this time.

"Go and see for yourself," Fiona demanded as before.

Richard entered the great hall and there on the hearth stones were his hounds, their limp bodies covered with blood. And again anger stabbed his breast, but still he said nothing to Marion.

On the next morning Fiona rose and shook her husband awake with piercing cries of anguish.

"What is it, wife?" Richard asked, frightened by Fiona's shrill wailing.

"I dreamed that Marion has murdered our son."

"It is but a dream," Richard replied, though his face grew pale.

Fiona turned to him, her green eyes red rimmed with weeping. "Go and see for yourself."

Richard rushed to his son's cradle. The white linens were stained red but there was no child to be seen. Then he threw back his head and howled in rage.

From her room, Marion shook with fear. The night before Fiona had given her candles that burned with such thick smoke that Marion had not been able to rouse herself from her bed, even when she saw Fiona come to her in the night and lay the small body beside her in the bed. Richard's anguished cry had released her from Fiona's spell and now there was blood on her sheets, blood on the sleeves of her nightdress, and on her pillow was laid the body of her murdered nephew and a silver blade.

Richard burst through the door of her room, his sword drawn. His black eyes glittered with malice. Marion could find no words to speak and he accepted her silence as confession of her guilt.

Richard dragged Marion by her hair across the garden until he came to the grove of thorns.

"Brother," she gasped, clinging to his wrist. "Brother, please listen to me."

"No," Richard shouted as he drew her up. "I will not." She raised her hand to touch him but he swung his sword and struck her right arm from her body. Marion gave a startled cry, as the arm fell lifeless on the branches. "And does it give you pain, my sister?" he shouted.

Marion nodded, weeping.

"It is the same that you gave to my hounds." Richard raised his sword and struck her other arm from her body.

"And again, does it hurt you, Sister?"

Marion nodded.

"It is the same hurt that you gave my son," he said bitterly. "I will leave you here, to die in this grove."

"I did not kill them," Marion said softly. "It was your own bride who did these things." Her golden hair fell across her face like threshed wheat. The blood from her shoulders spiraled around her waist. Slowly, Marion lifted her head and spoke: "Before you leave this grove, my brother, you will step on a thorn. And none but my hand shall free you of it."

Richard turned angrily from her and, seeing Fiona waiting for him in the courtyard, he began to hurry his steps. As he took the last step out of the grove, a thorn on a low-lying branch pierced his boot and entered the heel of his foot. Richard ignored the stab of pain, seeing only Fiona's smiling face beckoning him away from the grove.

In grove of thorns Marion wept with sorrow. The tears trickled down her cheeks and where they fell on the thorn bush, a few green leaves appeared. With the twilight came the dew, and the soft drops of healing water staunched the bleeding and soothed her wounds. Marion stopped her crying and, following the lighted path of the moon, entered into the forest.

Time passed like the slanting of moonlight in the forest, first silver, now black. Marion wandered through the trees, her feet treading wearily along an unknown path. The animals came to her, for she was a strange creature that, unlike other men, had no arms with which to hurt them. At night she lay down among the deer, their warm hides sheltering her from the night's chill. Birds and squirrels brought her berries and hulled nuts, leaving them on stones where she might bend to eat.

But it was not enough. How she longed for the sound of a human voice, for the kind touch of another's hand on her cheek. She was growing thin with hunger, her clothing was torn and ragged, and her once-golden hair was a dirty brown, matted with moss and twigs.

And then one morning she was awakened by the scent of apples carried on the breeze. She followed the sweet aroma until she came to a wall of stones. Looking up she saw apple trees, their boughs ladened with ripe fruit. Her mouth watered at the memory of the taste. Quickly she began searching for an opening along the stone wall, and found a tunnel that an animal had furrowed out beneath the wall.

It was a narrow tunnel, and she wriggled through it, her body covered with dirt, and her face scratched by the small stones. So great was Marion's hunger that she didn't care, but forced her way through to the promise of apples on the other side. Once in the orchard, Marion tried to stand, but she was too weak from hunger. Instead, she rolled herself to the base of a tree, and ate the apples that had fallen on the ground.

After Marion had eaten, a measure of strength returned to her and she was able to sit up, leaning gratefully against the trunk of an apple tree. From where she sat, Marion could see the tall spires of a castle rising over the treetops. On the spires blue and green flags snapped gaily in the wind.

Suddenly, Marion heard loud voices. Servants were coming to the orchard to gather apples. Fearful of being seen, Marion fell to the ground and tried to roll away to the stone wall again.

"Look! Over there!" Marion heard someone shout and her heart began to race. "What kind of animal is it?" another shouted. "Quick! Catch it!"

Marion was surrounded by servants, their eyes staring curiously at her. One man held a long stick, prepared to strike her if she proved dangerous.

"Please," Marion called, "please, help me."

"Bless me, it can speak!" said a serving woman, and she came a little closer.

"Careful now," the man with the stick warned.

"I mean no harm," Marion answered.

Another man pushed through the circle of servants, and they straightened as he spoke. "What is it?" he demanded.

"My Prince," said the servant with the stick, "we found a creature in your orchard stealing apples."

"I wasn't stealing them," Marion answered angrily. "How can I steal apples when I have no hands!" Tears brimmed in her eyes.

The man approached her and bent to look into her face. As she gazed back, Marion felt a mixture of gladness and shame, for the man was young and handsome. His eyes were a clear blue, and the look he gave her was one of kindness, but also pity. *How wretched I must seem to him,* she thought and quickly lowered her eyes.

"This is no creature," the young man said softly, "but a woman. Bring her back to the castle. There is nothing that can be done for her wounds, but at least she can be washed and fed."

"As you wish, my Prince," the servant answered and Marion felt herself being lifted from the ground and carried through the orchard. Only then did she raise her eyes to follow the young man's back, with his broad shoulders that tapered into a narrow waist.

The serving women scrubbed Marion's skin with sand and soap, taking off the forest dirt and dried blood. Twice they washed her hair and combed out the tangles until it shone again like newly spun gold.

"But she is a pretty child," one woman murmured to another. "Too bad about her arms."

They dressed her in a blue gown, and over her shoulders they draped a cloak of soft green, so that it seemed her arms were not missing at all. When Marion entered the Great Hall and stood before the Prince, she saw his eyes open wide with surprise. He came down from his throne and looked at her closely.

"Can it be that you are the same creature from the orchard?"

"Yes," she answered quietly, shy in his presence.

"Tell me how you came to be like this," he said gently, and drew her to a chair.

Marion's voice trembled at first and then grew steady as she told the Prince of Fiona's treachery and Richard's cruel attack. The Prince's face darkened with anger.

"Be at rest," he said firmly. "There is no one here that will harm you. That I promise."

Marion smiled at the Prince, and in his eyes she saw pity ignite the spark of love.

They spent their days walking through the gardens of the castle, sharing their thoughts, and finding happiness in each others' company. The Prince saw to it that Marion was well cared for; servants dressed her each day, combed her hair, and the Prince himself fed her slices of bread dipped in milk. At times her helplessness troubled Marion, but she was too dazed by her good fortune to remain worried.

All who saw Marion and the Prince together nodded their heads, knowing it would not be long before the Prince offered marriage. Indeed, soon after in the garden, he crowned Marion with a wreath of white roses and asked if she would be his bride. And though Marion's heart was overjoyed, a sliver of doubt remained.

"I am not whole, my Prince. Can you you love me as I am?" Marion asked.

"Always," the Prince replied.

"Then I accept," said Marion and banished all doubt from her heart.

The King and Queen approved of the match, though secretly they had hoped the Prince would marry someone else—a woman with arms, at least. The Prince and Marion were married quietly, with only the servants and the King and Queen present to bear witness. The Prince placed Marion's wedding ring on a gold chain around her neck.

Time passed like the summer flowers, first blooming and then fading. One day a messenger arrived, bringing the Prince news of war. And though he hated the thought of leaving Marion, newly pregnant with their first child, the Prince was obliged to go. As he packed his supplies, he called on the King and Queen to guard well his wife and to write as soon as the child was born.

Marion watched a servant hold the stirrup steady for the Prince as he mounted his horse. That should be my duty, she thought sadly as she stood helplessly beside his horse. The Prince bent down and kissed her on the forehead. And then he was gone, the steel of his armor glistening in the sun as he rode away. Marion felt the tears that washed her cheeks and waited for the servant to wipe them away.

When the time came, Marion gave birth to a beautiful son: his face shining like the moon, his hair like threads from the sun. The Queen wrote to the Prince to give him the glad tidings. She entrusted the letter to a serving man and sent him on his way through the woods to where the Prince was engaged in battle.

The way was long and tiring, and when the servant came upon a fine house made of white stone with windows of glass, he decided to stop and rest. He knocked on the door and a woman answered, startling him with her bright green eyes.

"Come in," she cried. "I have been without company since the war began. Let me offer you food and wine. I am called Fiona," she said sweetly.

The tired servant was grateful for a meal and joined her at the table. There was roasted chicken and beef, bowls of vegetables in creamy sauces, and all nature of sweet cakes. Fiona poured the servant a glass of wine and they began to talk.

"What brings you here?" she asked.

The servant saw no harm in answering and told Fiona of the Prince and his wife, a woman fair to look at but with no arms. He told her of the letter he was carrying with the news of the birth of their first child. So intent was the servant on his plate of food that he did not see the hard gleam in Fiona's green eyes, nor the way her hands tightened into angry fists. Over and over, she poured the wine until the servant had drunk so much that he grew tired and, laying his head in the crook of his arm, fell asleep.

Fiona slipped the letter from his pouch and read it quickly. Then she tossed it on the fire and sat down to write a new one. When that was done, she carefully tucked the new letter into the servant's bag.

In the morning she woke the servant, and sent him on his way with a loaf of bread and cheese. "Please stop this way on your return," she said to him, "and I shall see that you are well fed once more."

The servant agreed to the pleasant offer and hurried on his way to the Prince.

At the battle camp the servant approached the Prince with his letter. The Prince looked weary, blood rusting on his bright armor. The servant was pleased to think he had brought good news and hoped he would be well rewarded. He gave the Prince the letter and waited.

The Prince read the letter, his eyes moving eagerly at first over the words. Then, abruptly, they clouded with pain, and to the servant's astonishment, he saw the Prince become haggard. "Your wife has given birth to a monster," Fiona had written, "an armless monster so terrifying that no one can look upon him without fear. And now your wife sleeps with this monster in the stables and feeds like an animal at the kitchen door."

The Prince folded the letter and the servant saw how his hand trembled. But the Prince called for paper and a pen to write a reply. "As before," the Prince wrote, "take care of my wife and child. Give them shelter and all that they need. When I return, I will see what is to be done." He folded the letter and gave it to the servant.

"Go now with and return to the castle," he said sharply.

"But Prince," the servant protested, "I have traveled a long way. Am I to get no rest? Nothing to eat?"

"Go now," the Prince ordered and his armor rattled dangerously.

The servant left with the new letter, grumbling as he did. "Well," he thought, "at least I can stop the night at that house. The mistress there will see to it I am well fed." And the servant marched quickly, thinking of roast beef and sweet wine.

"Well met, good man," Fiona called out when she saw the servant approaching. "And are you returning from the Prince?"

"Indeed, I am the ungrateful man. He gave me no reward for my labor, just penned his reply and sent me on my way without so much as a thank you."

"Too bad," Fiona clucked sympathetically. "Come in and eat. I have a lamb here that is done to a turn and needs only to be eaten."

The servant was happy to sit and eat and he didn't mind as Fiona poured glass after glass of wine. And then when he felt overcome at last with food and wine, he laid his head in the crook of his arm on the table and slept.

Fiona withdrew the letter and read. She hissed angrily when she read the Prince's words. "No," she whispered. "This will not do. I shall give you another answer and settle it once and for all." She took a new piece of paper and wrote. "I no longer care for my wife or child. I can see now how foolish I was to love a creature with no arms, one that can not even feed herself. I do not wish to see them on my return. Send them away into the woods where they belong." Smiling to herself, Fiona folded the letter and placed it in the servant's bag.

The servant arrived at the castle in the morning, and handed the Prince's letter to the King. At least the King knows how to reward a good servant, the man thought, and great was his surprise when the King stood angrily and waved the servant away.

"What shall we do?" the King asked the Queen.

"Marion is a good girl, but our son is right. She can do nothing for herself. Even the child must be cared for by another." She sighed unhappily. "We must have been mistaken when we approved of this marriage."

Marion was called for and when she came, the King showed her the letter. Marion's cheeks paled and her eyes glistened with unshed tears. She remembered her doubt, and felt the pain of it now in her heart. But she raised her chin and when she spoke, her voice was clear and strong.

"I shall leave. I ask only that you tie my son to my back."

"At least leave the baby," the Queen pleaded. "We can give him to a serving woman to raise. You will not be able to care for him."

"No. He is my child. I shall care for him. Tie him to my back and I shall leave."

A servant helped Marion to change her clothes. She left behind the gowns of silk and linen and the finely embroidered shoes. She wore only a brown woolen shift and her feet were bare. Her little son was tied with a length of white cloth to her back and he slept with his cheek pressed against her shoulder.

She walked with head held high, past the line of whispering servants and through the gates of the castle wall. Without a glance backwards, Marion entered again into the forest.

And only when she was alone among the trees did she weep bitterly.

She walked along the unknown paths, letting her feet take her deeper into the forest. The baby woke hungry and began to cry. Marion bent her face, her cheeks flushed. But there was nothing she could do. The baby on her back was there to stay, for without arms there was no way she could take him down and feed him. The baby soiled his diapers and Marion could feel the wetness seeping through the length of cloth and making her back cold. But still she walked on. And when his cries grew weaker and more piteous, Marion felt her heart would break.

The night came, and weary with walking and crying, Marion sat, bowing her head on her knees to sleep. The baby on her back slept too, though his arms thrashed beneath the tight bounds of the cloth.

When she woke Marion was weak with hunger and her lips were parched with thirst. She stood and the baby, roused by her movements, began to cry again for food. Marion continued walking, searching for the tiny pockets of water that collected in the crevices of rocks. But the rocks were dry and even the lichens had faded to a brittle gray.

Desperation drove Marion through the brambles, until at last her feet stepped onto a path overhung with ferns about the edges. She stared at it, puzzled at first, and then made up her mind to follow it. The sweet trill of a bird led her on, reassuring her as she travelled the ferny path. Late in the day as the sun was dipping behind the trees, Marion heard the sound of water lapping against a shore. It was a soft rustling noise and her feet hurried down the path. As she pushed through the branches, she gasped, seeing before her the smooth crystal surface of a lake. In the fading sunlight, the water glowed like a jewel.

Marion bent over a rock and peered into the water. She could see no bottom, only the shining surface of the water reflecting the image of her weary face and the baby, his tear-stained cheek resting on her shoulder.

She stared long at the reflection of her face, arrested by the changes time had worked. Her features were still pretty, her hair a bright gold, but her eyes were lined with sadness. And an old pain returned, the memory throbbing in her shoulders. Would the shame and sorrow of that moment never leave her? She stared at herself in the clear water and wished in her heart for wholeness. The water stirred, inviting her to drink.

She bent slowly and carefully, afraid now that the baby might slip from her back. Her lips were close to the water when the baby woke and began to struggle on her back. The cloth came undone, and in an instant the baby tumbled in with hardly a splash.

"No!" Marion cried, and she dove into the water after her son.

She shuddered as the icy-cold water closed around her. She opened her eyes and saw her baby, slowly drifting down, the water swirling around him with bubbles of quicksilver. Marion kicked her legs but it was not enough to reach him. Her lungs burned, demanding air, but still she kicked, driving her body downward toward her baby.

And then before her a huge fish threshed the water with shimmering waves. Its scales were pale green tipped with silver. Its amber eyes stared curiously at her. From its gaping mouth hung two long whiskers.

"As spirit of this lake, I would save you if you wish. Or I can save your child. You must chose," said the fish, its whiskers quivering as it spoke.

"My arms," Marion cried. "Give me hands and I will save us both!"

The fish paused, its tail slowly undulating as it thought. And then it thrashed, arching its spine as it dove again to the bottom of the lake.

The water began to seethe and boil, turning Marion over and over in a whirlpool of silvery water. Her shoulders tingled as if tiny fishes rubbed their scaled sides across her old wounds. She searched through the churning water, trying to see her baby. And when she saw him still drifting, his moon-white face upturned, she gave a desperate cry and lunged toward him.

With no other thought but to save him, Marion reached out and saw a hand—her own hand—plunge through the churning water. She reached again, this time with her other hand, and clutching the baby to her breast, she swam upward.

As their heads broke the surface, Marion gave a cry of joy. The baby sputtered and coughed and then cried. She lifted him out of the water, marveling at the sight of her two hands, fingers clasped around his chest.

On the shore again, Marion cradled her son, marvelling at the heavy feel of his body in the crook of her arms. She nursed him, one hand stroking his cheek until he slept. But the newness of her arms kept her awake and so she tickled him until he cried, and then she hugged him again, lifting him to her face as she kissed his soft, downy cheeks. Then she rocked him back to sleep and when she lay down, she hugged him close within the shelter of her arms.

In the morning when she woke, Marion had decided she would return. But not to the castle. Not yet.

With her child on her back, she faced the silent lake to offer thanks and farewell. The water stirred and from the depths she saw the huge fish rising. Its whiskers floated along the surface of the water and it spoke to her.

"There is no need of thanks. It was your own courage that reached out and took back that which was once severed from you. Grafted again to the old stock, the new tree bears fruit. Go in peace," the fish rumbled. Then it leaped high into the air, its huge jade-green body breaching the surface of the lake. It flashed brightly and then was gone. Just a circle of tiny waves marked its passing.

Marion followed the ferny path away from the lake until she came to a poor woodcutter's cottage. The woodcutter was old, and as he lived alone, he agreed to let Marion and her son stay. She tucked her skirts up and with a broom swept the cottage clean. Next she kneaded the dough and set the round loaves to baking. She mended the woodcutter's torn clothes and then fed his chickens and pig. And when that was done, she settled down with her son to wait.

Time passed like flashing swords, first sharp and then blunt. The Prince returned from the war, weary with killing and anxious to see his wife and son.

"But she is gone," the King told him. "You told us to send her into the forest."

"Never," the Prince shouted. "You told me she had given birth to a monster! I told you to care for them until I returned."

"Someone has lied to all of us," the Queen cried out.

The Prince called the servant before him. "Tell me," the Prince demanded, "did you stop anywhere before delivering the messages?"

"Yes," the servant answered fearfully. "A house in the forest. A woman named Fiona gave me food."

The Prince groaned, for he knew well Fiona's name and could guess what she had done. "And did you sleep there?"

"Yes, my Prince," the servant answered wretchedly, bowing his head.

"Then you will not sleep again until my wife is found," the Prince answered. "Go and pack the horses. We shall search for her."

"But surely you cannot hope to find her," the King said gently. "How would she have survived?"

But the Prince refused to believe that Marion was dead. "I would know it in my heart," he told the servant, "and my heart tells, she is still alive."

The servant wasted no time in saddling two horses. Together he and the Prince left the castle and headed into the deep woods. They searched for days, never stopping long to eat, never resting more than a brief moment. They turned over the bushes for signs, looked into the mouths of caves, and watched for branches that had been bent to permit a woman to pass.

One morning, after the forest mist had cleared and the sun was lighting the forest floor, the Prince looked up to see a thin line of blue smoke rising over the trees. Though exhausted, he urged his horse through a clearing, where he saw the smoke coming from a cottage chimney. As he entered the clearing, the Prince's lips parted in surprise.

A woman, her back to him, played with a child. She stood in a circle of sunlight and her long hair shimmered like gold down her back. She was laughing and the sound of it pierced the Prince's heart with recognition. He wanted to run to her, turn her around, and look into her face. But he didn't, confused by what he saw. With the sleeves of her dress pushed back, the Prince saw she had arms and long white hands that tossed the happy child into the air, and caught him again as he fell.

The Prince approached the woman, each step more eager and confused. The woman turned at the sound of his horse, and when the Prince saw her face, he stopped in astonishment.

"Marion," he sighed with relief. "I have been searching for you."

"You sent me away," Marion answered softly.

At this the servant rushed before Marion and fell to his knees. Grabbing the hem of her dress, he began pleading for her forgiveness. Marion clasped him by the shoulders and raised him. Seeing the miracle of her hands made the servant more miserable, and the words of his confession rushed out of his mouth in furious haste. At the mention of Fiona's name, Marion's hands gripped his shoulders more tightly. But when he was done speaking, Marion released him, and again the servant begged for Marion's forgiveness.

She nodded, one hand on his shoulder, and granted him her forgiveness.

"Come home, Marion," the Prince said.

"Not yet," replied Marion, smiling sadly. "When I first came to you, I was a creature of the woods. You pitied me and gave me shelter. But now I am a woman and you must court me as a woman."

The Prince nodded, understanding, and though he was reluctant to leave her he mounted his horse and bid her good-bye. "Tomorrow," he promised.

The next morning the woodcutter woke Marion, shaking her excitedly by the shoulder. "Come and see, Mistress. Come quick."

Marion came to the door and saw the line of horses, each ladened with bridal gifts. There were bolts of fine silk and creamy white linen, a chest of gold coins, and baskets of silver dishes. There were geese, brood hens, a milk cow, and a fine bull with an orange speckled hide. The Queen left her horse and Marion saw that she carried a small crown of sapphires. She placed the crown on Marion's head and there were tears in her eyes as she took Marion by the hands and kissed her on the cheeks.

"Take what you need," Marion said to the woodcutter, "for you have been kind and generous to me and my son."

Marion mounted a gray horse, his mane braided with little bells. The woodcutter lifted up her son and as she took him, his chubby hands eagerly reached out to jingle the bells. With one white arm around her son and the other holding the reins of her horse, Marion returned to the castle.

They were married the next day, and this time the church was crowded. Marion wore a dress of white silk stitched about the neck and sleeves with tiny pearls and stars of sapphire. The Prince stood straight and tall, his blue eyes shining at the sight of her. And when he placed the ring of gold on her finger, Marion sighed. "Now we are well and truly wed," she said, smiling at the Prince.

The bells pealed loudly the joy of the day, and only her son cried, afraid at first of their booming voices.

But one thing yet troubled Marion.

"I wish to go to my brother," Marion told the Prince. "I must go and see him."

The Prince was not pleased at this request, but he would not refuse his wife. They rode their horses through the woods until they came to the white stone house. Marion looked around sadly. It had become ravaged and poor in the time she was gone. Nothing grew in the gardens and only a few starving chickens scratched at the dust that swirled around her feet.

Marion called at the door and heard a weak voice answer. She pushed open the door and entered into the hall. She saw no one, but the frail voice continued to call her forth. She walked through the musty, empty house until she came to the kitchen.

And there, sitting in the ashes of a cold hearth, Marion found her brother, Richard.

From the single thorn in his heel a bush of thorns had sprouted, covering all but his face with a dense thicket of branches and thorns, and with every move he made the thorns dug into his arms and sides. His skin seemed as pale and lifeless as the prison of thorns surrounded him.

Richard looked at her from eyes that were hollowed with pain and sadness. "Though I do not deserve it, forgive me, sister," he asked.

With tears, Marion rushed to his side and kneeling, she plucked the single thorn from his heel.

No sooner was it removed than the thorns about his body began to wither. The fierce branches curled and dried into brittle twigs. What was left of the thorns fell away and Richard was freed.

Weakly, Richard bent on his knees and took Marion by the hands. He shook his head in amazement. "I was blind, foolish and cruel. I know now what manner of woman I married, and my own deeds were no better than hers. But these hands that once I took from you have given back to me my life."

"Where is Fiona?" Marion asked.

"I am here!" a sharp voice answered. Marion saw Fiona standing in the shadow of the kitchen. "But you won't have me!" Fiona said and ran out the open door.

Marion chased after her, but Fiona ran faster. And when she came to the grove of the thorn, Fiona leapt, diving into the thickest tangle of branches.

As Marion watched, Fiona was transformed. Her arms and legs grew gray as they stretched into branches. Her brown hair coiled into tendrils. Her torso twisted and curved as her skin darkened with bark. And on her face was the merest whisper of a smile as her features faded into the wood. Only the green eyes seemed to stare back at Marion—until Marion realized that it was not Fiona's eyes at all, but the sprouting of brilliant green leaves on the branch.

Marion stepped back and saw that throughout the once-barren thorn grove, leaves were growing, thick and green. The thorns changed to stems, and at the end of every stem appeared a rose. The roses bloomed pink and fragrant, lifting their petaled faces to the sun. As Marion walked back to the where her husband and her brother stood waiting for her, rose petals drifted in the wind and swirled around her. She laughed as she caught them in her upturned hands.

# The Hero's Journey

### ✦ Midori Snyder ✦

In hero narratives, a young man leaves the familiar home of his birth and ventures into the unknown world where the fantastic waits to challenge him. Along the journey, his worth as a man and as a hero is tested. But when the trials are done, he returns home again in triumph, bringing to his society newfound knowledge, maturity—and often a magic bride. The transformation of a young man into a responsible adult is sealed when the hero marries his magic bride and assumes kingship.

While no less heroic, how different is the journey of young women. In folk tales, the rite of passage from adolescence to adulthood is confirmed by marriage and the assumption of adult roles. In an exogamous society, young women must leave forever the familiar home of their birth to become brides elsewhere. Venturing out into the dangerous world of the fantastic, they know they will never return home. Instead they will eventually arrive in new kingdoms and villages. There, disguised as dirty-faced servants and goose girls, they struggle to complete their initiation into adulthood by carving out new identities in foreign lands. With their re-emergence as adult women, they too bring the gifts of knowledge, maturity, and fertility to their new communities.

In the language of folk tales, abstract ideas are represented by concrete images.° Traditional storytellers have used terrifying events to cre-

---

°Harold Scheub, "Oral Narrative Process and the Use of Models," *New Literary History,* VI, 2, (Winter 1975): 353–377; and Harold Scheub, "Body and Image in Oral Narrative Traditions," *New Literary History,* VIII, 2 (Winter 1977): 345–367.

ate the emotional experience of grief and abandonment, in which a young woman is not only set out on her journey away from home, but assured of the impossibility of ever returning. In the "Armless Maiden" narratives a girl is mutilated by a trusted family member and then thrust like a wounded animal into the forest. There can be no return to this home corrupted by violence. The girl must move forward in her journey to a new destination where she will reconstruct, not only her severed arms, but her identity as an adult woman as well.

My first experience with the "Armless Maiden" narrative was a powerful version performed by Mrs. Nongenile Masithatu Zenani, a Xhosa storyteller from South Africa.† Her version is frightening and brutal. A widowed father tries to coerce his young daughter into filling the sexual role of his deceased wife. When the girl refuses to have sex with him, he takes her into the woods and cuts off her arms, leaving her to die. The horror of this opening passage is balanced only by its dramatic ending, when the girl's arms are restored on the shore of a magic lake and she is able at last, as a whole woman, to take her baby into her arms.

The "Armless Maiden" narrative stayed with me for many years and I found myself hunting down other versions. What surprised me the most was discovering how ubiquitous this complex and violent story was. There were versions told all over Europe and Asia, some less sexual in their tone, but every bit as gruesome; fathers and brothers hacking away the limbs of young girls, either in rage or in payment to the Devil. And there would always be that complicated twist in the middle of the story, the false exchange of letters that forces the armless girl back into nature where the final act of initiation occurs.

It is a narrative with a strange hiccup in the middle. The brutality of the opening scene seems resolved as the armless girl is rescued in a garden and then married to the Prince. But she has not completed her journey of transformation. She is not whole, not the girl she was nor the woman she was meant to be. The narratives make it clear that without her arms, she is unable to fulfill her role as an adult. She can do nothing for herself, not even care for her own child. Conflict is reintroduced into the narrative to send the girl back on her journey of initiation alone. Every narrative version concludes with what is in effect a second marriage. The woman, now whole, her arms restored by an act of magic, has become herself the magic bride, aligned with the creative power of nature. She does not return to the Prince's castle, but waits in the forest for him to find her. When he comes to propose marriage this second time, it is a marriage of equals, based on respect and not pity.

Although I believe that the "Armless Maiden" narratives are about rites of passage to adulthood, within the story is the echo of abuse. Heroes may be impoverished or robbed of their royal birthrights, but rarely are

---

†Nongenile Masithatu Zenani, "A Father Cuts Off His Daughter's Arms," *The World and The Word* (Madison: University of Wiscosin Press, 1992): 61–78

they so vindictively mutilated before they are turned out into their jour-
neys. Storytellers know well the constant underlying fear and threat that
surrounds the lives of women in their communities from childhood into
adulthood. The exploitation of these terrifying images in the narrative
may be extreme, but they are the dark threads pulled out of the fabric of
our shared experiences as women. We are repulsed and angered by the
brutal actions, not because such events could never happen, but because
they do. The fantastic emerges quickly in the story to magically soften the
pain of the mutilation, and move the listener away from the horror of the
event and into the journey of self-discovery. Though the terror of the attack is short, as long as the girl remains mutilated we are reminded of the
continuing painful isolation that such blows inflict. Survivors of abuse
know that isolation well—whether as a child stripped of innocence among
those still cloaked, or as an adult unable to bridge the fear of betrayal, and
trust in the love of another.

It takes acts of self-determination and power to restore a sense of
wholeness after abuse. In a number of European versions of the "Armless
Maiden" the girl, mutilated by her brother or father in a thorn grove,
speaks out against the crime with the calm assurance of a prophet. Armless and bleeding, she tells him that the thorn he is about to step on will be
removed only by her hand. In that moment of intense pain and betrayal
she envisions her life restored to wholeness. And, what is more, she envisions her forgiveness of his terrible crime. The narrative is not about her
survival as a victim, rather it is about her journey as a committed traveler
fully aware of her destination.

The need for restoration and reconciliation are not the armless girl's
alone in the versions employing the motif of the thorn grove. Abusers too
are isolated by the shame and brutality of their violent acts. The brother
or father in the thorn grove versions barely survives in the armless
maiden's absence, their bodies imprisoned and pierced by a punishing
vine of thorns that grows from the offending thorn in their heel. When the
armless maiden returns, her transformation from a girl into a woman possessed of creative power is confirmed as she frees her brother or father
from the prison of thorns with the touch of her restored hands. In so
doing she removes forever the corrupting taint of violence, allowing them
both to continue in their new lives, unshackled by the past.

In finding my own voice for the retelling of this story, I selected those
images that perhaps more strongly addressed the underlying threat of
abuse and its forgiveness. But in one aspect of the narrative I created a
scene that is not found as part of the traditional versions of the "Armless
maiden." Since traditional storytellers have accepted at the outset that the
girl would have her arms restored at the proper time, indicating her re-
emergence as an adult, they were not as concerned with how her arms
were restored. Only that the girl must be returned to nature, and there
nature would determine when she had reached the apex of her journey.
Though nature would still make it happen, I wanted the armless maiden

to recognize and literally grab that moment for herself. When she demands of the magic fish to restore her arms that she may save herself and her child, it is the first real step in her reemergence as an adult. It is also the moment when the adult identity is grafted onto the once-wounded stock of childhood, making whole again the girl's history. In one luminous moment, her past is restored, her present made manifest in the power of her hands, and her future assured, as she lifts her child out of the foaming water.

# Bedtime Story

Lisel Mueller

♦

The moon lies on the river
like a drop of oil.
The children come to the banks to be healed
of their wounds and bruises.
The fathers who gave them their wounds and bruises
come to be healed of their rage.
The mothers grow lovely; their faces soften,
the birds in their throats awake.
They all stand hand in hand
and the trees around them,
forever on the verge
of becoming one of them,
stop shuddering and speak their first word.

But that is not the beginning.
It is the end of the story,
and before we come to the end,
the mothers and fathers and children
must find their way to the river,
separately, with no one to guide them.
That is the long, pitiless part,
and it will scare you.

The German fairy tale "Allerleirauh," found in the Brothers Grimm collections, is quite similar to the better-known French tale from Perrault called "Donkeyskin." Its overtly incestuous theme of a king determined to marry his own daughter, much to her terror and despair, is another common one that can be found in folk tales from cultures all around the world.

# Allerleirauh

### ◆ Jane Yolen ◆

**H**er earliest memory was of rain on a thatched roof, and surely it was a true one, for she had been born in a country cottage two months before time, to her father's sorrow and her mother's death. They had sheltered there, out of the storm, and her father had never forgiven himself nor the child who looked so like her mother. *So* like her, it was said, that portraits of the two as girls might have been exchanged and not even Nanny the wiser.

So great had been her father's grief at the moment of his wife's death, he might even have left the infant there, still bright with birth blood and squalling. Surely the crofters would have been willing, for they were childless themselves. His first thought was to throw the babe away, his wife's Undoing as he called her ever after, though her official name was Allerleirauh. And he might have done so had she not been the child of a queen. A royal child, whatever the crime, is not to be tossed aside so lightly, a feather in the wind.

But he had made two promises to the blanched figure that lay on the rude bed, the woolen blankets rough against her long, fair legs. White and red and black she had been then. White of skin, like the color of milk after the whey is skimmed out. Red as the toweling that carried her blood, the blood they could not staunch, the life leaching out of her. And black, the color of her eyes, the black seas he used to swim in, the black tendrils of her hair.

"Promise me." Her voice had stumbled between those lips, once red, now white.

He clasped her hands so tightly he feared he might break them, though it was not her bones that were brittle, but his heart. "I promise," he said. He would have promised her anything, even his own life, to stop the words bleeding out of that white mouth. "I promise."

"Promise me you will love the child," she said, for even in her dying she knew his mind, knew his heart, knew his dark soul. "Promise."

And what could he do but give her that coin, the first of two to close her dead eyes?

"And promise me you will not marry again, lest she be . . ." and her voice trembled, sighed, died.

"Lest she be as beautiful as thee," he promised wildly in the high tongue, giving added strength to his vow. "Lest she have thy heart, thy mind, thy breasts, thy eyes . . ." and his rota continued long past her life. He was speaking to a dead woman many minutes and would not let himself acknowledge it, as if by naming the parts of her he loved, he might keep her alive, the words bleeding out of him as quickly as her lost blood.

"She is gone, my lord," said the crofter's wife, not even sure of his rank except that he was clearly above her. She touched his shoulder for comfort, a touch she would never have ventured in other circumstances, but tragedy made them kin.

The king's litany continued as if he did not hear, and indeed he did not. For all he heard was the breath of death, that absence made all the louder by his own sobs.

"She is dead, Sire," the crofter said. He had known the king all along, but had not mentioned it till that one moment. Blunter than his wife, he was less sure of the efficacy of touch. "Dead."

And this one final word the king heard.

"*She is not dead!*" he roared, bringing the back of his hand around to swat the crofter's face as if he were not a giant of a man but an insect. The crofter shuddered and was silent, for majesty does make gnats of such men, even in their own homes. Even there.

The infant, recognizing no authority but hunger and cold, began to cry at her father's voice. On and on she bawled, a high, unmusical strand of sound till the king dropped his dead wife's hand, put his own hands over his ears, and ran from the cottage screaming, "I shall go mad!"

He did not, of course. He ranged from distracted to distraught for days, weeks, months, and then the considerations of kingship recalled him to himself. It was his old self recalled: the distant, cold, considering king he had been before his marriage. For marriage to a young, beautiful, foreign-born queen had changed him. He had been for those short months a better man, but not a better ruler. So the counselors breathed easier, certainly. The barons and nobles breathed easier, surely. And the peasants— well, the peasants knew a hard hand either way, for the dalliance of kings has no effect on the measure of rain nor the seasons in the sun, no matter what the poets write or the minstrels pluck upon their strings.

Only two in the kingdom felt the brunt of his neglect. Allerleirauh, of course, who would have loved to please him; but she scarcely knew him. And her Nanny, who had been her mother's Nanny, and was brought across the seas to a strange land. Where Allerleirauh knew hunger, the nurse knew hate. She blamed the king as he blamed the child for the young queen's death, and she swore in her own dark way to bring sorrow to him and his line.

The king was mindful in his own way of his promises. Kingship demands attention to be paid. He loved his daughter with the kindness of kings, which is to say he ordered her clothed and fed and educated to her station. But he did not love her with his heart. How could he, having seen her first cloaked in his wife's blood? How could he, having named her Undoing?

He had her brought to him but once a year, on the anniversary of his wife's death, that he might remind himself of her crime. That it was also the anniversary of Allerleirauh's birth, he did not remark. She thought he remembered, but he did not.

So the girl grew unremarked and unloved, more at home in the crofter's cottage where she had been born. And remembering each time she sat there in the rain, learning the homey crafts from the crofter's stout wife, that first rain.

The king did not marry again, though his counselors advised it. But memory refines what is real. Gold smelted in the mind's cauldron is the purer. No woman could be as beautiful to him as the dead queen. He built monuments and statues, commissioned poems and songs. The palace walls were hung with portraits that resembled her, all in color—the skin white as snow, the lips red as blood, the hair black as raven's wings. He lived in a mausoleum and did not notice the live beauty for the dead one.

Years went by, and though each spring messengers went through the kingdom seeking a maiden "white and black and red," the king's own specifications, they came home each summer's end to stare disconsolately at the dead queen's portraits.

"Not one?" the king would ask.

"Not one," the messengers replied. For the kingdom's maidens had been blonde or brown or redheaded. They had been pale or rosy or tan. And even those sent abroad found not a maid who looked like the statues or spoke like the poems or resembled in the slightest what they had all come to believe the late queen had been.

So the king went through spring and summer and into snow, still unmarried and without a male heir.

In desperation, his advisers planned a great three-day ball, hoping that—dressed in finery—one of the rejected maidens of the kingdom might take on a queenly air. Notice was sent that all were to wear black the first night, red the second, and white the third.

Allerleirauh was invited, too, though not by the king's own wishes. She was told of the ball by her nurse.

"I will make you three dresses," the old woman said. "The first dress will be as gold as the sun, the second as silver as the moon, and the third one will shine like the stars." She hoped that in this way, the princess would stand out. She hoped in this way to ruin the king.

Now if this were truly a fairy tale (and what story today with a king and queen and crofter's cottage is not?) the princess would go outside to her mother's grave. And there, on her knees, she would learn a magic greater than any craft, a woman's magic compounded of moonlight, elopement, and deceit. The neighboring kingdom would harbor her, the neighboring prince would marry her, her father would be brought to his senses, and the moment of complete happiness would be the moment of story's end. Ever after is but a way of saying: "There is nothing more to tell." It is but a dissembling. There is always more to tell. There is no happy *ever* after. There is happy *on occasion* and happy *every once in a while*. There is happy *when the memories do not overcome the now*.

But this is not a fairy tale. The princess is married to her father and, always having wanted his love, does not question the manner of it. Except at night, late at night, when he is away from her bed and she is alone in the vastness of it.

The marriage is sanctioned and made pure by the priests, despite the grumblings of the nobles. One priest who dissents is murdered in his sleep. Another is burned at the stake. There is no third. The nobles who grumble lose their lands. Silence becomes the conspiracy; silence becomes the conspirators.

Like her mother, the princess is weak-wombed. She dies in childbirth surrounded by that silence, cocooned in it. The child she bears is a girl, as lovely as her mother. The king knows he will not have to wait another thirteen years.

It is an old story.

Perhaps the oldest.

# Snow White to the Prince

## Delia Sherman

♦

I'm beautiful, you say, sublime,
Black and crystal as a winter's night,
With lips like rubies, cabochon,
My eyes deep blue as sapphires.
I cannot blame you for your praise:
You took me for my beauty, after all;
A jewel in a casket, still as death,
A lovely effigy, a prince's prize,
The fairest in the land.

But you woke me, or your horses did,
Stumbling as they bore me down the path,
Shaking the poisoned apple from my throat.
And now you say you love me, and would wed me
For my beauty's sake. My cursed beauty.
Will you hear now why I curse it?
It should have been my mother's—it had been,
Until I took it from her.

I was fourteen, a flower newly blown,
My mother's faithful shadow and her joy.
I remember combing her hair one day,
Playing for love her tire-woman's part,
Folding her thick hair strand over strand
Into an ebon braid, thick as my wrist,
And pinned it round and round her head
Into a living crown.

I looked up from my handiwork and saw
Our faces, hers and mine, caught in the mirror's eye.
Twin white ovals like repeated moons
Bright amid our midnight hair. Our eyes

*Like heaven's bowl; our lips like autumn's berries.*
*She frowned a little, lifted hand to throat,*
*Turned her head this way and then the other.*
*Our eyes met in the glass.*

*I saw what she had seen: her hair white-threaded,*
*Her face and throat fine-lined, her eyes softened*
*Like a mirror that clouds and cracks with age;*
*While I was newly silvered, sharp and clear.*
*I hid my eyes, but could not hide my knowledge.*
*Forty may be fair; fourteen is fairer still.*
*She smiled at my reflection, cold as glass,*
*And then dismissed me thankless.*

*Not long after the huntsman came, bearing*
*A knife, a gun, a little box, to tell me*
*My mother no longer loved me. He spared me, though,*
*Unasked, because I was too beautiful to kill.*
*And the seven little men whose house*
*I kept that winter and the following year,*
*They loved me for my beauty's sake, my beauty*
*That cost me my mother's love.*

*Do you think I did not know her,*
*Ragged and gnarled and stooped like a wind-bent tree,*
*Her basket full of combs and pins and laces?*
*Of course I took her poisoned gifts. I wanted*
*To feel her hands coming out my hair,*
*To let her lace me up, to take an apple*
*From her hand, a smile from her lips,*
*As when I was a child.*

In the earliest known versions of the "Sleeping Beauty" tale, such as Strapola's Italian retelling, the prince does not chastely kiss the lovely maid he finds sleeping in the enchanted castle. He fornicates with her sleeping body and leaves. She does not wake until she has given birth to twins, for they attempt to suckle at her fingers and in doing so pull out the spinning wheel's splinter that has caused her enchanted sleep. The following story is one of the dark versions of the tale.

# She Sleeps in a Tower
## ♦ Tanith Lee ♦

Through the dark wood, the man rides on his horse. Birds sing sometimes in the heavy boughs, among the brackish leaves, but he is not looking out for birds. Nor for hares, though once a pale one ran across his path.

Then he reaches the clearing. It is as they had described it. The fallen tree and beyond, the stone sundial, and there the ruined garden, in which still the tall and somber roses grow, and from which they have climbed up into the trees. Up the walls of the towers the roses have risen also, among the black-green ivy. Roses with terrible thorns.

And presently, the old woman, the hag, comes creeping out in her gray old mantle.

She bows low. "Good day, Sir Prince. Do you know where it is you've come to?"

"The tower," he says, the man on the horse.

"And do you know the story?"

Excited, the man twitches in the saddle.

"Tell me, old dame."

"A young girl, little more than a child. A princess. Bewitched. She lies in the tower, sleeping a sleep that may not be broken—save by her true prince."

"I'll wake her," says the man. He swings from the horse. "If she's *young,* and beautiful."

"Oh yes. There is the way then. Through that door. You must cut your path with your knife."

As he passes her, the man puts a silver coin into the old woman's hand. It is the usual amount.

Sex isn't for women. I always knew. My mother told me first. No, sex is for men. But women are the vessels.

You have to survive. God says you must, and then God tests you by making it very hard.

My father used to beat my mother, she was always black and blue, and sometimes he'd lay into me, but never so much. My uncle, my father's brother, used to protect me. "Get behind me," he'd say. Or, "Run to the well house. I'll tell him you've gone into the woods."

When I was ten, and in the well house, a year or so after my mother had died, my uncle came and sat beside me.

He told me I was a pretty girl and he played with my hair. When he put his hand on the little mound of my coming breast, I knew at once what he wanted and what would happen . . . and I knew it was only what must always happen.

So when he suggested it, I lay down, and first he put his finger inside me, and then he put his penis in. It was agonizing, but I didn't cry, and he said afterward that I was his special little girl and he'd never let any harm come to me.

He did protect me too, from my father. But one day my father broke his leg, and it went bad and he died. I was nearly thirteen by then, and my uncle was losing interest in me, so he married me to a rich man's son, but the son wasn't right in the head, so no questions were asked.

That was how I came to live in the grand house with the three towers, which belonged to my husband.

My husband, who was a booby, was also hearty in bed, and very big, so I was glad I had already been with my uncle.

Inside a few months I was in the family way, and when I gave birth to a daughter, the rich man, my husband's father, cast us off, saying I was a slut and worthless. My husband, though a fool, would often beat me as my father had. However, because he had no mind, I could now and then outwit him and keep the baby safe.

In the next two years I had another two, both girls. By then the house was going to wrack and ruin, the roof leaking and ivy growing in through the walls. Great stones had fallen out, and all the servants had gone away, but for one old woman. She hated me, and usually tried to poison me. In the end, she made a mistake, and poisoned my moron husband instead. Then she ran off, and I was all alone with my three little girls.

I lived as best I could, but I found the only way I could pay for anything was by opening my legs. And so I did. A great many men had me, and every year I grew thinner and more wrinkled, and my hair turned gray and was like straw.

But my little girls were bonny. They were dressed only in rags, but their hair shone like copper and their skin was fresh and white as milk.

One night there was a storm, the rain rushed and split the leaves and in the house it rained too, and up in the three old towers the rats rattled in the leaves and thorns that had broken through the walls.

A stranger came knocking near midnight. When I let him in, he stood before the poor fire and said, "I'd heard there was a woman here who served men. But you're an old crone. Where is she?" I said, "I fear she's gone away, sir." Just then my eldest daughter, ten years of age, came into the hall. She had been out gathering sticks to dry for the fire, and rain hung like crystals in her hair. "What's this?" said the man. "This is nice. I'll take her."

My first thought was *No*. Most mothers would think this, although it wasn't wise. But then he took out a silver piece and put it on the table. "I'll give you that for a go with her. But I like it a particular way."

What he wanted was that she go up and lie on a bed and pretend to be asleep. And then he would slip in and mount her, and at the end she would wake up and fling her arms around him and cry out he was her long-lost love.

I could see she was listening carefully, so I took her aside. I told her it would hurt, but that she must pretend to be happy, and praise him. She was always a good girl.

When he came down he was sullen, but many of them are, after they've come, so I didn't worry, and indeed he let me keep the silver piece. My daughter had survived, though she bled for a week. She was cheerful, however, and boasted to the other girls that she'd been clever. Then they wanted to do it too.

Well, their chance came for that, though not right away. A month later another man came knocking. It was in the afternoon, and he was pleasant enough. He said he'd heard a girl lay asleep who could be woken by a kiss—that was the story that had gone round apparently, rather like some of the old legends of the wood. And he said that the girl was in a tower.

So I asked my eldest if she'd go up into the west tower. She agreed, and she lay on the old bed there that had been my husband's mother's bed. She said, my girl, she was glad when the traveler came up, because, lying so quiet as she had to, the rats were skulking about. But he scattered them with his boot, and cut the thorns away from the bed—though in a fortnight they were back again.

It went on from there. And the story became a little more elaborate. And, as time went by, my other girls . . . well, they know the way of it, how life is.

I come out to them in the garden, and I ask, do they know where they've come to? And they don't say, "The brothel," no, they play along, these kinky fellows. They say they've come to the tower. And some of them even say, "Is she sleeping here?" And of course she always is. Three shes. One in each tower. I go by how they talk of her youth, whether they want the youngest now, who's ten, or the middle girl of eleven, or my eldest, who's just twelve years.

We never have any trouble, and I've never been shortchanged. Once even a rich man came a gave me a piece of gold. Perhaps he thought that was the fee, and I, obviously, didn't say no.

The man climbs up the stone stair of the east tower, his heart hammering. He lops the deadly murderous thorns with his long steel knife, but he breathes fast from hope, not exertion.

At last he reaches the wooden door, and thrusts it wide. A mad skitter of rats.

He takes the chamber in. Even in the summer light it is damp and chill, yet the roses have blossomed in the walls, and all about the mildewed bed. And on the bed she lies. Oh . . . but she is lovely.

Slim as a wand, upon a cloud of dark red gleaming hair. Her skin like cream. Her hands crossed below her bosom—and oh, she is so young, only the faintest swelling there, like two sweet kisses.

She wears, the princess, a dress of white silk, a little stained and worn, but this he does not see. In any case, she has been sleeping years—decades—perhaps a century, awaiting the true touch of love.

He goes to the bed and pulls away her skirt—easy, it might have been arranged for him to do it.

As he enters her pliant body he can barely wait. Such joy. She must feel it.

And she does. Her eyes fly open. She clasps him with her slender little-girl arms.

And in her bird's voice, ten years of age, she softly cries: "At last! My prince!"

# Briar Rose (Sleeping Beauty)

Anne Sexton

♦

*Consider*
*a girl who keeps slipping off,*
*arms limp as old carrots,*
*into the hypnotist's trance,*
*into a spirit world*
*speaking with the gift of tongues.*
*She is stuck in the time machine,*
*suddenly two years old sucking her thumb,*
*as inward as a snail,*
*learning to talk again.*
*She's on a voyage.*
*She is swimming further and further back,*
*up like a salmon,*
*struggling into her mother's pocketbook.*
*Little doll child,*
*come here to Papa.*
*Sit on my knee.*
*I have kisses for the back of your neck.*
*A penny for your thoughts, Princess.*
*I will hunt them like an emerald.*
*Come be my snooky*
*and I will give you a root.*
*That kind of voyage,*
*rank as honeysuckle.*

*Once*
*a king had a christening*
*for his daughter Briar Rose*
*and because he had only twelve gold plates*
*he asked only twelve fairies*
*to the grand event.*
*The thirteenth fairy,*

her fingers as long and thin as straws,
her eyes burnt by cigarettes,
her uterus an empty teacup,
arrived with an evil gift.
She made this prophecy:
The princess shall prick herself
on a spinning wheel in her fifteenth year
and then fall down dead.
Kaputt!
The court fell silent.
The king looked like Munch's Scream.
Fairies' prophecies,
in times like those,
held water.
However the twelfth fairy
had a certain kind of eraser
and thus she mitigated the curse
changing that death
into a hundred-year sleep.
The king ordered every spinning wheel
exterminated and exorcized.
Briar Rose grew to be a goddess
and each night the king
bit the hem of her gown
to keep her safe.
He fastened the moon up
with a safety pin
to give her perpetual light
He forced every male in the court
to scour his tongue with Bab-o
lest they poison the air she dwelt in.
Thus she dwelt in his odor.
Rank as honeysuckle.

On her fifteenth birthday
she pricked her finger
on a charred spinning wheel
and the clocks stopped.
Yes indeed. She went to sleep.
The king and queen went to sleep,
the courtiers, the flies on the wall.
The fire in the hearth grew still
and the roast meat stopped crackling.
The trees turned into metal
and the dog became china.
They all lay in a trance,

*each a catatonic*
*stuck in the time machine.*
*Even the frogs were zombies.*

*Only a bunch of briar roses grew*
*forming a great wall of tacks*
*around the castle.*
*Many princes*
*tried to get through the brambles*
*for they had heard much of Briar Rose*
*but they had not scoured their tongues*
*so they were held by the thorns*
*and thus were crucified.*
*In due time*
*a hundred years passed*
*and a prince got through.*
*The briars parted as if for Moses*
*and the prince found the tableau intact.*
*He kissed Briar Rose*
*and she woke up crying:*
*Daddy! Daddy!*
*Presto! She's out of prison!*
*She married the prince*
*and all went well*
*except for the fear—*
*the fear of sleep.*

*Briar Rose*
*was an insomniac . . .*
*She could not nap*
*or lie in sleep*
*without the court chemist*
*mixing her some knock-out drops*
*and never in the prince's presence.*
*If it is to come, she said,*
*sleep must take me unawares*
*while I am laughing or dancing*
*so that I do not know that brutal place*
*where I lie down with cattle prods,*
*the hole in my cheek open.*
*Further, I must not dream*
*for when I do I see the table set*
*and a faltering crone at my place,*
*her eyes burnt by cigarettes*
*as she eats betrayal like a slice of meat.*

I must not sleep
for while asleep I'm ninety
and think I'm dying.
Death rattles in my throat
like a marble.
I wear tubes like earrings.
I lie as still as a bar of iron.
You can stick a needle
through my kneecap and I won't flinch.
I'm all shot up with Novocain.
This trance girl
is yours to do with.
You could lay her in a grave,
an awful package,
and shovel dirt on her face
and she'd never call back: Hello there!
But if you kissed her on the mouth
her eyes would spring open
and she'd call out: Daddy! Daddy!
Presto!
She's out of prison.

There was a theft.
That much I am told.
I was abandoned.
That much I know.
I was forced backward.
I was forced forward.
I was passed hand to hand
like a bowl of fruit.
Each night I am nailed into place
and I forget who I am.
Daddy?
That's another kind of prison.
It's not the prince at all,
but my father
drunkenly bent over my bed,
circling the abyss like a shark,
my father thick upon me
like some sleeping jellyfish.

What voyage this, little girl?
This coming out of prison?
God help—
this life after death?

In Boston several years ago, The Endicott Studio mounted an art exhibition on the theme of child abuse, titled "Surviving Childhood." That exhibition sparked a dialogue among writers and artists that resulted in the formation of this book. It is fitting then that in the following story the author has re-created such an exhibition, setting it in Newford, the magical North American city that is the setting for many of his stories.

# In the House of My Enemy
### ♦ Charles de Lint ♦

*We have not inherited the Earth from our fathers, we are borrowing it from our children.*

*—Native American saying*

## 1

The past scampers like an alleycat through the present, leaving the pawprints of memories scattered helter-skelter—here ink is smeared on a page, there lies an old photograph with a chewed corner, elsewhere still, a nest has been made of old newspapers, the headlines running one into the other to make strange declarations. There is no order to what we recall, the wheel of time follows no straight line as it turns in our heads. In the dark attics of our minds, all times mingle, sometimes literally.

I get so confused. I've been so many people; some I didn't like at all. I wonder that anyone could. Victim, hooker, junkie, liar, thief. But without them, I wouldn't be who I am today. I'm no one special, but I like who I am, lost childhood and all.

Did I have to be all those people to become the person I am today? Are they still living inside me, hiding in some dark corner of my mind, waiting for me to slip and stumble and fall and give them life again?

I tell myself not to remember, but that's wrong, too. Not remembering makes them stronger.

## 2

The morning sun came in through the window of Jilly Coppercorn's loft, playing across the features of her guest. The girl was still asleep on the

Murphy bed, sheets all tangled around her skinny limbs, pulled tight and smooth over the rounded swell of her abdomen. Sleep had gentled her features. Her hair clouded the pillow around her head. The soft morning sunlight gave her a Madonna quality, a nimbus of Botticelli purity that the harsher light of the later day would steal away once she woke.

She was fifteen years old. And eight months pregnant.

Jilly sat in the windowseat, feet propped up on the sill, sketchpad on her lap. She caught the scene in charcoal, smudging the lines with the pad of her middle finger to soften them. On the fire escape outside, a stray cat climbed up the last few metal steps until it was level with where she was sitting and gave a plaintive meow.

Jilly had been expecting the black and white tabby. She reached under her knees and picked up a small plastic margarine container filled with dried kibbles, which she set down on the fire escape in front of the cat. As the tabby contentedly crunched its breakfast, Jilly returned to her portrait.

"My name's Annie," her guest had told her last night when she stopped Jilly on Yoors Street just a few blocks south of the loft. "Could you spare some change? I really need to get some decent food. It's not so much for me. . . ."

She put her hand on the swell of her stomach as she spoke. Jilly had looked at her, taking in the stringy hair, the ragged clothes, the unhealthy color of her complexion, the too-thin body that seemed barely capable of sustaining the girl herself, little say nourishing the child she carried.

"Are you all on your own?" Jilly asked.

The girl nodded.

Jilly put her arm around the girl's shoulder and steered her back to the loft. She let her take a shower while she cooked a meal, gave her a clean smock to wear, and tried not to be patronizing while she did it all.

The girl had lost enough dignity as it was and Jilly knew that dignity was almost as hard to recover as innocence. She knew all too well.

### 3

*Stolen Childhood, by Sophie Etoile. Copperplate engraving. Five Coyotes Singing Studio, Newford, 1988.*

*A child in a ragged dress stands in front of a ramshackle farmhouse. In one hand she holds a doll—a stick with a ball stuck in one end and a skirt on the other. She wears a lost expression, holding the doll as though she doesn't quite know what to do with it.*

*A shadowed figure stands behind the screen door, watching her.*

I guess I was around three years old when my oldest brother started molesting me. That'd make him eleven. He used to touch me down between my legs while my parents were out drinking or sobering up down in the kitchen. I tried to fight him off, but I didn't really know that what he was doing was wrong—even when he started to put his cock inside me.

I was eight when my mother walked in on one of his rapes and you know what she did? She walked right out again until my brother was finished and we both had our clothes on again. She waited until he'd left the room, then she came back in and started screaming at me.

"You little slut! Why are you doing this to your own brother?"

Like it was my fault. Like I *wanted* him to rape me. Like the three-year-old I was when he started molesting me had any idea about what he was doing.

I think my other brothers knew what was going on all along, but they never said anything about it—they didn't want to break that macho code-of-honor bullshit. When my dad found out about it, he beat the crap out of my brother, but in some ways it just got worse after that.

My brother didn't molest me anymore, but he'd glare at me all the time, like he was going to pay me back for the beating he got soon as he got a chance. My mother and my other brothers, every time I'd come into a room, they'd all just stop talking and look at me like I was some kind of bug.

I think at first my dad wanted to do something to help me, but in the end he really wasn't any better than my mother. I could see it in his eyes: He blamed me for it, too. He kept me at a distance, never came close to me anymore, never let me feel like I was normal.

He's the one who had me see a psychiatrist. I'd have to go and sit in his office all alone, just a little kid in this big leather chair. The psychiatrist would lean across his desk, all smiles and smarmy understanding, and try to get me to talk, but I never told him a thing. I didn't trust him. I'd already learned that I couldn't trust men. Couldn't trust women either, thanks to my mother. Her idea of working things out was to send me to confession, like the same God who let my brother rape me was now going to make everything okay so long as I owned up to seducing him in the first place.

What kind of a way is that for a kid to grow up?

4

"Forgive me, Father, for I have sinned. I let my brother . . ."

5

Jilly laid her sketchpad aside when her guest began to stir. She swung her legs down so that they dangled from the windowsill, heels banging lightly against the wall, toes almost touching the ground. She pushed an unruly lock of hair from her brow, leaving behind a charcoal smudge on her temple.

Small and slender, with pixie features and a mass of curly dark hair, she looked almost as young as the girl on her bed. Jeans and sneakers, a dark T-shirt and an oversized peach-colored smock only added to her air of slightness and youth. But she was halfway through her thirties, her own teenage years long gone; she could have been Annie's mother.

"What were you doing?" Annie asked as she sat up, tugging the sheets up around herself.

"Sketching you while you slept. I hope you don't mind."

"Can I see?"

Jilly passed the sketchpad over and watched Annie study it. On the fire escape behind her, two more cats had joined the black and white tabby at the margarine container. One was an old alleycat, its left ear ragged and torn, ribs showing like so many hills and valleys against the matted landscape of its fur. The other belonged to an upstairs neighbor; it was making its usual morning rounds.

"You made me look a lot better than I really am," Annie said finally.

Jilly shook her head. "I only drew what was there."

"Yeah, right."

Jilly didn't bother to contradict her. The self-worth speech would keep.

"So is this how you make your living?" Annie asked.

"Pretty well. I do a little waitressing on the side."

"Beats being a hooker, I guess."

She gave Jilly a challenging look as she spoke, obviously anticipating a reaction.

Jilly only shrugged. "Tell me about it," she said.

Annie didn't say anything for a long moment. She looked down at the rough portrait with an unreadable expression, then finally met Jilly's gaze again.

"I've heard about you," she said. "On the street. Seems like everybody knows you. They say . . ."

Her voice trailed off.

Jilly smiled. "What do they say?"

"Oh, all kinds of stuff." She shrugged. "You know. That you used to live on the street, that you're kind of like a one-woman social service, but you don't lecture. And that you're—" she hesitated, looked away for a moment "—you know, a witch."

Jilly laughed. "A witch?"

That was a new one on her.

Annie waved a hand towards the wall across from the window where Jilly was sitting. Paintings leaned up against each other in untidy stacks. Above them, the wall held more, a careless gallery hung frame to frame to save space. They were part of Jilly's ongoing "Urban Faerie" series, realistic city scenes and characters to which were added the curious little denizens of lands which never were. Hobs and fairies, little elf men and goblins.

"They say you think all that stuff's real," Annie said.
"What do you think?"

When Annie gave her a "give me a break" look, Jilly just smiled again.
"How about some breakfast?" she asked to change the subject.

"Look," Annie said. "I really appreciate your taking me in and feeding
me and everything last night, but I don't want to be a freeloader."

"One more meal's not freeloading."

Jilly pretended to pay no attention as Annie's pride fought with her
baby's need.

"Well, if you're sure it's okay," Annie said hesitantly.

"I wouldn't have offered if it wasn't," Jilly said.

She dropped down from the windowsill and went across the loft to the
kitchen corner. She normally didn't eat a big breakfast, but twenty minutes later they were both sitting down to fried eggs and bacon, home fries
and toast, coffee for Jilly and herb tea for Annie.

"Got any plans for today?" Jilly asked as they were finishing up.

"Why?" Annie replied, immediately suspicious.

"I thought you might want to come visit a friend of mine."

"A social worker, right?"

The tone in her voice was the same as though she was talking about a
cockroach or maggot.

Jilly shook her head. "More like a storefront counselor. Her name's
Angelina Marceau. She runs that drop-in center on Grasso Street. It's pri-
vately funded, no political connections."

"I've heard of her. The Grasso Street Angel."

"You don't have to come," Jilly said, "but I know she'd like to meet
you."

"I'm sure."

Jilly shrugged. When she started to clean up, Annie stopped her.
"Please," she said. "Let me do it."

Jilly retrieved her sketchpad from the bed and returned to the windowseat while Annie washed up. She was just adding the finishing touches
to the rough portrait she'd started earlier when Annie came to sit on the
edge of the Murphy bed.

"That painting on the easel," Annie said. "Is that something new
you're working on?"

Jilly nodded.

"It's not like your other stuff at all."

"I'm part of an artist's group that calls itself the Five Coyotes Singing
Studio," Jilly explained. "The actual studio's owned by a friend of mine
named Sophie Etoile, but we all work in it from time to time. There's five
of us, all women, and we're doing a group show with a theme of child
abuse at the Green Man Gallery next month."

"And that painting's going to be in it?" Annie asked.

"It's one of three I'm doing for the show."

"What's that one called?"

" 'I Don't Know How To Laugh Anymore.' "
Annie put her hands on top of her swollen stomach.
"Me, neither," she said.

### 6

*I Don't Know How to Laugh Anymore, by Jilly Coppercorn. Oils
and mixed media. Yoors Street Studio, Newford, 1991.*

*A life-sized female subject leans against an inner city wall in
the classic pose of a prostitute waiting for a customer. She wears
high heels, a micro-miniskirt, tube-top and short jacket, with a
purse slung over one shoulder, hanging against her hip from a
narrow strap. Her hands are thrust into the pockets of her jacket.
Her features are tired, the lost look of a junkie in her eyes
undermining her attempt to appear sultry.*

*Near her feet, a condom is attached to the painting, stiffened
with gesso.*

*The subject is thirteen years old.*

I started running away from home when I was ten. The summer I turned
eleven I managed to make it to Newford and lived on its streets for six
months. I ate what I could find in the dumpsters behind the McDonald's
and other fast food places on Williamson Street—there was nothing
wrong with the food. It was just dried out from having been under the
heating lamps for too long.

I spent those six months walking the streets all night. I was afraid to
sleep when it was dark because I was just a kid and who knows what
could've happened to me. At least being awake I could hide whenever I
saw something that made me nervous. In the daytime I slept where I
could—in parks, in the back seats of abandoned cars, wherever I didn't
think I'd get caught. I tried to keep myself clean, washed up in restaurant
bathrooms and at this gas bar on Yoors Street where the guy running the
pumps took a liking to me. Paydays he'd spot me for lunch at the grill
down the street.

I started drawing back then and for awhile I tried to hawk my pictures
to the tourists down by the Pier, but the stuff wasn't all that good and I
was drawing with pencils on foolscap or pages torn out of old school note-
books—not exactly the kind of art that looks good in a frame, if you know
what I mean. I did a lot better panhandling and shoplifting.

I finally got busted trying to boost a tape deck from Kreiger's Stereo—
it used to be where Gypsy Records is. Now it's out on the strip past the
Tombs. I've always been small for my age, which didn't help when I tried
to convince the cops that I was older than I really was. I figured juvie
would be better than going back to my parents' place, but it didn't work.
My parents had a missing persons out on me, God knows why. It's not like
they could've missed me.

But I didn't go back home. My mother didn't want me and my dad didn't argue, so I guess he didn't either. I figured that was great until I started making the rounds of foster homes, bouncing back and forth between them and the Home for Wayward Girls. It's just juvie with an old-fashioned name.

I guess there must be some good foster parents, but I never saw any. All mine ever wanted was to collect their check and treat me like I was a piece of shit unless my case worker was coming by for a visit. Then I got moved up from the mattress in the basement to one of their kids' rooms. The first time I tried to tell the worker what was going down, she didn't believe me and then my foster parents beat the crap out of me once she was gone. I didn't make that mistake again.

I was thirteen and in my fourth or fifth foster home when I got molested again. This time I didn't take any crap. I booted the old pervert in the balls and just took off out of there, back to Newford.

I was older and knew better now. Girls I talked to in juvie told me how to get around, who to trust and who was just out to peddle your ass.

See, I never planned on being a hooker. I don't know what I thought I'd do when I got to the city—I wasn't exactly thinking straight. Anyway, I ended up with this guy—Robert Carson. He was fifteen.

I met him in back of the Convention Center on the beach where all the kids used to all hang out in the summer and we ended up getting a room together on Grasso Street, near the high school. I was still pretty fucked up about getting physical with a guy but we ended up doing so many drugs—acid, MDA, coke, smack, you name it—that half the time I didn't know when he was putting it to me.

We ran out of money one day, rent was due, no food in the place, no dope, both of us too fucked up to panhandle, when Rob gets the big idea of selling my ass to bring in a little money. Well, I was screwed up, but not that screwed up. But then he got some guy to front him some smack and next thing I know I'm in this car with some guy I never saw before and he's expecting a blow job and I'm crying and all fucked up from the dope and then I'm doing it and standing out on the street corner where he's dumped me some ten minutes later with forty bucks in my hand and Rob's laughing, saying how we got it made, and all I can do is crouch on the sidewalk and puke, trying to get the taste of that guy's come out of my mouth.

So Rob thinks I'm being, like, so fucking weird—I mean, it's easy money, he tells me. Easy for him maybe. We have this big fight and then he hits me. Tells me if I don't get my ass out on the street and make some more money, he's going to do worse, like cut me.

My luck, I guess. Of all the guys to hang out with, I've got to pick one who suddenly realizes it's his ambition in life to be a pimp. Three years later he's running a string of five girls, but he lets me pay my respect—two grand which I got by skimming what I was paying him—and I'm out of the scene.

Except I'm not, because I'm still a junkie and I'm too fucked up to work, I've got no ID, I've got no skills except I can draw a little when I'm not fucked up on smack which is just about all the time. I start muling for a couple of dealers in Fitzhenry Park, just to get my fixes, and then one night I'm so out of it, I just collapse in a doorway of a pawn shop up on Perry Street.

I haven't eaten in, like, three days. I'm shaking because I need a fix so bad I can't see straight. I haven't washed in Christ knows how long, so I smell and the clothes I'm wearing are worse. I'm at the end of the line and I know it, when I hear footsteps coming down the street and I know it's the local cop on his beat, doing his rounds.

I try to crawl deeper into the shadows but the doorway's only so deep and the cop's coming closer and then he's standing there, blocking what little light the streetlamps were throwing and I know I'm screwed. But there's no way I'm going back into juvie or a foster home. I'm thinking of offering him a blow job to let me go—so far as the cops're concerned, hookers're just scum, but they'll take a freebie all the same—but I see something in this guy's face, when he turns his head and the streetlight touches it, that tells me he's an honest joe. A rookie, true blue, probably his first week on the beat and full of wanting to help everybody and I know for sure I'm screwed. With my luck running true, he's going to be the kind of guy who thinks social workers really want to help someone like me instead of playing bureaucratic mind-fuck games with my head.

I don't think I can take anymore.

I find myself wishing I had Rob's switchblade—the one he liked to push up against my face when he didn't think I was bringing in enough. I just want to cut something. The cop. Myself. I don't really give a fuck. I just want out.

He crouches down so he's kind of level with me, lying there scrunched up against the door, and says, "How bad is it?"

I just look at him like he's from another planet. How bad is it? Can it get any worse I wonder?

"I . . . I'm doing fine," I tell him.

He nods like we're discussing the weather. "What's your name?"

"Jilly," I say.

"Jilly what?"

"Uh. . . ."

I think of my parents, who've turned their backs on me. I think of juvie and foster homes. I look over his shoulder and there's a pair of billboards on the building behind me. One's advertising a suntan lotion—you know the one with the dog pulling the kid's pants down? I'll bet some old pervert thought that one up. The other's got the Jolly Green Giant himself selling vegetables. I pull a word from each ad and give it to the cop.

"Jilly Coppercorn."

"Think you can stand, Jilly?"

I'm thinking, if I could stand, would I be lying here? But I give it a try. He helps me the rest of the way up, supports me when I start to sway.

"So . . . so am I busted?" I asked him.

"Have you committed a crime?"

I don't know where the laugh comes from, but it falls out of my mouth all the same. There's no humor in it.

"Sure," I tell him. "I was born."

He sees my bag still lying on the ground. He picks it up while I lean against the wall and a bunch of my drawings fall out. He looks at them as he stuffs them back in the bag.

"Did you do those?"

I want to sneer at him, ask him why the fuck should he care, but I've got nothing left in me. It's all I can do to stand. So I tell him, yeah, they're mine.

"They're very good."

Right. I'm actually this fucking brilliant artist, slumming just to get material for my art.

"Do you have a place to stay?" he asks.

Whoops, did I read him wrong? Maybe he's planning to get me home, clean me up, and then put it to me.

"Jilly?" he asks when I don't answer.

Sure, I want to tell him. I've got my pick of the city's alleyways and doorways. I'm welcome wherever I go. World treats me like a fucking princess. But all I do is shake my head.

"I want to take you to see a friend of mine," he says.

I wonder how he can stand to touch me. I can't stand myself. I'm like a walking sewer. And now he wants to bring me to meet a friend?

"Am I busted?" I ask him again.

He shakes his head. I think of where I am, what I got ahead of me, then I just shrug. If I'm not busted, then whatever's he's got planned for me's got to be better. Who knows, maybe his friend'll front me with a fix to get me through the night.

"Okay," I tell him. "Whatever."

"C'mon," he says.

He puts an arm around my shoulder and steers me off down the street and that's how I met Lou Fucceri and his girlfriend, the Grasso Street Angel.

## 7

Jilly sat on the stoop of Angel's office on Grasso Street, watching the passersby. She had her sketchpad on her knee, but she hadn't opened it yet. Instead, she was amusing herself with one of her favorite pastimes: making up stories about the people walking by. The young woman with the child in a stroller, she was a princess in exile, disguising herself as a nanny in a far distant land until she could regain her rightful station in some suitably romantic dukedom in Europe. The old black man with the cane was a physicist studying the effects of Chaos theory in the Grasso Street traffic. The Hispanic girl on her skateboard was actually a mermaid, having exchanged the waves of her ocean for concrete.

She didn't turn around when she heard the door open behind her. There was a scuffle of sneakers on the stoop, then the sound of the door closing again. After a moment, Annie sat down beside her.

"How're you doing?" Jilly asked.

"It was weird."

"Good weird, or bad?" Jilly asked when Annie didn't go on. "Or just uncomfortable?"

"Good weird, I guess. She played the tape you did for her book. She said you knew, that you'd said it was okay."

Jilly nodded.

"I couldn't believe it was you. I mean, I recognized your voice and everything, but you sounded so different."

"I was just a kid," Jilly said. "A punky street kid."

"But look at you now."

"I'm nothing special," Jilly said, suddenly feeling self-conscious. She ran a hand through her hair. "Did Angel tell you about the sponsorship program?"

Annie nodded. "Sort of. She said you'd tell me more."

"What Angel does is coordinate a relationship between kids that need help and people who want to help. It's different every time, because everybody's different. I didn't meet my sponsor for the longest time; he just put up the money while Angel was my contact. My lifeline, if you want to know the truth. I can't remember how many times I'd show up at her door and spend the night crying on her shoulder."

"How did you get, you know, cleaned up?" Annie asked. Her voice was shy.

"The first thing is I went into detox. When I finally got out, my sponsor paid for my room and board at the Chelsea Arms while I went through an accelerated high school program. I told Angel I wanted to go on to college, so he cosigned my student loan and helped me out with my books and supplies and stuff. I was working by that point. I had part-time jobs at a couple of stores and with the Post Office, and then I started waitressing, but that kind of money doesn't go far—not when you're carrying a full course load."

"When did you find out who your sponsor was?"

"When I graduated. He was at the ceremony."

"Was it weird finally meeting him?"

Jilly laughed. "Yes and no. I'd already known him for years—he was my art history professor. We got along really well and he used to let me use the sunroom at the back of his house for a studio. Angel and Lou had shown him some of that bad art I'd been doing when I was still on the street and that's why he sponsored me—because he thought I had a lot of talent, he told me later. But he didn't want me to know it was him putting up the money because he thought it might affect our relationship at Butler U." She shook her head. "He said he *knew* I'd be going the first time Angel and Lou showed him the stuff I was doing."

"It's sort of like a fairy tale, isn't it?" Annie said.

"I guess it is. I never thought of it that way."

"And it really works, doesn't it?"

"If you want it to," Jilly said. "I'm not saying it's easy. There's ups and downs—lots more downs at the start."

"How many kids make it?"

"This hasn't got anything to do with statistics," Jilly said. "You can only look at it on a person to person basis. But Angel's been doing this for a long, long time. You can trust her to do her best for you. She takes a lot of flak for what she does. Parents get mad at her because she won't tell them where their kids are. Social services says she's undermining their authority. She's been to jail twice on contempt of court charges because she wouldn't tell where some kid was."

"Even with her boyfriend being a cop?"

"That was a long time ago," Jilly said. "And it didn't work out. They're still friends but—Angel went through an awful bad time when she was a kid. That changes a person, no matter how much they learn to take control of their life. Angel's great with people, especially kids, and she's got a million friends, but she's not good at maintaining a personal relationship with a guy. When it comes down to the crunch, she just can't learn to trust them. As friends, sure, but not as lovers."

"She said something along the same lines about you," Annie said. "She said you were full of love, but it wasn't sexual or romantic so much as a general kindness towards everything and everybody."

"Yeah, well . . . I guess both Angel and I talk too much."

Annie hesitated for a few heartbeats, then said, "She also told me that you want to sponsor me."

Jilly nodded. "I'd like to."

"I don't get it."

"What's to get?"

"Well, I'm not like you or your professor friend. I'm not, you know, all that creative. I couldn't make something beautiful if my life depended on it. I'm not much good at anything."

Jilly shook her head. "That's not what it's about. Beauty isn't what you see on TV or in magazine ads or even necessarily in art galleries. It's a lot deeper and a lot simpler than that. It's realizing the goodness of things, it's leaving the world a little better than it was before you got here. It's appreciating the inspiration of the world around you and trying to inspire others.

"Sculptors, poets, painters, musicians—they're the traditional purveyors of Beauty. But it can as easily be created by a gardener, a farmer, a plumber, a caseworker. It's the intent you put into your work, the pride you take in it—whatever it is."

"But still. . . . I really don't have anything to offer."

Annie's statement was all the more painful for Jilly because it held no self-pity, it was just a laying out of facts as Annie saw them.

"Giving birth is an act of Beauty," Jilly said.

"I don't even know if I want a kid. I . . . I don't know what I want. I don't know who I am."

She turned to Jilly. There seemed to be years of pain and confusion in her eyes, far more years than she had lived in the world. When had that pain begun? Jilly thought. Who could have done it to her, beautiful child that she must have been? Father, brother, uncle, family friend?

Jilly wanted to just reach out and hold her, but knew too well how the physical contact of comfort could too easily be misconstrued as an invasion of the private space an abuse victim sometimes so desperately needed to maintain.

"I need help," Annie said softly. "I know that. But I don't want charity."

"Don't think of this sponsorship program as charity," Jilly said. "What Angel does is simply what we all should be doing all of the time—taking care of each other."

Annie sighed, but fell silent. Jilly didn't push it any further. They sat for awhile longer on the stoop while the world bustled by on Grasso Street.

"What was the hardest part?" Annie asked. "You know, when you first came off the street."

"Thinking of myself as normal."


8

Daddy's Home, *by Isabelle Copley. Painted Wood. Adjani Farm, Wren Island, 1990.*

*The sculpture is three feet high, a flat rectangle of solid wood, standing on end with a child's face, upper torso and hands protruding from one side, as though the wood is gauze against which the subject is pressing.*

*The child wears a look of terror.*


Annie's sleeping again. She needs the rest as much as she needs regular meals and the knowledge that she's got a safe place to stay. I took my Walkman out onto the fire escape and listened to a copy of the tape that Angel played for her today. I don't much recognize that kid either, but I know it's me.

It's funny, me talking about Angel, Angel talking about me, both of us knowing what the other needs, but neither able to help herself. I like to see my friends as couples. I like to see them in love with each other. But it's not the same for me.

Except who am I kidding? I want the same thing, but I just choke when a man gets too close to me. I can't let down that final barrier, I can't even tell them why.

Sophie says I expect them to just instinctively know. That I'm waiting for them to be understanding and caring without ever opening up to them. If I want them to follow the script I've got written out my head, she says I have to let them in on it.

I know she's right, but I can't do anything about it.

I see a dog slink into the alleyway beside the building. He's skinny as a whippet, but he's just a mongrel that no one's taken care of for awhile. He's got dried blood on his shoulders, so I guess someone's been beating him.

I go down with some cat food in a bowl, but he won't come near me, no matter how soothingly I call to him. I know he can smell the food, but he's more scared of me than he's hungry. Finally I just leave the bowl and go back up the fire escape. He waits until I'm sitting outside my window again before he goes up to the bowl. He wolfs the food down and then he takes off like he's done something wrong.

I guess that's the way I am when I meet a man I like. I'm really happy with him until he's nice to me, until he wants to kiss me and hold me, and then I just run off like I've done something wrong.

## 9

Annie woke while Jilly was starting dinner. She helped chop up vegetables for the vegetarian stew Jilly was making, then drifted over to the long worktable that ran along the back wall near Jilly's easel. She found a brochure for the Five Coyotes Singing Studio show in amongst the litter of paper, magazines, sketches, and old paint brushes and brought it over to the kitchen table where she leafed through it while Jilly finished up the dinner preparations.

"Do you really think something like this is going to make a difference?" Annie asked after she'd read through the brochure.

"Depends on how big a difference you're talking about," Jilly said. "Sophie's arranged for a series of lectures to run in association with the show and she's also organized a couple of discussion evenings at the gallery where people who come to the show can talk to us—about their reactions to the show, about their feelings, maybe even share their own experiences if that's something that feels right to them at the time."

"Yeah, but what about the kids that this is all about?" Annie asked.

Jilly turned from the stove. Annie didn't look at all like a young expectant mother, glowing with her pregnancy. She just looked like a hurt and confused kid with a distended stomach, a kind of Ralph Steadman aura of frantic anxiety splattered around her.

"The way we see it," Jilly said, "is if only one kid gets spared the kind of hell we all went through, then the show'll be worth it."

"Yeah, but the only kind of people who are going to go to this kind of thing are those who already know about it. You're preaching to the converted."

"Maybe. But there'll be media coverage—in the papers for sure, maybe a spot on the news. That's where—if we're going to reach out and wake someone up—that's where it's going to happen."

"I suppose."

Annie flipped over the brochure and looked at the four photographs on the back.

"How come there isn't a picture of Sophie?" she asked.

"Cameras don't seem to work all that well around her," Jilly said. "It's like"—she smiled—"an enchantment."

The corner of Annie's mouth twitched in response.

"Tell me about, you know . . ." She pointed to Jilly's Urban Faerie paintings. "Magic. Enchanted stuff."

Jilly put the stew on low to simmer then fetched a sketchbook that held some of the preliminary pencil drawings for the finished paintings that were leaning up against the wall. The urban settings were barely realized—just rough outlines and shapes—but the faerie were painstakingly detailed.

As they flipped through the sketchbook, Jilly talked about where she'd done the sketches, what she'd seen, or more properly glimpsed, that led her to make the drawings she had.

"You've really seen all these . . . little magic people?" Annie asked.

Her tone of voice was incredulous, but Jilly could tell that she wanted to believe.

"Not all of them," Jilly said. "Some I've only imagined, but others . . . like this one." She pointed to a sketch that had been done in the Tombs where a number of fey figures were hanging out around an abandoned car, pre-Raphaelite features at odds with their raggedy clothing and setting. "They're real."

"But they could just be people. It's not like they're tiny or have wings like some of the others."

Jilly shrugged. "Maybe, but they weren't just people."

"Do you have to be magic yourself to see them?"

Jilly shook her head. "You just have to pay attention. If you don't you'll miss them, or see something else—something you expected to see rather than what was really there. Fairy voices become just the wind, a bodach, like this little man here"—she flipped to another page and pointed out a small gnomish figure the size of a cat, darting off a sidewalk—"scurrying across the street becomes just a piece of litter caught in the backwash of a bus."

"Pay attention," Annie repeated dubiously.

Jilly nodded. "Just like we have to pay attention to each other, or we miss the important things that are going on there as well."

Annie turned another page, but she didn't look at the drawing. Instead she studied Jilly's pixie features.

"You really, really believe in magic, don't you?" she said.

"I really, really do," Jilly told her. "But it's not something I just take on faith. For me, art is an act of magic. I pass on the spirits that I see—of people, of places, mysteries."

"So what if you're not an artist? Where's the magic then?"

"Life's an act of magic, too. Claire Hamill sings a line in one of her songs that really sums it up for me: 'If there's no magic, there's no meaning.' Without magic—or call it wonder, mystery, natural wisdom—nothing has any depth. It's all just surface. You know: What you see is what you get. I honestly believe there's more to everything than that, whether it's a Monet hanging in a gallery or some old vagrant sleeping in an alley."

"I don't know," Annie said. "I understand what you're saying, about people and things, but this other stuff—it sounds more like the kinds of things you see when you're tripping."

Jilly shook her head. "I've done drugs and I've seen Faerie. They're not the same."

She got up to stir the stew. When she sat down again, Annie had closed the sketchbook and was sitting with her hands flat against her stomach.

"Can you feel the baby?" Jilly asked.

Annie nodded.

"Have you thought about what you want to do?"

"I guess. I'm just not sure I even want to keep the baby."

"That's your decision," Jilly said. "Whatever you want to do, we'll stand by you. Either way we'll get you a place to stay. If you keep the baby and want to work, we'll see about arranging daycare. If you want to stay home with the baby, we'll work something out for that as well. That's what this sponsorship's all about. It's not us telling you what to do; we just want to help you be the person you were meant to be."

"I don't know if that's such a good person," Annie said.

"Don't think like that. It's not true."

Annie shrugged. "I guess I'm scared I'll do the same thing to my baby that my mother did to me. That's how it happens, doesn't it? My mom used to beat the crap out of me all the time, didn't matter if I did something wrong or not, and I'm just going to end up doing the same thing to my kid."

"You're only hurting yourself with that kind of thinking," Jilly said.

"But it *can* happen, can't it? Jesus, I . . . You know I've been gone from her for two years now, but I still feel like she's standing right next to me half the time, or waiting around the corner for me. It's like I'll never escape. When I lived at home, it was like I was living in the house of an

enemy. But running away didn't change that. I still feel like that, except now it's like everybody's my enemy."

Jilly reached over and laid a hand on hers.

"Not everybody," she said. "You've got to believe that."

"It's hard not to."

"I know."

## 10

This Is Where We Dump Them, *by Meg Mullally. Tinted photograph. The Tombs, Newford, 1991.*

*Two children sit on the stoop of one of the abandoned buildings in the Tombs. Their hair is matted, faces smudged, clothing dirty and ill-fitting. They look like turn-of-the-century Irish tinkers. There's litter all around them: torn garbage bags spewing their contents on the sidewalk, broken bottles, a rotting mattress on the street, half-crushed pop cans, soggy newspapers, used condoms.*

*The children are seven and thirteen, a boy and a girl. They have no home, no family. They only have each other.*

The next month went by awfully fast. Annie stayed with me—it was what she wanted. Angel and I did get her a place, a one-bedroom on Landis that she's going to move into after she's had the baby. It's right behind the loft—you can see her back window from mine. But for now she's going to stay here with me.

She's really a great kid. No artistic leanings, but really bright. She could be anything she wants to be if she can just learn to deal with all the baggage her parents dumped on her.

She's kind of shy around Angel and some of my other friends—I guess they're all too old for her or something—but she gets along really well with Sophie and me. Probably because, whenever you put Sophie and me together in the same room for more than two minutes, we just start giggling and acting about half our respective ages, which would make us, mentally at least, just a few years Annie's senior.

"You two could be sisters," Annie told me one day when we got back from Sophie's studio. "Her hair's lighter, and she's a little chestier, and she's *definitely* more organized than you are, but I get a real sense of family when I'm with the two of you. The way families are supposed to be."

"Even though Sophie's got faerie blood?" I asked her.

She thought I was joking.

"If she's got magic in her," Annie said, "then so do you. Maybe that's what makes you seem so much like sisters."

"I just pay attention to things," I told her. "That's all."

"Yeah, right."

♦♦♦

The baby came right on schedule—three-thirty, Sunday morning. I probably would've panicked if Annie hadn't been doing enough of that for both of us. Instead I got on the phone, called Angel, and then saw about helping Annie get dressed.

The contractions were really close by the time Angel arrived with the car. But everything worked out fine. Jillian Sophia Mackle was born two hours and forty-five minutes later at the Newford General Hospital. Six pounds and five ounces of red-faced wonder. There were no complications.

Those came later.

## 11

The last week before the show was simple chaos. There seemed to be a hundred and one things that none of them had thought of, all of which had to be done at the last moment. And to make matters worse, Jilly still had one unfinished canvas haunting her by Friday night.

It stood on her easel, untitled, barely sketched-in images, still in monochrome. The colors eluded her. She knew what she wanted, but every time she stood before her easel, her mind went blank. She seemed to forget everything she'd ever known about art. The inner essence of the canvas rose up inside her like a ghost, so close she could almost touch it, but then fled daily, like a dream lost upon waking. The outside world intruded. A knock on the door. The ringing of the phone.

The show opened in exactly seven days.

Annie's baby was almost two weeks old. She was a happy, satisfied infant, the kind of baby that was forever making contented little gurgling sounds, as though talking to herself; she never cried. Annie herself was a nervous wreck.

"I'm scared," she told Jilly when she came over to the loft that afternoon. "Everything's going too well. I don't deserve it."

They were sitting at the kitchen table, the baby propped up on the Murphy bed between two pillows. Annie kept fidgeting. Finally she picked up a pencil and started drawing stick figures on pieces of paper.

"Don't say that," Jilly said. "Don't even think it."

"But it's true. Look at me. I'm not like you or Sophie. I'm not like Angel. What have I got to offer my baby? What's she going to have to look up to when she looks at me?"

"A kind, caring mother."

Annie shook her head. "I don't feel like that. I feel like everything's sort of fuzzy and it's like pushing through cobwebs to just to make it through the day."

"We'd better make an appointment with you to see a doctor."

"Make it a shrink," Annie said. She continued to doodle, then looked down at what she was doing. "Look at this. It's just crap."

Before Jilly could see, Annie swept the sheaf of papers to the floor. "Oh, jeez," she said as they went fluttering all over the place. "I'm sorry. I didn't mean to do that."

She got up before Jilly could and tossed the lot of them in the garbage container beside the stove. She stood there for a long moment, taking deep breaths, holding them, slowly letting them out.

"Annie . . . ?"

She turned as Jilly approached her. The glow of motherhood that had seemed to revitalize her in the month before the baby was born had slowly worn away. She was pale again. Wan. She looked so lost that all Jilly could do was put her arms around her and offer a wordless comfort.

"I'm sorry," Annie said against Jilly's hair. "I don't know what's going on. I just . . . I know I should be really happy, but I just feel scared and confused." She rubbed at her eyes with a knuckle. "God, listen to me. All it seems I can do is complain about my life."

"It's not like you've had a great one," Jilly said.

"Yeah, but when I compare it to what it was like before I met you, it's like I moved up into heaven."

"Why don't you stay here tonight?" Jilly said.

Annie stepped back out of her arms. "Maybe I will—if you really don't mind . . . ?"

"I really don't mind."

"Thanks."

Annie glanced towards the bed, her gaze pausing on the clock on the wall above the stove.

"You're going to be late for work," she said.

"That's all right. I don't think I'll go in tonight."

Annie shook her head. "No, go on. You've told me how busy it gets on a Friday night."

Jilly still worked part-time at Kathryn's Cafe on Battersfield Road. She could just imagine what Wendy would say if she called in sick. There was no one else in town this weekend to take her shift, so that would leave Wendy working all the tables on her own.

"If you're sure," Jilly said.

"We'll be okay," Annie said. "Honestly."

She went over to the bed and picked up the baby, cradling her gently in her arms.

"Look at her," she said, almost to herself. "It's hard to believe something so beautiful came out of me." She turned to Jilly, adding before Jilly could speak, "That's a kind of magic all by itself, isn't it?"

"Maybe one of the best we can make," Jilly said.

## 12

How Can You Call This Love? *by Claudia Feder. Oils. Old Market Studio, Newford, 1990.*

*A fat man sits on a bed in a cheap hotel room. He's removing his shirt. Through the ajar door of the bathroom behind him, a thin girl in bra and panties can be seen sitting on the toilet, shooting up.*

*She appears to be about fourteen.*

I just pay attention to things, I told her. I guess that's why, when I got off my shift and came back to the loft, Annie was gone. Because I pay such good attention. The baby was still on the bed, lying between the pillows, sleeping. There was a note on the kitchen table:

*I don't know what's wrong with me. I just keep wanting to hit something. I look at little Jilly and I think about my mother and I get so scared. Take care of her for me. Teach her magic.*

*Please don't hate me.*

I don't know how long I sat and stared at those sad, piteous words, tears streaming from my eyes.

I should never have gone to work. I should never have left her alone. She really thought she was just going to replay her own childhood. She told me, I don't know how many times she told me, but I just wasn't paying attention, was I?

Finally I got on the phone. I called Angel. I called Sophie. I called Lou Fucceri. I called everybody I could think of to go out and look for Annie. Angel was at the loft with me when we finally heard. I was the one who picked up the phone.

I heard what Lou said: "A patrolman brought her into the General not fifteen minutes ago, ODing on Christ knows what. She was just trying to self-destruct, is what he said. I'm sorry, Jilly. But she died before I got there."

I didn't say anything. I just passed the phone to Angel and went to sit on the bed. I held little Jilly in my arms and then I cried some more.

I was never joking about Sophie. She really does have faerie blood. It's something I can't explain, something we've never really talked about, something I just know and she's never denied. But she did promise me that she'd bless Annie's baby, just the way fairy godmothers would do it in all those old stories.

"I gave her the gift of a happy life," she told me later. "I never dreamed it wouldn't include Annie."

But that's the way it works in fairy tales, too, isn't it? Something always goes wrong, or there wouldn't be a story. You have to be strong, you have to earn your happily ever after.

Annie was strong enough to go away from her baby when she felt like all she could do was just lash out, but she wasn't strong enough to help herself. That was the awful gift her parents gave her.

I never finished that last painting in time for the show, but I found something to take its place. Something that said more to me in just a few rough lines than anything I've ever done.

I was about to throw out my garbage when I saw those crude little drawings that Annie had been doodling on my kitchen table the night she died. They were like the work of a child.

I framed one of them and hung it in the show.

"I guess we're five coyotes and one coyote ghost now," was all Sophie said when she saw what I had done.


### 13

In the House of My Enemy, *by Annie Mackle. Pencils. Yoors Street Studio, Newford, 1991.*

*The images are crudely rendered. In a house that is merely a square with a triangle on top, are three stick figures, one plain, two with small "skirt" triangles to represent their gender. The two larger figures are beating the smaller one with what might be crooked sticks, or might be belts.*

*The small figure is cringing away.*


### 14

In the visitor's book set out at the show, someone wrote: "I can never forgive those responsible for what's been done to us. I don't even want to try."

"Neither do I," Jilly said when she read it. "God help me, but neither do I."

# Fear of Falling

Susan Palwick

♦

*My father taught me men are dangerous.*
*Women invite lewd looks if they reveal*
*an inch of thigh, contempt if they should feel*
*righteous and raise an eyebrow or a fuss*
*when flesh is bared—for sex is beautiful*
*and healthy. He said that aloud. The rest*
*we learned from winks and nudges, and we guessed*
*our dizzy way to safety, dutiful*
*daughters treading the tightrope as we grew,*
*teetering between prude and prostitute,*
*unsure of nets. We learned the safest way*
*was plainness. When uncertain what to do,*
*we fade. Admiration and pursuit*
*can make me lose my balance to this day.*

In the older versions of "Cinderella" (and other "Ash Girl" tales dating back to ancient China, found in cultures throughout the world), our heroine does not wait drooping by the fireside until she is saved by fairy godmothers and talking mice. She is a quick-witted and angry young woman, determined to reclaim her life. The following modern story reflects these older tales, although it does so with tongue firmly in cheek.

# Princess in Puce

### ◆ Annita Harlan ◆

*nce upon a time there was a not-too-successful storyteller. He woke up one morning to find the sun in his eye and an alarming thought in his head. "Omigosh, it's Sunday already! I've got a deadline to-morrow, and I haven't put word one on paper!" As is the way with those in tight corners, adrenaline rushed to his head and he said, with great relief, "I've got it! I'll cheat!" So, he wrote down this old, familiar tale and was saved one more time.*

In a land not too far away, in a time not too distant from our own, there lived a happy little family of three—Mom, Dad, and a bouncy little girl named Priscilla (for Dad's wealthy aunt). Their little house was a homey shade of blue with white shutters, a thatch roof that also housed saucy, plump swallows, and ruffled yellow curtains that blew about in the sweet breezes that always seemed to grace their orchard and fields. The whole family was cheerful and fat and full of laughter and loved each other.

And then Mom died, and right away Dad married another lady who was not fat at all. She already had two daughters. They were older than Priscilla, and not very fat, either. The three of them looked down their long, thin noses at Priscilla and were not amused.

"My beloved Elmer," the stepmother said. "You've really overfed this child frightfully. All that milk! Why, she has all the signs of serious obesity at only seven years! Look at that ruddy complexion! She'll be a heart case by twelve if she lasts that long. Diet and exercise—yes, that's the only thing for it. I'll see to it at once."

Pretty soon there wasn't a scrap of fat on Priscilla's plate, nor on her body, either. She missed both. It was cold without them. And as for the exercise part, well, that seemed to mean Stepmom had her doing a lot of scrubbing and sweeping and hoeing weeds and running errands for her and her daughters. Priscilla had Mom's brain, so she knew she was getting the shit end of the stick. Dad's brain was where it had always been, so he didn't notice her plight. Things went on like this until Priscilla reached puberty.

"Uh-oh," the stepsisters said in unison.

"Priscilla's got prettier hair than I do, even though I curl mine every day!" wailed Elaine Elizabeth.

"Yeah, and that's not all. It's all that exercise and lean diet you've had her on, Mom. Do something!" demanded Margaret Mary Faye.

Stepmom looked at her own daughters and then at Priscilla and said, "You're right. The girl is drop-dead beautiful."

To Dad she said, "Darling Elmer, Love of My Life, little Priscilla needs new clothes. I thought perhaps something up-to-date for her crowd—like puce rags with pop-top earrings?"

"Whatever," Dad said from his newspaper. "Nothing's too good for my kids."

"My darling stepdaughter," Stepmom began. Priscilla knew she was in trouble. "Here's your new outfit. I know you'll love it. And you know how you've said you need more food so you won't sleep so cold at night? Well, I have a wonderful idea. The warmest place in the house is the fireplace. And all the latest advice is to keep your bed as firm as possible! I'm going to move you right to the hearth! I'm sure it's the best thing for you!"

So there she was, camping out on the fireplace stones in her puce handkerchief skirt and puce T-shirt. If only Dad wasn't such a dodo.

Then Stepmom got a bad cold that lasted two weeks. Dad decided to go off to town to do the shopping. Before he left, he said to Priscilla and her stepsisters, "Hey, girls, whatcha want from the mall? I'll bring each of you one—count it, one—present."

Elaine Elizabeth said, "Pearls! Chartreuse and fuchsia ones with a gold and silver clasp and a sparkly dangly thing in the middle."

"That's a diamond, you idiot," Margaret Mary Fay interrupted. "I want diamonds, too. I want a whole necklace of diamonds that says 'Kiss me, Dude!' "

Then her dad actually looked at Priscilla and smiled and said, "How about you, babe?"

"Flowers," she said. "Bring me the first red flower you see."

"Flowers! What a world-class dope!" her stepsisters chimed.

Priscilla herself wondered why she'd said that. On the other hand, a steady wardrobe of puce clothing would make any girl long for a good, vivid red.

Dad might be a dodo but he brought home the bacon. Elaine and Margaret snatched their goodies and were gone to their rooms in an instant. In the relative quiet that followed Dad presented Priscilla with a branch broken off somebody's vine.

"Hey, it was the only red thing I saw. Old George won't miss it off his trellis. Your mom used to call 'em hummingbird trumpets. Enjoy, babe." And he was off to "comfort" Stepmom.

Priscilla hardly noticed the red flowers she had asked for. Instead she looked at the green stem and felt the cool juice within it and then went straight out into the orchard. There she found a spot where an old tree had died and left a stump where squirrels and owls sometimes nested. She dug a hole and planted the sprig of red trumpet flowers at the base of the stump. She couldn't help the tears that dripped into the dirt as she patted it down. Her mom had loved that old tree, and now both of them were gone.

Summer turned to winter. By then the vine had wound all the way up the stump. Better yet, in the cool of autumn after the heart-shaped leaves turned as scarlet as the flowers had been, they did not fall, but stayed on unfaded. Priscilla visited the vine every day no matter what the weather. She knew a miracle when she saw one.

Everybody else was bored with winter, so not surprisingly, their local King decided it was time for a ball. Besides, his son, the Prince, was dragging his feet on producing an heir. Therefore and by decree, every eligible woman in the countryside was invited. Informally, everyone understood this was a chance to be seen, and perhaps be chosen, by the Prince. The invitations were hardly in the mail before Elaine Elizabeth and Margaret Mary Faye and all the other young ladies of the land descended on the stores and made the shopkeepers very happy.

Royal purple, amethyst, lavender, and white satin sold out instantly. Priscilla watched while her stepsisters and stepmom went through all the possibilities. Should they appear kindred royalty? The princess in disguise? The bride-apparent? For her part, she thought of round pink rosebuds trailing across a white sheer underlain with petticoats that seemed so much a breath of early spring that you could smell the damp wind and feel the pulse of life returning.

"You want to do what?" Stepmom exclaimed. "Don't be ridiculous. I don't believe you've been invited. You have too much housework to do. You haven't a thing to wear. And somebody has to stay home and keep the fire lit."

"Every girl in the whole kingdom got an invitation," Priscilla said somewhat testily. "And I could have something to wear if you worked on it."

"Well, that's just it, isn't it, child? You see how worn out I already am trying to get your sisters ready. It's really too much to ask."

"I could fix something up myself, couldn't I?"

"Don't be silly. You never have extra time. You never get your chores finished as it is."

That was true enough, since Stepmom made sure of it. Still, Priscilla did want to go to the ball. "How about if I really did get everything done? Then could I go?"

"Oh, I suppose so. Elaine Elizabeth, stop picking your face! You don't want to have a case of zits for the prince!"

Priscilla had some reason to hope that Stepmom might let her tag along after all, so the day of the ball she worked like a demon. She finished everything around the house by late afternoon. Almost breathless she presented herself and her old dress at the door of the sewing room. The three other women were still furiously busy sewing themselves into their finery.

"Yoo-hoo," she said, tentatively. "Could I borrow a needle and thread?"

Dead silence as they all turned and regarded her.

"Of course, my dear," Stepmom said. "Elaine Elizabeth. Find her one. Excuse me a minute." She brushed by, headed for the stairs to the kitchen.

Elaine Elizabeth just glared at her and made no move to loan her anything. Almost at once from the kitchen came, "Priscilla, come here, please." Priscilla could tell she'd been had.

Something else to do. She walked heavily down the stairs, trailing her old dress behind her.

"Clumsy me. It must be the excitement. I've managed to spill lentils into the fireplace. We've really got to pick them up and wash them and get them in to soak or there's no supper tomorrow night, is there? There's a good girl. See to it, won't you?"

Stepmom went back up the stairs. Priscilla looked at the empty lentil jar—at least a gallon of lentils "spilled" in the ashes and coals? Right. If they ate that many lentils for supper they could all float to the palace on the gas they produced. But there wasn't any way around for it.

She had less than a pint of lentils and more than one burn apiece for her fingers when her stepsisters and her stepmom paraded into the kitchen and prepared to depart in the rented carriage.

"I thought we'd get an early start, to get around the parking problems," Stepmom remarked by way of explanation. "Ta-ta! Wish us good luck!"

Priscilla watched them leave, sat back with her singed fingers, and began to sniffle.

At the window there was a commotion. She scrambled up and looked out. The songbirds of the garden were gathered there, hopping up and down, chirping and looking impatient. She opened the door to see what was happening. At once they all came indoors and flew straight to the hearth. In a short while they had the gallon of lentils back in the jar. They all lined up on the sink and while she washed away the soot, they picked out the bad lentils and ate them.

No sooner did she put the cover on the bean pot than the birds congregated at the door. She opened it and watched as they danced in the air, seeming to beckon her onward into the cold dusk. She had to see what they were so excited about.

The crowd of them led her to the old tree and the scarlet vine. For its part, it was fairly glowing with color. It *was* a miracle after all. "Oh vine of mine, I do so want to go to the ball!" she blurted out. "Couldn't you help me, please?"

By way of reply, the leaves on the vine shook themselves. A dazzling shower of light fell from their tips and puddled at her feet. She reached down to touch it, and wow! It was no longer a puddle of light, but a full-length, fully appointed ball gown, glistening white with a tracery of pink rosebuds strewn across it like the very promise of spring.

She rushed indoors and put it on without a thought for her usual grubbiness. "Oh, gosh!" she murmured catching sight of her suddenly romantic hairdo in the hall mirror. Even the burns on her fingers and the soot under her nails were gone.

A knock sounded at the door. "Come in!" she exclaimed.

"Your carriage, mademoiselle," the liveried stranger announced. "If we go now, we will arrive fashionably late."

That *was* an advantage. At the palace, Priscilla lightly climbed the marble stairs to the reception without encountering anyone that she knew. Already there was a floor full of dancers moving to the beat of a full orchestra. Such wonderful music she had never heard before. Classical, perhaps.

A face across the ballroom caught her eye. What a handsome man! Why was he looking her way? At someone behind her, maybe? She half-turned to look, and saw her own reflection in the mirrored wall. She was simply gorgeous, in form, face, and apparel. A splendid match for the tall, uniformed gentleman who had seen her and was now making his way through the crowd. She turned from the glass to the man and basked in the breathtaking smile he gave her.

He looked deep into her eyes and held out his hand. "Please, beautiful princess. Will you dance with me?"

She took his hand; it was all warm and tingly as it touched hers. She gave him the widest smile of her entire life, and with a hint of a curtsy she sailed with him into the sea of dancers.

Later, the dance whirled them out onto a balcony where the cold night air kept them close even after the music ended.

"Princess," the Prince said, looking puzzled. "Is this a new kind of makeup?" He lifted a finger to touch her nose, and off came a glowing bit of light that shimmered as dew and disappeared while she watched.

*Oops,* she thought. She laughed gracefully. "I think it's one of the stars in your eyes, Highness."

The Prince laughed, too. "I think it's magic," he said, giving her a tender look. "Like meeting you."

Priscilla decided she would never need a coat again.

It was all magical. In fact, annoyingly so. Her liveried escort appeared at her elbow as the wee hours approached, and said, "Time to go, mademoiselle. If we leave now, we'll beat your family home."

That *was* a good idea. They left with little problem, except for her left glove. She lost it somewhere in the hurry, but they couldn't stop to hunt for it. She was on the hearth in soot and rags, the ball gown was gone back to Fairyland, the fire was a comfortable bed of coals, and the kitchen was cozy warm before the rest of the family returned.

"All that expense for nothing!" Stepmom was saying over and over.

"She had to be a foreigner. I never saw her before," Elaine Elizabeth insisted.

"Probably an illegal alien. We should close our borders and keep our jobs for our own people!" Stepmom replied.

"She was really, really pretty. I wish I could glow like that. I wonder how she does it?" Margaret flopped into the rocking chair.

"I wish I could have been there," Priscilla put in for effect. No one paid any attention to her or to her remark.

"We're not dead yet, girls," Stepmom declared as she paced up and down. "I heard the Duchesses talking among themselves. That—girl—disappeared before the ball was over. She didn't tell the Prince good-bye, and it seems no one, even his Highness, knows who she was."

"What a dumb thing to do," said Elaine Elizabeth. "I wouldn't have left until he popped the question."

"Or at least asked me who I was," Margaret Mary Faye mused, picking her nose.

"Nevertheless, off to bed with you. Get your beauty sleep. We haven't heard the last of this business." Stepmom finally turned her attention to Priscilla. "Breakfast at noon, sharp, Priscilla. And it had better not be lentils."

By afternoon the day after the ball, nobody was talking about the dance anymore. Instead, the news was full of special bulletins about the Prince's Quest. There were interviews with the Queen Mom and the King himself. And hasty shots of the Prince at the steps of the palace, looking dazed and clutching a white glove to his breast.

"Oh wow, what a buff!" Elaine Elizabeth groaned.

"And he looks so sad! I could just die." Margaret Mary Faye swooned into an overstuffed chair that suited her well.

"Priscilla!" Stepmom snapped. "Stop watching TV and mind the supper."

"Such a tragedy," remarked the commentator. "After three weeks of looking for just the right woman for the job, to have her disappear before the Prince could speak his mind."

And then a copy of the Royal Decree scrolled across the television screen: the search for the Prince's One True Love who had dropped her glove on the stairs. The glove, a left one, was shown in close-up. "And the Prince has declared that whoever fits the glove will be his royal bride."

"He's addled in the brain," Stepmom muttered. "There must be dozens of girls in this kingdom who could wear that ridiculous little glove. Look at it. Obviously size six and a half."

"That's okay. Maybe he wants more than one wife," Dad put in cheerfully.

All four women in the room glared at him, so he wiped the grin off his face. "Well, there's probably a trick to it."

"Yes," Stepmom said. "There's probably a trick, and maybe we can come up with a trick or two ourselves."

*Uh-oh*, Priscilla thought.

"Yes. Elaine Elizabeth, you have the smallest hands in the house. You may have the best chance. But I think the forefinger will be too long. Still"—she moved a little closer to Elaine Elizabeth on the sofa—"you know, you don't really need that last joint. After all, you don't play the piano that well. And when you're Queen, any music you want you can order. It would certainly be in your best career interests if, before the Prince and his men come to this house, you do something about it."

"You mean cut off the end of my finger?" Elaine Elizabeth exclaimed. "That's gross!"

Stepmom smiled sweetly, reached over and patted Elaine's hand. "No, dear. That's love."

"As for you, Margaret My Dear, I think there's a chance, also, if Elaine isn't chosen first, of course. I took a sculpturing class once. I was rather good, if I do say so myself."

*Oh my gosh.* Priscilla got up from the hearth and scooted for the door. "I think I'll go get another log from the woodpile."

No one paid any attention to her. Even from several paces away she could hear Margaret Mary Faye whining, "But Mom, that'll hurt. Really it will."

Priscilla ran all the way to the vine. "Ooog," she kept saying to herself, glad for once that she had an empty stomach. At least out here in the quiet orchard, in the clear light of winter, she could believe in beauty, peace, and Prince Charming again.

She threw herself down on the ground beside the old stump. "Tell me this is all a bad dream," she said to the defiant red hearts. "It's too gruesome. Even if the Prince shows up here, he's going to take one look at my mutilated stepsisters and my greedy, grinning parents, and gallop away like a shot. At least he will if he's got a brain in that wonderful head!" She burst into tears and hid her face in the leaf mold at the root of the vine.

At least she did until she heard footsteps approaching. Then she sat bolt upright and wrapped the old blanket she was wearing as a coat high up around her face. There was a guy trespassing in the orchard. He strode along pretty fast, looking all around, until he saw he wasn't alone. Then he slowed down and came toward her. He was wearing a heavy short jacket that looked like something a tank commander might don against the cold, except it wasn't camouflaged. Between it and the furry mink hat on his head, all she could make out of his face was the plume of white breath when he spoke. But when he did, she knew he was a young man.

"Good morning," he said. "I wonder if you could tell me which way is Kingston?"

"Are you from out of town?" She stood up, trying to look more like a confident landowner than a miserable girl. "You're going in exactly the wrong direction for Kingston." She found herself staring hard at him. "I'll show you to the road. It's close." His riding boots were fabulous, even with cow manure on them.

"I'd be grateful, miss. Hey, I'm sorry about the trespassing." He followed her stare and looked down at his muddy boots. "I was out riding to cheer myself up, going too fast I guess, and Old Meg got a burr up her ass—I mean—sorry for the language—she's my dad's mare and she always thinks I need my comeuppance. That is, well, she throws me at least once every time I ride her."

"Maybe you should ride your own horse, instead," Priscilla said without thinking.

He laughed and looked embarrassed. "Well, yes, that would save me bruises. Uh, that's an unusual plant you've got there. Why hasn't it thrown off its leaves?"

"Oh, it *belongs* to me," Priscilla blurted. "I would be so sad if I couldn't see it all bright and glowing every day!"

At that he just stood there looking at her broken-down shoes and the sickly purplish brown of her skirt. Priscilla blushed. "Well, anyway, the road's over here." She started off, looking to see if he was following.

Once on the macadam, Priscilla cautioned him. "Don't take the left fork, or you'll wind up in our orchard again. The right one goes straight out to Highway 1. It's only about a quarter-mile."

A look of concern came over his face. "Oh shit. Old Meg's half deaf. If she gets out on the highway she'll get confused and bag herself a dozen cars before she's hit. Gotta go." He held out his hand, hand-stitched leather glove and all. When he reached toward her, the collar pulled away from his face. For the first time she could see and hear him plainly. "Thank you, miss . . . ?"

Priscilla just stared wide-eyed at her Prince.

"Shake? I didn't mean to trespass."

*He doesn't recognize me.* "Bye," she said, and fled.

The reek of charred meat met her at the door. Stepmom was at the hearth, poking at something in the coals. "Open the windows for a little, Priscilla. The supper must have burned on the bottom. Put down that wood and see to it."

Priscilla stirred the innocently simmering supper and tried to think of something more pleasant than what Stepmom was burning in the fireplace.

Over the following days there was another flurry of dressmaking. Priscilla was not invited into her stepsisters' rooms. For once she was glad. She sewed what they brought to her and ironed what they ordered. And made teas and poultices when they said, and spent every spare minute outside.

The Prince's footprints were still in the orchard. Priscilla and the birds looked at them a lot.

"Vine mine," she said, more than once. "Please help me."

Then the seventh day of the Prince's Quest arrived. About nine in the morning a knock sounded on the front door. Priscilla dried her hands and went to answer it.

"Not so fast." Stepmom dashed by and put her own hand on the doorknob. "Go to your room, Priscilla. And stay there."

"But I don't *have* a room," Priscilla protested.

"Don't argue with me. Improvise."

Priscilla jumped out of the way just in time as her stepsisters, swathed in unbelievably genteel finery, thundered down the stairs and assumed rehearsed poses at the door beside Stepmom.

Stepmom stamped her foot. "Go on, Priscilla!"

There was no use arguing. Priscilla trudged into the downstairs bathroom, closed the door, and listened through the keyhole.

Sure enough, it was the Royal Search Committee, quite a lot of them. She couldn't hear the Prince. They seemed to be filling out a lot of forms. Then came the trying-on-the-glove part. There was a hush. Then Stepmom said, "Oh that, just a hangnail gone bad. As you can see it's getting better quite fast since we trimmed it."

There was another hush. Priscilla began to feel queasy.

"Well, Miss Elaine," a male voice as brisk as Stepmom's said. "It seems the glove fits perfectly, except for the forefinger. That's a bit short. You're not the girl we're looking for."

"Yes," a kind of giggly female voice continued on, "maybe you should have left the hangnail on. Better luck next time."

The crowd in the living room tittered.

"Next resident eligible female," the brisk voice called.

So where was the Prince? Priscilla began to wish she had not been so obedient. Too bad the bathroom didn't have a back door. Or even a window.

A collective gasp sounded through the door. It didn't seem all that joyous.

"See, gentlemen!" Stepmom declared triumphantly. "It fits perfectly! Absolutely, down to the millimeter, perfectly!"

Nobody said anything right away. Priscilla's heart was in her shoes, and feeling just as scuffed as they were.

"Yes." The brisk voice wasn't pleased. "It would seem so. Down to the millimeter."

"Where are the marriage certificate forms? I get to do those now, don't I?" It was Dad's voice.

"Yes, of course. Please read the fine print on the back before you sign on the bottom line."

Dad made a sort of squeak. "You mean there's a dowry to be paid?"

"Is there some problem?" the brisk voice asked. "It is the custom, is it not?"

"Elmer My Lovebird, whatever it is, pay it! I'll get her bags. Stay right where you are, Margaret Mary Faye. I'll only be a moment."

Priscilla sank down on the bathroom floor and listened to Stepmom climb the stairs. Then a bit of bright blue in the ceiling caught her attention. Through the ventilation fan she could see sky—and birds peeking down at her. "Scram, kid!" a male cardinal said. "While the going's good."

Priscilla blinked. It was good advice. She heard Stepmom close Margaret Mary's door. Priscilla hurried to open the bathroom door. She slid out into the hall and tiptoed through the kitchen. Nobody in the living room was looking her way. The crowd was around Dad and Margaret Mary.

Priscilla ducked out the back door and sprinted for the orchard. But no, there was a huddle of Royal Troops in the way. She dodged behind the toolshed. It was rotten cold, and she didn't have her blanket, but there *was* a view of the front door.

It opened, and Margaret Mary and Dad and the whole Royal Committee came out into the yard. There was a carriage waiting. A footman reached underneath to pull down the steps so the new princess could climb in. But it wouldn't come down. At all. Not for anybody.

The footmen struggled and tugged, but the steps stayed stuck. Another attendant tried to open the door and just give Mary Margaret a leg up. But the carriage door didn't open either. No tugging, jiggling, pounding, or cussing budged it. The door behaved as though enchanted. Priscilla began to smile.

Margaret Mary Faye began to look worried. She kept fiddling with her left hand. She was still wearing the white glove Priscilla had dropped on the palace steps.

Thundering hoofbeats echoed in the lane. Priscilla peered through the fence to see her Prince, half unseated, his walkie-talkie jouncing wildly around his neck and his dad's mettlesome mare barely under his knees. Priscilla laughed. She couldn't help it.

Old Meg rounded the gate, lurched into the yard, and came to a halt. Priscilla admired the dignified way the Prince dismounted, considering the ride. It was the constant practice, she supposed. He straightened his tunic and strode to the door to meet his betrothed. But when he caught sight of Margaret Mary Faye he stopped short.

Everyone looked worried. No one said a thing. Then the front door popped open and Stepmom popped out, waving the marriage papers. "It's all legal and proper. The glove fits perfectly, Your Highness. You said yourself, only your True Love could wear it."

The Prince looked again at Margaret Mary Faye. Priscilla could almost hear him gulp. "You don't look the same—my love." He hesitated, then held out his hand.

Priscilla imagined the Prince's life with Margaret Mary Faye and Stepmom. She was glad she couldn't see his face. "Oh, vine mine," she said under her breath. "He's in for it now. Please help him out."

Margaret Mary performed a curtsy and then, all at once, the flock of birds that had been sitting on the edge of the roof watching the whole show took off as if commanded, and dived like a squadron of fighter planes right at her.

The Prince tried to pull her away from the danger. But when he did, her whole hand, glove and all, came off in his. Margaret Mary screamed in fright, not in pain. After all, the amputation was a week old by now. Stepmom shrieked with rage. The man who belonged to the brisk voice said, "Aha!" and snatched the marriage papers out of Stepmom's grasp. Then he took the grisly object away from the Prince. He peeled the glove off the hand before he tossed it to Dad. "Your prosthetic, sir."

To the Prince he gave Priscilla's glove and said, "Your treasure, My Liege. Shall we away?"

"Yes, good officer," the Prince said.

Priscilla's heart sank again. He would go away, just as she feared. But just as she hoped, too. At least he would be safe from Stepmom and the rest. "Thank you, vine mine."

The crowd began to move away from the door, but then the Prince hesitated, "No. Wait." He turned to his officer. "Is there no other eligible woman in this household? No other daughter, or maidservant we have not yet tested?"

"Well," Dad began, looking nervous.

"No. Absolutely not," Stepmom declared.

"Huh-uh," Elaine Elizabeth echoed.

"No way," Margaret agreed, shaking her curls.

The officer fixed her family with a steely glare. "If there be such, His Royal Highness requests, indeed *commands*, that she be brought forth." Then he looked straight at Dad.

Dad face turned red. "Uh—nope. Not here, Your Highness. Not this house."

"Yet I believe I've seen such a woman," the Prince said hopefully. "I think it was here. In an orchard. She was a little thing, dressed in repulsive puce rags. But there was something about her . . . She had a pet vine. It seemed to be all she owned. It was blooming even in winter. Just as she bloomed, even in rags . . ."

Stepmom shook her head fiercely.

The Prince sighed and half-turned from the house. Priscilla could see how his face became sad. Elaine and Margaret Mary were ready to swoon. Stepmom was up to something; she didn't take her eyes off Dad, but she spoke to the officer. "I do believe all these trials have affected our Prince. His Royal Highness must be hallucinating."

The Prince interrupted her. "She was no hallucination, madam, but I can believe no such girl is to be found in this house."

"Then, my lord," said the officer—he seemed a smart cookie, if there ever was one—"let us search the grounds. The lady you saw may be homeless, or a runaway, and in need of rescue in any case."

*Now wait,* Priscilla thought, *why can't I run right now into my Prince's arms?* It was true he didn't recognize her as his One True Love before, but still—He thought her interesting enough to mention. She stood up.

Dad was between her and the Prince, and the look on his face was like one of Stepmom's. *Oh no, if I show up now, they'll know Dad's a liar and creep!* She crouched back down in the weeds.

The soldiers with the Prince's entourage took instructions and divided up. They were soon off to all points of the compass.

"I believe it was this way." The Prince set off on his steed with the group going in exactly the opposite direction from where he had seen Priscilla and her vine.

Clearly his Royal Highness was a better dancer than a geographer. Priscilla thought that was sweet, even if Old Meg found it exasperating. He seemed as much of a misfit in his Royal family as she was here in hers.

As soon as the soldiery were on their way, Priscilla saw Dad exchange looks with Stepmom. Then he left the front door and strolled toward the toolshed. At once the flock of birds reappeared and began chirping angrily, following in the air behind him.

Priscilla's heart leaped into her throat. He had seen her. He was coming for her! She tried to imagine herself a mere mushroom in the grass. But no, he simply opened the toolshed door and pulled out a shovel. He plopped it over his shoulder and walked off into the orchard after the troops. She didn't understand what he was up to, but she was saved again.

But, if she was saved, why were the birds still shrieking just above her head? She turned around.

"So there you are, you naughty child!" Stepmom sounded as if she had just caught Priscilla reading again.

Elaine Elizabeth and Margaret Mary Faye were there too, and among them they had her escape cut off.

"You'll have to lock her in the closet again, Mom," Elaine Elizabeth said, rubbing her sore finger. "The one where I spilled the bubble-gum perfume."

Priscilla recoiled. She had to get out of here, somehow. She dove through the barbed wire of the property fence, ripping whatever had been whole in her clothing into yet more unbecoming rags. But Stepmom nabbed her ankle and held her fast like a rabbit in a trap.

Still she struggled and kicked. It was some satisfaction to hear her stepsisters yell when she kicked mud on their fancy dresses. Then she caught sight of Dad returning. The shovel was caked with mud and in his hand he dragged his kill. "Oh no, you didn't! How could you!" She began to cry out of pure despair, seeing her vine limp on the ground. "It was the only thing of mine!"

"And more than you deserved." Stepmom looked smug as a stuffed trout. "Besides, girls your age shouldn't dabble in the black arts. That comes later in a proper upbringing."

"I *knew* it was all her fault somehow! What a nasty weed!" Margaret Mary ripped off a leaf from the limp stem in Dad's hand, and threw it on the ground.

Elaine Elizabeth snatched it away before Priscilla's hand could close on it. "Quick, let's burn it up before anyone sees it." In an unaccustomed display of helpfulness, she grabbed Priscilla's other leg and they began dragging her back to the front door.

Dad didn't offer to help. He walked along behind knotting the vine into a ball for the fire, saying, "Pretty smart all right. No girl. No magic vine. No evidence."

Stepmom jerked open the front door.

"We're home free," Dad said happily.

"Not so fast," a brisk voice said from the inside of the house. "Hands up, all of you."

Stepmom and Elaine Elizabeth dropped Priscilla unceremoniously on the door mat. The vine fell within reach, so she grabbed it.

"That's not fair!" Margaret Mary Faye began to whine. "You tricked us. You sneaked in the back way."

The officer said, "Your Majesty, I believe this is the girl you sought."

Priscilla wanted to crawl under the doormat. But she wouldn't fit. On the other hand, she couldn't just lie there, eye-to-eye with the toe of the Prince's riding boot. She got up slowly, and lifted her wet eyes.

"The glove, my lord. Try it."

"Yes. The glove," the Prince said, as if remembering his manners. Priscilla felt his eyes trying to see through her tear-stained misery. "Miss—" he held out his hand. "Did you happen to drop this at the ball last week?"

Priscilla put out her left hand, broken nails, scratches, dirt and all. She could feel every person in the room holding his breath.

The little white glove, size six and a half, slid onto Priscilla's hand as though it had been made for such a chance. The Prince began to smile. "It's really you. I've got you back," he said. "My little Princess in Puce."

To the wonder of all, and to Priscilla's everlasting relief, the rags and grime of her past life then fell away like old leaves. She stood revealed, radiant in bud pink and white, ready to exchange the hand and the heart held out to her for her own.

"My Prince," she said, putting both her hands in his.

"My Princess," he said. "Now, er, how do we get out of here?"

Rather than attempt to open the carriage door, the Royal couple rode away on Old Meg. They were followed by the Royal Quest Committee, the Prince's soldiery, and a multicolored flock of little songbirds.

After them, down the lane, floated Dad's parting words. "Well, hey. That's my girl. The future Queen!" he said proudly.

*"Do you think that ending's too easy on Dad?" the storyteller asked his agent, Al.*

*"Nah," replied Al, sorting through the paperwork on his desk. "Fella signed for a bundle in dowry, didn't he? He'll never get it back from the bureaucrats. . . . Here, sign this."*

*"I guess you're right," the storyteller mused, signing yet another disadvantageous contract. "I mean, everybody know it's the stepmother who's the wicked one, right?"*

*And so the occasional storyteller went off to bed with a clean conscience, and slept happily ever after.*

# The Stepsister's Story

## Emma Bull

♦

*I knew you, dancing.*
*She said, "Who is that?"*
*The others said it, too,*
*But I knew.*

*I thought the word she would not let me say.*
*Sister. You danced by so close*
*I could have touched the tiny buttons down your back.*
*I kept your secret, as true sisters do.*

*You were not more beautiful*
*Spinning in a cloud of silk,*
*Laughing in spangle-light,*
*Than on that cold hearth.*

*Not more beautiful*
*Than when my eyes crept secretly toward you*
*To the line of your bent white neck*
*And I thought, Sister.*

*Not more beautiful*
*Than your fair closed ash-marked face.*
*Ash-bruised fingers took the poker, made the fire dance*
*And I thought, I love you.*

*Who closed the tiny buttons down your back?*
*I would have done that sister's work.*
*You would have made the boys who loved you*
*Dance with me first.*

*Oh, tomorrow, don't let her see*
*That fallen sequin, that unguarded smile.*

*She'll be wild to think that you were happy.*
*Never be happy out loud*
*And I'll keep the secret.*

*The shoe came.*
*She locked you in the pantry.*
*She brought it to me, still full of spangle-light*
*And the chime of your laugh.*

*I did it to share your laugh and the cloud of silk*
*For don't true sisters share?*
*I did it to dance away from fear, from her,*
*To dance you away in my arms and call you sister.*
*True sisters ride to rescue, and I would*
*If only the shoe fit.*

*We'll make it fit, she said.*
*The kitchen knife was not full of spangle-light*
*And this is not how I meant to share with you.*

*Light-headed, I rode away,*
*My arms around a prince's waist,*
*Blood welling from your shoe*
*To stain the white horse flank.*

*And as the spangles danced before my eyes*
*I thought I might be you, riding safe away,*
*That I was the one she'd shut in darkness,*
*That we'd both slipped from her grasp at last.*

*I can't dance now.*
*But I would sit on your hearth*
*And stir the fire to dancing with a crutch.*
*Let me sit near your happiness.*
*Let me warm myself at your laughter.*
*Let me say at last, where she can't hear,*
*Sister, sister, sister.*

A common element in many fairy tales is the guide, the wise helper. They can take many forms: fairy godmother, talking snake, therapist . . .

# The Session

♦ Steven Gould ♦

he armchair is nice. *Some people like to sit or stretch out on the couch. Whatever you're most comfortable with.*
Well, lying down makes me nervous. I think . . . the chair. It was good of you to see me on such short notice.
*I don't "see" people. I help them to see themselves.*
I feel quite strange coming here like this. I'm not sick, you know. I'm not.
*Nobody said you were. Sometimes we all need someone to talk to, to sort things out in our heads. It doesn't mean we're sick. It often means, though, that we're unhappy with some aspect of our lives.*
Well, I guess that's right. It's not as if I shouldn't be happy. I have the whole happy-ever-after package: wonderful husband, wonderful baby girl, servants, fine clothes. I don't know why I shouldn't be happy.
*Yet you aren't happy.*
Right. I'm not. There's tension between me and my husband.
*Tell me about it.*
The first year was wonderful. All honeymoon and roses and parties. All my problems were over. Then Father died, which hit me pretty damn hard, and, of course, we moved back here to take over running things. It was expected, you know, and it was interesting at first, but there were all my stepmother's old friends and, of course, all the childhood memories.
My husband became more and more involved in administration and

we were apart longer, but I was pregnant by then and nesting, picking out the baby clothes and remodeling the nursery and interviewing nannies. For a while, after she was born, my husband and I spent more time together, but then he was back to work and I was taking care of her and supervising servants.

It was when she turned one that I started getting these fits of depression. I'd goad my husband and we'd get into these awful shouting fights that would end up in passionate reconciliation. The sex was wonderful but then I'd get depressed again, crying suddenly in the middle of the day, usually while I watched my daughter play.

*What did you feel? Grief? Anger?*

Sad, I guess. Though sometimes there was anger as well. I lose my temper. I have to leave my daughter to the nanny because there are times that I don't trust myself with her. When she's being bad.

*Being bad?*

Crying all the time, pulling things off of tables, throwing things.

*How old is your daughter?*

Two. And I know—that's normal behavior for a two-year-old. My temper is probably not normal.

*Why do you think that is?*

Can't you tell me? I mean, this is what you do, isn't it?

*Yes and no. I know a great many things and I suspect others, but for me to tell you what I know or suspect is not going to do any good unless you're ready to see it for yourself. I know this seems roundabout, but what we're doing is exploring things in a way that lets you discover what causes you to feel and behave as you do. So, if I reflect things back at you or ask questions, it's to steer you to where you can find insight.*

Oh.

*So, why do you think your temper isn't normal?*

Well, uh, I react to things way out of proportion. Something that I know is a trivial annoyance still causes me to fly into a rage. The servants have stopped talking to me about anything "bad." If there's a problem, they go to my husband.

I guess that's as it should be. After all, he's the reasonable one. Sometimes it feels like if I let myself get really angry, I'll destroy things.

*It sounds like you've been holding anger back for a long time.*

Well, yes. I guess that's right. I remember thinking I'd explode long before I ran away from home.

*Let's talk about that.*

About what?

*Well, why don't we start with how you met your husband? That was after you ran away.*

Oh, everybody knows that.

*I want your viewpoint.*

Well, okay. He saved my life. I was choking, you see, on some fruit. I was pretty far gone. I'd even passed out, suffocating, and the next thing I know this guy is giving me mouth-to-mouth. Apparently, he did the Heimlich maneuver to dislodge the obstruction, then CPR to get me going again. We weren't anywhere near a hospital and those bozos I was working for at the time were useless for something like that.

*Bozos?*

I was doing housework for these miners. After I ran away from home, they took me in, and I was grateful, but I never met such slobs. Took me a month to clean their house the first time. All I was getting out of it was room and board and the odd pinch on the fanny. They were a randy bunch, but I used a rolling pin on one of them and they left me alone after that. You know all of this.

*Viewpoint, remember? How long did you stay with the, uh, bozos?*

Well, I was sixteen when I ran away . . . uh, a year and a half. We still talk. They come by for Christmas dinner, and they always bring my daughter something nice, but they're still slobs. Embarrassing.

*Do they embarrass you in front of your husband?*

Oh, no. *He* likes them.

*Why did you run away from home?*

Oh, come on! You talked to my stepmother all the time. You know how crazy she was.

*My relationship with your, uh, stepmother, was not a two-way thing. I know details, but it's your perspective that we need here.*

I don't see why she has anything to do with my problems with my husband!

*Don't you?*

No!

*You're angry right now. Why?*

I'm not angry!

—

Well, maybe I am! I've got every right to be angry when I think about that bitch.

*She abused you.*

Hell, yes, she abused me. She tried to kill me. And it got worse the older I got. She thought I was competing with her in some way. She'd spend all that time with all those creams and things. Spa treatments. But even before she thought I was competing with her, she abused me. She was so cold. When my complexion got so pale and clear and the zits went away it was even worse.

*Tell me about the time she tried to kill you. Your viewpoint, please.*

Well, I don't know why we have to go over the thing again but if you want . . .

*Please.*

I was braiding my hair, trying it some of the ways she used to, when she burst into my room, raging, furious about something. She took my mirror away long before, so I was using the water in the wash basin to see how it looked. If you put the lamp just right, so it casts a shadow over the water but not over you, it makes a fair mirror. She took the mirror away because she said it would make me "vain."

*Vain. I see. Go on.*

She grabbed me by the back of the neck—that's how she liked to handle me—and dragged me down the stairs to the kitchen. Karl was there—he's the groundskeeper—and she said I was to go with him, and no whining. He'd tell me what was wanted.

Karl looked white, almost as white as my skin, and really grim, so I thought something had happened to Father. I didn't want to ask, afraid I'd learn something awful, and Karl didn't offer.

*She* stayed behind, and I was so relieved to be away from her that I didn't ask Karl any questions until we were out in the woods.

"What's going on?" I finally said. We'd always gotten along. I was the only one besides him that his dog would let near.

"It's that woman, lassie, she's gone crazy."

"Too late," I said.

"Well, she says I'm to take you out into the forest and kill you or she'll tell your father that I've been sleeping with her. Your father's a fair man, but he sets far too much by her word. He'd kill me."

"I'll back you up, Karl. I know you wouldn't do anything so nasty."

Karl looked ashamed. "But, lassie, I did. Long ago and only once. Your father was away and she was bored."

"What are you going to do?"

He was silent and walked faster, going deeper into the woods. I had to run to keep up with him and the lamp.

Finally, deep in the woods, farther than I'd ever gone, he left me, saying, "I'll try to convince her that you're dead, now. Run away, or we're both dead."

*How did you feel about that?*

Feel? How do you think I felt?! I was so mad that I wanted both of them dead. Not only was Karl an idiot, caving in to that bitch, but he'd had the extreme bad taste to sleep with her. I fully intended to find my father and tell him everything, but Karl took the lamp with him when he left and he walked too fast for me to keep up. I got lost.

Anyway, that's when I found the house of the seven bozos.

*So, she abused you, betrayed you, yet again. You're pretty angry right now, remembering it, aren't you?*

Yes.

*How angry?*

Extremely angry. I feel like I'm going to ex—

*Explode?*

—

*There's handkerchiefs on the end table.*

Sorry. I don't know what came over me.

*Don't you?*

Is that what you mean? That I had to see things for myself?

*This is a start.*
So this rage I have is really against my stepmother?
*Well, let's talk about that, too.*
What do you mean?
*What happened to your mother?*
She died when I was little, but I remember her. She was beautiful and kind and she'd sing me lullabies.
*So, your father remarried?*
Yes. But it's like she cast a spell on him. She must have, for him to marry her. I don't remember the wedding, but I remember the first time she came into the nursery. I'd spilled some paint on my clothes and she grabbed me by the back of the neck and screamed at me. "Look what you've done! Look what you've done!" She hit me. Later that year she pushed me down the stairs.
*Why?*
I was bad.
*Do you really believe a child deserves to be pushed down a stairway? Whatever they've done?*
Well, no, but sometimes kids get out of hand. A little discipline is necessary. My father said that he couldn't go against her. Discipline, he said, is what wins battles. He did say she got "carried away," sometimes.
*Discipline. I see. What do you remember of the funeral?*
I don't think I went.
*You don't remember the funeral?*
No.
*Why do you think that is?*
Uh, because it was horrible. My mother died and I didn't want to deal with it. I read in *Damsels Who Love Too Much* that one can suppress memories like that.
*So why do you remember all the things that your "stepmother" did? Surely they were horrible memories, worthy of suppression.*
Maybe after the death of my mother—someone who loved me—the abuse by someone who didn't care wasn't significant.
*I think it's very significant. Do you accept that I've been around long enough to have met your mother?*
You knew my mother?
*Oh, yes.*
What does that mean?
*Your father never remarried. Your mother didn't die when you were little.*
What are you talking about? What is this nonsense?
*I don't lie. I've never lied. What I just said is the truth.*
But—but, that doesn't make sense. Of course she died. Or that creature wouldn't have come to ruin my childhood.
*Mothers love their children.*
Of course.

*Your mother would never push you down the stairs.*
No, she wouldn't.
*Your mother held you and sang lullabies and was kind.*
Yes!
*I'm sorry. Check the court history. Your mother didn't die until she "overdid it" at your wedding. Your father never remarried. This is the truth.*

—

*Sometimes it's easier to believe that a parent has died and been replaced by an evil creature than to believe they would—*
No! It's not true, it isn't!
*You know I don't lie. Why are you crying? Why does it hurt so much? Why? Why would she hurt me so? Oh, God—*
*I don't know why. I only know that she did. And a child doesn't deserve to be hurt. A child deserves to be loved and cared for.*

—

*I see we're going to need more handkerchiefs. Don't stop. It's a good thing to cry, a healing thing. I'd hold you if I could, but that's hardly possible. You deserve to be held, just as you deserved to be loved and held as a child. That's something you need to grieve for, a pain you haven't let yourself feel, for a childhood you weren't allowed to have.*

—

*Try the couch. It's almost like a hug. There's a comforter in the chest . . . Is that better? Good.*
Oh, God. . . . Why?
*Nothing forgives abuse, but sometimes it's because of similar abuse in the abuser's past. A vicious, nasty cycle that doesn't stop until a generation breaks out of the grip of the past and deals with it.*
Are you saying that my daughter is in danger?
*To some extent. Every bit of self-knowledge helps avoid that, but until you deal with the pain, the grief, and the anger, yes, your child and marriage are in danger.*
Oh, God!
*Your concern is valid but I want to reassure you—you're already farther from the danger than you were when you walked into this room. Recovery takes work, but it isn't impossible. Overcoming denial is a major step and you've already done that. You can do the rest.*

—

*It's all right. I'll help you all I can.*
Really?
*I don't lie. I can't. That's what started this whole mess in the first place, isn't it?*
Oh. I guess so. But it wasn't your fault. She didn't have to ask. She was the one who was obsessed with asking the question.
*Yes.*

I hope my daughter is as beautiful as she was. I mean, that's all *I* ever wanted—to be like her, to please her, and she hated me for it.

*Better hope for your daughter's happiness, instead.*

Could I just ask? I mean, would it be too much trouble if I checked?

*Checked?*

You know—mirror, mirror, on the—

*You really don't want to do that.*

I guess not. It's so hard.

*One day at a time.*

When should I see you again?

*Same time next week?*

All right. I'll have a servant bring up more handkerchiefs—and I'll have him clean your glass while he's at it.

*Thank you, Your Highness.*

No, no—thank *you*, Mirror.

# The Mirror Speaks

Jane Yolen

♦

I have reflected upon abuse
all of my life
and the vanity of loving.
Mothers see their worth
in the bones of a child,
in soft lineaments, gentle curves
like new-formed planets
not yet jutting into rock.
"Was I ever so fair?" they ask.
"Was I ever so new?"

—I cannot speak lies,
—but each truth is half-told;
—hot is not warm but warming,
—Age by planet's count not old.

Where does the threat begin—
in the cradle? In the heart?
Under the breastbone?
Behind the eyes,
where the time-crow plants
its uncaring feet, toes splayed,
etching the fine lines?
I show you what you would see:
bleached eyes, yellow teeth,
the lines of gray hair.
You were never so fair.

—I cannot speak lies,
—but each truth is half-told;
—hot is not warm but warming,
—green is but part of gold.

Is it the child's fault?
Is it the glass?
Is it the fault of winter
and summer and winter again?
All childhoods pass.
I have reflected upon abuse
all of my life,
the answer is truth:
oh queen, all Snow Whites
are fairer still,
as you were, in your youth.

—I cannot speak lies,
—but each truth is half-told:
—hot is not warm but warming,
—death is but cool, not cold.

"The Juniper Tree," found in the German folk tales gathered and edited by the Brothers Grimm, is one of the most horrifying of traditional fairy tales, and is often left out of collections published for children. In it, a young boy is killed by his stepmother, chopped into pieces, and hidden in a trunk. Later the woman cooks him up and serves him to his unwitting (and unprotective) father, who cries, "Mmm. This is good! Give me more!" The spirit of the boy haunts the family, however, and eventually gets his revenge. In Peter Straub's version of the story, it is the boy himself, grown to adulthood now, who is haunted by the child he has been.

# The Juniper Tree

### ♦ Peter Straub ♦

It is a schoolyard in my Midwest of empty lots, waving green and brilliant with tiger lilies, of ugly new "ranch" houses set down in rows in glistening clay, of treeless avenues cooking in the sun. Our schoolyard is black asphalt—on June days, patches of the asphalt loosen and stick like gum to the soles of our high-top basketball shoes.

Most of the playground is black empty space from which heat radiates up like the wavery images on the screen of a faulty television set. Tall wire mesh surrounds it. A new boy named Paul is standing beside me.

Though it is now nearly the final month of the semester, Paul came to us, carroty-haired, pale-eyed, too shy to ask even the whereabouts of the lavatory, only six weeks ago. The lessons baffle him, and his Southern accent is a fatal error of style. The popular students broadcast in hushed, giggling whispers the terrible news that Paul "talks like a nigger." Their voices are *almost* awed—they are conscious of the enormity of what they are saying, of the enormity of its consequences.

Paul is wearing a brilliant red shirt too heavy, too enveloping, for the weather. He and I stand in the shade at the rear of the school, before the cream-colored brick wall in which is placed at eye level a newly broken window of pebbly green glass reinforced with strands of copper wire. At our feet is a little scatter of green, edible-looking pebbles. The pebbles dig into the soles of our shoes, too hard to shatter against the softer asphalt. Paul is singing to me in his slow, lilting voice that he will never have

friends in this school. I put my foot down on one of the green candy peb
bles and feel it push up, hard as a bullet, against my foot. "Children are s
cruel," Paul casually sings. I think of sliding the pebble of broken glas
across my throat, slicing myself wide open to let death in.

Paul did not return to school in the fall. His father, who had beaten a man
to death down in Mississippi, had been arrested while leaving a movie
theater near my house named the Orpheum-Oriental. Paul's father had
taken his family to see an Esther Williams movie costarring Fernando
Lamas, and when they came out, their mouths raw from salty popcorn,
the baby's hands sticky with spilled Coca-Cola, the police were waiting for
them. They were Mississippi people, and I think of Paul now, seated at a
desk on a floor of an office building in Jackson filled with men like him at
desks: his tie perfectly knotted, a good shine on his cordovan shoes, a necessary but unconscious restraint in the set of his mouth.

In those days I used to spend whole days in the Orpheum-Oriental.

I was seven. I held within me the idea of a disappearance like Paul's, of
never having to be seen again. Of being an absence, a shadow, a place
where something no longer visible used to be.

Before I met that young-old man whose name was "Frank" or "Stan" or
"Jimmy," when I sat in the rapture of education before the movies at the
Orpheum-Oriental, I watched Alan Ladd and Richard Widmark and
Glenn Ford and Dane Clark. *Chicago Deadline.* Martin and Lewis, tangled up in the same parachute in *At War with the Army.* William Boyd
and Roy Rogers. Openmouthed, I drank down movies about spies and
criminals, wanting the passionate and shadowy ones to fulfill themselves,
to gorge themselves on what they needed.
    The feverish gaze of Richard Widmark, the anger of Alan Ladd, Berry
Kroeger's sneaky eyes, girlish and watchful—vivid, total elegance.

When I was seven, my father walked into the bathroom and saw me looking at my face in the mirror. He slapped me, not with his whole strength,
but hard, raging instantly. "What do you think you're looking at?" His
hand cocked and ready. "What do you think you see?"
    "Nothing," I said.
    "Nothing is right."
    A carpenter, he worked furiously, already defeated, and never had
enough money—as if, permanently beyond reach, some quantity of
money existed that would have satisfied him. In the morning he went to
the job site hardened like cement into anger he barely knew he had.
Sometimes he brought men from the taverns home with him at night.
They carried transparent bottles of Miller High Life in paper bags and set
them down on the table with a bang that said: Men are here! My mother,

who had returned from her secretary's job a few hours earlier, fed my brothers and me, washed the dishes, and put the three of us to bed while the men shouted and laughed in the kitchen.

He was considered an excellent carpenter. He worked slowly, patiently; and I see now that he spent whatever love he had in the rented garage that was his workshop. In his spare time he listened to baseball games on the radio. He had professional, but not personal, vanity, and he thought that a face like mine should not be examined.

Because I saw "Jimmy" in the mirror, I thought my father, too, had seen him.

One Saturday my mother took the twins and me on the ferry across Lake Michigan to Saginaw—the point of the journey was the journey, and at Saginaw the boat docked for twenty minutes before wallowing back out into the lake and returning. With us were women like my mother, her friends, freed by the weekend from their jobs, some of them accompanied by men like my father, with their felt hats and baggy weekend trousers flaring over their weekend shoes. The women wore blood-bright lipstick that printed itself onto their cigarettes and smeared across their front teeth. They laughed a great deal and repeated the words that had made them laugh. "Hot dog," "slippin' 'n' slidin'," "opera singer." Thirty minutes after departure, the men disappeared into the enclosed deck bar; the women, my mother among them, arranged deck chairs into a long oval tied together by laughter, attention, gossip. They waved their cigarettes in the air. My brothers raced around the deck, their shirts flapping, their hair glued to their skulls with sweat—when they squabbled, my mother ordered them into empty deck chairs. I sat on the deck, leaning against the railings, quiet. If someone had asked me: What do you want to do this afternoon, what do you want to do for the rest of your life? I would have said, I want to stay right here, I want to stay here forever.

After a while I stood up and left the women. I went across the deck and stepped through a hatch into the bar. Dark, deeply grained imitation wood covered the walls. The odors of beer and cigarettes and the sound of men's voices filled the enclosed space. About twenty men stood at the bar, talking and gesturing with half-filled glasses. Then one man broke away from the others with a flash of dirty blond hair. I saw his shoulders move, and my scalp tingled and my stomach froze and I thought: Jimmy. "Jimmy." But he turned all the way around, dipping his shoulders in some ecstasy of beer and male company, and I saw that he was a stranger, not "Jimmy," after all.

I was thinking: Someday when I am free, when I am out of this body and in some city whose name I do not even know now, I will remember this from beginning to end and then I will be free of it.

The women floated over the empty lake, laughing out clouds of ciga-

rette smoke, the men, too, as boisterous as the children on the sticky asphalt playground with its small green spray of glass like candy.

In those days I knew I was set apart from the rest of my family, an island between my parents and the twins. Those pairs that bracketed me slept in double beds in adjacent rooms at the back of the ground floor of the duplex owned by the blind man who lived above us. My bed, a cot coveted by the twins, stood in their room. An invisible line of great authority divided my territory and possessions from theirs.

This is what happened in the morning in our half of the duplex. My mother got up first—we heard her showering, heard drawers closing, the sounds of bowls and milk being set out on the table. The smell of bacon frying for my father, who banged on the door and called out my brothers' names. "Don't you make me come in there, now!" The noisy, puppyish turmoil of my brothers getting out of bed. All three of us scramble into the bathroom as soon as my father leaves it. The bathroom was steamy, heavy with the odor of shit and the more piercing, almost palpable smell of shaving—lather and amputated whiskers. We all pee into the toilet at the same time. My mother frets and frets, pulling the twins into their clothes so that she can take them down the street to Mrs. Candee, who is given a five-dollar bill every week for taking care of them. I am supposed to be running back and forth on the playground in Summer Play School, supervised by two teenage girls who live a block away from us. (I went to Play School only twice.) After I dress myself in clean underwear and socks and put on my everyday shirt and pants, I come into the kitchen while my father finishes his breakfast. He is eating strips of bacon and golden-brown pieces of toast shiny with butter. A cigarette smolders in the ashtray before him. Everybody else has already left the house. My father and I can hear the blind man banging on the piano in his living room. I sit down before a bowl of cereal. My father looks at me, looks away. Angry at the blind man for banging at the piano this early in the morning, he is sweating already. His cheeks and forehead shine like the golden toast. My father glances at me, knowing he can postpone this no longer, and reaches wearily into his pocket and drops two quarters on the table. The high-school girls charge twenty-five cents a day, and the other quarter is for my lunch. "Don't lose that money," he says as I take the coins. My father dumps coffee into his mouth, puts the cup and his plate into the crowded sink, looks at me again, pats his pockets for his keys, and says, "Close the door behind you." I tell him that I will close the door. He picks up his gray toolbox and his black lunch pail, claps his hat on his head, and goes out, banging his toolbox against the door frame. It leaves a broad gray mark like a smear left by the passing of some angry creature's hide.

✦✦✦

Then I am alone in the house. I go back to the bedroom, close the door and push a chair beneath the knob, and read *Blackhawk* and *Henry* and *Captain Marvel* comic books until at last it is time to go to the theater.

While I read, everything in the house seems alive and dangerous. I can hear the telephone in the hall rattling on its hook, the radio clicking as it tries to turn itself on and talk to me. The dishes stir and rattle in the sink. At these times all objects, even the heavy chairs and sofa, become their true selves, violent as the fire that fills the sky I cannot see, and races through the secret ways and passages ben⌐ath the streets. At these times other people vanish like smoke.

When I pull the chair away from the door, the house immediately goes quiet, like a wild animal feigning sleep. Everything inside and out slips cunningly back into place, the fires bank, men and women reappear on the sidewalks. I must open the door and I do. I walk swiftly through the kitchen and the living room to the front door knowing that if I look too carefully at any one thing, I will wake it up again. My mouth is so dry, my tongue feels fat. "I'm leaving," I say to no one. Everything in the house hears me.

The quarter goes through the slot at the bottom of the window, the ticket leaps from its slot. For a long time, before "Jimmy," I thought that unless you kept your stub unfolded and safe in a shirt pocket, the usher could rush down the aisle in the middle of the movie, seize you, and throw you out. So into the pocket it goes, and I slip through the big doors into the cool, cross the lobby, and pass through a swinging door with a porthole window.

Most of the regular daytime patrons of the Orpheum-Oriental sit in the same seats every day—I am one of those who comes here every day. A small, talkative gathering of bums sits far to the right of the theater, in the rows beneath the sconces fastened like bronze torches to the walls. The bums choose these seats so that they can examine their bits of paper, their "documents," and show them to each other during the movie. Always on their minds is the possibility that they might have lost one of these documents, and they frequently consult the tattered envelopes in which they are kept.

I take the end seat, left side of the central block of seats, just before the broad horizontal middle aisle. There I can stretch out. At other times I sit in the middle of the last row, or the first; sometimes when the balcony is open I go up and sit in its first row. From the first row of the balcony, seeing a movie is like being a bird and flying down into the movie from above. To be alone in the theater is delicious. The curtains hang heavy, red, anticipatory; the mock torches glow on the walls. Swirls of gilt wind through the red paint. On days when I sit near a wall, I reach out toward the red, which seems warm and soft, and find my fingers resting on a chill dampness. The carpet of the Orpheum-Oriental must once have been a bottomlessly rich brown; now it is a dark non-color, mottled with the pink and gray smears, like melted Band-Aids, of chewing gum. From about a third of the seats dirty gray wool foams from slashes in the worn plush.

On an ideal day I sit through a cartoon, a travelogue, a sequence of previews, a movie, another cartoon, and another movie before anyone else enters the theater. This whole cycle is as satisfying as a meal. On other mornings, old women in odd hats and young women wearing scarves over their rollers, a few teenage couples, are scattered throughout the theater when I come in. None of these people ever pays attention to anything but the screen and, in the case of the teenagers, each other.

Once, a man in his early twenties, hair like a haystack, sat up in the wide middle aisle when I took my seat. He groaned. Rusty-looking dried blood was spattered over his chin and his dirty white shirt. He groaned again and then got to his hands and knees. The carpet beneath him was spotted with what looked like a thousand red dots. The young man stumbled to his feet and began reeling up the aisle. A bright, depthless pane of sunlight surrounded him before he vanished into it.

At the beginning of July, I told my mother that the high-school girls had increased the hours of the Play School because I wanted to be sure of seeing both features twice before I had to go home. After that I could learn the rhythms of the theater itself, which did not impress themselves upon me all at once but revealed themselves gradually, so that by the middle of the first week, I knew when the bums would begin to move toward the seats beneath the sconces—they usually arrived on Tuesdays and Fridays shortly after eleven o'clock, when the liquor store down the block opened up to provide them with the pints and half-pints that nourished them. By the end of the second week, I knew when the ushers left the interior of the theater to sit on padded benches in the lobby and light up their Luckies and Chesterfields, when the old men and women would begin to appear. By the end of the third week, I felt like the merest part of a great, orderly machine. Before the beginning of the second showing of *Beautiful Hawaii* or *Curiosities Down Under,* I went out to the counter and with my second quarter purchased a box of popcorn or a packet of Good 'N Plenty candy.

In a movie theater nothing is random except the customers and hitches in the machine. Filmstrips break and lights fail; the projectionist gets drunk or falls asleep; and the screen presents a blank yellow face to the stamping, whistling audience. These inconsistencies are summer squalls, forgotten as soon as they have ended.

The occasion for the lights, the projectionist, the boxes of popcorn and packets of candy, the movies, enlarged when seen over and over. The truth gradually came to me that this deepening and widening out, this enlarging, was why movies were shown over and over all day long. The machine revealed itself most surely in the exact, limpid repetitions of the actors' words and gestures as they moved through the story. When Alan Ladd asked "Blackie Franchot," the dying gangster, "Who did it, Blackie?" his voice widened like a river, grew *sandier* with an almost unconcealed tenderness I had to learn to hear—the voice within the speaking voice.

*Chicago Deadline* was the exploration by a newspaper reporter named "Ed Adams" (Alan Ladd) of the tragedy of a mysterious young woman, "Rosita Jandreau," who had died alone of tuberculosis in a shabby hotel room. The reporter soon learns that she had many names, many identities. She had been in love with an architect, a gangster, a crippled professor, a boxer, a millionaire, and had given a different facet of her being to each of them. Far too predictably, the adult me complains, the obsessed "Ed" falls in love with "Rosita." When I was seven, little was predictable—I had not yet seen *Laura*—and I saw a man driven by the need to understand, which became identical to the need to protect. "Rosita Jandreau" was the embodiment of memory, which was mystery.

Through the sequences of her identities, the various selves shown to brother, boxer, millionaire, gangster, all the others, her memory kept her whole. I saw, twice a day, for two weeks, before and during "Jimmy," the machine deep within the machine. Love and memory were the same. Both love and memory accommodated us to death. (I did not understand this, but I saw it.) The reporter, Alan Ladd, with his dirty blond hair, his perfect jawline, and brilliant, wounded smile, gave her life by making her memory his own.

"I think you're the only one who ever understood her," Arthur Kennedy—"Rosita" 's brother—tells Alan Ladd.

Most of the world demands the kick of sensation, most of the world must gather and spend money, hunt for easier and more temporary forms of love, must feed itself, sell newspapers, destroy the enemy's plots with plots of its own. . . .

"I don't know what you want," "Ed Adams" says to the editor of *The Journal.* "You got two murders . . ."

". . . and a mystery woman," I say along with him. His voice is tough and detached, the voice of a wounded man acting. The man beside me laughs. Unlike his normal voice, his laughter is breathless and high pitched. It is the second showing today of *Chicago Deadline,* early afternoon—after the next showing of *At War with the Army* I will have to walk up the aisle and out of the theater. It will be twenty minutes to five, and the sun will still burn high over the cream-colored buildings across wide, empty Sherman Boulevard.

I met the man, or he met me, at the candy counter. He was at first only a tall presence, blond, dressed in dark clothing. I cared nothing for him, he did not matter. He was vague even when he spoke. "Good popcorn." I looked up at him—narrow blue eyes, bad teeth smiling at me. Stubble on his face. I looked away and the uniformed man behind the counter handed me popcorn. "Good for you, I mean. Good stuff in popcorn—comes right out of the ground. Grows on big plants tall as I am, just like other corn. You know that?"

When I said nothing, he laughed and spoke to the man behind the counter. "*He* didn't know that—the kid thought popcorn grew inside poppers." The counterman turned away. "You come here a lot?" the man asked me.

I put a few kernels of popcorn in my mouth and turned toward him. He was showing me his bad teeth.

"You do," he said. "You come here a lot."

I nodded.

"Every day?"

I nodded again.

"And we tell little fibs at home about what we've been doing all day, don't we?" he asked, and pursed his lips and raised his eyes like a comic butler in a movie. Then his mood shifted and everything about him became serious. He was looking at me, but he did not see me. "You got a favorite actor? I got a favorite actor. Alan Ladd."

And I saw—both saw and understood—that he thought he looked like Alan Ladd. He did, too, at least a little bit. When I saw the resemblance, he seemed like a different person, more glamorous. Glamour surrounded him, as though he were acting, impersonating a shabby young man with stained, irregular teeth.

"The name's Frank," he said, and stuck out his hand. "Shake?"

I took his hand.

"Real good popcorn," he said, and stuck his hand into the box. "Want to hear a secret?"

A secret.

"I was born twice. The first time, I died. It was on an Army base. Everybody *told* me I should have joined the Navy, and everybody was right. So I just had myself get born somewhere else. Hey—the Army's not for everybody, you know?" He grinned down at me. "Now I told you my secret. Let's go in—I'll sit with you. Everybody needs company, and I like you. You look like a good kid."

He followed me back to my seat and sat down beside me. When I quoted the lines along with the actors, he laughed.

Then he said—

Then he leaned toward me and said—

He leaned toward me, breathing sour wine over me, and took—

No.

"I was just kidding out there," he said. "Frank ain't my real name. Well, it was my name. Before. See? Frank *used* to be my name for a while. But

now my good friends call me Stan. I like that. Stanley the Steamer. Big
Stan. Stan the Man. See? It works real good."

You'll never be a carpenter, he told me. You'll never be anything like
that—because you got that look. *I* used to have that look, okay? So I know.
I know about you just by looking at you.

He said he had been a clerk at Sears; after that he had worked as the
custodian for a couple of apartment buildings owned by a guy who used to
be a friend of his but was no longer. Then he had been the janitor at the
high school where my grade school sent its graduates. "Good old booze
got me fired, story of my life," he said. "Tight-ass bitches caught me
drinking down in the basement, in a room I used there, and threw me out
without a fare-thee-well. Hey, that was my *room*. My *place*. The best
things in the world can do the worst things to you; you'll find that out
someday. And when you go to that school, I hope you'll remember what
they done to me there."

These days he was resting. He hung around, he went to the movies.

He said: You got something special in you. Guys like me, we're funny,
we can tell.

We sat together through the second feature, Dean Martin and Jerry
Lewis, comfortable and laughing. "Those guys are bigger bums than us,"
he said. I thought of Paul backed up against the school in his enveloping
red shirt, imprisoned within his inability to be like anyone around him.

You coming back tomorrow? If I get here, I'll check around for you.

Hey. Trust me. I know who you are.

You know that little thing you pee with? Leaning sideways and whispering
into my ear. That's the best thing a man's got. Trust me.

The big providential park near our house, two streets past the Orpheum-
Oriental, is separated into three different areas. Nearest the wide iron
gates on Sherman Boulevard through which we enter was a wading pool
divided by a low green hedge, so rubbery it seemed artificial, from a playground with a climbing frame, swings, and a row of seesaws. When I was a
child of two and three, I splashed in the warm pool and clung to the chains
of the swings, making myself go higher and higher, terror and joy and
grim duty so woven together that no one could pull them apart.

Beyond the children's pool and playground was the zoo. My mother
walked my brothers and me to the playground and wading pool and sat
smoking on a bench while we played; both of my parents took us into the
zoo. An elephant extended his trunk to my father's palm and delicately
lipped peanuts toward his maw. The giraffe stretched toward the con-

stantly diminishing supply of leaves, ever fewer and higher, above his cage. The lions drowsed on amputated branches and paced behind the bars, staring out not at what was there but at the long, grassy plains imprinted on their memories. I knew the lions had the power not to see us, to look straight through us to Africa. But when they saw you instead of Africa, they looked right into your bones, they saw the blood traveling through your body. The lions were golden brown, patient, green-eyed. They recognized me and could read thoughts. The lions neither liked nor disliked me, they did not miss me during their long weekdays, but they took me into the circle of known beings.

("You shouldn't have looked at me like that," June Havoc ["Leona"] tells "Ed Adams." She does not mean it, not at all.)

Past the zoo and across a narrow park road down which khaki-clothed park attendants pushed barrows heavy with flowers stood a wide, unexpected lawn bordered with flower beds and tall elms—open space hidden like a secret between the caged animals and the elm trees. Only my father brought me to this section of the park. Here he tried to make a baseball player of me.

"Get the bat off your shoulders," he says. "For God's sake, will you try to hit the ball, anyhow?"

When I fail once again to swing at his slow, perfect pitch, he spins around, raises his arm, and theatrically asks everyone in sight, "Whose kid is this, anyway? Can you answer me that?"

He has never asked me about the Play School I am supposed to be attending, and I have never told him about the Orpheum-Oriental—I will never come any closer to talking to him than now, for "Stan," "Stanley the Steamer," has told me things that cannot be true, that must be inventions and fables, part of the world of children wandering lost in the forest, of talking cats and silver boots filled with blood. In this world, dismembered children buried beneath juniper trees can rise and speak, made whole once again. Fables boil with underground explosions and hidden fires, and for this reason, memory rejects them, thrusts them out of its sight, and they must be repeated over and over. I cannot remember "Stan's" face—cannot even be sure I remember what he said. Dean Martin and Jerry Lewis are bums like us. I am certain of only one thing: Tomorrow I am again going to see my newest, scariest, most interesting friend.

"When I was your age," my father says, "I had my heart set on playing pro ball when I grew up. And you're too damned scared or lazy to even take the bat off your shoulder. Kee-rist! I can't stand looking at you anymore."

He turns around and begins to move quickly toward the narrow park road and the zoo, going home, and I run after him. I retrieve the softball when he tosses it into the bushes.

"What the hell do you think you're going to do when you grow up?" my father asks, his eyes still fixed ahead of him. "I wonder what you think life is all *about*. I wouldn't give you a job, I wouldn't trust you around carpenter tools, I wouldn't trust you to blow your nose right—to tell you the truth, I wonder if the hospital mixed up the goddamn babies."

I follow him, dragging the bat with one hand, in the other cradling the softball in the pouch of my mitt.

At dinner my mother asks if Summer Play School is fun, and I say yes. I have already taken from my father's dresser drawer what "Stan" asked me to get for him, and it burns in my pocket as if it were alight. I want to ask: Is it actually true and not a story? Does the worst thing always have to be the true thing? Of course, I cannot ask this. My father does not know about worst things—he sees what he wants to see, or he tries so hard, he thinks he does see it.

"I guess he'll hit a long ball someday. The boy just needs more work on his swing." He tries to smile at me, a boy who will someday learn to hit a long ball. The knife is upended in his fist—he is about to smear a pat of butter on his steak. He does not see me at all. My father is not a lion, he cannot make the switch to seeing what is really there in front of him.

Late at night Alan Ladd knelt beside my bed. He was wearing a neat gray suit, and his breath smelled like cloves. "You okay, son?" I nodded. "I just wanted to tell you that I like seeing you out there every day. That means a lot to me."

"Do you remember what I was telling you about?"

And I knew: It was true. He had said those things, and he would repeat them like a fairy tale, and the world was going to change because it would be seen through changed eyes. I felt sick—trapped in the theater as if in a cage.

"You think about what I told you?"

"Sure," I said.

"That's good. Hey, you know what? I feel like changing seats. You want to change seats too?"

"Where to?"

He tilted his head back, and I knew he wanted to move to the last row. "Come on. I want to show you something."

We changed seats.

For a long time we sat watching the movie from the last row, nearly alone in the theater. Just after eleven, three of the bums filed in and proceeded to their customary seats on the other side of the theater—a rumpled graybeard I had seen many times before; a fat man with a stubby, squashed face, also familiar; and one of the shaggy, wild-looking young men who hung around the bums until they became indistinguishable from them. They began passing a flat brown bottle back and forth. After a second I remembered the young man—I had surprised him awake one morning, passed out and spattered with blood, in the middle aisle.

Then I wondered if "Stan" was not the young man I had surprised that morning; they looked as alike as twins, though I knew they were not.

"Want a sip?" "Stan" said, showing me his own pint bottle. "Do you good."

Bravely, feeling privileged and adult, I took the bottle of Thunderbird and raised it to my mouth. I wanted to like it, to share the pleasure of it with "Stan," but it tasted horrible, like garbage, and the little bit I swallowed burned all the way down my throat.

I made a face, and he said, "This stuff's really not so bad. Only one thing in the world can make you feel better than this stuff."

He placed his hand on my thigh and squeezed. "I'm giving you a head start, you know. Just because I liked you the first time I saw you." He leaned over and stared at me. "You believe me? You believe the things I tell you?"

I said I guessed so.

"I got proof. I'll show you it's true. Want to see my proof?"

When I said nothing, "Stan" leaned closer to me, inundating me with the stench of Thunderbird. "You know that little thing you pee with? Remember how I told you how it gets real big when you're about thirteen? Remember I told you about how incredible that feels? Well, you have to trust Stan now, because Stan's going to trust you." He put his face right beside my ear. "Then I'll tell you another secret."

He lifted his hand from my thigh and closed it around mine and pulled my hand down onto his crotch. "Feel anything?"

I nodded, but I could not have described what I felt any more than the blind men could describe the elephant.

"Stan" smiled tightly and tugged at his zipper in a way even I could tell was nervous. He reached inside his pants, fumbled, and pulled out a thick, pale club that looked like nothing human. I was so frightened I thought I would throw up, and I looked back up at the screen. Invisible chains held me to my seat.

"See? Now you understand me."

Then he noticed that I was not looking at him. "Kid. Look. I said, look. It's not going to hurt you."

I could not look down at him. I saw nothing.

"Come on. Touch it, see what it feels like."

I shook my head.

"Let me tell you something. I like you a lot. I think the two of us are friends. This thing we're doing, it's unusual to you because this is the first time, but people do this all the time. Your mommy and daddy do it all the time, but they just don't tell you about it. We're pals, aren't we?"

I nodded dumbly. On the screen, Berry Kroeger was telling Alan Ladd, "Drop it, forget it, she's poison."

"Well, this is what friends do when they really like each other, like your mommy and daddy. Look at this thing, will you? Come on."

Did my mommy and daddy like each other? He squeezed my shoulder, and I looked.

Now the thing had folded up into itself and was drooping sideways against the fabric of his trousers. Almost as soon as I looked, it twitched and began to push itself out like the slide of a trombone.

"There," he said. "He likes you, you got him going. Tell me you like him too."

Terror would not let me speak. My brains had turned to powder.

"I know what—let's call him Jimmy. We'll say his name is Jimmy. Now that you've been introduced, say hi to Jimmy."

"Hi, Jimmy," I said, and, despite my terror, could not keep myself from giggling.

"Now go on, touch him."

I slowly extended my hand and put the tips of my fingers on "Jimmy."

"Pet him. Jimmy wants you to pet him."

I tapped my fingertips against "Jimmy" two or three times, and he twitched up another few degrees, as rigid as a surfboard.

"Slide your fingers up and down on him."

If I run, I thought, he'll catch me and kill me. If I don't do what he says, he'll kill me.

I rubbed my fingertips back and forth, moving the thin skin over the veins.

"Can't you imagine Jimmy going in a woman? Now you can see what you'll be like when you're a man. Keep on, but hold him with your whole hand. And give me what I asked you for."

I immediately took my hand from "Jimmy" and pulled my father's clean white handkerchief from my back pocket.

He took the handkerchief with his left hand and with his right guided mine back to "Jimmy." "You're doing really great," he whispered.

In my hand "Jimmy" felt warm and slightly gummy. I could not join my fingers around its width. My head was buzzing. "Is Jimmy your secret?" I was able to say.

"My secret comes later."

"Can I stop now?"

"I'll cut you into little pieces if you do," he said, and when I froze, he stroked my hair and whispered, "Hey, can't you tell when a guy's kidding around? I'm really happy with you right now. You're the best kid in the world. You'd want this, too, if you knew how good it felt."

After what seemed an endless time, while Alan Ladd was climbing out of a taxicab, "Stan" abruptly arched his back, grimaced, and whispered, "Look!" His entire body jerked, and too startled to let go, I held "Jimmy" and watched thick, ivory-colored milk spurt and drool almost unendingly onto the handkerchief. An odor utterly foreign but as familiar as the toilet or the lakeshore rose from the thick milk. "Stan" sighed, folded the handkerchief, and pushed the softening "Jimmy" back into his trousers. He leaned over and kissed the top of my head. I think I nearly fainted. I felt lightly, pointlessly dead. I could still feel him pulsing in my palm and fingers.

When it was time for me to go home, he told me his secret—his own real name was Jimmy, not Stan. He had been saving his real name until he knew he could trust me.

"Tomorrow," he said, touching my cheek with his fingers. "We'll see each other again tomorrow. But you don't have anything to worry about. I trust you enough to give you my real name. You trusted me not to hurt you, and I didn't. We have to trust each other not to say anything about this, or both you and me'll be in a lot of trouble."

"I won't say anything," I said.

I love you.

I love you, yes I do.

Now *we're* a secret, he said, folding the handkerchief into quarters and putting it back in my pocket. A lot of love has to be secret. Especially when a boy and a man are getting to know each other and learning how to make each other happy and be good, loving friends—not many people can understand that, so the friendship has to be protected. When you walk out of here, he said, you have to forget that this happened. Otherwise people will try to hurt us both.

Afterward I remembered only the confusion of *Chicago Deadline,* how the story had abruptly surged forward, skipping over whole characters and entire scenes, how for long stretches the actors had moved their lips without speaking. I could see Alan Ladd stepping out of the taxicab, looking straight through the screen into my eyes, knowing me.

My mother said that I looked pale, and my father said that I didn't get enough exercise. The twins looked up from their plates, then went back to spooning macaroni and cheese into their mouths. "Were you ever in Chicago?" I asked my father, who asked what was it to me. "Did you ever meet a movie actor?" I asked, and he said, "This kid must have a fever." The twins giggled.

Alan Ladd and Donna Reed came into my bedroom together late that night, moving with brisk, cool theatricality, and kneeled down beside my cot. They smiled at me. Their voices were very soothing. I saw you missed a few things today, Alan said. Nothing to worry about. I'll take care of you. I know, I said, I'm your number-one fan.

Then the door cracked open, and my mother put her head inside the room. Alan and Donna smiled and stood up to let her pass between them and the cot. I missed them the second they stepped back. "Still awake?" I nodded. "Are you feeling all right, honey?" I nodded again, afraid that Alan and Donna would leave if she stayed too long. "I have a surprise for you," she said. "The Saturday after this, I'm taking you and the twins all the way across Lake Michigan on the ferry. There's a whole bunch of us. It'll be a lot of fun." Good, that's nice, I'll like that.

"I thought about you all last night and all this morning."

When I came into the lobby, he was leaning forward on one of the padded benches where the ushers sat and smoked, his elbows on his knees and his chin in his hand, watching the door. The metal tip of a flat bottle protruded from his side pocket. Beside him was a package rolled up in brown paper. He winked at me, jerked his head toward the door into the theater, stood up, and went inside in an elaborate charade of not being with me. I knew he would be just inside the door, sitting in the middle of the last row, waiting for me. I gave my ticket to the bored usher, who tore it in half and handed over the stub. I knew exactly what had happened yesterday, just as if I had never forgotten any of it, and my insides began shaking. All the colors of the lobby, the red and the shabby gilt, seemed much brighter than I remembered them. I could smell the popcorn in the case and the oily butter heating in the machine. My legs moved me over a mile of sizzling brown carpet and past the candy counter.

Jimmy's hair gleamed in the empty, darkening theater. When I took the seat next to him, he ruffled my hair and grinned down and said he had been thinking about me all night and all morning. The package in brown paper was a sandwich he'd brought for my lunch—a kid had to eat more than popcorn.

The lights went all the way down as the series of curtains opened over the screen. Loud music, beginning in the middle of a note, suddenly jumped from the speakers, and the Tom and Jerry cartoon "Bull Dozing" began. When I leaned back, Jimmy put his arm around me. I felt sweaty and cold at the same time, and my insides were still shaking. I suddenly realized that part of me was glad to be in this place, and I shocked myself with the knowledge that all morning I had been looking forward to this moment as much as I had been dreading it.

"You want your sandwich now? It's liver sausage, because that's my personal favorite." I said no thanks, I'd wait until the first movie was over. Okay, he said, just as long as you eat it. Then he said, look at me. His face was right above mine, and he looked like Alan Ladd's twin brother. You have to know something, he said. You're the best kid I ever met. Ever. The man squeezed me up against his chest and into a dizzying funk of sweat and dirt and wine, along with a trace (imagined?) of that other, more animal odor that had come from him yesterday. Then he released me.

✦✦✦

You want me to play with your little "Jimmy" today?

No.

Too small, anyhow, he said with a laugh. He was in perfect good humor.

Bet you wish it was the same size as mine.

That wish terrified me, and I shook my head.

Today we're just going to watch the movies together, he said. I'm not greedy.

Except for when one of the ushers came up the aisle, we sat like that all day, his arm around my shoulders, the back of my neck resting in the hollow of his elbow. When the credits for *At War with the Army* rolled up the screen, I felt as though I had fallen asleep and missed everything. I couldn't believe that it was time to go home. Jimmy tightened his arm around me and in a voice full of amusement said *Touch me.* I looked up into his face. Go on, he said, I want you to do that little thing for me. I prodded his fly with my index finger. "Jimmy" wobbled under the pressure of my fingers, seeming as long as my arm, and for a second of absolute wretchedness I saw the other children running up and down the school playground behind the girls from the next block.

"Go on," he said.

*Trust me,* he said, investing "Jimmy" with an identity more concentrated, more focused, than his own. "Jimmy" wanted "to talk," "to speak his piece," "was hungry," "was dying for a kiss." All these words meant the same thing. *Trust me:* I trust you, so you must trust me. Have I ever hurt you? No. Didn't I give you a sandwich? Yes. Don't I love you? You know I won't tell your parents what you do—as long as you keep coming here, I won't tell your parents anything because I won't *have* to, see? And you love me, too, don't you?

There. You see how much I love you?

I dreamed that I lived underground in a wooden room. I dreamed that my parents roamed the upper world, calling out my name and weeping because the animals had captured and eaten me. I dreamed that I was buried beneath a juniper tree, and the cut-off pieces of my body called out to each other and wept because they were separate. I dreamed that I ran down a dark forest path toward my parents, and when I finally reached the small clearing where they sat before a bright fire, my mother was Donna and Alan was my father. I dreamed that I could remember everything that was happening to me, every second of it, and that when the teacher called on me in class, when my mother came into my room at night, when the policeman went past me as I walked down Sherman Boulevard, I had to spill it out. But when I tried to speak, I could not remember what it was that I remembered, *only that there was something to remember,* and so I walked again and again toward my beautiful parents in the clearing, repeating myself like a fable, like the jokes of the women on the ferry.

Don't I love you? Don't I show you, can't you tell, that I love you? *Yes.* Don't you, can't you, love me too?

He stares at me as I stare at the movie. He could see me, the way I could see him, with his eyes closed. He has me memorized. He has stroked my hair, my face, my body into his memory, stroke after stroke, stealing me from myself. Eventually he took me in his mouth and his mouth memorized me, too, and I knew he wanted me to place my hands on that dirty blond head resting so hugely in my lap, but I could not touch his head.

I thought: I have already forgotten this, I want to die, I am dead already, only death can make this not have happened.

When you grow up, I bet you'll be in the movies and I'll be your number-one fan.

By the weekend, those days at the Orpheum-Oriental seemed to have been spent under water; or underground. The spiny anteater, the lyrebird, the kangaroo, the Tasmanian devil, the nun bat, and the frilled lizard were creatures found only in Australia. Australia was the world's smallest continent, its largest island. It was cut off from the Earth's great landmasses. Beautiful girls with blonde hair strutted across Australian beaches, and Australian Christmases were hot and sunbaked—everybody went outside and waved at the camera, exchanging presents from lawn chairs. The middle of Australia, its heart and gut, was a desert. Australian boys excelled at sports. Tom Cat loved Jerry Mouse, though he plotted again and again to murder him, and Jerry Mouse loved Tom Cat, though to save his life he had to run so fast he burned a track through the carpet. Jimmy loved me and he would be gone someday, and then I would miss him a lot. Wouldn't I? *Say you'll miss me.*

I'll—

"I'll miss—

*I think I'd go crazy without you.*

When you're all grown-up, will you remember me?

Each time I walked back out past the usher, tearing in half the tickets of the people just entering, handing them the stubs, every time I pushed open the door and walked out onto the heat-filled sidewalk of Sherman Boulevard and saw the sun on the buildings across the street, I lost my hold on what had happened inside the darkness of the theater. I didn't know what I wanted. I had two murders and a . . . My right hand felt as though I had been holding a smaller child's sticky hand very tightly between my palm and fingers. If I lived in Australia, I would have blond hair like Alan Ladd and run forever across tan beaches on Christmas Day.

I walked through high school in my sleep, reading novels, daydreaming in classes I did not like but earning spuriously good grades; in the middle of my senior year Brown University gave me a full scholarship. Two years later I amazed and disappointed all my old teachers and my parents and my parents' friends by dropping out of school shortly before I would have failed all my courses but English and history, in which I was getting A's. I was certain that no one could teach anyone else how to write. I knew exactly what I was going to do, and all I would miss of college was the social life.

For five years I lived inexpensively in Providence, supporting myself by stacking books in the school library and by petty thievery. I wrote when I was not working or listening to the local bands; then I destroyed what I had written and wrote it again. In this way I saw myself to the end of a novel, like walking through a park one way and then walking backward and forward through the same park, over and over, until every nick on every swing, every tawny hair on every lion's hide, had been witnessed and made to gleam or allowed to sink back into the importunate field of details from which it had been lifted. When this novel was rejected by the publisher to whom I sent it, I moved to New York City and began another novel while I rewrote the first all over again at night. During this period an almost impersonal happiness, like the happiness of a stranger, lay beneath everything I did. I wrapped parcels of books at the Strand Bookstore. For a short time, no more than a few months, I lived on Shredded Wheat and peanut butter. When my first book was accepted, I moved from a single room on the Lower East Side into another, larger single room, a "studio apartment," on Ninth Avenue in Chelsea, where I continue to live. My apartment is just large enough for my wooden desk, a convertible couch, two large crowded bookshelves, a shelf of stereo equipment, and dozens of cardboard boxes of records. In this apartment everything has its place and is in it.

My parents have never been to this enclosed, tidy space, though I speak to my father on the phone every two or three months. In the past ten years I have returned to the city where I grew up only once, to visit my mother in the hospital after her stroke. During the four days I stayed in my father's house I slept in my old room, my father upstairs. After the blind man's death my father bought the duplex—on my first night home he told me that we were both successes. Now, when we speak on the telephone, he tells me of the fortunes of the local baseball and basketball teams and respectfully inquires about my progress on "the new book." I think: This is not my father, he is not the same man.

My old cot disappeared long ago, and late at night I lay on the twins' double bed. Like the house as a whole, like everything in my old neighborhood, the bedroom was larger than I remembered it. I brushed the wall-paper with my fingers, then looked up to the ceiling. The image of two men tangled up in the ropes of the same parachute, comically berating each other as they fell, came to me, and I wondered if the image had a place in the novel I was writing, or if it was a gift from the as yet unseen novel that would follow it. I could hear the floor creak as my father paced upstairs in the blind man's former territory. My inner weather changed, and I began brooding about Mei-Mei Levitt, whom fifteen years earlier at Brown I had known as Mei-Mei Cheung.

Divorced, an editor at a paperback firm, she had called to congratu-late me after my second novel was favorably reviewed in the *Times,* and on this slim but well-intentioned foundation we began to construct a long and troubled love affair. Back in the surroundings of my childhood, I felt profoundly uneasy, having spent the day beside my mother's hospital bed without knowing if she understood or even recognized me, and I thought of Mei-Mei with sudden longing. I wanted her in my arms, and I yearned for my purposeful, orderly, dreaming adult life in New York. I wanted to call Mei-Mei, but it was past midnight in the Midwest, an hour later in New York, and Mei-Mei, no owl, would have gone to bed hours earlier. Then I remembered my mother lying stricken in the narrow hospital bed, and suffered a spasm of guilt for thinking about my lover. For a deluded moment I imagined that it was my duty to move back into the house and see if I could bring my mother back to life while I did what I could for my retired father. At that moment I remembered, as I often did, an orange-haired boy enveloped in a red wool shirt. Sweat poured from my fore-head, my chest.

Then a terrifying thing happened to me. I tried to get out of bed to go to the bathroom and found that I could not move. My arms and legs were cast in cement; they were lifeless and *would not move.* I thought that I was having a stroke, like my mother. I could not even cry out—my throat, too, was paralyzed. I strained to push myself up off the narrow bed and smelled that someone very near, someone just out of sight or around a corner, was making popcorn and heating butter. Another wave of sweat gouted out of my inert body, turning the sheet and the pillowcase slick and cold.

I saw—as if I were writing it—my seven-year-old self hesitating before the entrance of a theater a few blocks from this house. Hot, flat, yellow sunlight fell over everything, cooking the life from the wide boule-vard. I saw myself turn away, felt my stomach churn with the smoke of underground fires, saw myself begin to run. Vomit backed up in my throat. My arms and legs convulsed, and I fell out of bed and managed to crawl out of the room and down the hall to throw up in the toilet behind the closed door of the bathroom.

My age, as I write these words, is forty-three. I have written five novels over a period of nearly twenty years, "only" five, each of them more difficult, harder to write than the one before. To maintain this hobbled pace of a novel every four years, I must sit at my desk at least six hours every day; I must consume hundreds of boxes of typing paper, scores of yellow legal pads, forests of pencils, miles of black ribbon. It is a fierce, voracious activity. Every sentence must be tested three or four ways, made to clear fences like a horse. The purpose of every sentence is to be an arrow into the secret center of the book. To find my way into the secret center I must hold the entire book, every detail and rhythm, in my memory. This comprehensive act of memory is the most crucial task of my life.

My books get flattering reviews, which usually seem to describe other, more linear novels, and they win occasional awards—I am one of those writers whose advances are funded by the torrents of money spun off by best-sellers. Lately I have had the impression that the general perception of me, to the extent that such a thing exists, is that of a hermetic painter inscribing hundreds of tiny, grotesque, fantastical details over every inch of a large canvas. (My books are unfashionably long.) I teach writing at various colleges, give occasional lectures, am modestly enriched by grants. This is enough, more than enough. Now and then I am both dismayed and amused to discover that a young writer I have met at a PEN reception or a workshop regards my life with envy. Envy misses the point completely.

"If you were going to give me one piece of advice," a young woman at a conference asked me, "I mean, *real* advice, not just the obvious stuff about keeping on writing, what would it be? What would you tell me to do?"

I won't tell you, but I'll write it out, I said, and picked up one of the conference flyers and printed a few words on its back. Don't read this until you are out of the room, I said, and watched while she folded the flyer into her bag.

What I had printed on the back of the flyer was: GO TO A LOT OF MOVIES.

On the Sunday after the ferry trip I could not hit a single ball in the park. My eyes kept closing, and as soon as my eyelids came down, visions started up like movies—quick, automatic dreams. My arms seemed too heavy to lift. After I had trudged home behind my dispirited father, I collapsed on the sofa and slept straight through to dinner. In a dream a spacious box confined me, and I drew colored pictures of elm trees, the sun, wide fields, mountains, and rivers on its walls. At dinner loud noises, never scarce around the twins, made me jump. That kid's not right, I swear to you, my father said. When my mother asked if I wanted to go to Play School on Monday, my stomach closed up like a fist. I have to, I said, I'm really fine. I have to go. Sentences rolled from my mouth, meaning nothing, or meaning the wrong thing. For a moment of confusion I thought that I really was going to the playground, and saw black asphalt, deep as a field, where a few children, diminished by perspective, clustered at the far end. I went to bed right after dinner. My mother pulled down the shades, turned off the light, and finally left me alone. From above came the sound, like a beast's approximation of music, of random notes struck on a piano. I knew only that I was scared, not why. The next day I had to go to a certain place, but I could not think where until my fingers recalled the velvety plush of the end seat on the middle aisle. Then black-and-white images, full of intentional menace, came to me from the previews I had seen for two weeks—*The Hitchhiker,* starring Edmund O'Brien. The spiny anteater and nun bat were animals found only in Australia.

I longed for Alan Ladd, "Ed Adams," to walk into the room with his reporter's notebook and pencil, and knew that I had *something to remember* without knowing what it was.

After a long time the twins cascaded into the bedroom, undressed, put on pajamas, brushed their teeth. The front door slammed—my father had gone out to the taverns. In the kitchen, my mother ironed shirts and talked to herself in a familiar, rancorous voice. The twins went to sleep. I heard my mother put away the ironing board and walk down the hall to the living room.

I saw "Ed Adams" calmly walking up and down on the sidewalk outside our house, as handsome as a god in his neat grey suit. "Ed" went all the way to the end of the block, put a cigarette in his mouth, and leaned into a sudden, round flare of brightness before exhaling smoke and walking away. I knew I had fallen asleep only when the front door slammed for the second time that night and woke me up.

In the morning my father struck his fist against the bedroom door and the twins jumped out of bed and began yelling around the bedroom, instantly filled with energy. As in a cartoon, into the bedroom drifted tendrils of the odor of frying bacon. My brothers jostled toward the bathroom. Water rushed into the sink and the toilet bowl, and my mother hurried in, her face tightened down over her cigarette, and began yanking the twins into their clothes. "You made your decision," she said to me, "now I hope you're going to make it to the playground on time." Doors opened, doors slammed shut. My father shouted from the kitchen, and I got out of bed. Eventually I sat down before the bowl of cereal. My father smoked and did not meet my eyes. The cereal tasted of dead leaves. "You look the way that asshole upstairs plays piano," my father said. He dropped quarters on the table and told me not to lose that money.

After he left, I locked myself in the bedroom. The piano dully resounded overhead like a sound track. I heard the cups and dishes rattle in the sink, the furniture moving by itself, looking for something to hunt down and kill. *Love me, love me,* the radio called from beside a family of brown-and-white porcelain spaniels. I heard some light, whispery thing, a lamp or a magazine, begin to slide around the living room. *I am imagining all this,* I said to myself, and tried to concentrate on a *Blackhawk* comic book. The pictures jigged and melted in their panels. *Love me,* Blackhawk

cried out from the cockpit of his fighter as he swooped down to extermi-
nate a nest of yellow, slant-eyed villains. Outside, fire raged beneath the
streets, trying to pull the world apart. When I dropped the comic book
and closed my eyes, the noises ceased and I could hear the hovering stillness of perfect attention. Even Blackhawk, belted into his airplane within
the comic book, was listening to what I was doing.

In thick, hazy sunlight I went down Sherman Boulevard toward the Orpheum-Oriental. Around me the world was motionless, frozen like a
frame in a comic strip. After a time I noticed that the cars on the boulevard and the few people on the sidewalk had not actually frozen into place
but instead were moving with great slowness. I could see men's legs ad-
vancing within their trousers, the knee coming forward to strike the
crease, the cuff slowly lifting off the shoe, the shoe drifting up like Tom
Cat's paw when he crept toward Jerry Mouse. The warm, patched skin of
Sherman Boulevard. . . . I thought of walking along Sherman Boulevard
forever, moving past the nearly immobile cars and people, past the theater, past the liquor store, through the gates, and past the wading pool and
swings, past the elephants and lions reaching out to be fed, past the secret
park where my father flailed in a rage of disappointment, past the elms
and out the opposite gate, past the big houses on the opposite side of the
park, past picture windows and past lawns with bikes and plastic pools,
past slanting driveways and basketball hoops, past men getting out of cars,
past playgrounds where children raced back and forth on a surface shining black. Then past fields and crowded markets, past high yellow tractors
with mud dried like old wool inside the enormous hubs, past wagons piled
high with hay, past deep woods where lost children followed trails of
bread crumbs to a gingerbread door, past other cities where nobody
would see me because nobody knew my name, past everything, past everybody.

At the Orpheum-Oriental, I stopped still. My mouth was dry and my eyes
would not focus. Everything around me, so quiet and still a moment earlier, jumped into life as soon as I stopped walking. Horns blared, cars
roared down the boulevard. Beneath these sounds I heard the pounding
of great machines, and the fires gobbling up oxygen beneath the street. As
if I had eaten them from the air, fire and smoke poured into my stomach.
Flame slipped up my throat and sealed the back of my mouth. In my mind
I saw myself taking the first quarter from my pocket, exchanging it for a
ticket, pushing through the door, and moving into the cool air. I saw myself holding out the ticket to be torn in half, going over an endless brown
carpet toward the inner door. From the last row of seats on the other side
of the inner door, inside the shadowy but not yet dark theater, a shapeless
monster whose wet black mouth said *Love me, love me* stretched yearning
arms toward me. Shock froze my shoes to the sidewalk, then shoved me
firmly in the small of the back, and I was running down the block, unable

to scream because I had to clamp my lips against the smoke and fire trying
to explode from my mouth.

The rest of that afternoon remains vague. I wandered through the streets,
not in the clean, hollow way I had imagined but almost blindly, hot and
uncertain. I remember the taste of fire in my mouth and the loudness of
my heart. After a time I found myself before the elephant enclosure in the
zoo. A newspaper reporter in a neat gray suit passed through the space
before me, and I followed him, knowing that he carried a notebook in his
pocket, that he had been beaten by gangsters, that he could locate the
speaking secret that hid beneath the disconnected and dismembered
pieces of the world. He would fire his pistol on an empty chamber and
trick evil "Solly Wellman," Berry Kroeger with his girlish, watchful eyes.
And when "Solly Wellman" came gloating out of the shadows, the reporter would shoot him dead.
      Dead.
      Donna Reed smiled down from an upstairs window: Has there ever
been a smile like that? Ever? I was in Chicago, and behind a closed door
"Blackie Franchot" bled onto a brown carpet. "Solly Wellman," something like "Solly Wellman," called and called to me from the decorated
grave where he lay like a secret. The man in the gray suit finally carried his
notebook and his gun through a front door, and I saw that I was only a few
blocks from home.

Paul leans against the wire fence surrounding the playground, looking
out, looking backward. Alan Ladd brushes off "Leona" (June Havoc), for
she has no history that matters and exists only in the world of work and
pleasure, of cigarettes and cocktail bars. Beneath this world is another,
and "Leona's" life is a blind, strenuous denial of that other world.

My mother held her hand to my forehead and declared that I not only had
a fever but had been building up to it all week. I was not to go to the
playground the next day; I had to spend the day lying down on Mrs. Candee's couch. When she lifted the telephone to call one of the high-school
girls, I said not to bother, other kids were gone all the time, and she put
down the receiver.

I lay on Mrs. Candee's couch staring up at the ceiling of her darkened
living room. The twins squabbled outside, and maternal, slow-witted Mrs.
Candee brought me orange juice. The twins ran toward the sandbox, and
Mrs. Candee groaned as she let herself fall into a wobbly lawn chair. The
morning newspaper folded beneath the lawn chair said that *The Hitchhiker* and *Double Cross* had begun playing at the Orpheum-Oriental.
*Chicago Deadline* had done its work and traveled on. It had broken the
world in half and sealed the monster deep within. Nobody but me knew
this. Up and down the block, sprinklers whirred, whipping loops of water

onto the dry lawns. Men driving slowly up and down the street hung their elbows out of their windows. For a moment free of regret and nearly without emotion of any kind, I understood that I belonged utterly to myself. Like everything else, I had been torn asunder and glued back together with shock, vomit, and orange juice. The knowledge sifted into me that I was all alone. "Stan," "Jimmy," whatever his name was, would never come back to the theater. He would be afraid that I had told my parents and the police about him. I knew that I had killed him by forgetting him, and then I forgot him again.

The next day I went back to the theater and went through the inner door and saw row after row of empty seats falling toward the curtained screen. I was all alone. The size and grandeur of the theater surprised me. I went down the long, descending aisle and took the last seat, left side, on the broad middle aisle. The next row seemed nearly a playground's distance away. The lights dimmed and the curtains rippled slowly away from the screen. Anticipatory music filled the air, and the first letters appeared on the screen.

What I am, what I do, why I do it. I am simultaneously a man in his early forties, that treacherous time, and a boy of seven before whose bravery I shall forever fall short. I live underground in a wooden room and patiently, in joyful concentration, decorate the walls. Before me, half unseen, hangs a large and appallingly complicated vision I must explore and memorize, must witness again and again in order to locate its hidden center. Around me, everything is in its proper place. My typewriter sits on the sturdy table. Beside the typewriter a cigarette smolders, raising a gray stream of smoke. A record revolves on the turntable, and my small apartment is dense with music. ("Bird of Prey Blues," with Coleman Hawkins, Buck Clayton, and Hank Jones.) Beyond my walls and windows is a world toward which I reach with outstretched arms and an ambitious and divided heart. As if "Bird of Prey Blues" has evoked them, the voices of sentences to be written this afternoon, tomorrow, or next month stir and whisper, beginning to speak, and I lean over the typewriter toward them, getting as close as I can.

# Dolls

Guy Summertree Veryzer

◆

As a small boy I knew
that dogs once had wings
and that pigs
when they were first created
could produce gold
in perfect ingots
by dancing
The world as the gods intended it
has vanished
irretrievably
I realize that is no excuse
so before I am exposed
and humiliated
I will confess
I admit openly
I did have dolls

I used to poison them regularly
I sat them around the tiny tea set
and ladled heaping spoonfuls
of arsenic and cobra venom
into the rose-budded cups
They drank it all down
I made them
They thanked me very politely
then went into grotesque convulsions
screaming about the pain
of dying young
and the stains the grass
was getting on their tea gowns
Then I would strip them naked
placing them in an assortment

*of shocking positions*
*I painted strange designs*
*on their frozen faces*
*and their chubby innocent bodies*
*using a secret formula of melted lipstick*
*and Mercurochrome*

*One doll would try to play the heroine*
*attempting to rescue the others*
*That doll would suffer worst of all*
*She would be treated to a haircut*
*or a beating with a rolling pin*
*They never cried*
*I think it was because*
*they had religion*
*Often I used to be awakened in the night*
*by the chanting*
*from their prayer meetings*
*held beside the shoetree*
*in my closet*
*I would peer through the keyhole*
*at the lighted birthday candles*
*making tiny wax rivers*
*on the wooden floor*
*I could never see very much*
*They could have been praying*
*to a coat hanger or a piece of toast*
*or a Gumby*
*I let them be*

*One sultry afternoon in August*
*a dark-haired beauty*
*not unlike Merle Oberon*
*answered back at tea time*
*Of course I was compelled*
*to shoot her*
*(for the sake of discipline)*
*several times*
*with an old army revolver*
*I buried her*
*in a torn black lace negligee*
*I am not absolutely positive*
*she was dead*
*I think of those coy violet doll eyes*
*staring out of the pale plastic skin*
*in the dark*

*flexing in horror*
*at the sound of dirt being shoveled*
*on the lid of the shoebox*

*I suppose in my childish way*
*I was a monster*
*But you have to understand*
*I had been raised on fairy tales*
*and old Susan Hayward movies*
*Disney's Sleeping Beauty seemed real*
*I had my own t.v. and art lessons*
*summer theater school and large allowance*
*a 45 r.p.m. record collection*
*that asked*
*"How much is that doggie in the window?"*
*and told me in a warm resonant voice*
*that little boys are made of*
*"snails and puppy dogs tails"*
*and Hayley Mills sang the theme*
*from* The Castaways *(trust in your star)*
*What bliss!*
*I sang along*
*and lived in a reality all my own*
*Other children didn't understand*
*I was*
*tormented*
*laughed at*
*teased about my high pitched voice*
*and pretty face*
*I needed an outlet*
*in giving back a measure of what I received*
*I was doing no more than I'd been taught*

*I lied*
*the dolls did scream*
*they cried and begged and bled*
*broke and died*
*But I was in pain*
*I didn't realize*

*Often after a day of persecution*
*at grade school*
*I would take Maria Teresa*
*my favorite doll*
*away from the other ladies of the court*
*I would carefully dress her up*

*in rhinestone diamonds*
*and wrap her snugly*
*in scraps of satin and silk and fur*
*She would come and sleep*
*beside me as I napped*
*I would gently*
*Oh so very gently*
*so as not to wake her*
*slip my arm around her*
*whispering a hushed song*
*about the long ago days*
*when dogs had wings and could fly*
*as they were meant to do*
*and I was a handsome prince*
*We were two storybook children*
*lost in a great black cave*
*orphans of nightly sorrow*
*brother and sister*
*chaste and pure*
*I never violated her*
*Never ever abused*
*her perfect trust*

For most children television has replaced old-fashioned storytelling, and the archaic fairy-tale landscape of cottage and forest and castle has disappeared under a wave of name brands and fast video action. Nevertheless, as Mark Richards' verbally explosive tale demonstrates, children will still find and use and make the stories they need from the available materials.

# This Is Us, Excellent
◆ Mark Richards ◆

My brother gains his porpoise on my pony in our race along the alleys home. I handlebar-heave through some side-skidding garbage and hold him off at the turn. I back-jam my pedals for my famous gravel-scatter through our chain-link gate. I try to knee up fast to do my Duke McQuaid sidesaddle dismount but my toes catch on the crossbar and my brother slips in along my side. Either on TV it's "Danger: Duke McQuaid" or "Ocean Secrets," hundredth millionth. We elbow-to-rib wrestle up the back cement steps. I punch my brother in the boxwoods. I am pulling in the door.

I do the Duke McQuaid dive-from-the-back-of-the-buckboard through the den door down in front of the TV. The TV is already excellent, warmed up. My brother claws the wall coming in off the kitchen and surfs on the hall rug in on top of me. I'll break his wrist in one snap for him to touch that dial. But what we've missed coming in the alley the back way is our dad's car out front with our dad home, and with our dad home is our mom, backhanded backside down between the coffee table and the sofa for company we'd better keep our asses off of. What we've missed here is our dad helping our mom up for another blap across the mouth.

This is excellent! I do the Duke McQuaid drag-away-your-wounded partner with my brother, then we spin out with toenail traction on Mom's Shine-Rite floors down the hall to our room for shoes and shirts, leaving it all, leaving on the TV, it having sports on it on anyway. So much sports on makes it less the chance for our dad to have an interest in coming down the hall to beat our asses. It's just our mom this time.

This really is excellent. Now we get to go snag a 'za at Psycho Za, my brother and I getting to order the Manic Size Train Wreck 'za with double everything hot. We get two orders of Logjam Fries and two Gutbuster SuperSodas, no lids or sissy sticks, please!

Our mom just has coffee to go with her Jesus homework. The lady next door brings the homework over to her in little books. For us she brings usually some green apples and some Christian outlines you can cut out of God and the Apostles. My brother and I stick the cutouts in the spokes of our bikes with clothespins to rattle some clatter up and down our street until Mr. Murdock comes out and says, Stop it! He says, Here's a quarter for you and here's a dime for your brother, just, please, Stop it!

Our mom drinks her coffee cold, usually, not to burn the swole lip she has, the main reason for us going to Psycho Za. She sits while we eat and makes lines under the words in the little books the lady from next door brings over.

My brother and I have been snagging 'zas at Psycho Za when it was way before called Psycho Za, like the summer it was called Miss Romano's Pizza Palace, then Pizza Feast, then Earl's. When it was just Earl's I was little and my brother came in a sling and I would only have a soda or some snow cream and our beat-on mom just had cold coffee and cigarettes, no Jesus homework yet. Then our dad backhanding and giving our mom money for it after, I worked up through sodas and snow cream to pinball at Earl's, pizza burgers and playing with the knobs on the cigarette machine at Miss Romano's with my brother in a plastic chair, and finally us snagging some Manic Size 'zas at Psycho Za, leading to a ride on the Rocket Sling later in the park.

Talk about it, excellent! Sometimes on the ride my brother almost throws up the Train Wreck and sometimes he almost doesn't.

Then there are the nights when our mom calls up the lady from next door to come over to Psycho Za and this is not real excellent. Some nights our mom's pencil points break and we don't have a sharpener in her purse. Some nights her coffee soaks through her Jesus homework and her split lip beats in hiccups against her bent tooth. On these nights my brother and I know not to breathe Train Wreck breath on each other or jerk on the cigarette coin return over and over for pinball quarters until somebody says, Stop! We just sit there and work over our food while the lady from next door works over our mom, pulling tissues and gold sticks of make-up from her secret-compartment purse. Sometimes, if it is something we should not see that she should do, she and our mom go back into the ladies' room for a long time, taking along the purse we are never left long enough with to go through. Whenever we can, we look in it, but mostly all we ever see when our mom's head is tilted back and the lady's back is turned, mostly only all we ever see over the Train Wreck down inside her purse is something looking like God or an odd Apostle.

What else is not real excellent about the lady from next door coming over to Psycho Za is that later she won't get in the Rocket Sling down at the amusement park with us. She just sits on the railing talking to the man with the cast on his arm running the ride. You should tell him, whoever he is, every summer different, about the way the clutch handle slips and breaks your arm. Usually it happens into the summer when the ride has been pretty good ridden and the handle starts to click like one of those piano clocks, back and forth, back and forth, until one night the handle wants to lie down flat against the place where the men running the ride like to rest their arm, waiting for the ride to be run. Every summer somebody different has it happen, it's just always the same kind of cast over the same kind of arms, arms like with amusement-type tattoos that look deeper blue in winter when you see them doing some job else, like taking out restaurant trash or reaching for cigarettes through bars in the windows of the jail downtown.

And the next-door lady not getting on the Rocket Sling means that our mom will not get on either. And even with our mom behaving at home so our dad has to blap her, still me and my brother have to have her for the feeling we get when she screams excellent, us spinning around, tucked under the metal bar that other people eating fried mess and French fries have greased up, the rocket cockpit like a chicken wire box you can see through, you can almost stick your finger through the wire and touch the two bolts that hold you on, that keep the rocket on the ride. First you go up rocking slow and you can study the painted rust in the cracks of the metal arms with the bulbs lit in between where they are burned out, and then up, turning heavy, the rocket cockpit sloping me against my brother and my mother, you can smell Train Wreck and coffee, the ride taking your breath up until you spin around calm at the top at first, above our town and the ocean black ink you are on the edge of, and maybe a secret pinball quarter you were saving for yourself falls out of your shorts about now, you knowing the man running the ride can hear the silver bounce down while he watches in the sand for it to land, him waiting for it to rain change from people's pockets every time, like you wait all summer to show up and see his broken arm in a cast because nobody, even you, told him to watch out for that slipping stick on the clutch that starts and stops the ride.

And then, Down! you rocket-spin, going face first down. What you are seeing are just the bits out of a bigger thing, like when you and your best friend go through the trash behind the Ebb Tide Motel and find the instant camera pictures of naked people doing naked-people things, except when they get ready to go home from vacation they rip up all the naked pictures into the little bits you and your best friend find pieces of, hardly ever enough to put together, except for that one you don't even show your brother, the one of that fat lady with the scary titties, and how you keep one titty scrap and your best friend keeps the other, him also keeping the knees but you keeping what is real excellent scary, her happy face, you can

see how funny she thought her vacation was with scary titties and sun-
burn.

So on the Rocket Sling you are seeing these little pieces of the put-
together picture so that when the ride really gets excellent spinning fast,
mostly what you see are the spinning smears of the bulbs burning bright,
and like ripped scraps, sometimes maybe you see the shoes of the breakable-armed man and sometimes maybe you see a far summer star, all the
time smelling Train Wreck breath and coffee breath and breeze off the
ocean ink where it's deep black night and scary because you can still look
up and see the two rusted bolts that hold your rocket on and you think the
bolts might break and you are going to fly right off the rocket ride arm,
you are going to be slung right out of the park way out in the ink, all
strapped down and locked in, to blub-blub sink without no one's reach,
where nobody could ever possibly find you. That's the real excellent scary
part, that feeling, and that feeling won't come if the lady from next door is
there and your mom won't ride the ride, because what brings on that feeling most is when your mom rides wedged in tight with you and your
brother on nights like this, when your mom will scream the excellent
scream, the scream that people you see in snatches on the boardwalk stop
and stare for, the scream that stops the ride next door, the scream that
tells us to our hearts the bolts have finally broken.

My brother and I have been having off from school. Our mom won't let us
go because of my black eye. I took it like a Duke McQuaid. I like to look at
myself in the mirror and then spit in the sink like it ain't nothing to it at all.

We are at home alone so when we see the lady next door going up her
walk my brother and I put our mouths up to the window shade and yell,
Nosy Bitch! Then we lay down on the company sofa we're not allowed on
and laugh. Our dad has said that Nosy Bitch was the one who called our
school. They took us in the sick room and asked us was everything all right
at home, did we tend to fall down and hurt ourselves. I told them our dad
can beat up whoever he wants to. Nosy Bitch!

About an hour later that Nosy Bitch comes knocking at the back door
while we're watching TV. We crawl in the cave behind the company sofa
while the TV plays all the way up so I know she can hear it and I don't go
to the door. I ain't coming out to face a rope around my neck, Nosy Bitch,
you'll have to break down the door and shoot your way in. But she keeps
tapping the glass like I know she won't go away until I go see, so I get up
and go down the hall touching all the cousin pictures and then I make
sure the toilet isn't running where my brother had been in there for about
an hour and I take long linoleum slides in my socks across the kitchen
floor and still I see her shadow on the curtain in back. It could be the
shadow of a man with a loaf of bread under his arm.

It's just another bag of those green apples she's brought us and a book
of Jesus homework for our mom. She asks me, Is she here? and I say, Nah,
she ain't here, and she says, Well, tell her I came by, and then before she

leaves she looks over my head into the kitchen like she'd like to nose around in there so I close the door and watch her go back in her house through the shade.

Outside, me and my brother take some side-gnawing bites out of a couple of the green apples until we catch the Murdock cat in a run underneath some cars. We clobber him a few times with some apples to his brains until he makes a flat-eared dive into the storm drain. We see him down between the grates pushing against a ledge to keep out of the water so we chew some apples until they are the right size to throw through the grate. The cat has to swim away with apple mess all in his hair.

We make a few checks in the storm drain grates down the street but they run dry so I figure the Murdock cat has hit a turn in the pipe. We set back home when the mail truck stops and waits by a box while the mailman reads somebody's magazine. I line up for a shot like a bomb in a covered wagon but I'm off a little and the apple splits on the edge of the mailman's mirror and the mailman gets a face full of mess.

I don't do a Duke McQuaid. I run, pushing my little brother in front of me, pushing him so hard he starts to fall, then I grab him up before he does to push him ahead some more. The mailman has dropped the magazine in the middle of the street to chase us. I try to run us toward home without really going there. I run us the direction of our house where I know whose fence is weak and where whose garage will lock. We turn the alley two people's yards up from our chain-link gate and I figure: the dark of the magnolia next door! I throw my brother over the black-rotted whitewash and angle myself through a pushed-in plank and that is where we see them.

In that place, so always shady and the dirt is always damp, under where the magnolia has knotted limbs and leaves like plastic, the breakable-armed man is dragging a rake toward where the lady next door is bent over a basket. They both have stopped in mid what they're doing to look at us, and I see that the man's arm is white without his cast, his skin has been shaded by it from the sun. There is a tattoo of Jesus I would recognize anywhere on his white-shaded arm. The face of Jesus is blue ink and the beard is roughed with the real hair of the breakable-armed man. The tattoo looks somehow excellent, a wanted poster alive from the TV show I want to be.

Storm has come and taken our power off so we look into my brother's eyes with a flashlight for any change. His eyes are still like when you are bored at home on rainy days and you start to draw but you don't know what to draw so you just draw a dot and then you circle on and on the dot until it's a big black hole in the middle of the paper.

All around my brother's sick bed made up on the company sofa with a sheet and a pillow are stand-up Christian cutouts of God and the Apostles. We have two of one, the one with the sheep up his sleeve. Our mom has

made the green stuffed chair the place where she prays for my brother and waits in the dark with the flashlight.

Our dad is out in the car listening to the radio scores because the power is off to the TV. We know not to bother him. This afternoon Mr. Murdock came over and then my father grabbed me by my belt and collar like to clean a saloon bar with. I was lucky. When I hit by the TV I didn't taste blood or anything and when he came over I knew to stay down and just study his shoes, to just watch for the toe parts to swell, to get ready for him to bend down and pick up my head.

For my brother it was a simple palm-push but my brother's head was too close to the wall. I have told him a hundred million times to stay away from the walls even when the walls make corners. He was too close so when his head got pushed it sort of bounced off the wall and back to our dad's palm like to kiss it, and then he fell out on the floor like a girl on the playground having a spell.

There is brought-over apple pie from next door smelling up the kitchen. Before the storm the breakable-armed man was in the neighborhood looking down into the storm drain grates. He had both hands around the bars and was kneeling over them like a man in a face-down prison.

From the window where I sit near my brother I can hear Mr. Murdock calling his cat. The radio plays out in our dad's car. In the dashboard lights I can see his outline like a backwards Christian cutout. A candle is lit in the window next door. For as long as you look at it, it never flickers.

This is us, excellent, a family night out. Not even have we not had to go to Family Fish House to eat but we've come to Psycho Za to snag! Our mom has her hair fixed and has on the too-big red plastic parka with our dad's name on the front. Our dad has said for us to have anything we can think of we want on the list of things to eat. What I'd usually do is split the Manic Train Wreck with my brother but he is still acting funny about eating and stuff, like he's not all the way woken up and his eyes are like old fish-tank water. When he cries it's more like a hiss, like how a soft knife sounds when you split a green apple open.

Our dad has wads of quarters in his pockets for me and my brother to play pinball but my brother leans in the booth against our mom with his dead eyes while our mom pets his hair and our dad watches our car in the parking lot for somebody not to break in and steal it. There are still stacks of quarters when our food comes so I know I can tilt and push the pinball harder.

I eat my Brainbuster Burger heavy on the Super Goop and dig around in the catsup puddles with a Terminal Case of Logjam Fries but everyone else doesn't look down at their plates, like the food isn't good enough to eat. The family-night-out meal comes and goes with just me working on the platters, and then we get up and I show our dad where to pay while he strums quarters in his pockets and then we all stand out by the newspaper

racks in front of Psycho Za like nobody knows where we are or which way home.

I see this is excellent so I say Rocket Sling! Rocket SLING! and our mom looks at me and says, It's too late, way too late for the Rocket Sling. She says, It must be closed, and my brother mashes his face on her pants leg. Our dad says, Everybody get in the car.

I think at first our mom is right when we see the park shutting down with canvas wraps over the kiddie boats and there's just an ice cream crowd through the gate coming out. The more our mom says, No, the more our dad turns his fingers on her arm to lead us in.

This is excellent! Just us and the Rocket and the breakable-armed man. He is changing lights on the metal arms from a box of white-sleeved bulbs. He comes down climbing off the gears and hitches up his pants. He opens a rocket cockpit and he does it in a way to make us feel that if he had a watch he would look at it because it is late. The boardwalk is empty, the Roll-Go-Round next door is dark.

Our mom would no sooner get us in the rocket. My brother has his face in her pants zipper. She says, Please, to our dad. Our dad steps into the rocket and his weight works on the bolts that hold him on overhead. We stand by the ramp and wait. Come on, he says, we're going all the way tonight. He waits and we wait and then he starts to climb out to pull us in so I step up but the breakable-armed man moves faster and I watch his tattoo arm bring down the bar across our dad and snap the cockpit shut. I am still close as he slips in the clutch to bite a gear and our dad rocks a bit, porch-swinging, before the bolted-on arm lifts his rocket slowly to the top.

With his lopsided weight on the empty ride, the steel arms bend and bounce his one slow spin down, and in the bottom light I see a white-knuckled grip around the greased metal bar. Up he goes, his outline at the top before he rockets slung out full, to fall faster where we stand. The breakable-armed man leads us around behind the waiting line railing and then he drifts off backwards like as soon as he is in the dark he will run all the way home.

We are left alone in all this light. The bulbs running past throw shadows, the gears gnaw themselves against the motor. We cannot move to stop or move to go. We can only watch from behind the bars of the railings as around and around and around the rocket with our dad spins in perfect catching ups and perfect catching downs until there is the sound of metal breaking free. Something zings by my head like a bullet on TV. Things are starting to shake apart, things are coming loose, pieces of metal are rattling around the rockets and are being spun out of the light into the ink slapping the beach behind us.

Our mom takes a step toward where the breakable-armed man should stand. She has to drag my brother. He is green-apple screaming. We can hear more pieces falling as our dad rockets past. I look at the clutch handle I would never go near in a hundred million years. It is vibrating so fast it is a blurring thing in two places at once.

I see Dad up, I see Dad down. Breaking-loose metal hits against our clothes and we shield our eyes with our arms. We can't look and we can't not see what will happen next. I see something else and it is excellent, in the outline of Dad as he is slung up, still for a quick, quiet second before he is slung back down, and down I see him see the scrap of me, and then up I see his outline, his arms grabbing at the air and spreading space, and then down I see from his pockets the busted wads of silver sling into the sand, and then up I see him excellent, snatching in the dark at the things that will fall to our feet from heaven.

# Saturn

## Sharon Olds

♦

He lay on the couch night after night,
mouth open, the darkness of the room
filling his mouth, and no one knew
my father was eating his children. He seemed to
rest so quietly, vast body
inert on the sofa, big hand
fallen away from the glass.
What could be more passive than a man
passed out every night—and yet as he lay
on his back, snoring, our lives slowly
disappeared down the hole of his life.
My brother's arm went in up to the shoulder
and he bit it off, and sucked at the wound
as one sucks at the sockets of lobster. He took
my brother's head between his lips
and snapped it like a cherry off the stem. You would have seen
only a large, handsome man
heavily asleep, unconscious. And yet
somewhere in his head his soil-colored eyes
were open, the circles of the whites glittering
as he crunched the torso of his child between his jaws,
crushed the bones like the soft shells of crabs
and the delicacies of the genitals
rolled back along his tongue. In the nerves of his gums and
bowels he knew what he was doing and he could not
stop himself, like orgasm, his
boy's feet crackling like two raw fish
between his teeth. This is what he wanted,
to take that life into his mouth
and show what a man could do—show his son
what a man's life was.

"The Twelve-Windowed Tower" is an old fairy tale found in Germany and Eastern Europe. In the original story, an isolated princess can see through those windows into every corner of the world. In the following fairy tale, the author (who was born and raised in Austria) sets the story in Europe during more modern times—but the magical tower has endured despite the encroachment of urban streets.

# The Twelve-Windowed Tower
### ♦ Silvana Siddali ♦

Ilona was caught, rooted near the kitchen chair, transfixed by her mother's eyes. Now the trick wouldn't work. Face to face with that angry stare, she couldn't make herself invisible. The child stood waiting in the kitchen doorway, eyes cast carefully down.

Her mother held out the cracked china bowl. "Bugs in the flour! Your father's going to kill you. You think grocery money grows on trees?"

The weevils had invaded the old flour, which had been a charitable contribution from a schoolmate's mother. The nuns had sent Ilona and her brothers out of their classrooms one day and announced their family's poverty (and probably their father's shiftlessness as well) to everyone in the school. Stalky potatoes, rancid margarine, and this old flour had been the result of that announcement. Ilona's mother had known very well how to value such gifts, but she also had to make them do.

Now Ilona wondered how the bugs could have been her fault, since the children weren't allowed in the pantry. But that wouldn't have mattered to her mother. She avoided looking at her mother but she heard heels banging across the floor, and a ringing slap rocked her head. The world turned red for a moment. Ilona was able to keep her feet under her. *Don't move. It doesn't hurt. Don't cry.*

Her mother turned, shaking, her pretty face flushed an angry red, her hands twisting in her apron. She crashed her fist onto the table. The flour-filled bowl rocked wildly, then righted itself.

"For God's sake, you stupid girl, will you *leave?* Get out before I *do* something!"

But Ilona knew better than to go. That might start something even worse. Her mother would think she was being disrespectful, or perhaps was laughing at her. She took a deep breath, her face still stinging, and waited for the screaming to end. Ilona and her two younger brothers rarely knew just what to do at times like these. It was impossible to know what set their parents off, equally impossible to know what would calm them down. What worked one day might make everything worse the next. If only her mother would turn away, her attention caught by the vermin-ridden flour or lost in the gray city sky outside the kitchen window. Ilona needed the distraction to work her trick.

Some years before, when she was five years old, Ilona had learned the secret of invisibility. It had happened here, in the kitchen while she was playing with the burners on her mother's stove. As she was staring into the blue-white flame, a tiny capering figure appeared in the fire. It flickered in the circle of the gas flame, beckoning to Ilona. Not believing her eyes, she got up to move closer, and knocked over a chair. She froze then, but her mother hadn't noticed. In fact, she seemed to have forgotten Ilona's existence, staring at the fallen chair with a bewildered expression instead. Her mother sighed, picked up the chair, and left the kitchen, shaking her head.

It was then Ilona realized that she had become invisible while she was looking at the gas-flame fairy. That was when her mother's eyes had clouded over, and Ilona's own body had felt curiously vague, like a shadow on faded wallpaper, or a movement caught in a mirror.

Later that same evening, she tried it again. Standing in the middle of the living room while her father clenched his evening paper and her mother stared past her knitting into the night-darkened window, Ilona summoned the gas-flame fairy. Soon her parents' eyes unfocused, their attention wavered, and Ilona slipped away. Looking down, she could still see her legs, but she felt oddly empty and hollow. Her father sighed and began to read, while her mother shook her head and took up her needles.

Once she had practiced her skill enough so that it fit her like an old sweater, Ilona began to travel outdoors through their old European sea-coast city, looking for adventure. By the time she was nine, she knew her way through the city's secret passageways. She could find paths which led in and out of strange cellars, past neglected dockyards, and through weird and frightening ceramic waterfront drainpipes, nearly five feet high. She also learned the city's bus and tram routes by heart until she could travel them as confidently as the gray-suited people who flowed daily along the tracks. None of them ever seemed to wonder about a young girl riding the trams alone in the middle of the day, when she should have been in school. She knew she was still invisible. She could go wherever she liked.

Today, while her mother screamed herself into exhaustion, Ilona held perfectly still and eventually her mother forgot her presence. Ilona summoned the gas-flame fairy, then floated out of the apartment, down the stairs, and onto the sidewalk. She wasn't going to return to school that afternoon. The nuns probably wouldn't even notice.

For many weeks, Ilona had been wanting to explore the western reaches of the city's tram lines. Although she had wandered along most of the sidewalks which bounded the inner city, she had never travelled the westernmost end. Fishing her book of soft paper tickets out of the pocket of her worn blue jacket, Ilona climbed into the first trolley. Other girls her age had gone back to school, where they were learning how to sew striped skirts with tiny stitches, or struggling with irregular verbs in some impossible foreign language, or forcing numerals into narrow boxes on ruled paper. The tram was empty and quiet. Even the grey-suited people were gone. Ilona pictured them spending their day staring at account books, or displaying objects to one another in stores across the city, or fitting parts to a machine the name and use of which she could not fathom.

At first, the buildings and sidewalks outside the window looked familiar and ordinary: dark, gray, quiet, but beautiful to Ilona nonetheless. Then the buildings along the tram line began to thin and draw away from her eyes. She travelled for a long time. The last stop was nearing. The end of the western line.

Ilona was alone when the tram finally reached the its destination. A little apprehensive now, she climbed down the steps and stood on a windy, weedy street corner watching the tram make the difficult turn for the trip back into the city's heart. When the trolley rolled out of sight, Ilona felt for a moment as though her last friend had left her.

But ahead of her was adventure, a high ocean wind whipping up possibilities. The sky was white and clear. All around her were abandoned buildings, barren trees, and broken sidewalks suffering the quiet ravages of grass through cracks. Beyond the last empty lot, she spied a narrow path winding beyond a derelict warehouse and up a hill. A tall red tower was at the top. Ilona started to climb.

Up here, beyond the paved streets and buildings, the wind was freer and more playful, nudging her along, pulling at her sleeves, slapping her skirt against her legs. The air tasted fresh, the wind was wild, and the few scraggly trees which struggled for sunlight on the hill joined in the wind's dance.

Just ahead, as the path ended amid a litter of metal drums, Ilona saw the tall tower loom almost as high as a church. The tower was built of dark brick and a few broken windows were stuffed with rags. The door was secured with a padlock, fastened to a rusted hasp. Around the tower, leafless shrubs were hung with rags and bits of old paper. The wind was strong, wild, and sharp. The afternoon had already begun to darken. Ilona wasn't sure, suddenly, whether she was shivering from cold or fear. But something about the tower drew her closer.

She tugged at the tower's padlock, but it had long ago rusted quite shut. She wandered disconsolately around the tower, trying to find a way in. She noticed that one of the windows was lower to the ground than the others, and she dragged a can over. Standing on it, she pushed away the rags stuffed into a broken pane, and scraped her way through.

The upper windows of the tower were still whole, giving her plenty of light to pick her way around the bits and pieces littering the floor. She thought that if she could get to the top of the tower, she would have a magnificent view of the city. Maybe she could even see all the way to her school, where the other girls sat slaving over striped skirts and poisonous verbs.

Circling around inside the tower walls, stumbling over pieces of wood and metal, Ilona discovered a rusted set of rungs bolted into the wall. She dragged herself up the rungs one by one, scraping her hands, the rust stinging in the cuts. Her arms ached by the time she reached the top, where she found a narrow walkway encircling the tower just underneath the windows.

She stood for a minute to catch her breath, then looked out the first window. To the child's amazement, she was nearly blinded by the brilliance of the sun. Ilona blinked and closed her eyes tight. The wind had begun whistling, singing, an urgent note in its voice. When she opened her eyes, the light was as brilliant and dazzling as before.

Her heart began to pound in her chest. Beneath her, spread around the base of the tower, was a sea of vivid green grass and trees, and the sound of water splashing on stones. She felt a breath of fresh salt air against her cheek. Where was the city? And the tram lines?

*Never seen, you've never seen, oh, in your city. . . .*

"What was that? Who's talking?" Ilona called, searching the beautiful green scene beneath her. There was not a soul in sight.

*It's the Wind, the West Wind.*

"The West Wind," Ilona whispered. She stared into the branches, which had begun to stir softly. Her hand crept to her cheek, remembering the time she met the gas-flame fairy. "Where are you?" Ilona said.

The breeze grew stronger. Her hair was ruffled.

*Here, all around you. You're in one of my homes now, where you can look into other places. . . .*

She looked up, wondering. *Other places.* "West Wind, what am I seeing in the window? It's not what I saw when I climbed the hill from the tram station."

*A park in your city. Look again. . . .*

She clung to the window frame, crouching on the narrow catwalk, and tried to peer between the rustling green leaves beneath her. As she watched, she saw three dark-haired young women wearing convent school uniforms, walking together. Their heads were bent and their steps were quick. They appeared to be talking softly.

"Who are they, West Wind? What are you showing me?"

*The one in the middle may be your mother. That window looks into the possible past.*

Ilona frowned. "The possible past, West Wind? What do you mean?"

*The windows in this tower show you many parts of your city, my young friend. Some are only possible. This window allows you to look into the might-have-been.*

"The might-have-been," Ilona whispered. "I wonder if I can find it on the street car."

The wind fluttered in the leaves beneath her. *No, only through this window. Look, look; eleven other windows, and each is another world.*

"West Wind, may I look out of all of them?"

*Yes. Oh yes. But not now. In your own world, the sun is setting and soon it will be dark.*

Ilona sighed. "All right. But I'll come back as soon as I can. Will you be here the next time I visit?"

*Ah, I will. . . .*

Ilona looked out of her window again. The brilliant green beneath her began to shimmer, and then she found she was looking at the neglected landscape of the tower. The sky was shading into early evening. The tower looked dark and ordinary.

"Good-bye, West Wind," she said.

She scrambled down the rusted iron bars and out through the window, remembering to stuff the rags back into place. She dragged the can away, and then ran quickly back to the tram line. She seemed to have been away for hours. Ilona grew more and more apprehensive; surely, she hadn't missed the last train? While she waited, Ilona looked down and saw that her dress was torn, dirty, and stained with rust and grease. She began to feel sick with fear.

She tiptoed into her kitchen an hour later. Her mother's lovely face was stiff. She barely glanced at Ilona. "Oh, there you are. Hurry up and set the table. And call your brothers for dinner."

She turned her back on Ilona, hunching her shoulders over the stove. The odor of potatoes and boiled onions rose from the pot. Potatoes and onions again. Father wouldn't like that.

Ilona set down the last knife and fork and left the kitchen to call her brothers. Suddenly, she flinched and turned her head. From the bedroom came the sound of a thump and a whimper. Ilona's insides turned over.

The child closed her eyes then and summoned the gas-flame fairy. Cloaked in invisibility, she crept to the bedroom door and cracked it open. Her father, a big, heavy man, towered over Ilona's brother Benno. Her father was holding his fist clenched and circling it over his own head. "I'll show them! I'll show them all! They can't do this to me!" He spit out the words through clenched teeth, while the little boy on the floor tried very hard not to cry. Ilona saw that Benno had wet himself in fear. *Oh, God,* she prayed, *don't let Papa see that. Don't cry,* she thought. *Please, Bennie, don't cry. You know it only makes it worse.* The boy's face was white as chalk, his eyes were blinking rapidly, but he knew better than to make a single sound. He had never been able to learn Ilona's secret of invisibility, but she had at least managed to teach him the importance of keeping as still as possible.

Ilona leaned weakly against the door frame, hating herself for not helping the younger child. She was too afraid to enter the room. She wasn't so much afraid of being hit, but her father could hurt her in other ways. She hoped Benno understood.

"Ilona!" her mother's called from the kitchen. "Ilona, tell your father dinner's ready!" Ilona nearly fainted with relief. Perhaps her father had heard.

She ducked behind the door, and, yes, here he came. He strode purposefully out of the room, muttering to himself, "That will teach the little bastard to respect me."

Ilona peeked in at Benno, doubled over on the dark green rug. She crept over to him, put her arms around him, and whispered, "It's all right, Bennie. He's gone."

The boy's face was already purpling with bruises, and his head wobbled on his skinny neck. Ilona touched his hand. "Did he hurt you badly this time?"

Benno swallowed and shook his head no. "He just punched me a few times," he said, trying to be brave.

Ilona hugged him. "Listen, Benno, I have a wonderful story to tell you tonight. Just wait till after dinner, okay?" He nodded and got up. No time to change his pants. Neither of them dared to be late.

They crept into the kitchen, took their seats with the rest of the family, and ducked their heads while their father pronounced a solemn prayer. Egon, the youngest, was silent tonight. Ilona looked up at her mother. Her head was bent, dark hair hiding her pretty, tired face.

After the last dish was washed and dried, Ilona and her brothers got ready for bed. Benno had signaled to Egon that Ilona had a special story for them tonight. They would wait for their parents to fall asleep before whispering their stories to one another. Ilona told the best ones, about magical fairies, powerful spells, and animals who could conquer any evil sorcerer in the world.

That night, Ilona told her brothers about her adventures in the magic tower on the hill. But although her brothers loved the story, she could tell they didn't believe it, any more than they had believed her about the gas-flame fairy. Ilona begged them to come with her another day and see the tower for themselves, but the boys just smiled drowsily and snuggled into their blankets.

A week later, Ilona left school in the middle of the day after being made to clean the school's erasers once again. The dark, vinegary nun called Sister Edwig didn't like Ilona very much. The child's fingernails were often dirty and she didn't always pay attention like the other little girls. After another scolding, when the old nun's back was turned, Ilona thought about her gas-flame fairy and easily faded away.

When she reached the tower that afternoon, she climbed the rungs quickly and crept toward the second window.

"West Wind, I'm here! What are you going to show me today?" A cool breeze brushed her cheek.

*Look and see.*

Ilona looked through the second window and found she was staring directly into another window only a few yards away, set into a thick stone wall. Lace curtains were drawn back, permitting a glimpse into a quiet white room furnished with a solid maple bedstead and nightstand. The bed was piled with pillows and spread with a deep blue blanket.

"What's this place, West Wind?"

*The Hotel of Forgotten Dreams.*

"Why do you call it that?" Ilona wished she could build a bridge to the other window, climb in, and take a long nap.

*Because every time you fall asleep there, you undream a nightmare.*

"What do you mean, undream?"

*You forget or lose or undream one of your bad dreams. As though you never dreamed it at all.*

"Can I go there, West Wind? Can my brothers?" Ilona asked wistfully.

Her only answer was a whistling in the rafters. Soon the vision faded and was gone. Ilona climbed back down from the tower.

In the city, spring surrendered to summer. Although she tried often, Ilona never managed to convince her brothers to visit the West Wind's tower. Even when she told them about the green window, the white window, and all the other lovely and mysterious windows, her brothers never really believed her. They were comforted by her stories, and listened to them eagerly in the middle of the night, but when the morning came they forgot them, washed their faces, and trudged off to school.

And that was Ilona's greatest heartache. Benno's arm was purple with bruises, and little Egon's narrow, frightened face haunted her dreams. She wished there were some way she could get her brothers to visit the West Wind's tower. But they had never learned the trick of invisibility. Even when Ilona had turned on the burners to show them the dancing gas-flame fairy, they'd only shrugged and had seen nothing out of the ordinary.

The West Wind continued to show her the windows, one by one, until she looked out of them all. She saw other parts of the seacoast city; lovely, splendid parts, teeming with happy young people carrying books and laughing in a bright, silvery way that made Ilona long to join them. The West Wind told her that was the window of the possible future.

Then there was a window which showed her the innermost hearts of all the people she knew, but that was not a window the child cared to look out of for very long. There she saw her mother's lovely face staring up at her with wide, dark eyes, her mouth opened in a soundless scream. She saw Benno and Egon, watching clouds form and dissolve on the walls of their small bedroom. And she saw a few young girls from her school, feeding poisoned apples to one another. The Wind seemed to understand when she asked him not to show her that window again.

There was one window that frightened her at first and later became her favorite. It looked out onto midnight and showed Ilona a blue-black sky filled with stars. A glistening ribbon of light coiled and twisted through the velvety night. "What's that ribbon, West Wind?"

*The Gateway to the Stars. If you walk there, you can see the whole sleepy earth spread beneath you.*

The following week, on a scorching Wednesday afternoon, Ilona skipped Twistonometry and Pricklepin Embroidery, and clambered along the dusty path up to the tower clearing. She wore a sleeveless white dress with a rip where she'd caught herself on some nail or other, and her hair clung to the sweat on her forehead. The West Wind suddenly realized that he had forgotten to take care of the afternoon breezes, and in his enthusiasm to make up for lost time he overdid it a little. Sand, leaves, and bits of paper were hurled into Ilona's face.

Ilona stopped and stared up into the trees, trying to see the wind. "I came to ask you a question," she called.

The leaves stirred at her feet.

"Just a minute. Wait until I'm upstairs." Once she was perched on her window ledge, Ilona folded her hands and looked up at the sky expectantly. "Tell me, West Wind. What do I have to do to get into your other worlds?"

*Come here, live here forever.*

"Could I really come and live here—all the time? You mean I'd never have to go home?"

*It's not impossible to cross over. But you can only live, really live, not just gaze or dream or imagine or wonder, in one place at a time.*

"Can my brothers come too?"

*Anyone who believes can come.*

Ilona felt her excitement fade. Her brothers hadn't even believed in the little gas-flame fairy. How could she get them to come and look at her secret window worlds and believe what they saw?

Ilona sighed. "But Egon and Benno—could they come and visit me, at least? Could they look out the windows, and wave to me, or write letters and drop them down, or talk to me on two cans connected with strings?"

*Anything is possible, if they believe. But if they don't, all they will see is a dead patch of oily earth, an old brick tower, and a lot of trash.*

"Oh, dear. I was afraid of that. But maybe I can convince them. I'll go home tonight and tell them again, and maybe this time they'll believe me."

Before she left, Ilona crossed over to the twelfth window and opened it wide. She could smell the tang of fresh salt air out on the open sea, far from the city's harbor. Beneath her, a small fishing boat struggled on the waves. The child guessed the boat had strayed from the makeshift fleet which left the city's docks at dawn each day. An old man in a blue coat and a little boy in a striped sweater full of holes were yanking at a net over the side of the skiff. Ilona sat and watched them work, noticing that from time to time the old man would bend over the boy and explain something to him. The little boy would nod, shift his position, and move his hands, and then glance up at the old man with a shy, sweet smile. One time the old man gently slapped the boy on his back in approval, which made the boy drop his part of the net altogether. Ilona caught her breath, but the fisherman and his boy merely looked at the sinking net for a moment, and then burst out laughing. They laughed so loud that Ilona could hear it all the way up in her tower. With a sigh, she closed the window.

"Well, so long for now, West Wind. I'll see what I can do about Benno and Egon." She climbed down the rungs and hurried off to the tram station.

When Ilona opened the apartment door, she was slapped by the silence. At this time of day, an hour before dinner, she ought to have heard the clatter of lids on pots, her brothers' voices in the other room, or tinny music from the radio. But there was nothing. Something on the stove had bubbled over the side of an aluminum pan and burned to a black crust. Water slipped out of the faucet, drop by drop.

She heard a sigh in the other room. Oh, God, her father. What was he doing at home? He was supposed to be at work.

*Think about the gas-flame fairy. Don't move too fast. Look in the living room, don't breathe. Slowly, slowly, one step then another. Not a sound.*

Yes, that was her father on the couch, staring up at the ceiling and cradling his fist in his hand. An ugly bruise was forming across the knuckles. Ilona felt sick.

*Don't breathe, don't even think. Just tiptoe over to the other room.*

The door to the bedroom creaked on its hinges. The big man on the couch stirred and lifted his head, but he didn't see the little girl slip through the narrow crack of the door.

"Benno, Egon, what happened?" she whispered.

The two little boys cowered in the corner against the wall, their hands over their faces. Ilona sat down on their bed, reached toward them, afraid to touch.

"Ilona, where were you?" Benno said through his fingers, his voice choked. "We kept calling. He was looking for you. He *wanted* you. Why weren't you here? Nobody could find you!"

"What happened? What did he do?"

Benno lowered his hands from his face. His eyes were already swelling shut, and a long cut was crusted with blood.

"He got fired again. He came home and they . . . Mamma and Papa had a big fight. They kept screaming at each other."

Egon whispered, "He hit her really hard!"

"Where's Mamma now?"

"She left. She's downstairs with the neighbor lady. And then he started hitting us, because we didn't know where you were. Why did you stay away so long, Ilona?"

Ilona began to cry. This was all her fault. "I'm sorry, I didn't know, Benno. I was at the tower again."

Springs creaked from the living room and a heavy footfall sounded outside their door. All three children froze and tried to wipe all emotions from their faces. After an eternity, the footsteps retreated. Ilona and her brothers sighed with deep relief.

The setting sun touched a corner of the painted iron bedstead, and a door slammed somewhere. The children huddled together in their corner, and the young girl wrapped her arms around her brothers' shoulders. Egon snuggled against her, pressing his cheek against her arm.

She stroked his hair and took a deep breath. "Now listen very carefully, both of you. You'll have to put your socks and shoes on and come with me."

Benno and Egon looked up at their sister, confused but hopeful. "Where are we going, Ilona?" Benno wanted to know.

Ilona got up briskly. "There's no time to explain now. Hurry, boys!"

Egon sniffled. "Aren't you going to tell us a story tonight?"

Ilona began rooting under the bed for his socks. "Yes, I am. I'll tell you on the way."

Benno regarded his sister with serious eyes. "Are we coming back, Ilona?"

She paused for a moment while buttoning Egon's jacket, and looked at Benno. "We'll see."

When the children were dressed, Ilona peered through a narrow crack in the bedroom door. The living room was empty. She tiptoed into the kitchen, and that was empty too. Turning back, she placed her finger on her lips and gestured for the boys to follow her. "Come here," she whispered. "I have something to show you before we go."

The boys gathered around their sister, who was standing in front of the stove. "Now this time, watch very carefully. This is important." With that, the young girl reached out and turned on the front burner.

Holding hands, pressed close together, the three children stared intently into the blue flame.

# Now I Lay Me

## Sharon Olds

♦

*It is a fine prayer, it is an excellent prayer, really,*
Now I lay me down to sleep—
*the immediacy, and the power of the child*
*taking herself up in her arms*
*and laying herself down on her bed*
*as if she were her own mother,*
Now I lay me down to sleep,
I pray the Lord my soul to keep,
*her hands knotted together knuckle by knuckle,*
*feeling her heart beating in the knuckles,*
*that heart that did not belong to her yet*
*that heart that was just the red soft string in her*
*chest that they plucked at will.*
*Knees on the fine dark hair-like hardwood*
*beams of the floor—the hairs of a huge animal—*
*she commended herself to the care of some reliable keeper*
*above her parents, someone who had a*
*cupboard to put her soul in for the night,*
*one they had no key to, out of their reach*
*so they could not crack it with an axe, so that*
*all night there was a part of her*
*they could not touch. Unless when God had it*
*she did not have it, but lay there a raw*
*soulless animal for them to do their dirt on—*
*coming toward her room with those noises at night and their*
*fur and their thick varnished hairs.*
If I should die before I wake *seemed so*
*possible, so likely really,*
*the father with the blood on his face,*
*the mother down to 82 pounds, it was a*
*mark of doom and a benison*
*to be able to say* I pray the Lord

my soul to take—*the chance that, dead,*
*she'd be safe for eternity, which was so much*
*longer than those bad nights—*
*she herself could see each morning the*
*blessing of the white dawn, like some true god coming,*
*she could get up and wade in the false*
*goodness of another day.*
*It was all fine except for the word* take,
*that word with the claw near the end of it.*
*What if the Lord were just another one of those takers*
*like her mother, what if the Lord were no bigger than her father,*
*what if each night those noises she heard*
*were not her mother and father struggling to*
*do it or not do it, what if those*
*noises were the sound of the Lord wrestling with her father*
*on the round white bedroom rug,*
*fighting over her soul, and what if the*
*Lord, who did not eat real food,*
*got weaker, and her father with all he ate and*
*drank got stronger, what if the Lord*
*lost?* God bless Mommy and Daddy and
Trisha and Dougie and Gramma Hester and
Grampa Harry in Heaven, *and then the*
*light went out, the last of the terrible kisses,*
*and then she was alone in the dark*
*and the darkness started to grow there in her room*
*as it liked to do, and then the night began.*

The fairy-tale theme of the "Ash Girl" (best known in the French tale "Cinderella"), who stoically suffers unwarranted abuse while remaining pure at heart, is one that runs deep through our popular literature. Classic children's stories like Frances Hodgson Burnett's *The Little Princess* (about a warm-hearted young girl mistakenly put into a joyless boarding school) have been favorites with children of many backgrounds—for one needn't have suffered significant abuse in childhood to have felt at times like an orphaned child with no one in the world to turn to. The gentle tale that follows reads like one of those old-fashioned stories, reminding us of the comfort generations of lonely children have taken from the Cinderella theme. The villain is the kind of villain we've all known: that teacher who made our life hell in the third grade or that aunt whose house we hated to visit. The story evokes the ash girl and ash boy in all of us—the part of us that's never quite warm enough, the part always seeking to be loved.

# Now I Lay Me Down to Sleep

✦ Ellen Kushner ✦

**B**ump.

There it was again. Jerusha lay very still, willing it to go away. She kept her eyes shut tight, but it didn't help; she could still hear the sound of her room being torn apart.

She wanted to burrow under the covers, but the blankets were thin, and if she moved, the cold part of the sheets that she hadn't managed to warm yet would freeze her. Anyway, there weren't enough blankets to shut out the sounds. Even the feather pillow didn't work; she'd tried.

So she lay there, stiff with cold and fear, listening. *Whoosh*. There went all her clothes on the floor: her linsey-woolsey gown that she'd carefully folded on the chair, her petticoats that she'd laid out to air, her stockings and pantalettes for tomorrow . . . she knew she'd find them in the four corners of the room in the morning, or crumpled in a heap behind the door. Worse yet, Mrs. Minim would find them. She'd come in to wake her, and see the untidyness, and call her names Jerusha did not deserve.

Even the terrible bodyless motions in the dark were not enough to make her forget Mrs. Minim. If only she could stay awake tonight until the Thing was gone, stay awake and straighten up, so that Mrs. Minim could see just once that Jerusha was not a slattern, that she truly did appreciate the nice room she had, and the fine clothes her papa bought her . . .

At the thought of her papa, Jerusha's hands clenched into fists of misery. Papa was captain on a whaler; like the songs said, he "ploughed the stormy seas across the oceans wild," from Cape Hatteras where her Sunday shawl came from, to the cold and silent North Sea where the bears were white as milk, and women drove sleds pulled by teams of dogs. He had sailed out of New Bedford seven months ago, and it might be seven more months before his ship touched American shores again, laden with whale oil and tusks, and presents for his lonely girl. If papa were here, Jerusha thought, no Thing would dare come near me. He would chase it away with his pistol, as he did the mutineers in Barbaree. He would pick me up against his captain's coat of good broad cloth with the buttons that catch my hair . . .

Her whole bed frame shuddered as the trunk at the bed's foot was flung open. Jerusha clutched the sheets around her throat, too frightened to make a sound. The Thing had never gotten anything open before. The girl stared into the darkness to see pale white shapes flying across the room: her clothes, which had been neatly packed away in folds of lavender. Nightgowns, shifts, aprons: they floated through the darkness as if they were dancing at a ball . . . Jerusha had to fight the sudden urge to giggle. Dance of the Underthings! It wasn't funny, oh, it wasn't funny—it wouldn't be when Mrs. Minim saw.

"Stop," she whispered, "please stop." But it was useless. The trunk lid slammed shut. Jerusha shuddered. In her head she said her prayers again. Maybe it didn't count unless you said them kneeling on the hard floor. The Thing was still there.

She closed her eyes, thinking her prayers with all her might. "Matthew, Mark, Luke, and John, bless the bed that I lie on. Bless the bed that I lie on. Bless the bed that I lie on."

But the bed was cold, and Jerusha was alone. She fell into a sleep as thin and comfortless as the blankets in the Minim house.

By some miracle, Jerusha was awake before the dawn was fully come. Cold gray light flooded her room, revealing a devastation of clothes all over the floor. But at least no one else had seen it yet. There was a bump at the window. That was the sound that had woken her. It came again. Was the Thing waiting for her outside?

Jerusha pulled a blanket around her and set her feet on the icy floor. Stubbornly, she went to the window. Surely it couldn't harm her by day?

Standing under the window was a familiar figure: a girl wrapped in a blue cloak, her blonde curls escaping from the hood. Her rosy face was turned up to Jerusha's window, her hand raised to throw another snowball at the glass.

"Nancy!" Jerusha whispered. Nancy smiled and waved when she saw her friend. Jerusha's breath clouded the window. She rubbed it clear with her fist. So Nancy had not forgotten her. It made her feel like crying. Instead she smiled and waved back. Nancy was on her way to Miss Amelia's

Academy for Young Ladies, the school they'd attended together until last year, where they'd been best friends. Then everything changed. Her papa sold the house with the rooftop walkway where her mother had looked out for papa's ship to come home from sea, the house she'd lived in since she was born. Mama had died of the fever two years back. Now Papa was going off to sea again, and he decided that his motherless girl must be sent to live with her mother's old friend, Mrs. Minim. Mrs. Minim was the widow of another sea captain, and lived all alone in a fine house far from the sea. At first Jerusha didn't mind; she could still walk with Nancy to Miss Amelia's at the other end of town. But Mrs. Minim had other ideas.

"You are to be a lady," Mrs. Minim had said. "You will do your lessons here at home. There is nothing you can learn at the Academy that I cannot teach you. And your sewing is a positive disgrace!"

Worst of all, Mrs. Minim had some idea that the girls at Miss Amelia's were "not quite right." Whatever that meant, somehow Nancy was the un-rightest of all. "But Nancy's father, Phil Fogarty, saved papa's life in the Azores," Jerusha had tried to explain. "He is Papa's own coxswain."

"Exactly," Mrs. Minim sniffed. "You can do better than a common coxswain's daughter for a playmate. Why, if my dear Sarah were still alive, she could be an example for you. . . ."

Standing in the snow, Nancy looked so alive, so happy. Jerusha breathed on the window glass, and wrote in mirror-writing so Nancy could read it, "Friends forever. JF + NF" Nancy smiled and nodded. More blonde curls tumbled from her hood.

The stairs creaked. It was Ruth, the maid, on her way up to bring Mrs. Minim the morning hot wash water. Jerusha gasped. She had little time now. With a hasty wave at Nancy, she drew the curtains, and turned to the wreckage of her room.

She gathered up the clothes, shoved them back in the trunk. She'd just have to hope Mrs. Minim didn't look in there until she had time to refold them. The dress and apron she'd neatly arranged last night were under the bed. Jerusha put them on, and for once was all dressed and ready for the day to begin when Mrs. Minim came in to wake her.

After breakfast, Jerusha sat and sewed while Mrs. Minim read her from a book on manners for young people. It was full of useless information, things Jerusha already knew, like "Obey your elders" and "A respectful child speaks only when spoken to." It was easy not to speak, for Mrs. Minim never seemed interested in anything Jerusha ever said. But the Thing kept her awake at night with its bumping, and Jerusha had a hard time holding her eyes open this morning. She tried to concentrate on keeping her stitches even and neat, on sitting up straight in her hard chair. It was hard not to fidget when her feet were so cold. Although snow was falling again, Mrs. Minim refused to have a fire in the grate.

"Imagine, a fire in October! What would Captain Minim have said!"

Mrs. Minim seemed more interested in the opinions of dead people than in her own. "I suppose next you'll be wanting a feather quilt, and it not even November yet!"

Jerusha did want a feather quilt. She wanted two of them. But there was no point in asking. Mrs. Minim sat upright in her chair, in her gray dress. She wore no jewels except for a brooch containing locks of her dead husband's and daughter's hair. Her starched collar was as white as the falling snow, but there was not even an edge of lace on it. Jerusha was very fond of her own few inches of lace, which had been her mother's. Mrs. Minim's hair was pulled severely back from her face, and held in place behind her head with steel hairpins. Iron and starch, that was Mrs. Minim.

"*Do* sit still, Jerusha!" Mrs. Minim said. "I hope you are attending to this reading. Soon you will be a young lady, and must be a credit to your papa. Here, let me see your sewing."

Jerusha handed over the handkerchief she was hemming. Mrs. Minim peered at it and smiled thinly as if she felt sorry for Jerusha for being so hopeless. "I should make you pick these stitches out, but the fabric is so delicate, it might show. . . . Oh," she sighed for the ninth time that morning, "if only you could have had the benefit of my sainted Sarah's company. What an example she would have been for you! Dear Sarah sewed a seam with stitches so tiny you had to squint to see them. She was so good, God had to take her from me, she was too good for this world. . . ."

Jerusha thought she remembered Sarah Minim. When her mother was alive, they had come together to visit with Mrs. Minim, while both women's husbands were away at sea. Sarah had been a pale, thin girl, so quiet she seemed hardly there. Jerusha was so little then, Sarah Minim had appeared quite grown-up. But I suppose, Jerusha thought, that she would have been about the same age I am now. It's too bad she couldn't have stayed here and waited for me. Then there would be someone to play with.

But, she reflected, if Sarah was all Mrs. Minim says she was, I doubt she would have liked me. My hair gets so tangled, and I always forget to curtsy to my elders. She would probably just laugh at me, and her horrible mother would smile her starch-and-iron smile . . . I wonder if the sainted Sarah got to have quilts and fires when *she* was cold?

Angrily Jerusha jabbed the needle into the handkerchief. "Ouch!" Somehow, her thumb had been there on the other side. Jerusha sucked her thumb before the blood could get on the handkerchief. She'd had a wicked thought, and God had punished her. She couldn't remember God punishing her so much when her papa was home. Maybe she wasn't so wicked then.

"*Jeru*sha!" Mrs. Minim exclaimed. "A young lady does not cry out in that hoydenish fashion. And take your thumb out of your mouth at once! Really, sometimes one would take you for a kitchen maid. You were placed in my care not a moment too soon. These, I suppose, are the manners you learned from people like that Nancy Fogarty. My own sainted Sarah would never—"

"No!" Jerusha could not bear the injustice. "You wrong Nancy, ma'am, truly you do! A better, sweeter soul could not be found between here and Nantucket, and my papa says the Fogartys are good, decent people—"

But the rest of her defense melted like snowflakes on her lips. The look Mrs. Minim gave her was terrible.

"Jerusha. Let me see that handkerchief." She turned it over and over in her hard, cold fingers. "Just as I thought. Ruined. Utterly ruined." With a sudden movement, she tore the thread from the hem. The fine cloth raveled. Now the handkerchief indeed was ruined. "You are a stupid, wicked child. You cannot be trusted with the simplest task. And you pay no mind to my instruction. So be it. Return to work on your sampler. I shall leave you here alone to think about how to improve yourself. If you have made good progress by lunchtime, I will see about food for you."

Mrs. Minim left the room, shutting the door behind her with a decisive click. Jerusha took her sampler out of the sewing box. It was a square of linen, nowhere near finished. She was working on a poem of mourning, each of the letters to be worked out in cross-stitch, X after X after X, until it was done. It seemed to take forever.

> . . . *Since she has gone to her last home,*
> *Now let the weeping cease.*
> *For though we sigh and mourn for her,*
> *Her soul is now at peace.*

The poem had twelve lines in all. It had taken Jerusha five weeks to get to the last, *Her soul is now at peace.* All that had kept her going, besides Mrs. Minim's nagging, had been the picture the drawing master from Boston had drawn at the top of the sampler. Jerusha thought it was a lovely picture. A slender girl with ringlets as pretty as Nancy's leaned sadly on a Greek urn. Over her a willow tree's branches fell weeping. The initials on the urn were SM, Sarah Minim. When Jerusha finished her cross-stitches, she could begin on the picture. The willow's leaves would be in feather stitch, the girl's hair in long-and-short, her dress in chain stitch and elegant French knots. She would learn all the fancy stitches, and sew something really fine for Papa when he came home. Some slippers, maybe, or a case for his favorite pipe.

It was hard to work the Xs for *soul* when there was so much else she'd rather be doing. The room was full of books, not all of them on manners. She watched the snow fall gently on the trees outside. A cardinal made a bright splash of red. The color made her feel warmer for an instant. With a sigh, she turned back to her sampler. All the letters of the poem were in black thread, of course. But she'd make the girl's curls a golden blonde. Her dress could be blue, blue as the wide oceans her papa sailed on. Her papa was sailing to Zanzibar, which was near Africa. Jerusha suddenly needed to know the capital of Zanzibar. She was learning geography, and should know the answer. It was important for her education.

She put the sampler on the chair, went to the globe, and started to turn it. But a footstep in the hall sent her scuttling back to her work. She sat up straight, although her back ached—no telling when Mrs. Minim would return to check up on her.

Doggedly, Jerusha sewed on. *Her soul is now . . .* Suddenly, her fingers began to fly. She watched in amazement as the needle flashed in and out of the cloth, the thread spelling out the dreary letters. There it was! Mrs. Minim had been right after all: Jerusha had resisted temptation, applied herself to her work instead of being a lazy dreamer, and here were the results! Why, she was sewing almost as well as Sarah Minim, she thought, she *must* be!

*Her soul is now at peace.*

Some time later, Mrs. Minim entered the room. "Well, Miss," she asked angrily, "what do you think you're doing?"

Jerusha smiled up sweetly from the book she was reading. "I've finished stitching the poem, ma'am. Please look and see."

Mrs. Minim's iron face softened a hair. She picked up the sampler, nodding to herself. The she dropped it with an awful, strangled shriek, as though the cloth had burned her. "You wicked, wicked girl! You heathen monster!"

Jerusha darted to her skirts and picked up the sampler. She looked at the poem, and her own breath caught in her throat.

*Her soul is NOT at peace.*

"Oh, Mrs. Minim," she stammered, "it was an accident. I didn't mean—it was going so well—"

"Do you know what you have done? My dear Sarah is at rest with God and the angels." Mrs. Minim's face was as white as her collar. "How dare you—how dare you—you *wicked* child!"

And so it was that Jerusha sat through lunch over the picked-out letters, stitching X's until she saw them even when she closed her eyes. *Her soul . . . Her soul . . . Her soul is . . .*

Jerusha looked down to see what her hands had done. There, in neat and even cross-stitches, better than any she had ever done, were the letters again:

*Her soul is NOT at peace.*

Then Jerusha knew. As if a hand had come and touched it, the knowledge lay cold on the back of her neck.

Sarah Minim had returned to mess up her room at last.

All through the long afternoon Jerusha stitched and picked out, stitched and picked out. Her own sewing was slow and clumsy; but if she let her attention wander for an instant—to the window, to the globe, or even to the thought of the clothes in her trunk waiting to be folded—in that instant the sure and rapid stitches would return, the line finished as Sarah Minim wanted it finished.

Jerusha was near to weeping herself as the afternoon wore on. It was cruel of Sarah to be doing this to her! It was not her fault Sarah's mother thought she was a saint! Poor Sarah. Had Mrs. Minim worked her to death? Jerusha shivered, picturing her own punishment if she couldn't get the letters right: no lunch, no supper; sewing until her eyes went blind and starvation took its toll. Would anyone sew a mourning sampler for her? They could have this one, she thought wretchedly; just add my initials to the urn.

For the hundredth time she picked the T out of NOT. She was beginning another try at the W when Mrs. Minim came in.

"It's getting dark," Mrs. Minim said. "If you think I'm going to waste a candle on your foolishness, you're mistaken. You're to go off to bed, miss, without your supper. Hunger will sharpen your mind to think of your duty."

It was so cold in her room that Jerusha climbed into bed with all her clothes on. She curled herself in a hungry, miserable ball. Ruth hadn't even come in with the warming pan to warm the sheets.

When the chest lid flew open and the clothes began to scatter across the room, Jerusha hunched deeper under the covers, and covered her ears with her arms.

Mrs. Minim's cold hand woke her. Morning had come, with light enough to show the wreckage of her room. Her clothes were everywhere, crumpled and tangled. Her wash basin had been flung across the room, saved from breaking only because it had landed on a pile of nightgowns. Jerusha's hair ribbons were everywhere, bright blots of color like exclamation marks on the mess of bleached linen.

It looked awful—and, for the first time, Jerusha saw that it looked angry. Like someone who had been angry for years, but forced to act as if anger did not exist. Only now was it safe to show it. There was nothing they could do to Sarah Minim now. Nothing anyone could do.

Mrs. Minim's fingers bit into Jerusha's shoulders like iron nails. "I see," Mrs. Minim hissed, "that you still do not understand your duty. Come with me."

In the cold parlor she sat with a book of children's sermons to memorize. Reverend Arthur Eliezer Pennyfeather wrote, "I must obey my elders, for they punish me for my own good, to be closer to God, and know his love." The words caught like bile in her throat. At ten o'clock Ruth brought her some bread and milk, which reminded her of God's love more than the Reverend Arthur Eliezer Pennyfeather.

By evening she had memorized enough of the sermon to please Mrs. Minim. Jerusha was allowed to eat a hot supper at the dinner table, but the meal was served in silence, Mrs. Minim's eyes cold on her. Still, she was in no hurry to leave the dining room to go upstairs to the dark room she shared with Sarah.

She pulled the blankets up to her chin and stared resolutely into the darkness. Jerusha almost wished that Ruth had not tidied up the room this morning; would Sarah leave it alone if she found it not up to her mother's standards? or would she do something worse if messy clothing no longer mattered?

A sudden whish of air by her ear made Jerusha clutch the blankets to her more tightly. The unlit candle by her bed was wrenched out of its holder and flung against the far wall. Jerusha prayed that no one heard the bump it made.

"Now I lay me down to sleep," she began, bravely saying her prayers aloud. "I pray the lord my soul to keep—" An angry thump of the chest lid made her stop. Jerusha sat up straighter in bed, holding a pillow for courage.

"Sarah," she said. "Sarah Minim. Please hear me. I know it's you." The clothes stayed in the clothes chest, but the silence was rich with waiting. "I'm here, too, Sarah, and I'm alone. My papa is gone to sea, just like yours used to do. I miss him, and I miss my friend Nancy. Have you seen her? She came to the window yesterday. She has real curls, she doesn't need to use curl papers . . ." Jerusha stopped in fear. What would a spirit care about Nancy's curls? But the thumping had halted. And it felt so good to be talking to someone that she went on, in a rush of words, "You'd like Nancy. She has a dog named Tip that can do tricks. He can beg, and roll over, too. I don't suppose you ever had a dog. . . ."

A knocked-over chair was the answer.

"No, I didn't think so. This is a cold house, Sarah Minim, and I think you were as cold as I am. I hope you're not cold now. If I were you, I'd leave and never come back. My mother is in Paradise," Jerusha whispered into the dark, "with God and all the angels. And I truly want you to be happy there. But if you don't want to go there just yet, couldn't you stay and let us be friends?"

Jerusha waited. The room was quiet. No bumps, no knocks.

She heard a whisper on the air. A feather quilt floated over her bed to land softly on her. And another, and another . . . Mrs. Minim's precious feather quilts from the closet on the stairs; all the folded quilts, still smelling of the cedar chest and dried lavender flowers, falling like snowflakes, gentle as a hug, piled higher and higher.

And for the first time in the Minim house, Jerusha Farrier felt warm.

# Reading the Brothers Grimm to Jenny
## Lisel Mueller

♦

Dead means somebody has to kiss you.

*Jenny, your mind commands*
*kingdoms of black and white:*
*you shoulder the crow on your left,*
*the snowbird on your right;*
*for you the cinders part*
*and let the lentils through,*
*and noise falls into place*
*as screech or sweet roo-coo,*
*while in my own, real world*
*gray foxes and gray wolves*
*bargain eye to eye,*
*and the amazing dove*
*takes shelter under the wing*
*of the raven to keep dry.*

*Knowing that you must climb,*
*one day, the ancient tower*
*where disenchantment binds*
*the curls of innocence,*
*that you must live with power*
*and honor circumstance,*
*that choice is what comes true—*
*O, Jenny, pure in heart,*
*why do I lie to you?*

*Why do I read you tales*
*in which birds speak the truth*
*and pity cures the blind,*
*and beauty reaches deep*
*to prove a royal mind?*
*Death is a small mistake*
*there, where the kiss revives;*

*Jenny, we make just dreams*
*out of our unjust lives.*

*Still, when your truthful eyes,*
*your keen, attentive stare,*
*endow the vacuous slut*
*with royalty, when you match*
*her soul to her shimmering hair,*
*what can she do but rise*
*to your imagined throne?*
*And what can I, but see*
*beyond the world that is*
*when, faithful, you insist*
*I have the golden key—*
*and learn from you once more*
*the terror and the bliss,*
*the world as it might be?*

Sick children are one of the most powerless classes of people we have in this country. Historically, children have been the property of adults, just as women, until not very long ago, were the legal wards of their husbands. The danger of this lingering attitude of ownership can become most evident when a child is at its most helpless, as in the following dark fantasy story.

# Knives

### ✦ Munro Sickafoose ✦

The room was painted cornflower blue. High under the third floor gable, the dormered window caught the light of the sun, moon, and stars, and the light reflected from the leaves of the trees, in such a way as to make it seem that the room was filled with water: the clear water of a lagoon with a bottom of pure white sand, now gray with storm, now shimmering sky blue, now deep blue and dark as the bottom of a midnight well.

Mathilde's mother died when she was six, and the room became her world. Father said she was too frail to go to school, or to run and play with the other children; like her mother, he said, she possessed a weak heart and he feared he would lose her as well. So she lay abed and played alone with her dolls and her stuffed animals, and read from the book of fairy tales her mother had given to her. The bed was her world, along with the books her father taught her to read, and the peaked well of light from the window.

Through the window came the songs of birds, the sounds of cars, the barking of dogs, the voices of people walking by, and the faraway laughter of children. She would sit upon the window seat and look out into the trees that enclosed the house. The green leaves broke the light with their constant swaying motion, and she imagined they looked as seaweed would beneath the waves. She imagined the birds were fishes and she was the princess of the sea-kingdom, talking to the fishes and swimming in the great sea-forests.

One day there came the sounds of men and machines close by her window. The treetops began to shudder. She caught glimpses of men in red helmets, and then a great section of a tree was gone and she could see far away, across the world. She saw the tops of houses, the steeple of a church, and a broad expanse of green grass upon which children were running, laughing, jumping rope, and playing ball. Watching, she noticed one boy in particular. He had golden hair and tanned supple limbs. When the children cheered, he cheered the loudest, and his laughter rang out like a silver bell.

"What are you doing, Mathilde?" came her father's gentle voice behind her.

She replied, "Only watching the children play. See! The trees are cut and now I can see them."

He stood beside her and peered out the window. "And so you can, my love."

"Isn't it wonderful, Father? They are having so much fun! And look," she said, pointing, "at that boy. See how fast he runs! I would like to run like that."

"Indeed," said her father, reaching out to close the window. "But it is time for you to return to bed. You mustn't get up like this, my dear. You know you are frail. You could catch a chill."

She let him tuck her in among the fluffy pillows and the soft blue comforter. She lay listening to distant laughter as the light rippled across the ceiling and she read from her mother's book of tales.

Yet in the days to come the window beckoned her still. She loved to sit close to the window glass and watch the golden boy, daydreaming of cool green grass beneath her feet and the sun upon her face. Several times her father caught her watching and each time would chide her gently and put her back to bed. Mathilde gathered her courage to ask him if she could go out and sit in the meadow where the sun was shining and the other children played. But his face was grim and his voice filled with sadness as he spoke of the dangers she would face out of doors. The other children carried disease that could strike her down like her mother. Then he wept and begged her to promise him not to go to the window again.

The child tried to keep her promise, but she could not. She would perch upon the window seat, ears alert for the sound of her father's heavy tread upon the stair. But one day she did not hear him until the door opened behind her. She turned and saw the hurt upon his face and, chastened, climbed back into the bed. Her father did not say a word, only shook his head, and closed the door. She slept poorly that night, waking in the indigo stillness to the sound of her own heart beating.

In the morning when she opened her eyes, her father sat on the edge of the bed.

"Good morning, my sweet." He smiled down at her, his voice soft and comforting. "How are you feeling?"

Mathilde stretched. "I feel wonderful," she said.

He lay a hand upon her forehead and looked worried. "So I feared."

Her eyes widened in alarm. "Is something wrong, Father?"

"It is when we feel the best that we are most open to the evil around us, child. We are no longer so alert to its presence, and then it strikes us down."

He opened the little black bag at his feet.

"I fear your illness is getting worse, my love." He tapped the syringe in his hand, expelled a tiny jet of clear fluid. "Fortunately, there are medicines to aid us in our battle with evil."

He smiled at her.

"Roll up your sleeve, my darling."

"Will it hurt, Father?" she asked.

"Oh no, my dear. Only the tiniest prick, like a pin."

The medicine made Mathilde feel better, all drowsy and delicious. She lay in her bed while the blue light danced over her and the sound of laughter from the window hissed like waves upon the sand.

In the morning and the evening her father came and gave Mathilde her medicine, and for a long time she did not feel like going back to the window at all. The sounds of the other children were muffled and dreamlike now. She watched the changing of the light upon the walls, and read from her book of fairy tales, and dreamed she was a princess of the sea in her castle beneath the lagoon.

But after a while the medicine no longer worked its magic for quite so long, and sometimes in the afternoon she would hear the laughter, remember the bright green grass and the golden boy. On those days she would stare at the window and think of sitting there again. Then one day, when her medicine no longer made her feel quite so warm and sweet, the laughter beckoned and she did go; she walked shakily to the windowseat and sat and watched the children play in the meadow beyond the glass. She remembered how unhappy it had made her dear father, and so she tried to watch for only a little while . . . but once again she was caught, and once again her father wept and begged her promise him not to go. And once again she could not keep that promise.

When he caught her at the window once more, his face grew long and somber. He turned and left, reappearing some minutes later with his black bag.

"I don't mean to make you unhappy, Father," she said miserably from her nest among the pillows.

He stroked her forehead. "I know, my sweet. It's not your fault, evil enters wherever it can. Sometimes it enters through the eyes. Sometimes it enters through the mouth. Sometimes it enters through the feet. But we must be strong, and fight it."

The syringe was in his hands again. She rolled the sleeve of her night-gown up and the needle slipped gently in without the slightest prick of pain.

"Sleep tight, my child. When you wake, all will be well again. The evil expelled and peace upon us."

Mathilde saw his smiling face and felt his hand warm on her forehead, then her eyes closed and she slept. When she woke, her feet were swathed in white dressings, and she could not feel them at all. Her father now had to carry her to her toilet, but Mathilde did not mind, for the new medicine he gave her took her far away into lands of green grass and sun. At last the bandages came off, and her feet were still there at the end of her legs, but she could no longer command them and they flopped around like drown-ing fish.

Then her new medicine lost its magic as well, and no longer took her away from the room. She heard the laughter from the window and she knew there was evil in her still, for she had no will to resist it. She swung her legs from the bed and tried to walk to the window. It felt as if she balanced on the edge of a sword. The pain knifed upwards until it lodged itself in her heart. For an instant she tottered there, then she fell, hard upon the carpet. The child dragged herself back into bed, where she lay weeping.

What had been Mathilde's palace in the deep lagoon was now a prison, a sorcerer's tower. She lay in her bed and she no longer dreamed she was free to roam the deep. She was trapped in a hut on chicken legs, in a bundle of sticks with a golden cord. When the laughter drifted up she wished and wished for a prince to come and rescue her, the golden boy with the silver laugh. But all her wishing would not make it so, and a fire began to burn in her heart.

"I miss walking, Father," she ventured timidly when next he came to feed her.

He smiled and caressed Mathilde's brow. "But your feet carried you toward evil, child."

"My feet, Father? My feet?" she said. "I thought the weakness was in my heart!"

"And so it is," he replied somberly.

"Then why did you hurt my feet? Why didn't you cut out my heart?" she cried as the fire flared again in her breast.

Her father's eyes grew wide, then cold. "Never speak to me that way! Never again! Never!"

Mathilde turned away from him and silence grew thick around them. *Very well,* she thought, *I will not speak to you at all.*

At last he spoke, contritely. "All I do, I do for you. To keep you safe from evil. To keep you safe from harm. One day you will understand, my darling."

But she would not look at him. She thought: *It is my heart. My heart that guides my feet. My heart that makes me weak. My heart that longs to run and play, not my feet.* And it felt as if the fire consumed her, and she wept for a long time.

For many days thereafter she would not speak to her father. But she could not bear the reproach in his eyes; she missed his smile and his gentle touch, and so finally she forgave him.

Time passed, and the child grew into adolescence. She grew, but the room did not, nor her dolls, nor her stuffed animals. The pages of her mother's book grew worn from use, even though she knew the tales within word for word, for the pictures were her window now. And all the days ran into one long day, and the blue light came and went.

One day she awoke to a warmth and stickiness between her legs. When she touched her hand to it, it came away red. She screamed and her father ran to the room.

"What's wrong, Mathilde? What's wrong?"

"I'm dying, Father," she told him, weeping, holding out her bloody fingers.

"No. No. You will not die, my love. You are only becoming a woman."

He held her and rocked her until she stopped crying, then he got warm wet towels, soft and white, and began to bathe her clean.

"You see, my darling, when a girl becomes a woman, she takes on the evil that is the burden of all women. Women caused the Fall from Paradise and so they carry evil in them like a seed. Each month your body tries to expel this evil with the blood."

"Am I evil, Father?" she whispered.

"No, my sweet Mathilde. You could never be so. The evil tries to enter, but your body in its wisdom casts it out." He stroked her forehead as he explained about the cloth she would place between her legs to catch the evil, and how it would be burned and purified and all made clean again.

Now the time that used to pass in seamless dreaming was marked out by her flowing blood. Her father was right, there was evil in the world outside, evil that could lodge inside of her—each month she saw the proof of his words in the blood that flowed from between her legs. Her father burned the cloths as he'd promised, but she knew she was tainted and unclean.

One night she woke to find him in her bed.

"Mathilde, Mathilde," her father whispered as he touched her. It did not seem as though he talked to her, and she remembered then that Mathilde had been her mother's name as well.

"Mathilde, Mathilde," her father whispered as he rose above her. She hurt then in her deepest places, and cried out. He placed one large hand across her mouth. The blue moonlight washed over her and she knew that she was drowning, falling, drifting lifeless toward the depths that wrapped her mercifully in darkness.

He never came into her bed again, nor spoke of what had happened there. But at night she would wake, unable to breathe, drowning, a ghostly weight crushing the air from her lungs. By day she lay and watched the changing light; her world was her bed and her books and her dreams. She dreamed she was trapped in a witch's tower, and her hair was not long enough to touch the ground. She dreamed she was wrapped in a filthy donkey hide, with a trunk of fine gowns locked under her feet where she could not seem to reach them. She dreamed she was trapped in a glass coffin and the prince never came to wake her.

There was a day she began to grow warm, and then hot. Her bones seemed to ache and she whimpered until her father came, black bag in hand, shaking his head sadly.

"Oh, Mathilde. That same weakness that was in your mother has now claimed you, I fear. It grew inside of her until it ruled her body and her mind, and killed her."

"Will I die, Father?" she asked.

"No, my sweet." He stroked her forehead, as he liked to do. "For I am ever vigilant and skilled in battle with evil. I could not save your mother, but I will save you, sweet Mathilde. I will cut the evil out and you will be whole again."

She rolled her sleeve and offered up her arm to the needle. When she woke again she had an ache near her belly, and a pink cut sewn up with black thread on her side. Her skin grew hot, and cold, and hot; she dreamed of princes while shivering, and cats that talked while sweat poured from her brow. Her father held her hand and bathed her with cool cloths, talking of evil and the battle that she waged. She saw the golden boy float through her window on the wings of an angel; he tossed a ball to her to catch. She raised her hands to catch it, but then it became her father's face, and she wept.

Waking in darkness, she was alone. The light waxed from indigo to pale blue to indigo again as she lay too weak to move. Again the light changed and she grew hungry, and soiled the bed. Mathilde called and called out for her father, but the hours passed and he did not come. She drifted into exhausted sleep, then woke and cried out again, until at last she had no strength to call. She lay, watching the changing light, waiting for it to turn to deepest blue for one last time.

When the door opened, it seemed to Mathilde as if someone else watched it with her eyes. She was hovering somewhere over the bed, watching herself watching the door: watching as a boy peered round the door's edge. Watching as he moved to stand beside the bed. Watching as she opened her eyes and looked into his face.

"I heard you," he said. "Are you all right?"

Mathilde tried to speak but could only shake her head.

The boy's eyes were wide as saucers. "You don't look so good," he whispered. "I'll go get help."

And he turned and ran—before she could stop him, before she could ask his name, before she could ask him if he was a prince. He did not look like the princes in her book. His eyes were green. He had a thousand freckles. His front teeth were just a tiny bit crooked. But his hair was gold as the sun.

When next she woke, there were people in her room. A man in clothes of brown and tan, and a woman and a man wearing white. They stood beside her bed.

"Oh, my God," the woman said.

She turned to the man in white. "I need a glucose drip up here. Stat! And the goddamn gurney! Go!"

The men hurried from the room.

The woman knelt beside the bed. "Everything's going to be all right, honey," she whispered. "Can you tell me your name?"

Mathilde tried to speak. The woman placed her ear next to Mathilde's mouth. Mathilde tried again and felt her name pass outward, soft as a breeze.

"Well, Mathilde," said the woman, "we are going to take you to the hospital. Where we can help you get well again." She reached out and touched Mathilde's forehead.

Mathilde recoiled.

"You don't like that? All right, then, I won't do it." She held Mathilde's hand.

They're taking me away, Mathilde thought, suddenly very afraid. What will I do? Where is Father? She looked at her mother's book of tales beside the bed. She tried to reach out for it, but her arm barely moved.

"You want your book, honey?" said the woman, watching her closely. "Here you go." She placed the book on Mathilde's breast.

Mathilde clutched it tightly, and she sank back into unconsciousness. She dreamed that she floated out the window and into the world beyond the glass. She rode in a chariot filled with bright swords; it carried her to a bright white room, filled with people dressed in blue. She dreamed a prince had climbed up her hair, and she woke into the white room. She dreamed he had broken the bundle of sticks, and she woke into the white room. She dreamed he had placed a ring upon her finger, and she woke into the white room. She dreamed he had kissed her while she slept, and she woke into the white room.

Mathilde woke into the white room.

It was quiet. She lay on crisp white sheets. She wondered where she was, and then she knew this must be the hospital that the woman had spoken of. There was a sharp clean smell and beneath that, the subtle odor of illness. A soft humming sound rose and fell like the breathing of some enormous beast. The light reflected off every surface, cold, bright, and unforgiving, unprotecting. Panic seized her and she tried to rise, but she could not. She lay there with her heart pounding, until she noticed that beside her, on a table, lay her mother's battered book of tales. She wondered when her father would come. Then she went back to the world of dreams.

♦♦♦

Althea looked at the teenaged girl asleep in the hospital bed. She was perhaps fifteen, with pale skin that had never seen the sun, and long auburn hair that had never been trimmed. Beneath the thin hospital coverlet, her body was a pitiful contradiction. Above, a young woman's body, breasts and hips were beginning to fill out; below were the atrophied pipestem legs, twisted and useless.

Althea moved a corner of the girl's sleeve away to reveal the title of the book she grasped. *The Children's Fairy Tale Companion,* she read, and sighed softly. *What was to be done with this one?* The child had no family, no history, nothing, only ten years hidden away in an attic by a madman. *How many years without walking? How many years without speaking to another living soul?*

Damn the father! How could people do these things to their own children? It was a question she'd often asked herself in her years working on the hospital ward, and she still had no answer for it. This was one of the worst cases she'd seen. *Better the child had died with her father; died dreaming she was a princess.* There was very little chance of a happy ending for this one. She had no tools for living, no years with other children on a playground or in school, learning how to deal with the world. Only years of being kept like a canary in a cage.

The pale eyelids fluttered open, revealing frightened sea-green eyes.

"Hello, Mathilde," Althea said. "How are you feeling?"

"Where's Father?" the girl asked anxiously. "I want to see my father."

Althea felt her stomach clench. But the child's question had love laced with her fear, and Althea softened what she would have liked to say. "There is no easy way to tell you this, Mathilde. He can't come to see you anymore."

Tears poured down Mathilde's cheeks. Althea could see her thoughts upon her face: *Who would love her now?* It would be Althea's task to teach the child that love did not wield a knife.

She held Mathilde's hand for a long time, until the tears had passed. "You loved him very much, didn't you?"

Mathilde sniffled and nodded. "Where did he go?" she asked weakly.

Althea looked up at the bright white lights, then looked at the girl for a long time before she said, "There was a car accident, Mathilde. He died quickly, without pain."

*Too bad it was the truth,* Althea thought. *Died and left me with another wounded soul to heal. I should not think it, but I wish he had died horribly, in agony, suffering. I can only hope there is a Hell for him.*

Mathilde wept again, while Althea held her hand. When at last there were no more tears, she said gently, "My name is Althea. Can I be your friend, Mathilde? A friend to talk with? Everyone needs a friend to talk with, don't they?"

Mathilde looked up at her and red blood flushed the girl's pale cheeks. "Please," she said softly.

"Then we shall be good friends, loyal and true." She reached out to stroke Mathilde's brow, but the girl winced and shrank away. Althea nodded, and withdrew her hand. "Get some rest, child. We'll talk again soon."

When Althea came again there was more color in the girl's face and she was sitting up in bed, reading from a shiny new book."

"Look, Althea! Another book of fairy tales! The nurses brought it to me. I never knew there were so many!"

Althea made a mental note to speak to the nurses. Mathilde knew enough about the land of dreams; what she needed now was to learn about the world. She said, "Indeed, there are many wonderful stories. Shall I shall bring you books when I come again—stories about girls like you, who live in towns like this one?"

"Yes, please," Mathilde said shyly.

Althea drew close and smiled down into Mathilde's eyes. "I have talked to the doctors. The surgeons say they can try to make you walk again." She watched a faraway look come over Mathilde's face.

"Can they?" Mathilde looked up, eyes filled with hope, and trust.

"They'll try," replied Althea. "But most of it will be up to you. You will have to learn to use your legs. It will take a long time, and will be very, very painful. You'll have to work very hard, young lady. Harder than you have ever worked before."

"Then will I be able to run and play with the other children?"

Althea looked hard at the budding young woman who would never be a child again. She wanted to weep, but she kept her face calm as she said, "Of course you will."

Afterwards, she berated herself. *Why did I say that? If she never walks, I will have betrayed her.* She thought about Mathilde's book as she headed to her next appointment. There was something familiar about it. Althea shrugged off the feeling; she was too tired to think about it now, and another child was waiting for her down the hall.

Some weeks after Mathilde's surgery, Althea pushed Mathilde's wheelchair into another ward. It was a large open room with a dozen beds in it, each with a small dresser beside it. The walls were painted with bright colors and decorated with construction-paper hearts, flowers, stars, and pictures drawn by the children who stayed there. A few of the beds were unoccupied and covered only with a hospital blanket, but most of the others had a favorite quilt or pillow or stuffed animals on them. A large area by the window held a big table, chairs, a sofa, and a big box with a dark glass in it. Half a dozen children of various ages looked at Mathilde from beds or chairs. They were smiling at her, except for one boy.

"Sometimes children have to stay with us for a longer time," said Althea. "For treatment or special medicines or to recover from accidents. You'll be staying here with them."

"It's nice," whispered Mathilde.

A girl of about the same age walked up. "Hi, Althea. Who's your friend?" she asked.

Althea smiled. Mathilde stared at the girl's bald head.

"It's okay! I'm just on chemo. Makes your hair fall out." The girl laughed. "I'm Jamie. Who're you?"

"Mathilde."

"Welcome to the tough kids' ward. You must be a tough kid, too." Jamie winked.

"More like Death Row," sneered the boy who hadn't smiled. "Ward of the living dead."

Jamie rolled her eyes. "Don't pay any attention to Stan. He's got a bee up his butt 'cause he doesn't have anything really cool wrong with him." She looked up at Althea. "I'll take over from here, okay? Make sure she gets settled and stuff."

Althea nodded. "I thought you would," she said, standing back from the wheelchair.

Jamie spun the wheelchair around to face the other children. "Let me introduce you around. Stan, you met. That's Rico. He's got leukemia. That's Jessie. She's rehab, like you. Little Joanie there has major heart problems. Two more operations and they say she can go home. Bobby, he's accident rehab too. They had to practically rebuild him. That's Marco, he's got some kind of inoperable brain tumor, gives him seizures. There's a few others, but they're all down getting chemo or PT."

Jamie paused and took a deep breath. "So which bed do you want? Why don't you take the one next to mine? That way we can talk about stuff. Hey, you got any stuffed animals? No? You can borrow one of mine."

Althea smiled at the dumbfounded expression on Mathilde's face as Jamie wheeled Mathilde over to the empty bed, chattering away.

Valerie picked up the frail girl named Mathilde, turned her over, and began to massage the quadraceps on her thighs. Her thighs were barely as big around as one of Valerie's forearms.

Mathilde's eyes were far away, and with each stretching of the long muscles, she bit her lip. "It hurts."

"I know it hurts, honey," said Valerie sympathetically. "You haven't used them in too long. They shrank up pretty bad. Why don't you sing a song or something to take your mind off the pain?"

The girl considered this. "Can I tell you a story?"

Valerie nodded, and Mathilde began to tell her a story about a princess and a frog. When she was done, Valerie said, "That was a nice story. I like happy endings."

"Me, too," said Mathilde. "Can I go now?"

Valerie wheeled her back to the ward.

Mathilde sat in her wheelchair in Althea's office, looking out the window. The office was on the fourth floor and she could see a parking lot, the tops of other buildings and, far away, some houses and trees. A plane took off from the airport and thundered across the sky.

Althea watched her carefully. "Tell me again why your father hurt your feet," she prompted.

"So they would not carry me to evil," replied Mathilde.

"What evil is that?"

"The evil out the window." She paused. "But it didn't work. Evil came to me."

"Did it?"

"Uh-huh. It came out between my legs," the girl said, her face turning pink.

"Your monthly flow?" queried Althea. "That isn't evil. It's natural, child. I have a flow. All women of a certain age have a flow."

"I know. It's just . . ."

"Just what?" asked Althea.

"I don't know." Mathilde's eyes wandered in confusion.

Althea sighed. "Why do you want to walk?"

The girls face brightened. "To play with the other children."

Gently she asked, "What children, Mathilde? The children out the window?"

There was no answer. Mathilde squirmed in the wheelchair. "Can I go read now?" she pleaded.

Althea nodded. "Do you want me to wheel you back?"

"No, no," protested Mathilde. "I can manage. Just get the door, please."

Althea sat staring out the window for a long time.

Valerie held Mathilde upright in the pool of warm water.

"Go on, honey," she urged. "Put some weight down on those feet. Just a little bit. Just enough to feel. Come on."

Mathilde gingerly placed one foot on the tile. "It hurts."

"Take another step, honey. Come on now. I got you."

Mathilde took another step, and then another. She gasped. Her legs curled up and she floated in Valerie's arms. "It hurts too much. I can't do it!"

"Sure you can. Come on." Valerie pleaded. "You want to go play with the other kids, don't you, honey? Walk around in a pretty dress? Go to a movie?"

Mathilde gulped and nodded.

"Then take some more steps for me. Go on," she urged the girl.

"She won't try," said Valerie to Althea with exasperation. "She takes a few steps and she gives up."

Althea shook her head. She could understand the other woman's frustration. She rubbed her eyes, feeling tired. For every child she reached, every child she helped, there were three like Mathilde that she couldn't.

"I just want to shake her sometimes," continued Valerie. "She's such a pretty girl. Those legs of hers can work, I know it! I've seen people bounce back from so much worse."

"I know," said Althea. "We both have. But she doesn't want to. She's frightened. She never had to do anything before. And if she doesn't want to, then she won't."

There was a long silence.

"Let me come down and work with you," suggested Althea. "Maybe together we can get her going."

"It's worth a try," Valerie sighed.

Mathilde sat with her back to the window, looking pale and wan.

Althea cleared her throat. "Mathilde," she said carefully, "did your father ever touch you in your private places?"

There was a long silence. Althea waited. Finally Mathilde jerked her chin, almost imperceptibly. "Only once," she whispered.

"How did that make you feel?" asked Althea gently.

"It hurt."

Althea reached out and took the girl's hand. "Do you know that it wrong for him to do that?"

Mathilde looked stricken. "He loved me!" she said.

"But it was wrong."

Mathilde looked at Althea, her eyes wide, her breath rapid, fluttering. "I can't breathe!" she gasped. She clutched Althea's hand in a hard, painful grip.

"But it was wrong," insisted Althea. "He was wrong. Not you. *He* was wrong."

Mathilde nodded, silent tears falling in her lap.

Althea sat beside Mathilde's bed as she slept, the girl's books spread out before her. The nurses had listened to Althea and had brought no more books of fairy tales. Instead there were books about girls and horses. Girls in high school. Girls on vacation. Girls and their boyfriends. Girls having adventures in far-off lands.

In the middle of them was Mathilde's mother's book, *The Children's Fairy Tale Companion*. Althea held it in her lap. The other books were only so much paper. *Speak to me!* she demanded silently. *Tell me your secret! What do you know?* Without warning, a memory rose up inside her: She was sitting in her own mother's lap, listening to her read from fairy tale books. She had loved those stories of princesses, wicked witches, talking cats and enchanted swans; she had loved to touch those colorful illustrations with her pudgy little hand. *But I left all that behind, didn't I? When I was a child, I thought as a child, but now that I am grown, I have put away childish things . . .*

There was something missing here, something she could not grasp. Mathilde's book was silent. Whatever secrets it whispered to Mathilde, it would not speak to Althea. She threw the book back down into the middle of the pile in frustration. *Talking to books now, are we? It's late. Go home, you silly fool.*

The questions followed her as she fetched her coat and left the ward.

Mathilde struggled to hold herself erect between the parallel bars. The braces that helped support her legs were heavy; and clearly each step was painful. Weeks of erratic effort had made her a little bit stronger, but she gave up earlier and earlier in each session unless Valerie and Althea forced her to stay and work.

"Come on! Come on!" urged Althea.

"You can do it, honey," echoed Valerie.

Mathilde grimaced and took another step. "Oww, oww," she squeaked. The girl let her arms collapse, fell forward, and lay still.

Valerie and Althea looked at each other, grim expressions on their faces. They each bent over to take an arm and pull Mathilde to her feet.

"Come on, Mathilde," Althea said firmly. "No giving up."

Mathilde sobbed. "NO! No more! I can't do it. I can't!"

"Yes you can, honey," Valerie encouraged her.

She placed one of Mathilde's hands on each bar, and slowly let go and stood back.

Mathilde weighted one leg and buckled to the floor, crying again.

"It's all right, honey," Valerie said, moving to put an arm around her.

Althea stopped her. "Leave her be."

"But . . ."

Althea shook her head. "Come on. Leave her." She pulled Valerie away.

Behind them Mathilde sprawled on the floor alone, crying softly.

Mathilde sat up in bed, reading one of the books the nurses had brought her. Next to her, in the other bed, Jamie sat propped up by pillows. Her bald head carried no flesh; each bone stood out in high relief, and her face was thin and drawn. Stan sat on the edge of Jamie's bed, playing a board game with her.

"Come and play with us," Jamie begged Mathilde.

Mathilde looked up from her book. "Not tonight. Maybe tomorrow, okay?"

Stan snickered. "Don't be such a dumbass."

Mathilde stared at him.

"Don't you get it, stupid? She might not be here tomorrow."

Mathilde looked at Jamie, who wore a peaceful look on her thin face. "You'll be all right."

Jamie shook her head. "He's right. They've tried everything. I'm dying."

"We all die." said Stan, wearily. "All of us. You. Me. Her."

Mathilde shook her head. "She's going to be fine. We'll play tomorrow." She turned back to her book.

"What? You think some fairy fucking godmother is going to swish a wand?" Stan sneered. "A miracle will happen?" Angry tears began to fall from his eyes. "There are no fucking miracles!" he howled.

Mathilde stared woodenly at her book.

"Stan?" said Jamie. "It's okay. Let's play."

"Leave me alone! It's not okay! It's not!" He picked up the dice and threw them at Mathilde. One missed her completely, while the other hit her in the forehead. She stayed rigid, staring at the pages, ignoring him.

"Stupid!" he screamed at her. "Stupid, stupid, stupid!"

"Stan?" It was Jamie, tears on her face now too.

The boy turned to her, blue with grief. "Don't go," he sobbed, and ran from the ward.

"She won't come to PT anymore," Valerie said to Althea. "Every time I come to get her, she just smiles at me and tells me that it doesn't matter."

Althea rested her head in her hands. She was tired. She needed a good night's sleep. Lately her nights had been troubled by dreams full of talking cats and witches' towers. "I know. I know," she said to Valerie, "all she does is lie there in bed and read. She won't even use the wheelchair to get about."

"What are you going to do?"

Althea shook her head. "I don't know. I was hoping you had some brilliant suggestion."

Valerie flashed a smile at her. "Not my job. I just do bodies. You're the one that fixes brains."

Althea rolled her eyes. "Give me a break, will you?"

Valerie punched her lightly, affectionately, on the shoulder. "Give yourself one. You can't save them all."

"Mom? It's me," Althea sat behind her desk, looking out the window and watching a thunderstorm roll in over the city.

"You all right?" came her mother's voice from the speaker.

"Not really. I'm having a hard time with one of my kids. A young girl. She's trying to learn to walk. She can do it, but she won't." Althea paused. "Did I ever have a book of fairy stories called *The Children's Fairy Tale Companion*?"

"Oh, my goodness, yes. You loved that book. Your father and I could read it to you for hours." Her mother chuckled. "But that wasn't your favorite one."

"Really?" Althea watched as the rain began to gust against the heavy panes of glass.

"Well, maybe when you were really little. But your favorites were the

Brothers Grimm and Hans Christian Andersen. After you'd gotten older and could read to yourself. I remember feeling sad when you got too big to sit in our laps and wanted to read on your own." Her voice dropped. "Did you know that your father and I would read those to each other sometimes?"

"No, I didn't."

Lightning flashed. The boom rattled the window. Althea remembered sitting next to her father, bundled up in a blanket while the rain poured down outside. She was crying because the prince was going to marry a human princess, not the mermaid. Suddenly, in her office, Althea began to cry, her grief fresh and immediate.

"Thea? Thea? Are you all right?"

Her mother's voice brought her back to the present. "I'm just a little tired, Mom," she sniffled. "I'll be all right. Mom? I have to go. I have something I need to do. You've been a big help, really."

"If you say so, dear."

"I love you, Mom." Althea hungs up and gathered her things together. If she hurried, she could make it to the library before it closed for the day.

Althea was there when Mathilde woke. "Hello," she said. "I have a surprise for you."

Mathilde's eyes went wide. "What is it?"

"I have a new book of fairy tales for you. Two new books, in fact. Books I read when I was a child. Can I read you one of my favorite stories?"

Mathilde smiled. "Please!"

Althea opened the thick book and began to read. "Far out in the ocean, where the water is as blue as the prettiest cornflower, and as clear as crystal, it is very, very deep; so deep, indeed, that no cable could fathom it: many church steeples, piled one upon the other, would not reach from the ground beneath to the surface of the water above. There dwell the Sea King and his subjects . . ."

Mathilde listened with rapt attention. Althea read the tale through and when she finished she said, "Hans Christian Andersen wrote that tale over a hundred years ago. You aren't the only one who's ever had to walk on knives, Mathilde. Some of us choose to, and some us have no choice."

Althea paused. Mathilde lay there, puzzlement furrowing her brow. Althea bent close to her, took her chin, turned her head, and looked into her eyes.

"I cannot make you want to walk. I cannot take your pain away. I know you did not choose to be this way. But you can choose to stay this way. It must be your choice, and yours alone. There are many stories in these books. Enough to keep you company for many hours. Enough to while away a lifetime. A lifetime in a bed."

Althea dropped both heavy books onto the bed beside the girl and began to gather up the books that the nurses had brought Mathilde. The books about girls and horses. Girls in high school. Girls on vacation. Girls and their boyfriends. Girls having adventures in far-off lands.

"I made a mistake. I thought if you read about real girls in real life, it would help you. But these are fantasy tales too. Fantasy tales with happy endings." She grasped *The Fairy Tale Companion* and held it up. "*These* are not real fairy tales. *These* have been changed, and all the endings made happy."

"These, though," she continued, pointing at the two thick tomes, "*these* fairy tales are about real life. These are the real fairy tales, Mathilde. Not all of them have happy endings. There are evil stepmothers and horrible fathers and witches who eat little boys and girls. There are ogres and trolls and children who end up being torn apart by wolves. So if you're going to lie here and read, you might as well read the real ones."

She picked up the books. Mathilde was looking at her with a stunned expression. "One last thing," she said. "Unlike fairy tales, real people have something to say about the way their story might end. Understand?"

Mathilde looked frightened, and then angry, and then confused.

Althea walked away.

"How is she?" Althea asked Valerie.

"Better. She wouldn't talk to anybody but Stan for a week after Jamie died." Valerie sighed. "Talk to Stan and read those books you gave her. She read them from cover to cover, and then she read them again!"

"But will it do any good?" Althea wondered.

"I think so. I really do think so. Today when I came by she asked me if she could try the bars again. I told her no."

"No?"

"No way. I told her she had to start back in the pool after lying around on her lazy butt for so long."

Althea frowned. "But will she stick with it this time?"

"Don't know. I just don't know." Valerie shrugged. "Some do, some don't."

"When you can figure out which ones do, let me know will you?"

Valerie laughed. "If I knew that, I'd be God, not a PT."

Althea opened the car door. Mathilde got out and walked slowly across the grass. The sky was blue. The grass was green on the damp earth. The trees swayed gently in the breeze. Far away across the sward, children played at jump rope and tossed a ball.

Althea watched while Mathilde took her shoes off and dug her toes into the earth. She watched while Mathilde tasted the dirt. She watched as Mathilde made her way to one of the big trees and hugged it close. She watched as Mathilde spun in circles. She watched as Mathilde ran, hesitantly at first, then faster and faster. She watched while Mathilde played catch with a boy of about ten, a freckled kid with buck teeth, golden hair, and a high, shrill laugh.

At last Mathilde made her way back to where Althea stood beneath a tree, her feet dirty and her clothes sweaty, a touch of sun on her pale skin and a smile on her face.

She hugged Althea. "Thank you," she said.

Althea smiled. "Don't thank me. You did all the work."

She held the young woman at arms' length and looked into her eyes, seeing the pain deep within.

"It still hurts a lot, doesn't it?" she asked.

Mathilde looked down at her and nodded. Then she tossed off a shrug. "Race you back to the car?"

"No, I'm tired and my feet hurt . . ." Althea stopped abruptly.

"That's not really a very good excuse, is it?" said Mathilde icily. She turned and walked away, back stiff, limping slightly.

Althea stood frozen. *It never ends, does it,* she thought. The flesh had healed, but the heart still bled—and the tongue wielded its own thoughtless knives. As one wound was healed, another took its place. Healing and wounding. Wounding and healing. She got so tired of it all sometimes. It just never ended.

She roused herself ruthlessly from her self-pity. There was no time for that now.

She ran after Mathilde, ignoring her exhaustion, and the pain in her own feet.

# Scars
## Munro Sickafoose

♦

*This torn typography*
*of healed glyphs*
*a stuttered ancient*
*alphabet in skin*
*spells warrior tales*
*of battles lost*
*and gained*
*and homecomings*
*hard won*
*their meaning*
*barely touched*
*with fingertips*
*and gentle lips*
*to give them honor due*
*survivors*
*home to hearth*
*and loving arms*
*far-eyed survivors*
*who hear yet*
*the clash of arms*
*from distant corners*
*of the sky.*

Hans Christian Andersen's bitter tale of "The Little Mermaid," which inspired the previous story and the one that follows, bears little resemblance to the recent Walt Disney film version. In the original story, the mermaid gives up her voice and her tail to win the prince's love, attempting to walk and dance on the human legs he prefers even though it's as painful to her as walking on knives. In the end the prince marries a human woman anyway, and the mermaid drowns herself—for she is unable now, without her tail, to go back to a life in the sea. The following modern fairy tale is the story of the Little Mermaid's younger sister—a young woman, the author tells us, "of very different temper". . . .

# The Pangs of Love

### ✦ Jane Gardam ✦

It is not generally known that the good little mermaid of Hans Christian Andersen, who died for love of the handsome prince and allowed herself to dissolve in the foam of the ocean, had a younger sister, a difficult child of very different temper.

She was very young when the tragedy occurred, and was only told it later by her five elder sisters and her grandmother, the Sea King's mother with the twelve important oyster shells in her tail. They spent much of their time, all these women, mourning the tragic life of the little mermaid in the Sea King's palace below the waves, and a very dreary place it had become in consequence.

"I don't see what she did it for," the seventh little mermaid used to say. "Love for a man—ridiculous," and all the others would sway on the tide and moan, "Hush, hush—you don't know how she suffered for love."

"I don't understand this 'suffered for love,'" said the seventh mermaid. "She sounds very silly and obviously spoiled her life."

"She may have spoiled her life," said the Sea King's mother, "but think how good she was. She was given the chance of saving her life, but because it would have harmed the prince and his earthly bride she let herself die."

"What had he done so special to deserve that?" asked the seventh mermaid.

"He had *done* nothing. He was just her beloved prince to whom she would sacrifice all."

"What did he sacrifice for her?" asked Signorina Settima.

"Not a lot," said the Sea King's mother, "I believe they don't, on the whole. But it doesn't stop us loving them."

"It would me," said the seventh mermaid. "I must get a look at some of this mankind, and perhaps I will then understand more."

"You must wait until your fifteenth birthday," said the Sea King's mother. "That has always been the rule with all your sisters."

"Oh, shit," said the seventh mermaid (she was rather coarse). "Times change. I'm as mature now as they were at fifteen. Howsabout tomorrow?"

"I'm sure I don't know what's to be done with you," said the Sea King's mother, whose character had weakened in later years. "You are totally different from the others and yet I'm sure I brought you all up the same."

"Oh no you didn't," said the five elder sisters in chorus, "she's always been spoiled. We'd never have dared talk to you like that. Think if our beloved sister who died for love had talked to you like that."

"Maybe that's what she should have done," said the dreadful seventh damsel officiously, and this time in spite of her grandmother's failing powers she was put in a cave for a while in the dark and made to miss her supper.

Nevertheless, she was the sort of girl who didn't let other people's views interfere with her too much, and she could argue like nobody else in the sea, so that in the end her grandmother said, 'Oh for goodness' sake then—go. Go now and don't even wait for your *fourteenth* birthday. Go and look at some men and don't come back unless they can turn you into a mermaid one hundredth part as good as your beloved foamy sister."

"Whoops," said Mademoiselle Sept, and she flicked her tail and was away up out of the Sea King's palace, rising through the coral and the fishes that wove about the red and blue seaweed trees like birds, up and up until her head shot out into the air and she took a deep breath of it and said, "Wow!"

The sky, as her admirable sister had noticed, stood above the sea like a large glass bell, and the waves rolled and lifted and tossed towards a green shore where there were fields and palaces and flowers and forests where fish with wings and legs wove about the branches of green and so forth trees, singing at the tops of their voices. On a balcony sticking out from the best palace stood, as he had stood before his marriage when the immaculate sister had first seen him, the wonderful prince with his chin resting on his hand as it often did of an evening—and indeed in the mornings and afternoons, too.

"Oh help!" said the seventh mermaid, feeling a queer twisting around the heart. Then she thought, "Watch it." She dived under water for a time and came up on a rock on the shore, where she sat and examined her sea-green fingernails and smoothed down the silver scales of her tail.

She was sitting where the prince could see her and after a while he gave a cry and she looked up. "Oh," he said, "how you remind me of someone. I thought for a moment you were my lost love."

"Lost love," said the seventh mermaid. "And whose fault was that? She was my sister. She died for love of you and you never gave her one serious thought. You even took her along on your honeymoon like a pet toy. I don't know what she saw in you."

"I always loved her," said the prince. "But I didn't realize it until too late."

"That's what they all say," said Numera Septima. "Are you a poet? They're the worst. Hardy, Tennyson, Shakespeare, Homer. Homer was the worst of all. And he hadn't a good word to say for mermaids."

"Forgive me," said the prince, who had removed his chin from his hand and was passionately clenching the parapet. "Every word you speak reminds me more and more—"

"I don't see how it can," said the s.m., "since for love of you and because she was told it was the only way she could come to you, she let them cut out her tongue, the silly ass."

"And your face," he cried, "your whole aspect, except of course for the tail."

"She had that removed, too. They told her it would be agony and it was, so my sisters tell me. It shrivelled up and she got two ugly stumps called legs—I dare say you've got them under that parapet. When she danced, every step she took was like knives."

"Alas, alas!"

"Catch me getting rid of my tail," said syedmaya krasavitsa, twitching it seductively about, and the prince gave a great sprint from the balcony and embraced her on the rocks. It was all right until halfway down but the scales were cold and prickly. Slimy too, and he shuddered.

"How dare you shudder," cried La Septième. "Go back to your earthly bride."

"She's not here at present," said the p., "she's gone to her mother for the weekend. Won't you come in? We can have dinner in the bath."

The seventh little mermaid spent the whole weekend with the prince in the bath, and he became quite frantic with desire by Monday morning because of the insurmountable problem below the mermaid's waist. "Your eyes, your hair," he cried, "but that's about all."

"My sister did away with her beautiful tail for love of you," said the s.m., reading a volume of Descartes over the prince's shoulder as he lay on her sea-green bosom. "They tell me she even wore a disgusting harness on the top half of her for you, and make-up and dresses. She was the saint of mermaids."

"Ah, a saint," said the prince. "But without your wit, your spark. I would do anything in the world for you."

"So what about getting rid of your legs?"

"Getting rid of my *legs*?"

"Then you can come and live with me below the waves. No one has legs down there and there's nothing wrong with any of us. As a matter of fact, aesthetically we're a very good species."

"Get rid of my *legs*?"

"Yes—my grandmother, the Sea King's mother, and the Sea Witch behind the last whirlpool who fixed up my poor sister, silly cow, could see to it for you."

"Oh, how I love your racy talk," said the prince. "It's like nothing I ever heard before. I should love you even with my eyes shut. Even at a distance. Even on the telephone."

"No fear," said the seventh m., "I know all about this waiting by the telephone. All my sisters do it. It never rings when they want it to. It has days and days of terrible silence and they all roll about weeping and chewing their handkerchieves. You don't catch me getting in that condition."

"Gosh, you're marvellous," said the prince, who had been to an old-fashioned school, "I'll do anything—"

"The legs?"

"Hum. Ha. Well—the legs."

"Carry me back to the rocks," said the seventh little mermaid, "I'll leave you to think about it. What's more, I hear a disturbance in the hall which heralds the return of your wife. By the way, it wasn't your wife, you know, who saved you from drowning when you got shipwrecked on your sixteenth birthday. It was my dear old sister once again. 'She swam among the spars and planks which drifted on the sea, quite forgetting they might crush her. Then she ducked beneath the water, and rising again on the billows managed at last to reach you, who by now' (being fairly feeble in the muscles I'd guess, with all the stately living) 'was scarcely able to swim any longer in the raging sea. Your arms, your legs' (ha!) 'began to fail you and your beautiful eyes were closed and you must surely have died if my sister had not come to your assistance. She held your head above the water and let the billows drive her and you together wherever they pleased.' "

"What antique phraseology."

"It's a translation from the Danish. Anyway, 'when the sun rose red and beaming from the water, your cheeks regained the hue of life but your eyes remained closed. My sister kissed—'

("No!")

" '—your lofty handsome brow and stroked back your wet locks . . . She kissed you again and longed that you might live.' What's more, if you'd only woken up then she could have spoken to you. It was when she got obsessed by you back down under the waves again that she went in for all this tongue and tail stuff with the Sea Witch."

"She was an awfully nice girl," said the prince, and tears came into his eyes—which was more than they ever could do for a mermaid however sad, because as we know from H. C. Andersen, mermaids can never cry, which makes it harder for them.

"The woman I saw when I came to on the beach," said the prince, "was she who is now my wife. A good sort of woman, but she drinks."

"I'm not surprised," said the seventh mermaid. "I'd drink if I was married to someone who just stood gazing out to sea thinking of a girl he had allowed to turn into foam," and she flicked her tail and disappeared.

"Now then," she thought, "what's to do next?" She was not to go back, her grandmother had said, until she was one hundredth part as good as the little m. her dead sister, now a spirit of air, and although she was a tearaway and, as I say, rather coarse, she was not altogether untouched by the discipline of the Sea King's mother and her upbringing. Yet she could not say that she exactly yearned for her father's palace with all her melancholy sisters singing dreary stuff about the past. Nor was she too thrilled to return to the heaviness of water with all the featherless fishes swimming through the amber windows and butting into her, and the living flowers growing out of the palace walls like dry rot. However, after flicking about for a bit, once coming up to do an inspection of a fishing boat in difficulties with the tide and enjoying the usual drop-jawed faces, she took a header home into the front room and sat down quietly in a corner.

"You're back," said the Sea King's mother. "How was it? I take it you now feel you are a hundredth part as good as your sainted sister?"

"I've always tried to be good," said the s.m.; "I've just tried to be rationally good and not romantically good, that's all."

"Now don't start again. I take it you have seen some men?"

"I saw the prince."

At this the five elder sisters set up a wavering lament.

"Did you feel for him—"

"Oh, feelings, feelings," said the seventh and rational mermaid, "I'm sick to death of feelings. He's good-looking, I'll give you that, and rather sweet-natured and he's having a rough time at home, but he's totally self-centered. I agree that my sister must have been a true sea-saint to listen to him dripping on about himself all day. He's warm-hearted though, and not at all bad in the bath."

The Sea King's mother fainted away at this outspoken and uninhibited statement, and the five senior mermaids fled in shock. The seventh mermaid tidied her hair and set off to find the terrible cave of the Sea Witch behind the last whirlpool, briskly pushing aside the disgusting polyps, half-plant, half-animal, and the fingery seaweeds that had so terrified her dead sister on a similar journey.

"Aha," said the Sea Witch, stirring a pot of filthy black bouillabaisse, "you, like your sister, cannot do without me. I suppose you also want to risk body and soul for the human prince up there on the dry earth?"

"Good afternoon, no," said the seventh mermaid. "Might I sit down?"

(For even the seventh mermaid was polite to the Sea Witch.) "I want to ask you if, when the prince follows me down here below the waves, you could arrange for him to live with me until the end of time?"

"He'd have to lose his legs. What would he think of that?"

"I think he might consider it. In due course."

"He would have to learn to sing and not care about clothes or money or possessions or power—what would he think of that?"

"Difficult, but not impossible."

"He'd have to face the fact that if you fell in love with one of your own kind and married him he would die and also lose his soul as your sister did when he wouldn't make an honest woman of her."

"It was not," said the seventh mermaid, "that he wouldn't make an honest woman of her. It just never occurred to him. After all—she couldn't speak to him about it. You had cut out her tongue."

"Aha," said the s.w., "it's different for a man, is it? Falling in love, are you?"

"Certainly not," said Fräulein Sieben. "Certainly not."

"Cruel then, eh? Revengeful? Or do you hate men? It's very fashionable."

"I'm not cruel. Or revengeful. I'm just rational. And I don't hate men. I think I'd probably like them very much, especially if they are all as kind and as beautiful as the prince. I just don't believe in falling in love with them. It is a burden and it spoils life. It is a mental illness. It killed my sister and it puts women in a weak position and makes us to be considered second-class."

"They fall in love with us," said the Sea Witch. "That's to say, with women. So I've been told. Sometimes. Haven't you read the sonnets of Shakespeare and the poems of Petrarch?"

"The sonnets of Shakespeare are hardly all about one woman," said the bright young mermaid. "In fact some of them are written to a man. As for Petrarch" (there was scarcely a thing this girl hadn't read) "he only saw his girl once, walking over a bridge. They never exactly brushed their teeth together."

"Well, there are the Brownings."

"Yes. The Brownings were all right," said the mermaid. "Very funny-looking, though. I don't suppose anyone else ever wanted them."

"You are a determined young mermaid," said the Sea Witch. "Yes, I'll agree to treat the prince if he comes this way. But you must wait and see if he does."

"Thank you, yes I will," said the seventh mermaid. "He'll come," and she did wait, quite confidently, being the kind of girl well-heeled men do run after because she never ran after them, very like Elizabeth Bennet.

So, one day, who should come swimming down through the wonderful blue water and into the golden palaces of the Sea King and floating through the windows like the fish and touching with wonder the dry-rot flowers upon the walls, but the prince, his golden hair floating behind him and his golden hose and tunic stuck tight to him all over like a wet-suit, and he looked terrific.

"Oh, princess, sweet seventh mermaid," he said, finding her at once (because she was the sort of girl who is always in the right place at the right time). "I have found you again. Ever since I threw you back in the sea I have dreamed of you. I cannot live without you. I have left my boozy wife and have come to live with you for ever."

"There are terrible conditions," said the seventh mermaid. "Remember. The same conditions which my poor sister accepted in reverse. You must lose your legs and wear a tail."

"This I will do."

"You must learn to sing for hours and hours in unison with the other mermen, in wondrous notes that hypnotize simple sailors up above and make them think they hear faint sounds from Glyndebourne or Milan."

"As to that," said the prince, "I always wished I had a voice."

"And you must know that if I decide that I want someone more than you, someone of my own sort, and marry him, you will lose everything, as my sister did—your body, your immortal soul and your self-respect."

"Oh well, that's quite all right," said the prince. He knew that no girl could ever prefer anyone else to him.

"*Right,*" said the mermaid. "Well, before we go off to the Sea Witch, let's give a party. And let me introduce you to my mother and sisters."

Then there followed a time of most glorious celebration, similar only to the celebration some years back for the prince's wedding night when the poor little mermaid now dead had had to sit on the deck of the nuptial barque and watch the bride and groom until she had quite melted away. Then the cannons had roared and the flags had waved and a royal bridal tent of cloth of gold and purple and precious furs had been set upon the deck and when it grew dark, colored lamps had been lit and sailors danced merrily and the bride and groom had gone into the tent without the prince giving the little mermaid a backward glance.

Now, beneath the waves the sea was similarly alight with glowing corals and brilliant sea-flowers and a bower was set up for the seventh mermaid and the prince and she danced with all the mermen who had silver crowns on their heads and St. Christophers round their necks, very trendy like the South of France, and they all had a lovely time.

And the party went on and on. It was beautiful. Day after day and night after night and anyone who was anyone was there, and the weather was gorgeous—no storms below or above and it was exactly as Hans Christian Andersen said: "a wondrous blue tint lay over everything; one would be more inclined to fancy one was high up in the air and saw nothing but sky above and below than that one was at the bottom of the sea. During a calm, too, one could catch a glimpse of the sun. It looked like a crimson flower from the cup of which, light streamed forth." The seventh mermaid danced and danced, particularly with a handsome young merman with whom she seemed much at her ease.

"Who is that merman?" asked the prince. "You seem to know him well."

"Oh—just an old friend," said the seventh m., "he's always been about. We were in our prams together." (This was not true. The seventh m. was just testing the prince. She had never bothered with mermen even in her pram.)

"I'm sorry," said the prince, "I can't have you having mermen friends. Even if there's nothing in it."

"We must discuss this with the Sea Witch," said the seventh mermaid, and taking his hand she swam with him out of the palace and away and away through the dreadful polyps again. She took him past the last whirlpool to the cave where the Sea Witch was sitting eating a most unpleasant-looking type of caviar from a giant snail shell and stroking her necklace of sea snakes.

"Ha," said the Sea Witch, "the prince. You have come to be rid of your legs?"

"Er—well—"

"You have come to be rid of your earthly speech, your clothes and possessions and power?"

"Well, it's something that we might discuss."

"And you agree to lose soul and body and self-respect if this interesting mermaid goes off and marries someone?"

There was a very long silence and the seventh mermaid closely examined some shells round her neck, tiny pale pink oyster shells each containing a pearl which would be the glory of a Queen's crown. The prince held his beautiful chin in his lovely, sensitive hand. His gentle eyes filled with tears. At last he took the mermaid's small hand and kissed its palm and folded the sea-green nails over the kiss (he had sweet ways) and said, "I must not look at you. I must go at once," and he pushed off. That is to say, he pushed himself upwards off the floor of the sea and shot up and away and away through the foam, arriving home in time for tea and early sherry with his wife, who was much relieved. It was a very long time indeed before the seventh little mermaid returned to the party. In fact the party was all but over. There was only the odd slithery merman twanging a harp of dead fisherman's bones and the greediest and grubbiest of the deep-water fishes eating up the last of the sandwiches. The Sea King's old mother was asleep, her heavy tail studded with important oyster shells coiled round the legs of her throne.

The five elder sisters had gone on somewhere amusing.

The seventh mermaid sat down at the feet of her grandmother and at length the old lady woke up and surveyed the chaos left over from the fun. "Hullo, my child," she said. "Are you alone?"

"Yes. The prince has gone. The engagement's off."

"My dear—what did I tell you? Remember how your poor sister suffered. I warned you."

"Pooh—I'm not suffering. I've just proved my point. Men aren't worth it."

"Maybe you and she were unfortunate," said the Sea King's mother. "Which men you meet is very much a matter of luck, I'm told."

"No—they're all the same," said the mermaid who by now was nearly fifteen years old. "I've proved what I suspected. I'm free now—free of the terrible pangs of love which put women in bondage, and I shall dedicate my life to freeing and instructing other women and saving them from humiliation."

"Well, I hope you don't become one of those frowsty little women who don't laugh and have only one subject of conversation," said the Sea Witch. "It is a mistake to base a whole philosophy upon one disappointment."

"Disappointment—pah!" said the seventh mermaid. "When was I ever negative?"

"And I hope you don't become aggressive."

"When was I ever aggressive?" said Señorita Septima ferociously.

"That's a good girl then," said the Sea King's mother, "So now—unclench that fist."

# Brother and Sister
## Terri Windling

♦

*Do you remember, brother*
*Those days in the wood*
*When you ran with the deer*
*Falling bloody on my doorstep at dusk*
*Stepping from the skin*
*Grateful to be a man*
*And do you know, brother*
*Just how I longed*
*To wrap myself in the golden hide*
*Smelling of musk*
*Blackberries and rain*
*Tell me that tale*
*Give me that choice*
*And I'll choose speed and horn and hoof*
*Give me that choice*
*All you cruel, clever fairies*
*And I'll choose the wood*
*Not the prince*

The cruelty casually or accidently done to children can take many forms, as Alice Miller reminds us in "For Your Own Good," a psychological look at the history of child-rearing. Not all child abuse leaves bruises, or is actually meant to cause harm. The king in the fairy tale that follows loves his daughter dearly. But he is destroying her young life by insisting, because of his own needs, that she live in her mother's image instead of growing into herself.

# The Face in the Cloth
### ✦  Jane Yolen  ✦

here were once a king and queen so in love with one another that they could not bear to be parted, even for a day. To seal their bond, they desperately wanted a child. The king had even made a cradle of oak for the babe with his own hands and placed it by their great canopied bed. But year in and year out, the cradle stood empty.

At last one night, when the king was fast asleep, the queen left their bed. She cast one long, lingering glance at her husband, then, disguising herself with a shawl around her head, she crept out of the castle, for the first time alone. She was bound for a nearby forest where she had heard that three witch-sisters lived. The queen had been told that they might give her what she most desired by taking from her what she least desired to give.

"But I have so much," she thought as she ran through the woods. "Gold and jewels beyond counting. Even the diamond that the king himself put on my hand and from which I would hate to be parted. But though it is probably what I would least desire to give, I would give it gladly in order to have a child."

The witches' hut squatted in the middle of the wood, and through its window the queen saw the three old sisters sitting by the fire, chanting a spell as soft as a cradle song:

*Needle and scissors,*
*Scissors and pins,*
*Where one life ends,*
*Another begins.*

And suiting their actions to the words, the three snipped and sewed, snipped and sewed with the invisible thread over and over and over again.

The night was so dark and the three slouching sisters so strange that the queen was quite terrified. But her need was even greater than her fear. She scratched upon the window, and the three looked up from their work.

"Come in," they called out in a single voice.

So she had to go, pulled into the hut by that invisible thread.

"What do you want, my dear?" said the first old sister to the queen through the pins she held in her mouth.

"I want a child," said the queen.

"When do you want it?" asked the second sister, who held a needle high above her head.

"As soon as I can get it," said the queen, more boldly now.

"And what will you give for it?" asked the third, snipping her scissors ominously.

"Whatever is needed," replied the queen. Nervously she turned the ring with the diamond around her finger.

The three witches smiled at one another. Then they each held up a hand with the thumb and forefinger touching in a circle.

"Go," they said. "It is done. All we ask is to be at the birthing to sew the swaddling clothes."

The queen stood still as stone, a river of feeling washing around her. She had been prepared to gift them a fortune. What they asked was so simple, she agreed at once. Then she turned and ran out of the hut all the way to the castle. She never looked back.

Less than a year later, the queen was brought to childbed. But in her great joy, she forgot to mention to the king her promise to the witches. And then in great pain, and because it had been such a small promise after all, she forgot it altogether.

As the queen lay in labor in her canopied bed, there came a knock on the castle door. When the guards opened it, who should be standing there but three slouching old women.

"We have come to be with the queen," said the one with pins in her mouth.

The guards shook their heads.

"The queen promised we could make the swaddling cloth," said the second, holding her needle high over her head.

"We must be by her side," said the third, snapping her scissors.

One guard was sent to tell the king.

The king came to the castle door, his face red with anger, his brow wreathed with sweat.

"The queen told me of no such promise," he said. "And she tells me everything. What possesses you to bother a man at a time like this? Begone." He dismissed them with a wave of his hand.

But before the guards could shut the door upon the ancient sisters, the one with the scissors called out, "Beware, oh King, of promises given." Then all three chanted:

> *Needle and scissors,*
> *Scissors and pins,*
> *Where one life ends,*
> *Another begins.*

The second old woman put her hands above her head and made a circle with her forefinger and thumb. But the one with the pins in her mouth thrust a piece of cloth into the king's hand.

"It is for the babe," she said. "Because of the queen's desire."

Then the three left the castle and were not seen there again.

The king started to look down at the cloth, but there came a loud cry from the bedchamber. He ran back along the corridors, and when he entered the bedroom door, the doctor turned around, a newborn child, still red with birth blood, in his hands.

"It is a girl, Sire," he said.

There was a murmur of praise from the attending women.

The king put out his hands to receive the child and, for the first time, really noticed the cloth he was holding. It was pure white, edged with lace. As he looked at it, his wife's likeness began to appear on it slowly, as if being stitched in with a crimson thread. First the eyes he so loved; then the elegant nose; the soft, full mouth; the dimpled chin.

The king was about to remark on it when the midwife cried out, "It is the queen, Sire. She is dead." And at the same moment, the doctor put the child into his hands.

The royal funeral and the royal christening were held on the same day, and no one in the kingdom knew whether to laugh or cry except the babe, who did both.

Since the king could not bear to part with his wife entirely, he had the cloth with her likeness sewed into the baby's cloak so that wherever she went, the princess carried her mother's face.

As she outgrew one cloak, the white lace was cut away from the old and sewn into the new. And in this way the princess was never without the panel bearing her mother's portrait, nor was she ever allowed to wander far from her father's watchful eyes. Her life was measured by the size of the cloaks which were cut bigger each year, and the likeness of her mother, which seemed to get bigger as well.

The princess grew taller, but she did not grow stronger. She was like a pale copy of her mother. There was never a time that the bloom of health sat on her cheeks. She remained the color of skimmed milk, the color of ocean foam, the color of second-day snow. She was always cold, sitting huddled for warmth inside her picture cloak even on the hottest days, and nothing could part her from it.

The king despaired of his daughter's health, but neither the royal physicians nor philosophers could help. He turned to necromancers and stargazers, to herbalists and diviners. They pushed and prodded and prayed over the princess. They examined the soles of her feet and the movement of her stars. But still she sat cold and whey-colored, wrapped in her cloak.

At last one night, when everyone was fast asleep, the king left his bed and crept out of the castle alone. He had heard that there were three witch sisters who lived nearby who might give him what he most desired by taking from him what he least desired to give. Having lost his queen, he knew there was nothing else he would hate losing—not his fortune, his kingdom, or his throne. He would give it all up gladly to see his daughter, who was his wife's pale reflection, sing and dance and run.

The witches' hut squatted in the middle of the wood, and through its window the king saw the three old sisters. He did not recognize them, but they knew him at once.

"Come in, come in," they called out, though he had not knocked. And he was drawn into the hut as if pulled by an invisible thread.

"We know what you want," said the first.

"We can give you what you desire," said the second.

"By taking what you least wish to give," said the third.

"I have already lost my queen," he said. "So anything else I have is yours so long as my daughter is granted a measure of health." And he started to twist off the ring he wore on his third finger, the ring his wife had been pledged with, to give to the three sisters to seal his part of the bargain.

"Then you must give us—your daughter," said the three.

The king was stunned. For a moment the only sound in the hut was the crackle of fire in the hearth.

"*Never!*" he thundered at last. "What you ask is impossible."

"What *you* ask is impossible," said the first old woman. "Nonetheless, we promise it will be so." She stood. "But if your daughter does not come to us, her life will be worth no more than this." She took a pin from her mouth and held it up. It caught the firelight for a moment. Only a moment.

The king stared. "I know you," he said slowly. "I have seen you before."

The second sister nodded. "Our lives have been sewn together by a queen's desire," she said. She pulled the needle through a piece of cloth she was holding and drew the thread through in a slow, measured stitch.

The third sister began to chant, and at each beat her scissors snapped together:

> *Needle and scissors,*
> *Scissors and pins,*
> *Where one life ends,*
> *Another begins.*

The king cursed them thoroughly, his words hoarse as a rote of war, and left. But partway through the forest, he thought of his daughter like a waning moon asleep in her bed, and wept.

For days he raged in the palace, and his courtiers felt his tongue as painfully as if it were a whip. Even his daughter, usually silent in her shroud-like cloak, cried out.

"Father," she said, "your anger unravels the kingdom, pulling at its loosest threads. What is it? What can I do?" As she spoke, she pulled the cloak more firmly about her shoulders, and the king could swear that the portrait of his wife moved, the lips opening and closing as if the image spoke as well.

The king shook his head and put his hands to his face. "You are all I have left of her," he mumbled. "And now I must let you go."

The princess did not understand, but she put her small faded hands on his. "You must do what you must do, my father," she said.

And though he did not quite understand the why of it, the king brought his daughter into the wood the next night after dark. Setting her on his horse and holding the bridle himself, he led her along the path to the hut of the three crones.

At the door he kissed her once on each cheek and then tenderly kissed the image on her cloak. Then, mounting his horse, he galloped away without once looking back.

Behind him the briars closed over the path, and the forest was still.

Once her father had left, the princess looked around the dark clearing. When no one came to fetch her, she knocked upon the door of the little hut. Getting no answer, she pushed the door open and went in.

The hut was empty, though a fire burned merrily in the hearth. The table was set, and beside the wooden plate were three objects: a needle, a pair of scissors, and a pin. On the hearth wall, engraved in the stone, was a poem. The princess went over to the fire to read it:

> *Needle and scissors,*
> *Scissors and pins,*

*Where one life ends,*
*Another begins.*

"How strange," thought the princess, shivering inside her cloak.

She looked around the little hut, found a bed with a wooden headboard shaped like a loom, lay down upon the bed and, pulling the cloak around her even more tightly, slept.

In the morning when the princess woke, she was still alone, but there was food on the table, steaming hot. She rose and made a feeble toilette, for there were no mirrors on the wall, and ate the food. All the while she toyed with the needle, scissors, and pin by her plate. She longed for her father and the familiarity of the court, but her father had left her at the hut, and being an obedient child, she stayed.

As she finished her meal, the hearthfire went out, and soon the hut grew chilly. So the princess went outside and sat on a wooden bench by the door. Sunlight illuminated the clearing and wrapped around her shoulders like a golden cloak. Alternately she dozed and woke and dozed again until it grew dark.

When she went inside the hut, the table was once more set with food, and this time she ate eagerly, then went to sleep, dreaming of the needle and scissors and pin. In her dream they danced away from her, refusing to bow when she bade them.

She woke to a cold dawn. The meal was ready, and the smell of it, threading through the hut, got her up. She wondered briefly what hands had done all the work, but, being a princess and used to being served, she did not wonder about it very long.

When she went outside to sit in the sun, she sang snatches of old songs to keep herself company. The sound of her own voice, tentative and slightly off-key, was like an old friend. The tune kept running around and around in her head, and though she did not know where she had heard it before, it fitted perfectly the words carved over the hearth:

*Needle and scissors,*
*Scissors and pins,*
*Where one life ends,*
*Another begins.*

"This is certainly true," she told herself, "for my life here in the forest is different from my life in the castle, though I myself do not feel changed." And she shivered and pulled the cloak around her.

Several times she stood and walked about the clearing, looking for the path that led out. But it was gone. The brambles were laced firmly together like stitches on a quilt, and when she put a hand to them, a thorn pierced her palm and the blood dripped down onto her cloak, spotting the portrait of her mother and making it look as if she were crying red tears.

It was then the princess knew that she had been abandoned to the magic in the forest. She wondered that she was not more afraid, and tried out different emotions: first fear, then bewilderment, then loneliness; but none of them seemed quite real to her. What she felt, she decided at last, was a kind of lightness, a giddiness, as if she had lost her center, as if she were a balloon, untethered and ready—at last—to let go.

"What a goose I have become," she said aloud. "One or two days without the prattle of courtiers, and I am talking to myself."

But her own voice was a comfort, and she smiled. Then, settling her cloak more firmly about her shoulders, she went back to the hut.

She counted the meager furnishings of the hut as if she were telling beads on a string: door, window, hearth, table, chair, bed. "I wish there were something to *do*," she thought to herself. And as she turned around, the needle on the table was glowing as if a bit of fire had caught in its eye.

She went over to the table and picked up the needle, scissors, and pin and carried them to the hearth. Spreading her cloak on the stones, though careful to keep her mother's image facing up, she sat.

"If I just had some thread," she thought.

Just then she noticed the panel with her mother's portrait. For the first time it seemed small and crowded, spotted from the years. The curls were old-fashioned and overwrought, the mouth a little slack, the chin a touch weak.

"Perhaps if I could borrow a bit of thread from this embroidery," she whispered, "just a bit where it will not be noticed. As I am alone, no one will know but me."

Slowly she began to pick out the crimson thread along one of the tiny curls. She heard a deep sigh as she started, as if it came from the cloak, then realized it had been her own breath that had made the sound. She wound up the thread around the pin until she had quite a lot of it. Then she snipped off the end, knotted it, threaded the needle—and stopped.

"What am I to sew upon?" she wondered. All she had was what she wore. Still, as she had a great need to keep herself busy and nothing else to do, she decided to embroider designs along the edges of her cloak. So she began with what she knew. On the gray panels she sewed a picture of her own castle. It was so real, it seemed as if its banners fluttered in a westerly wind. And as it grew, turret by turret, she began to feel a little warmer, a little more at home.

She worked until it was time to eat, but as she had been in the hut all the while, no magical servants had set the table. So she hunted around the cupboards herself until she found bread and cheese and a pitcher of milk. Making herself a scanty meal, she cleaned away the dishes, then lay down on the bed and was soon asleep.

In the morning she was up with the dawn. She cut herself some bread, poured some milk, and took the meal outside, where she continued to sew. She gave the castle lancet windows, a Lady chapel, cows grazing in the outlying fields, and a moat in which golden carp swam about, their fins stroking the water and making little waves that moved beneath her hand.

When the first bit of thread was used up, she picked out another section of the portrait, all of the curls and a part of the chin. With that thread she embroidered a forest around the castle, where brachet hounds, noses to the ground, sought a scent; a deer started; and a fox lay hidden in a rambling thicket, its ears twitching as the dogs coursed by. She could almost remark their baying, now near, now far away. Then, in the middle of the forest—with a third piece of thread—the princess sewed the hut. Beneath the hut, as she sewed, letters appeared though she did not touch them.

> Needle and scissors,
> Scissors and pins,
> Where one life ends,
> Another begins.

She said the words aloud, and as she spoke, puffs of smoke appeared above the embroidered chimney in the hut. It reminded her that it was time to eat.

Stretching, she stood and went into the little house. The bread was gone. She searched the cupboards and could find no more, but there was flour and salt, and so she made herself some flat cakes that she baked in an oven set into the stone of the fireplace. She knew that the smoke from her baking was sending soft clouds above the hut.

While the bread baked and the sweet smell embroidered the air, the princess went back outside. She unraveled more threads from her mother's image: the nose, the mouth, the startled eyes. And with that thread she traced a winding path from the crimson castle with the fluttering banners to the crimson hut with the crown of smoke.

As she sewed, it seemed to her that she could hear the sound of birds—the rapid flutings of a thrush and the jug-jug-jug of a nightingale—and that they came not from the real forest around her but from the cloak. Then she heard, from the very heart of her lap work, the deep, brassy voice of a hunting horn summoning her home.

Looking up from her work, she saw that the brambles around the hut were beginning to part and there was a path heading north toward the castle.

She jumped up, tumbling needle and scissors and pin to the ground, and took a step toward the beckoning path. Then she stopped. The smell of fresh bread stayed her. The embroidery was not yet done. She knew that she had to sew her own portrait onto the white laced panel of the cloak: a girl with crimson cheeks and hair tumbled to her shoulders, walking the path alone. She had to use up the rest of her mother's thread before she was free.

Turning back toward the hut, she saw three old women standing in the doorway, their faces familiar. They smiled and nodded to her, holding out their hands.

The first old woman had the needle and pin nestled in her palm. The second held the scissors by the blades, handles offered. The third old woman shook out the cloak, and as she did so, a breeze stirred the trees in the clearing.

The princess smiled back at them. She held out her hands to receive their gifts. When she was done with the embroidery, though it was hard to part with it, she would give them the cloak. She knew that once it was given, she could go.

# Their Father

Gwen Strauss

♦

*I won't say it wasn't my idea.*
*I think of Hansel's first attempt,*
*pockets dribbling those white stones,*
*a tenuous trail to the home*
*that had ceased to hold him.*
*I was alone with two children*
*at the edge of a great wood.*

*Like that a man can be a fool*
*when it comes to a woman.*
*She used to beg for love-making.*
*Her anger was more*
*than I had courage for;*
*her eyes, soft beneath me,*
*could turn in a frenzy.*

*When they returned,*
*following the moon-pebbled path*
*I vowed never. There are stones*
*in my belly; they rattle*
*in my dreams.*

*The next time Gretel held my hand.*
*Hansel held back to watch*
*a cat on the roof. If I'd known*
*of his scant offerings,*
*could I have left them?*

*The time they were away is silent*
*but for the sawing of inward anger.*
*I dreamed of birds,*
*swooping down on their trail.*

*My wife ate and ate*
*but grew thin in front of me.*

*I did nothing. When she died*
*I drew inside the cottage,*
*shutters closed, a cage.*
*I lived in the smallest gestures:*
*sweeping, building a fire.*
*I moved as little as possible.*

*If I had the courage*
*I would enter the woods,*
*but I clung to cupboard habits.*

*Gretel, with her apron full of pearls,*
*has bought us a flock of geese.*
*Each morning I scatter crumbs for them;*
*Gretel likes it when I help:*
*either that, she says, or when I stay*
*out of her way.*

The following story takes Hans Christian Andersen's fairy tale "The Emperor's New Clothes" (originally published in Danish in the nineteenth century) and sets it in a magical version of old Japan. It is a haunting tale about a man of power, far removed from the world of childhood, who has forgotten that the life of a single child is ultimately more important than courtly politics and pride.

# The Chrysanthemum Robe
### ✦ Kara Dalkey ✦

O n the evening of the eighth day of the Long Month, in the dying of the year, the young Emperor sat watching the wind in the maple sapling just beyond his open shoji. The vermilion leaves held defiantly to their slender branches despite the approaching frosts and the buffeting of the breezes. *As they are, so must I be,* thought the young Emperor.

He sat in his private residence, the Seiryo Den, awaiting his Imperial Chamberlain, Fujiwara no Yabuimu, the most powerful elder of the Fujiwara clan. "Beware the Fujiwara, my son," the Old Emperor had said to the young Emperor, just before retiring into monkhood on Mount Kurama. "The Fujiwara are like cats at your dinner table. They will accept the fish scraps you give them, and steal whatever else they can, as well."

The young Emperor was still bristling from the treatment he received at the Submission of Reports on Unfit Land the day before. The purpose of the ceremony was to inform the Imperial Majesty which lands had suffered from natural disaster and would not be producing a full harvest this year. This was so that the Emperor would charitably remit the tax that had been paid for that land. However, the young Emperor suspected that there were more reports of crop failures due to flood and earthquake than had in fact occurred. Many of the lands cited were holdings of the Fujiwara family or its related clans—not to mention that the reports were presented with a sloppiness of form and language that bordered on disrespect.

This evening, the young Emperor was to be presented with a special gift from the Fujiwara; something to do with the Procession to View Chrysanthemums the next day. The gifts brought by the Fujiwara tended to be two-sided. They would be too elegant to be rejected out of hand, and yet would contain some subtle joke, a sharp reminder of the Fujiwara's power. The young Emperor had reigned for a little over a year now and he had learned how to spot these tricks. He wondered what the Chamberlain would have hidden within his copious black sleeves this time.

In the distance, a temple bell tolled its low, sad tones, a reminder that the World of the Ancestors is never as far as the living choose to believe. It made the hairs on his neck prickle. The Young Emperor noted how the steam of his breath drifted before him, a momentary lost spirit until it vanished in the chill autumn air. He felt a touch of *aware*, the melancholy knowledge that all things of beauty must die. The young Emperor shook himself. *A suitable feeling for autumn, but this leaf shall not fall until he is so withered he can no longer hold to his bough.*

As if summoned by the tolling of the temple bell, the Imperial Chamberlain arrived, bustling in officiously. Yabuimu-sama was dressed as befitted a noble of the First Rank, in voluminous black robes lined with red silk and a tall black silk hat, and bearing the flat wood baton of his office. He bowed only so low as to avoid offense to the young Emperor and knelt to one side. Behind him came a weasel-like fellow carrying a large red-lacquered box emblazoned with the Kikumon, the Imperial Chrysanthemum crest. A waiting-woman closed the shoji behind them for privacy.

"Majesty," began the Imperial Chamberlain, "I have brought you a gift from my family, that we may do you the honor on tomorrow's joyous occasion, as we have done for your father and generations before."

*Yes, I know your clan has been in power a long time.* "As always, Yabuimu-sama, I am surprised and touched by the homage of your family. What gift could possibly express the affections our families have for one another?"

"Surely, none," said the Imperial Chamberlain with a knowing smile. "But I have made a feeble attempt with the item this tailor, Bakasai-san, has brought to us. If you will please us by making the presentation, Bakasai-san."

The weasely man, who wore an undistinguished gray and purple robe, prostrated himself on the polished cypress floorboards. "Great Majesty, Son of Heaven, I pray that this insignificant garment I bring will prove worthy of your approval."

"Garment?" said the young Emperor, raising his brows at the Chamberlain.

"Yes, Majesty," said the Fujiwara. "An *Ue no Kinu* that I hope you will find suitable to wear as your over-robe in tomorrow's procession. It has been embroidered with the Kikumon, fitting for the occasion, as well as your imperial state."

*Ah,* thought the young Emperor, *is that the joke—that the Imperial gown is a gift of the Fujiwara—that I am clothed in their power, or that it is only by their generosity that I am named Emperor?* "Well, I am full of curiosity, Bakasai-san. Show me your gift."

Reverently lifting the top of the red box, Bakasai said, "The cloth of this robe, Most Great Majesty, was woven by a sorceress of the western mountains and washed three times in the waters of Lake Biwa. The sorceress told me that the robe I would make from this cloth would be of such purity and quality, that only the wise could apprehend its true beauty. To fools, the robe would seem nothing at all."

*Considering the number of fools at court,* thought the young Emperor, *I am not sure of the wisdom of this gift.* "Go on," he told the tailor.

"Majesty, I shall let the garment speak for itself." Bakasai reached into the box and pulled out what appeared to the Emperor to be a loose bundle of gold wire and thread. When the tailor unfolded the bundle, it became a shimmering framework, the outline of a robe—but there was no cloth between. The young Emperor felt his mouth drop open. *Never have the Fujiwara been so bold as this!*

"I see you appreciate its beauty," said the Imperial Chamberlain. "I think the motif of cranes flying above the clouds is quite elegant, as well as pleasing in its symbolism, neh?"

*I must not give in to this taunting,* thought the young Emperor. *I must preserve my dignity above all. I will play along with their stupid game— but I will make them regret it.* Putting on his most welcoming smile, the young Emperor said, "I find its beauty . . . indescribable, Yabuimu-sama. Truly, your family has never given me such an astonishing gift as this. I will be pleased to wear it for tomorrow's procession."

The Chamberlain bowed, also smiling. "Then you do my family honor, Majesty. It gives me great joy that the gift pleases you."

*Yes, because now you can spread rumors that the Emperor is mad and thus justify further restrictions on my powers.* "However, I must make one condition to my wearing this."

"Majesty?"

"If what Bakasai-san has said is true, there may be fools who do not see its beauty. I cannot allow such people to belittle the person of the Emperor and thereby the taste and good judgment of the Fujiwara. Therefore, I will make a decree stating that should anyone claim that the Emperor wore no robe during the Chrysanthemum Procession, that person shall be put to death."

The Imperial Chamberlain sat silent for a moment and blinked.

*Hah!* thought the young Emperor. *Got you this time.*

The Fujiwara looked at the golden framework then back at the Emperor, frowning. "That would seem rather extreme, Majesty. Are you certain of the wisdom of this decree?"

"As certain as I have ever been of anything, Yabuimu-sama. After all, we cannot abide fools in the Imperial Palace, can we? This robe is so extraordinary that I will not have anyone speak against it. I will not wear it without the decree."

The Imperial Chamberlain raised his brows and sighed. "Let it be as you wish, Majesty."

So that night, as the ladies of the court were laying out swaths of silk on the flower beds to catch the chrysanthemum dew that would ensure long life, the decree to shorten the life of any who derided the imperial garb was written by the Bureau of Secretaries and posted everywhere in the palace. The irony was not lost on the young Emperor. The atmosphere of imperial presence and power seemed even more enhanced. He hoped the Fujiwara would take note.

The following day, the ninth day of the Ninth Month, the young Emperor set forth on the procession through the various gardens of the palace to view the chrysanthemums in bloom. He wore only his formal under-robe surmounted by the golden framework "cloak." He noticed occasional stares from the nobles and servants, but because of his decree, no one said a word of insult. The young Emperor smiled and walked with all the dignity of a man clothed in gold.

It was not until the procession reached the gardens of the Plum Pavilion, where the Emperor's second wife resided, that his decree was breached. From behind the bamboo screens, there came the laughter of ladies and suddenly a tiny hand pointed out. "Look! The Emperor-sama wears no cloak!"

The entire procession stopped, silent, and stared at the screen.

The young Emperor felt his heart beat like a taiko drum as two Imperial Guards brought forth from behind the screen Shikiko, his fourth little daughter, wide-eyed in her pink and orange kimono.

The young Emperor, bent down on one knee to her and whispered, "Little one, do you know what you have done? What you will make me do?" He looked at the courtiers surrounding him, waiting. He wanted with all his heart to be merciful to the child. *But will that not make me seem unjust, decreeing a dire fate for any but my family? Will my law be made worthless? The Fujiwara would like that, no doubt.*

With great heaviness of spirit, the young Emperor stood and signaled to his guards that the decree was to be carried out on the spot. One of the lengths of dew-catching silk was laid out before the little girl and she was forced to kneel upon it. The young Emperor steeled himself to ignore the cries and pleas of the women behind the bamboo screens. Two guards had to stay at the screen to prevent his second wife from coming out and making a unseemly public display.

Little Shikiko looked up at him as her kimono was loosened around her neck. She glanced around in fright. "Papa-chan?"

The young Emperor felt tears beginning in the corners of his eyes.

"Be brave," he whispered to her fiercely. To the guard who had drawn a long tachi sword, he growled, "Make it swift."

The guard nodded once and with a single stroke severed the child's head from her body. Her blood fountained into the chrysanthemums, staining the golden blossoms a bright crimson.

The young emperor turned away. "Take the kimono and hang it on the palace gate as an example and warning to those who would disobey my will." For a moment, his gaze met that of the Chamberlain, who seemed stunned. *You see, Fujiwara, I have the courage to wield my power justly, no matter that I suffer loss thereby.* The young Emperor continued to walk the rest of the procession as though he had done no more than swat a fly, though his gait might have been swifter and his gaze a trace more distant than before.

That night, the young Emperor did not attend the banquet at which his courtiers would drink chrysanthemum wine and write poetry. Nor did he watch the dances of the Palace Girls or accept their gifts of white trout cooked in sake. Instead, he retired early, claiming weariness from the procession. He did not speak of the execution of his daughter at all. He had the framework golden robe placed on a special wooden rack and set up in the main chamber of his private quarters, "as a memento of this wondrous day," he told his dubious servants. Then, after a light meal, the young Emperor curled up on his tatami mat and drifted off to sleep.

He was awakened by the sound of drops on his shoji. *Ah, an autumn rain.* A voice from elsewhere in his mind said, *The gods weep for Shikiko.* But he rubbed his head and shook the thought away. He propped himself up on one elbow and looked at the translucent paper panels of the shoji, bright with moonlight, hoping to see the pattern of the raindrops. Instead, the drops were dark and thick, going *spat, spat, spat* in a viscous line down the pure white paper as if it were—

The young Emperor sat up and slid the shoji open. He peered outside. There was, indeed, dark liquid dripping down from the eaves. He stepped out onto the veranda and placed a finger into one of the drops and brought it to his nose to be certain. It was blood. He looked up into the eaves, but saw nothing that could be the source. It seemed to come from nowhere.

*This is a Fujiwara trick. They want to disturb my rest and torment me. They have stuck a freshly killed bird in the eaves while I slept. So. I will not let it upset me. Dignity above all.* The young Emperor wiped the blood on his white silk under-robe and walked back into the room, shutting the shoji behind him. He saw a glittering by the far wall, then realized it was only the golden framework robe reflecting stray beams of moonlight. The young Emperor returned to his sleeping mat. But he did not rest well that night. He kept hearing the high-pitched keening of the wind in the bare-boughed trees.

The next morning, the young Emperor rose early, feeling stiff and uncomfortable. He looked at the shoji—it was clean and unstained in the light of the rising sun. *Humph* thought the Emperor, *they even changed the paper while I slept. Clever.* A serving woman entered with his morning meal of rice and pickled vegetables.

"Good morning!" said the young Emperor, trying to sound hearty.

"Yes. Morning, Majesty. If you say it is good, then it is so." As the woman set down the tray before him, she seemed pale and distracted.

"What is the matter, woman?"

She glanced up at him then quickly looked down again. "It is the silk, Majesty. For catching the chrysanthemum dew."

"Well? What about it?"

"We have had to throw it all away, Majesty."

"That seems wasteful. Why?"

"Because we caught no dew, Majesty. Instead, each piece of silk was—" She stopped and put her sleeve to her face to stifle a sob.

"Was dry?" said the young Emperor impatiently.

"Was soaked in blood, Majesty. In blood!"

"Ridiculous!" said the young Emperor, too loudly.

"Yes," said the woman, bowing until her forehead met the floor. "Ridiculous, Majesty. Clearly we were mistaken. All is well. Good morning." The woman shuffled backwards out of the room, still bowing, until she shut the shoji behind her.

*Another bit of trickery*, thought the young Emperor, seething. *Either the Fujiwara talked the woman into telling me this nonsense, or someone splashed all the silk with red ink last night. Perhaps the same one who put the bleeding animal in the eaves.* The Emperor sighed and picked up his chopsticks. And found he had no stomach for eating.

He went through the day pretending nothing was amiss, yet he noticed that the servants and courtiers seemed wary and anxious behind their smiling countenances. There were murmurs of bad luck and inauspicious times. *Ah, it must have been the red ink on the silk. I will give some small acknowledgment to help soothe their disquiet.* So the young Emperor dressed in solemn gray robes that evening and hung ivory prayer tags from his sleeves, announcing that he would sequester himself for a while in prayer and meditation. A message came from his second wife, but he sent it away unread. *It is probably only more hysteria about the silk.*

That night, the young Emperor was again awakened by the sound of *spat, spat, spat* on his shoji. With trepidation, he opened one eye and again saw the dark liquid dripping down the white paper. His pang of fear was quickly replaced with a flash of anger, and he leapt from the sleeping mat, flinging the shoji open. He grabbed his long sword from its stand and stepped outside. He stared up at the eaves a moment, then ran the sword, still in its sheath, up along the underside of the eaves. Nothing was there. The blood came from nowhere, still dripping *spat, spat, spat* down the white paper. The young Emperor took two steps backward and shuddered. Something cool and damp brushed the back of his neck and he whirled around. Nothing was there. But as he looked, he saw wisps and tendrils of mist drifting over the chrysanthemum beds in the garden. Some of them swirled into columns above the flowers, as if they were coalescing into human form.

Before he was quite aware of his actions, the young Emperor was back in his chamber, slamming the shoji closed behind him. He was trembling. *It is nothing. Only tricks, fog and mist.* It occurred to him that as puissant as the Fujiwara were said to be, they were not known to have power over the weather. Something glittered in the dark ahead of him, but it was only the golden framework robe. He flung himself onto his sleeping mat, still clutching the sheathed sword, and curled up with his knees nearly to his chin. "It is nothing. It is nothing," he kept thinking to himself, as he tried to will himself to sleep. But no sleep came.

That morning, on rising, the young Emperor looked again at the shoji. It was clean. And he had heard no one come to replace it. When the serving woman came in with the morning meal, she again looked distracted.

"Well? Is it a good morning, woman?"

"Yes, Majesty. So it would seem."

"What do you mean by that? Do you have any more bloodied silks?"

"No, Majesty. And that is the strange thing. A beggar woman came this morning to take the silk away. And when she held it up, there was no stain at all. She was very pleased and grateful." The woman spoke lightly, staring off at nothing.

"So. The ladies have been foolish. This will be a lesson to them."

"Yes, Majesty." The woman put down the tray and left, saying nothing more.

The young Emperor decided to remain in his chambers that day. *It is the lack of sleep,* he told himself, *that will not let me think clearly.* He decided it would not be seemly to go about in such a state. Another note arrived from his second wife, but the young Emperor put it aside, unread. *No doubt it concerns the miracle with the silk this morning.* He tried to sit in calm contemplation, but found it difficult. He did not want to stare out at the garden. He did not want to look at the gleaming framework cloak on its stand. Staring at the plain wall only invited his mind to bring forth unpleasant scenes. The day felt very long.

Yet, long as it was, when the shoji paper turned golden as an autumn leaf from the light of the setting sun, the young Emperor wished the day would not end, for he did not look forward to the night. He laid himself down and at last drifted off into a restive slumber.

The young Emperor again awoke in the middle of the night to the *spat, spat, spat* of drops on the shoji. Furious, he leapt from his sleeping mat and flung the shoji open. Mists were again coiling among the flower beds in the garden, drifting from the direction of the Plum Pavilion. *The Fujiwara are boiling pots of water in the shadows. I shall find them and give them a scalding for their knavery!*

He grabbed his sword and went running through the gardens, the same route as his procession two days before. At last he arrived at the garden beside the Plum Pavilion, where the mists seemed to gather into a column over the chrysanthemum bed. *I have found you now!* thought the young Emperor, and he swung his sword, still in its sheath, into the flowers. Something caught on it and he pulled the sword out of the mist. Draped over it was a long swath of silk, with a pattern of pink and orange blossoms. The young Emperor realized he was standing on the spot where Shikiko had been killed.

Suddenly the silk rose up off the end of his scabbard and stood on end above the chrysanthemums. Like a piece of origami paper in the hands of a puppeteer, the silk wrapped and folded itself into the shape of a small kimono. A face coalesced out of the mist above it and the sleeves sprouted small white hands.

"Shikiko," whispered the young Emperor.

The apparition stared out over the garden as if watching something. The kimono sleeve lifted and a misty white hand pointed. "Look!" said the apparition in a voice like the echoes of mountain winds. "The Emperor-sama wears no cloak!"

The young Emperor gasped and stepped back.

The apparition floated down to kneel before the flower beds. The kimono loosened around the misty neck. The apparition looked wide-eyed and afraid.

"No," whispered the young Emperor.

The apparition looked straight into his eyes. "Papa-chan?" Then it opened its mouth to scream and the head of mist vanished. The silk dropped to the ground in a heap. It was covered in blood.

As fast as he had come, the young Emperor turned and ran back to his quarters, slamming the shoji shut behind him. He saw a glimmering in the shadows before him, but it was only—

The young Emperor rushed to the stand where hung the golden framework robe. He tore it from the rack, crying, "You thing of evil! This is because of you!" Savagely, he tried to pull it apart, then he fell to his knees, gasping. "Oh, Shikiko, forgive me. My pride was not worth the sacrifice of your life!" He closed his eyes and felt tears rush into them. He lowered his head and sobbed into the cloth in his hands.

The cloth in his hands.

The young Emperor opened his eyes and looked at what he held. It was a ceremonial over-robe of silk embroidered with golden thread. Blue cranes soared over silver clouds in the pattern at the sleeves and hem. A large gold chrysanthemum was stitched in black thread on the back, now divided by a tear in the back seam. "It was truly a robe," he whispered, "truly—"

Something white fluttered out of the sleeve and the young Emperor picked it up. It was the note from his second wife that he had set aside. He opened it now and read,

202 ◆◆◆ Kara Dalkey

*"The tailor did not mean*
*for his shears to cut short*
*the life of a child.*

*"I beg you, my lord, speak to Bakasai again. And do not be*
*angry with him, but listen to what he has to say."*

At once the young Emperor shouted for his servants. When they shuffled in, sleepy eyed and bewildered, he said, "Go to the home of the tailor
Bakasai and bring him to the palace immediately!"

"That is not necessary, Majesty," said one of the servants. "Bakasai has
been sleeping just outside the palace by the Western Gate every night
since . . . since . . ."

"Yes. Good. Bring him here."

When the miserable tailor was brought before the young Emperor, he
flung himself flat against the polished cypress floor as if wanting to melt
into the woodgrain. "Please, Almighty Son of Heaven, forgive this lowly
one! I did not know!"

The Chamberlain Fujiwara Yabuimu swept into the room. "What is
the matter, Majesty? What is all the disturbance?" Then he looked at the
tailor prostrate on the floor and the Fujiwara sank warily to his knees
before the young Emperor.

"I did not know!" wailed the tailor.

"Did not know what?" growled the Fujiwara.

"My Lord, I thought the weaver woman was only boasting and telling
tales when she said what the robe could do. I did not think it could truly
only be seen by the wise and not the foolish."

The Fujiwara rubbed his chin. "Children are sometimes foolish. That
is why adults must teach them. But our Majesty's lesson seems harsher
than most."

"No," said the young Emperor, though it took all his courage to get
the words past his lips. "I am the fool."

The Fujiwara raised his brows slightly. The tailor looked up from the
floor.

"I could not see the robe, Bakasai-san. I saw only a golden framework.
I thought my Chamberlain was . . . having a holiday jest with me. I did not
see the beautiful cloth with the blue cranes and silver clouds until this
very hour."

For a moment there was only stunned silence. Then the tailor covered
his face with his hands. "Forgive me, Great Majesty. I . . . it was never my
intention—"

"No, Bakasai-san. It is I who need to be forgiven. For your skill, I will
see that you are given seven bars of gold and seven bags of rice from the
Imperial Treasury."

When the tailer left them, the young Emperor went over to the

Fujiwara, took his hand and sighed heavily. "Yabuimu-san, from now let us work together in harmony, not in contention."

"Great Majesty," said the Fujiwara, "that is my hope also."

"I shall send investigators to some of the provinces that claim to have been so hard-pressed this year."

The Fujiwara looked at him and lifted a brow.

The young Emperor smiled tightly. "To use too much caution is foolish. But to use no caution at all is distinctly unwise."

The Chamberlain nodded. "I shall remember that, Majesty."

"One more thing, Yabuimu-san. Please send to my second wife appropriate gifts in recognition of her grief, and tell her I shall come to visit her soon, if she is willing to see me. And now I have other matters I must attend to."

The young Emperor crossed the room and put on the golden robe. It felt heavier than when he had worn it for the chrysanthemum procession, but it draped on his form perfectly, a testament to the tailor's skill. He swept past the astonished chamberlain and went directly to the Imperial Shrine in the center of the palace grounds. There he knelt and prayed before the Sacred Mirror, begging his ancestors all the way back to Amaterasu for forgiveness.

He remained there throughout the next day until midnight when he went to the garden of the Plum Pavilion. As the ghost of Shikiko appeared and cried, "Look!" he caught her small cold hand in his.

"Look at me now, Shikiko. Your Emperor-sama wears a robe."

She turned and stared, her mouth wide open. "I am sorry, Papa-chan. I am wrong."

"No, Shikiko-chan. I was wrong. And may your father in your next life be wiser than to put his pride before his child." A tear slid down his cheek as the apparition bowed to him and faded away into the mist.

As the young Emperor turned away, he saw Fujiwara Yabuimu standing at the edge of the garden. The Emperor could not be sure, but it seemed the Imperial Chamberlain, too, had trails of tears on his face.

# Watching the Bobolinks

Caroline Stevermer

♦

When I last went home to the farm, I had a chance to walk in the fields with my father. It was a great pleasure for us both, high summer on the hillside, with the grass deep, almost to our waists, green with a mist of gold laid over it, where the alfalfa and the timothy grass went to seed.

We were watching the bobolinks. Throwing themselves upward on their song, bobolinks arch into the wind and hover, their flight nearly motionless, an equipoise of wings and wind. When the song dies, they drop out of the wind, back to the world, and take up station on the grass itself. A bobolink can perch on a stalk of grass and ride it as it sways in the wind, bending the stalk scarcely more than the wind bends it.

Oh, it was beautiful. We counted twelve pairs. They were yarding up for the flight south. They fly to Brazil and stay there all winter long. But in spring, when the wheel of the year turns to the proper moment, they set off northward again.

On those same small wings that can meet the breeze of high summer and match it, they fly to our hayfield, and after that journey of astonishing length, of amazing speed, they all arrive within a day or two of each other. Then they scatter and they nest. They hatch their eggs and they raise their young, all in our hayfield, until the correct day comes in high summer, when they gather and go back to Brazil, leaving the field empty for another year.

Until this year, the bobolinks troubled my father. They nest in the strips of hay he harvests to feed our cattle and they hatch their young as the timothy grass and the alfalfa blossom. The crop is ready just as the bobolinks are teaching their young to fly.

A day or two of weather makes a lot of difference to a hay crop. Wait too long after the blossoms set and the stalks grow tough and wiry. The virtue of the hay fades visibly.

But mow when the crop is at its peak, and you mow the grass where the bobolinks live. Grown birds rise up before the tractor as *you go, shrieking. Young birds fly in abrupt, dangerous arcs, staggering out of danger or into it.*

*When the hay is cut, the bobolinks don't go back to their nests. They live on the wing for a week or so longer, then the day arrives when they must set forth southward and they are gone, completely gone.*

*And when they return in the spring, the sight of them—coming from so far back to their same strip of hay—lifts the heart. But that lift of the heart is hard to enjoy when, each year, my father knows what he will see. So, come time to make hay, he waits a day, or two days, or as long as he can wait, while the young bobolinks learn to fly. Some years he can't afford to wait to keep the bobolinks from danger. Some years he can't afford to waste a day. But no matter what, the years go by, twenty or thirty or forty, and every year, no matter what, the bobolinks come back.*

*Two years ago, my father had surgery for cancer. Among the changes the cancer demanded, one year ago he put some land into an "Idle Acres" program, setting part of our farm aside to go uncultivated for ten years. In ten years, my father will be seventy-five. In ten years, we hope we will still own our farm. Nothing is certain.*

*But for ten years, one thing is as certain as the law can make it. The land will rest. Unplowed, unseeded, unmown, it will lie undisturbed, season after season.*

*The land my father chose to set aside is the bobolinks' hayfield. This year, the bobolinks taught their young to fly untroubled. This year, the alfalfa and the timothy grass are tough and wiry, burnt green gold by the summer sun. The bobolinks rise from it singing, as they wait for their day, the day they set off together for Brazil.*

*This year, my father and I stood side by side, silent in the deep grass, and watched them. Soon they leave us. For a while.*

Many of us have a favorite fairy tale, one that evokes the dark and bright magic of childhood better than any other. Often that tale will be one that resonates closely with the themes of one's own life. The protagonist in the following story has lost his favorite fairy tale. He's also losing his wife and child, and all that is precious to him. Here we see what fairy tales can mean to a parent rather than a child—although of course all parents contain the child *they* once were, somewhere deep inside.

# The Boy Who Needed Heroes
### ✦ Kristine Kathryn Rusch ✦

en woke up in the morning thinking about the story. Strange that he hadn't thought about it in—what, twenty, twenty-five years? But now, on the morning after Janice had left him, taking little Casey with her, he lay in bed thinking of fairy tales.

He sat up, hugged his knees to his chest. The satin sheets were soft, the room suffused with early morning light. If he closed his eyes, he could imagine Janice in the shower, Casey still sprawled in sleep under her Spiderman comforter. But they were on the road somewhere—Michigan, probably—and he was here, in the remnants of their lives. He had let them go. All the screaming in the world hadn't stopped them—it had just egged Janice on.

In the end, he had stood helplessly by as the Audi pulled out of the driveway, thinking that they would be back.

They had always come back before.

And when they came, he would have a new story for Casey.

The first time Ben had read the story, he had been at his grandmother's house. Grandmother's always seemed like a haven, with her large antique furniture, old photographs, and quilt-covered beds. Her bedroom smelled of mothballs, ointment, and perfume. The rest of the house smelled like baking bread.

The story was in a book he had found in her attic—fairy tales, or perhaps a collection of stories; he didn't know. All he remembered was the tattered green cover, and the mildewy smell that rose from the pages.

It was called "The Boy Who Needed Heroes," and he stared at it for a long time, afraid that the story wouldn't live up to the title. Then he sprawled in the sunshine on his grandmother's bed, let the quilt warm his underside, and read.

"No," he said to the reference librarian later that day, "it's a story about a little boy who goes searching for heroes. He finds a man with a sword, but that man isn't the kind of hero the little boy wants. He finds a king, but that man isn't the kind of hero the little boy wants. Then he finds a merchant, who isn't heroic enough for the little boy, either. The story goes on and on until he finally discovers what he's looking for."

The librarian punched key words and parameters into her computer. She shoved her glasses to the top of her head and pushed aside some papers on her desk. A flourescent hum filled the silence. The library was empty, save for a few students studying for exams.

"It's not in Grimm's," she said, "unless you have the title wrong. And I don't believe it's one of Andersen's or Lang's. Are you sure it's a fairy tale?"

He leaned against the counter, feeling the blond wood dig into his arms. He hadn't worked with a librarian since he was in graduate school. It had been years since he searched for something outside his area. Maybe he had gotten a few of the details wrong. "It begins 'Once upon a time.' I remember it as a fairy tale."

"All right." The woman scrawled some numbers on a piece of paper. She slid the paper across the desk. "These are the reference numbers for the likeliest areas. Look there first. Come back if you don't find anything."

He took the paper, and glanced at the elevator. He had trapped himself in his own specialty, so much so that going to a new floor made him nervous. The librarian was watching him. He didn't like her attitude or her tone. She obviously didn't believe he had remembered a fairy tale. But he did.

Janice always tried to tell him his memory was wrong as well.

Janice. Her name sent a dagger through his heart. No word yet, and it had been a couple days. He had even left a message with her parents, and though they sounded reluctant, they promised to have her call if she and Casey showed up.

"Fourth floor," the librarian said, mistaking his confusion.

He turned, nodded. "Thanks," he said.

He took the elevator to the fourth floor, spent three hours there, and found nothing.

"Are you sure she's not there, Helen?" he asked. Boxes of family treasures surrounded him, old memories scattered across the unvacuumed living-room floor. It had been nearly a week, and still he hadn't heard. They had never been gone this long before.

"I promise, Ben, I'll let you know if she shows up." Janice's mother, Helen, had a tiny voice, and it sounded even tinier across the phone lines from Michigan. Was there a tremor that hadn't been in the voice two days ago?

"I'm sorry to worry you like this," he said, not sorry at all.

"It's okay," Helen said, and that's when he realized what was wrong. It *was* okay. She knew where Janice was.

"If she's not there, Helen, do you have any idea where she might be?" He held his breath. Old memories, smelling of mothballs and must, rose from the boxes.

"No." Helen did sound nervous. "Oh," she said, "that's the doorbell. I promise to let you know, Ben." And with that she hung up.

She was lying. Just like her daughter, she was lying. He slammed his fist against the box, overturned the coffee table, and was satisfied at the clink and clatter. Damn them for conspiring against him. His wife, his daughter, his family. They had no right to leave him.

He kicked the coffee table again and was startled by the sound of breaking glass. He raised the table, saw one of Casey's precious dolls, head smashed beyond recognition. He picked it up, cradled it against him as if it were his own daughter. "Sorry," he whispered. "I'm so sorry."

Dale, the folklore professor, looked like a wizard out of one of the paintings that dominated his office. He was short, squat, with long silver hair and too many teeth. He wore tweed, and kept an elaborate pipe on his desk, more for show than for use. A cat slept on top of the filing cabinet, and books on myths, religions, and fairy tales dominated his shelves.

Ben had never liked Dale much. He acted superior in staff meetings, as if he deserved special treatment because he had a good reputation in his field. He had written a pop nonfiction study of literature, human nature, and fairy tales that outsold both *The Tao of Pooh* and Bettelheim's classic *The Uses of Enchantment*.

Ben could never remember the name of the book.

Yet here he sat, in Mr. Famous's office, asking for help.

"Fairy tales are important to children," Dale was saying, "because they are one of the few literatures of truth. Today's children's literature is beginning to bring fantasy back, along with the harsh issues, but when you and I were children, our parents protected us from the evils of the world. They wouldn't let us read about things that would distress them. Children's literature was pap. Except fairy tales. Fairy tales are filled with tragedy, and with ways to cope."

Ben waved his hand. He hadn't wanted a lecture. He wanted to find the story. "Have you heard of my fairy tale?"

"By that title, no." Dale leaned back on two chair legs, reached up and scratched the chin of the sleeping cat. "And I doubt I've ever seen it. Tell me, Ben. Why did you become an English professor?"

The rage returned, smoldering beneath the surface. He was doing this for Casey, but Casey was gone, stolen by Janice. "I don't know what that has to do with anything."

"I think it has to do with everything. You read a lot as a child. Escaped into imaginary worlds. Created a few of your own?"

The cat raised its head, letting a stream of sunlight through the window. The office smelled faintly musty, like dustballs. Ben wanted out. "You're saying I made the story up."

"Our subconscious works in metaphors, stories, and word play. That's why a particular story or movie may mean more to some people than to others. Have you considered why you quest for this tale now?"

"To share with my daughter." The words were clipped. Ben felt himself stiffen. Dale's question had been much too private.

"And she is what age?"

"Six." A fragile six. Always sick, always complaining. He clenched his fists. Sometimes he didn't know why he wanted his family back.

"And she loves stories?"

"She used to." When Ben told them. *I want a story, Daddy,* Casey used to say, and then she would giggle as her father pulled the covers up to her neck in preparation for the evening's tale. In the past year, though, she would cringe when her father sat on the bed, and when he would offer a story, she glance at her mother for approval, then nod once, lips a thin line.

"But no longer." Dale's voice remained neutral, his expression intense, as if Ben's answer held the secret to all literature.

Ben stood. If he wanted to be psychoanalyzed, he would go to a shrink. "This isn't getting anywhere. I want to know if you've heard of the story, and if not, if you could help me find it. That's all."

"Hmmm." Dale picked up his pipe and stuck it in his teeth. He puffed, even though the pipe wasn't lit. "Thought I was helping."

Ben had found the story at the age of eight. Eight was an age where a boy needed to admire someone, something. He couldn't admire his father. His father had been a large, beefy man who smelled of spoiled fish. A longshoreman with a temper shorter than his name, Ben's father had done nothing heroic.

Ben pressed his hand to his forehead. He hadn't thought of his father since the man had died, nearly fifteen years ago. Ben pushed aside the boxes still littering his living-room floor. The book wasn't inside any of them. He had had Dale call the NYPL information line, and they knew nothing. Dale promised to contact a few other sources, but he had no hopes of the story turning up.

He leaned back, frustration making him shake. The house was filthy. He needed to hire a service. He couldn't believe how Janice had let it go. She had never patched the hole in the wall where his fist smashed the plaster, nor had she scrubbed away the stains Casey had left on the rug before her last trip to the doctor. He should have known Janice was going to leave, just from the way she was letting things go.

The phone rang, and Ben jumped. No one had called since Janice left. His hand hovered over the white receiver. The last time he had answered the phone, home alone like this, it had been the hospital. *Casey's going to be all right,* Janice had said, her tone shaking with fury. *Thank God,* he replied.

He picked up the receiver, cradled its coolness against his ear. "Yes?"

"Ben?" The voice belonged to Helen. She sounded scared. "I heard from Janice. She asked me to call you."

His stomach muscles clenched. He could barely swallow. "Is she all right?"

"She's fine. Little Casey's fine, too. She asked—" Helen's voice broke. He was hearing fear. "—that you not try to find them. She has a lawyer here who will be handling everything. His name is—"

Papers rustled on the other end. Ben couldn't move. A lawyer. But he had told her that marriage was forever. That they could never divorce each other, no matter what happened.

"—Joshua Kutler. He'll be calling you."

"I'll contest it." He was amazed that he could sound so calm.

"She expects that, I think."

"Is she there? Let me talk to her."

"She thinks—she thinks it better that you not know where she and Casey are. Casey almost died the last time—"

He hung up the receiver. Of course, Janice would bring that up. She always threw that in his face. No matter how many times he promised, no matter how hard he tried, she always threatened to have him put away for hurting their little girl.

He looked in the box in front of him, at an old G.I. Joe and a worn-out stuffed dog that stared at him one-eyed. He didn't want to hurt Casey. All he wanted to do was tell her stories.

Ben had never sat in a bar before without taking a drink, but he knew that if he started drinking now he'd never stop. His fingers played with his Coke glass. The bar was nearly empty in the middle of the afternoon. He wondered what he was doing here. It had been a spur-of-the-moment decision when he saw Dale in the hall. Ben had been thinking of Casey and Janice when Dale passed, and half an hour later he found himself in a campus bar sharing drinks and conversation. "What makes you think I made the fairy tale up?" he asked.

Dale took a sip of his Guinness, then leaned back against the rough wood wall. A cloud of cigarette smoke wafted over them from the next table. "Because you remembered the story in such detail, and I wasn't familiar with any of it."

"You're familiar with every fairy tale ever written?"

Dale smiled, ignoring the sarcasm. "No. But I know a great many of them, and I have friends who know the ones I don't know. I've generally found that when we can't track down a story, it doesn't exist."

"This has happened before, then." Water dripped down the side of Ben's glass. He wiped his fingers on his linen pants.

"I've been collecting tales like this for a book I'm doing that should be out next fall. I've seen this a hundred times. Just last week, I had a woman in one of my classes that wanted to write about 'The Lady and the Tiger.' Only her version had a happy-ever-after ending."

"But it doesn't end," Ben said. He remembered reading that story in high school and loving the ambiguous ending. For days he tried to decide who emerged from the closed door—the lady or the tiger.

Dale smiled. "Right. That's the beauty of the tale."

Ben took a sip, frowned at the lemony sweetness. "You're saying I'm like that woman."

"I'm saying you could be." Dale was watching him, little pig eyes appearing over the beer stein.

Ben shivered. Dale made him uncomfortable, as if Dale had the power to uncover all of Ben's secrets—even the ones he kept from himself.

A gust of laughter echoed in the room behind them. Kenny Rogers played on the jukebox. "Tell you what," Dale said. "Write it down. You'll probably have a strong tale that comes from the subconscious."

Ben started to take another sip, then realized that his throat was so tight he couldn't swallow. "What happens if I get it wrong?"

"You won't," Dale said. "I suspect you'll get it just right."

*Once upon a time . . .*

. . . his father used to read to him, huddled on the edge of Ben's bed, smelling of fish and sweat, cigarettes and grease . . .

*. . . there lived a little boy . . .*

Those were the best times, when his father read to him. Otherwise he yelled, or broke things, or slammed his fist into Ben.

*. . . who had no heroes.*

In the stories, someone always saved the beleaguered child. Perhaps a prince, riding in from the north, or a funny-looking little man with a funny name. Ben would wake up in the morning, praying for his hero.

*His mother died while he was still a child . . .*

His mother never protected him. She washed his cuts, told him that his father was under pressure, and turned away when Ben screamed.

*. . . and his father worked day and night, stopping only to sleep and eat.*

The readings ended when Ben started school. He was old enough, his father said, to read to himself. And then there were no more good times.

*The little boy knew that in the night, an evil wizard would get him. He had no one to protect him, with his father away. The little boy needed a hero . . .*

Ben read to himself and discovered stories. Children saved by others, children saved by magic. Children saved by themselves. He loved "The Brave Little Tailor" and "Rapunzel." But when that fist came crashing down, nothing he did saved him.

"Mr. Lockheart?"

Phone voices. He hated phone voices. Ben sat on the couch, clutching a cup of aromatic coffee, broken doll beside him, afghan across his legs. "Yes."

"I'm Joshua Kutler. I'm representing your wife in the matter of your divorce. Do you have a lawyer?"

Weary. He was so weary. Three days with no sleep. He did have a draft of the fairy tale, though. And more understanding than he ever wanted. "No," he said.

"I suggest you get one, sir. Your wife plans to play hardball."

"Hardball?" The words were just beginning to make sense.

"She wants full custody of your daughter, with no visitation rights to you. Child support in excess of $25,000 per year, paid through my office—"

"Wait." Ben ran his hand over his face. His skin felt greasy. "No visitation. You mean I can't see Casey?"

"You can't even know where she is," the laywer said. "So I suggest you get legal assistance. I would prefer to deal with another attorney on this."

"Look." He glanced around the room, looked for assistance in the lamp he and Janice had bought on their honeymoon, in the books scattered across the built-in shelves. There was a hand-sized hole in the wood near the base. He frowned. He couldn't remember that happening. He took a deep breath. "Look," he repeated. "I've been a bastard, and I've hurt my daughter. I'll go into treatment. I'll do anything Janice wants. Only I can't lose them. Please—"

"I'll tell her." The lawyer sounded brusque. He'd heard this before. "Only I doubt it will make any difference."

Ben sucked in air. It had to make a difference. He understood now. He was imitating his father, being his father, and hurting his little girl like his father had hurt him. He would stop. He would make it up to her. If he didn't, maybe she would go on, hurt her own children. "Please . . ."

"I'll send you my card. I expect to hear from your attorney within the week." The lawyer hung up. Ben clutched the receiver, listening to the hum of the wire, then the series of clicks informing him that the call had ended. Soon the operator would come on, asking him to hang up the phone.

He did, gently.

What good did it do, understanding everything? It changed nothing.

Except his perspective.

He got up, flung the afghan aside, and began cleaning up the living-room. If he could get them back, the place had to be clean. And he wanted them back. He wanted them back badly.

He set the coffee table upright, then grabbed the broken doll from the couch, and clutched it to him. Still didn't explain why he woke up thinking about the story after so many years, why he thought it so important to share with Casey.

The doll was like her, fragile, thin. A few more tosses across the room, and there would be no more Casey to share anything with. He had almost killed her the last time. No wonder Janice took her. Janice rescued her . . .

Then he inhaled, bringing with the air a pain so deep that he doubled over. Jealousy and anger. That's why the story came back. Inside him, a little boy lived, a little boy who wanted to be rescued, who grew angry when his wife rescued someone else.

*She was supposed to be my hero,* he thought. *For life. Till death . . .*

That was why he vowed no divorce, why he punished Casey for taking her mother's attention away from him. He sat down, still clutching the doll. This one was too big to handle alone, for inside he was as fragile as Casey.

Janice was supposed to rescue him.

But she was gone, and he was alone.

Like he had always been.

Alone. Without a hero. Unable to save himself.

He put his head down, wishing he had never gone to Dale, wishing he had never tried to understand . . .

. . . He remembered the hole in the bookshelf. Casey had taken his book of fairy tales from the shelf and was smearing it. He had struck at her, but she ducked, and his fingers went through the wood as if it were glass. She had run from him, screaming, and Janice had come out of the kitchen, her eyes a reproach. She hated him. How could she save him when she hated him?

So he would remain, like the lawyer believed. A man stuck in time, with no solutions. He had promised to get help. He had to get help, only no one was coming in on a white horse with an army behind him and magic at his fingertips.

He had to figure out his own rescue.

And he did have someone he could ask.

He hugged his knees to his chest and thought a minute, then stood and returned to the phone.

His fingers dialed almost without thought. "Dale," he said when the professor answered. "I know where the fairy tale comes from, and"—these words were harder—"I know what it means . . ."

# Wolves

Sonia Keizs

♦

In Jamaica I called him Uncle Dud. The ABC book he gave me
spelled happiness along with making mud pies under our stilted
house, terrifying the lizards, climbing the mango tree and making
brown paper kites. When I arrived in England from Jamaica I was
reunited with my mother and Uncle Dud. We had been separated
for a year. He took me aside and said from then on I should call
him Papa Dud. I understood from this change of name that his
status and my relationship to him had also changed, and that it
had to do with a new baby who turned out to be my half-brother.
After five years had passed another baby arrived. Harlesden,
northwest London, was our new home.

It was cold, gray, and smog-consumed, and I grew to love it.
The streets of Victorian terraced houses, named after the poets
Shakespeare, Milton, Carlyle, Shrewsbury, were now populated
by a substantial West Indian community. The houses had strange
smells foreign to my nose, of chips and overcooked cabbage. Our
two-story house, which Papa Dud had secured with three hundred
pounds he earned on a cotton farm in America, was packed solid.
Our family lived in two rooms while the other rooms were rented
out: one to Papa Dud's brother, another to a single man, and a
room each to two couples. The kitchen downstairs was shared except by the upstairs tenants, who used a cooker on the landing.

From the kitchen all sorts of chat and gossip would filter out
along with the aroma of rice and peas and chicken. The "peas"
were actually beans: kidney beans or black-eyed beans seasoned
with coconut cream, thyme and onions and rice added, eaten with
spicy fried chicken. Later on, West Indian food products were im-
ported and breakfast of ackee and saltfish could be eaten just like
back home. Sundays in the kitchen were lively with gossiping,
cooking, and hymn-singing, alternating with high-pitched wailing
renditions of country-western songs, Jim Reeves being a favorite at

*the time. Then the congregation at 28 Carlyle Avenue would say grace, weep silent homesick tears, beg the Lord to have mercy on their souls, and eat heartily.*

*Now, a lifetime later, as I walk along the road to my new home, these old memories of London and Jamaica ride on each other's backs. I look them over, looking for some resemblance to myself so that I can have my young self back again. The road to my house becomes a dirt track, smelling of the heat and dust of Jamaica. Dark, dense trees line my way, allowing only snippets of sunlight through, dappling the path and lifting my spirits. The dirt, dry and terra-cotta, holds the aroma of thyme and rosemary. As I reach the house I can see the rocking chair on the blue verandah. I climb the steps that bring me to the dark coolness of the verandah with its pots of fired earth from which jasmine and honeysuckle fill the space with scent. These scents mingle with the smell of wood resin from the polished wooden floorboards. I move through to a darker, cooler space where, as I open the wooden shutters, sunlight explodes, bouncing off the white walls. In its aftermath the sea breeze from several miles away quietly creeps in and the curtains breathe in and out.*

*Memory is exhaled in a deep sigh. The London street where I used to live stretches and yawns before me again. I see an accident of grazed limbs; their ghostly impressions dangle over silent walls, boundaries between silent front yards and silent pavements. Most of the houses on the street kept their secrets behind their black ballot-box doors and even my imagination could not unlock them, but the secret of one house would reveal itself to me quite soon. Along with other scabby-kneed residents I used to bang hard on these doors. "Knock down ginger" this was called; I never knew why. The sudden loud knocks provoked guilty starts and awakened others from their daydreams, as we ran away to the bomb site down the street to scavenge for more excitement among the broken cars and pointed glass, forgetting our mothers waiting to feed us.*

*Sometimes a friendly knock was followed by "Can Faith come out to play?" Then she would come and we would play on roller skates, carts, and red-and-yellow scooters. We would hopscotch and scuff the chalk numbers scrawled on paving stones. We would juggle balls, bounce balls, beat balls held in stockings against walls, while we overheard the wheeling dealing of young teddy boys. Faith came from a religious family that occasionally took me to meetings. I enjoyed Faith's friendship, but I wasn't so sure about the meetings. Living with Catholic sin and Hell and my mother lamenting if anybody had seen her dying trial was enough; to be a Jehovah's Witness like Faith's parents seemed too much. I did however feel something pleasant when I sang along in her Sunday school and made actions to "Joy, joy, joy/With joy my heart is ringing (or is it wringing?)/My heart is bubbling over/With this joy, joy, joy."*

*One day, one playtime, when I knocked on Faith's door I was told she was not in but that I could wait for her. While I waited for Faith her father laughed and joked and charmed; and I've wondered since: do you call your girl child Faith when you've lost your own? Marveling at the athletic tricks and kicks youngsters could perform, he inquired if I could do these acrobatic turns. I glowed in the pride and pleasure that I certainly could perform them. He asked me to bend over backwards; I was compliant and pliable. When he offered to support me and I felt his hardness against me, an uneasiness enveloped me; and although I didn't know what this hardness meant, an instinct older than my years, older than my mother and her mother before her, older than time, whispered in my ear. It was my only protector. It spoke of Little Red Riding Hood and wolves and fables of deception.*

*I left his house, and the streets were now transformed to jungle paths; the lamp posts were trees for hiding behind, and their lights were shafts of sunlight illuminating the shame of it all, casting shadows. Where wildcat cars roared furiously I saw a solitary wolf, bare breasted, returning from his day's labor. In his clan the girl children were for his own fancy; "I fancy that," he says and takes her. A slow rising fire burned my young face, the redness radiating out in heartbeat pulses. Was it anger or embarrassment that had conjured up that heat? Its haze before my eyes left my friend's father's face a forgotten blur, an ill-defined spot, a blemish diminished and gone.*

*The fire burns down to ash. In ashes there is softness, a cooling transformation. The specks of gray-white particles float on the breeze, then down to the ground, reunited with the earth once more. And so I remember the man now without the heat of anger, but with compassion. The rocking chair soothes, its rhythmic groans send molecules rippling through the floorboards, waving back and forth, back and forth, back.*

*Back to the eve of my womanhood. A hot and bloody school day. It was a lonely rite of passage, reluctantly performed by every young girl. Times were difficult then for my mother and Papa Dud, and the silences they experienced were shattered by flying cups and saucers, crockery falling to the floor. My uncle Des used to visit quite regularly—my favorite uncle, his dark mustachioed face showing some Asian ancestry. He had a bright and charming smile, which he used to his advantage many times. I looked forward to his visits when, on arrival, he would dip his hands into his pocket and offer its abundance to me.*

*On that hot school day he reminded me of my little girl fears, of* how I had been frightened of animals, of dogs. He taunted and teased me and the fear revived itself. "Dawg gwine bite yuh, Soan . . . Mind de dawg doan bite." He laughed. Then he kissed me hard on the lips, taking my breath away and forcing his own into my body. Laughing louder he said it was time I experienced an older man. In that moment a new acquaintance was struck like a slap in the face. Now I was forced to be intimate with the tobacco smell of his breath and hair, intimate with the taste of his saliva and the roughness of his hands. I was infected with shame and went into hiding, avoiding his eyes whenever he came to visit, keeping silent. In that silence the ancestral voices spoke again and reminded me that charm and deception know each other very well. My uncle heard those voices too; he got the message: No Trespassing. I haven't seen him again since he went back to Jamaica twenty-six years ago, but I have forgiven his trespass against me. And I know now to be wary of charm and the smile of the wolf.

The following story takes imagery from "Hansel and Gretel" and several other classic fairy tales, then shapes it into a brand-new story—yet one would swear this too is a tale that has been retold for generations. It tells of the relationship of siblings in an abusive household, and the "survivor's guilt" often felt by siblings who once stood helplessly by while abuse was meted out to another in the family.

# Wolf's Heart

### ◆ Tappan King ◆

Once, long ago, a woodcutter and his wife lived in a cottage by the edge of the wood with two young children, a daughter and a son. The couple was very poor, and there was barely enough food to keep body and soul together from year to year. One winter, a fierce snowstorm came up, cutting the woodcutter's cottage off from the road that led to the town. The woodcutter could no longer sell his wood, and the couple's meager store of food dwindled.

One day, the woodcutter said to his wife:

"Wife, I am hungry and sick to death of porridge. Go and kill the chickens and we will feast."

"But husband," the wife protested, "if we kill the chickens, we will feast tonight and fast tomorrow, for there will be no eggs for ourselves and our little babes."

"Enough!" roared the woodcutter. "Do as I say, or I will cut off your feet with my axe!"

So the woodcutter's wife, fearing for her life, did as she was told, and wrung the chicken's necks and cooked them, and placed them on the table before her husband. But when she went to take a piece of chicken for herself, the woodcutter threw her a chicken bone, saying, "Faithless wife! This is all you deserve for your disobedience!"

In seven days, the woodcutter had eaten all of the chickens. But the woodcutter's wife had saved the pot liquor for herself and her babies, and so they did not starve.

When the chickens were gone, the woodcutter said to his wife:

"Wife, I am hungry and sick to death of chicken. Go and kill the cow and we will feast."

"But husband," the wife answered, "if we kill the cow we will feast tonight and fast tomorrow, for there will be no milk or cheese for ourselves and our little babes."

"Silence!" roared the woodcutter. "Do as I say, or I will cut off your hands with my axe!"

So the woodcutter's wife, with fear in her heart, did as she was told, and struck the cow dead, and butchered it, and served it to her husband. But when she went to take a piece for herself, he struck her and threw her a hoof instead, saying, "Faithless wife! This is all you deserve for your disobedience!"

In a fortnight, the woodcutter had eaten all of the cow. But the woodcutter's wife had saved the blood for herself and her babies, and so they did not starve.

When the last of the cow was gone, the woodcutter said to his wife:

"Wife, I am hungry, as hungry as a man has ever been. Bring me some meat that I might eat."

"But husband," she answered, "we have killed the chickens and the cow, and there is no more meat to eat."

"Be still!" he roared. "Then go and kill our two young babes and we will feast!"

"I would rather die myself than kill our two young babes," she answered.

"Do as I say, or I will cut your head off with my axe!" cried the woodcutter.

But the woodcutter's wife would not kill her children. Fearing for their lives, she put them in a basket made of rushes, and took them out into the wood, and left them under a great oak tree. "Perhaps the spirits of the wood will take pity on you, and find you here," she said, "for I can do no more."

And when she came back, she carved an image of the children out of a log, and served it to her husband. But when he bit into the wooden children, he got splinters in his mouth, and flew into a rage, and struck off her head with his axe. And where the poor woman's blood flowed into the snow, roses bloomed there the next spring. Soon thereafter, the woodcutter starved to death, for there was no one to care for him; and the rats gnawed on his bones.

Now in the depths of the wood there lived an old wolf bitch whose cubs had died in the storm. One day, as she was coming back from a fruitless day of hunting, she smelled the two children in the basket under the tree.

"What is this?" she asked. "Is it meat or mate?" And because her eyesight was poor, she thought she saw two wolf cubs lying in the basket.

"The poor darlings!" she cried. "I will take them home with me." So she took the basket in her mouth and brought them home to her den. Soon after, the wolf bitch realized her mistake, but because they were small and helpless, she decided to raise the children as her own. The girl she named Thistle, for her hair was like thistledown, and the boy she named Thorn, for he had once pulled a thorn from her coat.

A fortnight later, her mate came home from many days hunting. And when he smelled the two babies, his mouth began to water. "I smell sweet young meat!" he growled. "Give it to me!" But the old bitch quickly wrapped the babies in the skins of her dead cubs, and passed them under the wolf's nose.

"You old fool!" she cried. "Don't you know your own cubs? See the fine ears and long tails? How could cubs as handsome as these be anything but your own?"

The wolf, flattered by her words and confused by the smells, turned aside and let them stay. And the wolf bitch spoke to Thistle and Thorn in the language of wolves, saying:

"From this day forth you must always wear these skins when my mate is at home. For if he finds you without them, he will surely devour you whole!" And the children, frightened of the great wolf, did as they were told.

When they were old enough, the wolf bitch took Thistle and Thorn out hunting with her, clad in the skins of her dead cubs. They learned to kill without mercy and take what they needed, and they grew up as wolves are raised, fast and fierce, and cunning and strong.

One day, Thistle and Thorn came home from hunting to find the wolf bitch lying on the ground, with an arrow through the heart.

"A hunter has killed me," she cried. And Thorn began to cry, and Thistle to weep. But the wolf bitch told them sternly: "Listen to me! When I am dead, you must skin me, and share my skin between you, and wear it so that my mate will not know you are human children." For the children had long since outgrown the skins of the wolf cubs.

And when she died, the two children cried loud and long, and then did as she bid them with her dying wish, and dressed themselves in her skin.

For a long time, they were able to fool the wolf. But one fine spring day, he returned home from many days of hunting to find Thistle and Thorn playing naked in the sun, without the wolf skin on.

"I smell sweet young meat!" he cried, and sprang upon Thorn, who was nearest. But Thistle threw herself between the wolf and her brother, calling out:

> *"Run, Thorn! Run away!*
> *I will keep the wolf at bay!"*

And the wolf turned upon Thistle, and Thorn was able to escape. But the wolf was too fast, and Thistle was unable to outrun the wolf. Thorn wanted to save his sister, but his heart was filled with fear of the great wolf, and so he ran away instead. And the wolf swallowed Thistle whole, and then ran after Thorn.

Now a hunter, who was hunting in the wood, heard Thorn's cries, and found the boy, with the wolf at his throat, at the door of the woodcutter's cottage at the edge of the wood. Seizing the woodcutter's axe, the hunter cut the wolf open, and Thistle sprang out alive. And the hunter took the wolf's skin as a trophy, and brought the two children home with him to the town where he lived.

The hunter and his wife adopted Thorn as their own child, for he was as fair of face as an angel, but they scorned Thistle, for her face had been marked and scarred by the sharp teeth of the wolf. And when they asked her how she had come by the scars, she would not speak, so they banished her to the stables, where she lived among the animals like a dumb beast, and cared for them.

Thorn never came to see his sister there, for the scars on her face reminded him of his fear, and her wretched condition filled him with shame. And because he could not speak of his shame, his heart grew hard and cold.

As Thorn grew into a young man, the hunter taught him to hunt. And because he had lived as an animal and knew their ways, Thorn soon became the greatest hunter in all of that kingdom. All of the young men of that town admired Thorn for his courage and skill at hunting, and longed for his friendship. And all of the young women dreamed of him, and hoped he would ask for their hand. But he would have none of them, for his heart was as hard as stone.

By day, Thorn would go out into the woods with his quiver and bow, and bring back game for the village. But by night, he would put on the wolf's skin, and go hunting as a wolf beneath the silvery moon, killing deer and cattle, and sometimes, when the blood lust was upon him, peasants who had strayed too far from the town.

Now the fairest woman in all that country was a young princess called Elisande, who was as good of heart as she was beautiful, and as fair as she was wise. Of all the women in that town, only she had a kind word for poor Thistle, and often brought her cakes and tea while she worked in the stables.

The moment he saw her, Thorn wanted Elisande for his own, and he went to the king to ask for her hand. And though he was fair of face, and charming, and renowned throughout the kingdom, the princess feared him, for reasons she could not explain.

"Elisande, Elisande!" cried her father the king. "It is time and long past that you should be wed. For three hot summers and three long winters you have been courted by the finest and fairest lads in all the kingdom, and you will have none of them. What will it take to please you?"

"By the law of this land, my husband will one day be king," Elisande answered. "To be worthy of that office, the man that I marry must be at once as brave as a lion and as gentle as a lamb, as strong as an oak and as tender as a reed."

"Daughter, be reasonable!" cried the king. "There is no man in all the world who is all these things at once. This young man seems stronger than some, and braver than most. What will I tell him?

"For seven long years, a great, fierce wolf has roamed this land, killing cattle and deer, and filling the people with fear," Elisande answered. "The greatest hunters in all this kingdom have hunted it, by day and by night, but none has ever captured it. Tell the young man this: Only he who brings me the heart of this wolf will have my own."

The king summoned Thorn, and told him what the princess had said. When Thorn heard Elisande's words, he howled in agony, for though his heart was hard and cold, he loved Elisande more than life itself.

That night, he ranged over all the countryside, but he could not find a wild wolf to kill. So he slew one of the king's own deer, and tore out its heart, and brought it next morning to the king.

"Sire, I have slain the wolf, and here is its heart," said Thorn. "Pray, honor your word and give me your daughter's hand."

The king brought the heart to his daughter, but she held him off, saying, "Tell him to return at cock's crow tomorrow, and I will give him his answer." The king sent Thorn away, and the princess went to the stable where Thistle toiled, and showed her the heart.

"Tell me, you who are wise in the ways of birds and beasts, whose heart is this?"

Thistle could not speak but she could sing. And she answered:

> *"It is not a wolf's heart you hold here,*
> *Thorn has brought you the heart of a deer."*

The princess returned to the castle, and told her father what Thistle had said. When Thorn returned at first light the next morning for his answer, the king cried angrily: "How dare you try to deceive my daughter!"

"Last night the sky was dark, and my arrow missed its mark," Thorn answered. "But tonight, by the love I bear your daughter, I swear I will slay the wolf."

That night, Thorn hunted twice as far and twice as wide, but could not find a wild wolf to kill. So just before dawn, he slew his finest hunting hound, and tore out its heart, and brought it to the king.

"Tonight I have slain the wolf, and brought you its heart," said Thorn. "Now you must honor your word and give me your daughter's hand."

Again the king brought the heart to his daughter, but again she put him off, saying, "Tell him to return at cock's crow tomorrow, and I will give him his answer." The king sent Thorn away, and the princess went again to Thistle's stable, and showed her the heart.

"Tell me, you who know the ways of every living thing, whose heart is this?"

And Thistle sang:

> "This is no wolf's heart Thorn has found,
> The heart you hold is the heart of a hound."

When the princess told her father what Thistle had said, the king told Thorn angrily, "Twice you have attempted to deceive my daughter. Now I say this. If you do not bring me the wolf's heart by cock's crow tomorrow, you will lose not only Elisande's hand, but your life as well!"

The king's words filled Thorn with grief and fear. That night he roamed far and wide across the kingdom, searching for a wild wolf whose heart he could steal, but his quest was fruitless. And because the king's men were hunting him, he sought refuge at last in the stable where his sister Thistle lived.

The king's men found him at first light, asleep on the hay, naked save for the wolf's skin that covered him, and summoned the king. When the king came with his daughter to the stable, he ordered Thorn to stand.

"Get up, you scoundrel, and prepare to die!" cried the king. "Twice your life is forfeit to me—once for your wanton slaughter, and twice for deceiving my daughter!"

Thorn rose slowly, covering his nakedness with the wolf's skin. Thistle placed herself between her brother and the king, but Thorn put her gently aside, and spoke to the king, and to Elisande, tears flowing from his eyes for the first time in many years:

"Though dawn has broken, the cock has not yet crowed," he said. "I have given you my word that I would bring you the heart of a wolf, and while I live I will keep that word."

So saying, he plunged his hunting knife into his own heart, crying:

> "I have kept my word to the one I love best.
> The wolf's heart lies within my own breast."

As he fell, his sister, Thistle, knelt beside him. And the blood from his heart and the tears from his eyes washed the scars from her face, though they left deep marks on his own. And from that day forward, Thistle could speak again, and when the story of her ordeal was told, she was loved and honored by all the people in the village.

Now you may think that Thorn died from that wound in his heart, and indeed, for many a day he lay as one dead in that stable. But Elisande, who was indeed a wise woman, nursed him back to health. And the next spring, when he had recovered, she pleaded with her father to pardon him for all the harm he had done.

"But Elisande," her father protested. "This man is as scarred on the inside as he is without. He has lived as an animal, hard and fierce, and cold and cruel. Why do you waste your pity on a man such as this?"

"A man whose heart is filled with rage and fear and shame, but does not know it, has a wolf's heart, Father," she answered with a smile. "But a man who has felt rage and fear and shame, and has cut his heart with his own hand, is at once as brave as a lion and as gentle as a lamb, as strong as an oak and as tender as a reed."

And, in time, Thorn and Elisande were married, and became king and queen of that realm. And if they were not the best rulers that kingdom had ever seen, they were surely not the worst. And if they did not live happily ever after, they were not so unhappy as most. And he that can claim better, may God bless him, and the Devil not call him a liar.

# The Story I Hadn't Planned to Write
### ♦  Tappan King  ♦

"Wolf's Heart" wasn't the story I was planning to write.

When Terri Windling invited me to submit a story for this anthology, I accepted immediately, even though I had no clear idea what tale I would tell.

I knew that I wanted to explore some basic issues that men from abusive backgrounds share, especially men whose female relatives are also abused: the accommodations they make just to survive; the "survivor guilt" they experience if their abuse is less harsh simply because they are male; the powerlessness and shame they feel when they are unable to protect their sisters; and the deadening of feeling that occurs when they can't acknowledge those emotions, especially in a male culture where weakness is condemned.

The result, for many men with this sort of history, is a division of the personality into a day self that is pleasant and accommodating, and a night self that is given license to express forbidden rage through such avenues as irresponsibility, substance abuse, and violence. Some men yield entirely to their night selves, becoming abusers themselves.

I've come to believe that the only way to heal these kinds of wounds is to know, and embrace, that night self. There's a dangerous notion current in our society today that to be good is to be innocent, unaware of the darker side of the world around us, and ourselves. This idea enables all

226 ◆◆◆ Tappan King

manner of evil, including the cycle of abuse, by allowing us to deny that we are responsible for the actions of that darker side.

I believe goodness comes instead from self-knowledge. If we admit to ourselves that we possess and have control over the power to hurt others as well as to help them, and then deliberately choose not to exercise that power in a harmful way, we regain and reintegrate both sides of our nature.

The story I'd chosen to write to illustrate those points was going to be a contemporary fantasy about an ambitious young filmmaker who uses an old fairy tale he read when he was young as the basis for a low-budget supernatural thriller. The making of the film invokes the ghost of his older sister, who killed herself when he was in his teens. She forces him to recall, and confront, the abuse they both received as children from their father, a well-known actor.

Weeks went by, and I couldn't bring myself to write the story. Part of the problem was that I couldn't find a fairy tale like the one I recalled from my own childhood, of a boy and girl raised by wolves in the heart of a forest. I began to realize that I had to create (or re-create) that fairy tale before I could write the story itself.

One afternoon, a few hours before a meeting of a writer's group Terri Windling and I both belong to, I sat down and wrote the first half of "Wolf's Heart," and brought it to the group. I finished it the following week.

Shortly afterward, Terri asked me if I'd be willing to submit "Wolf's Heart" itself for the anthology. I was surprised at first, until I realized that everything I'd been struggling to express in the modern story was there in the fairy tale.

# Gretel in Darkness

## Louise Gluck

♦

This is the world we wanted.
All who would have seen us dead
are dead. I hear the witch's cry
break in the moonlight through a sheet
of sugar. God rewards.
Her tongue shrivels into gas . . .

        Now far from women's arms
and memory of women, in our father's hut
we sleep, we are never hungry.
Why do I not forget?
My father bars the door, bars harm
from the house, and it is years.

No one remembers. Even you, my brother,
summer afternoons you look at me as though
you meant to leave,
as though it never happened.
But I killed for you. I see armed firs,
the spires of that gleaming kiln . . .

Nights I turn to you to hold me
but you are not there.
Am I alone? Spies
hiss in the stillness, Hansel,
we are there still and it is real, real
that black forest and the fire in earnest.

One of the most painful things a child can deal with is to be noticeably different than other children. Children who are handicapped (or visibly scarred, or invisibly damaged) require extra courage when they cross the rough terrain of childhood—and the difficulties they encounter don't necessarily disappear when they grow up. Instead they must find a way to face these difficulties with strength and ingenuity. The following story is a new fairy tale woven together with imagery from the old ones. It's a story we can all relate to, for we've all felt "different" at some point in our lives; we've all been the one-eyed weaver.

# The Lily and the Weaver's Heart

### ♦ Nancy Etchemendy ♦

When one-eyed Jacinth was ten years old and had just begun to weave tapestries, her mother took her and her two sisters to see the young men of Aranho set off in search of lilies. Jacinth pressed close to her mother as they stood in the noisy crowd at the edge of the village. Sunshine fell down like golden thread from a cloudless summer sky, and the thick grass of the meadows lay heavy with morning dew. Even the straw roofs of the houses and shops seemed bright and magical as Jacinth watched the parade of Aranho's tall, handsome youths. Some of them had hair the color of flax, and others had hair as dark as ravens' feathers. Some sported the soft beards of early manhood, and others had shaven chins. They carried pouches of fragrant bread at their belts, and their knives and bows flashed gaily as they passed. They walked with their shoulders swaying, like men who are glad to be off and expect to return triumphant.

As she watched, Jacinth thought of the tapestry that hung unfinished on her loom at home. She had already woven into it a picture of her father grinding flour at his mill. Now she wondered if she could add this street, and the stone cottages, and the lines of proud young men striding away on their adventure.

Jacinth's older sister, Wynna, rose on her tiptoes, lifting both hands in the air. "There goes Sten!" she cried. "I see him!" Then louder, "Good luck, Sten. Bring me a lily. I'll be waiting."

From the far edge of the passing ranks, Jacinth could just make out a strong, tan arm waving in reply.

"What does a lily look like?" she asked, for in fact she had never seen one, and now she wondered if the lilies themselves could also be added to the scene in the tapestry.

"A lily looks like a bell," said her mother. "A very beautiful bell, yellow as fire or ripe peaches or the sun when it rises."

Jacinth frowned, trying hard to imagine such a flower. "Why does Wynna want Sten to bring her one? Just because it's pretty?" she asked.

Wynna looked down at her and smiled and ruffled her hair. "It's more than that," she said. "You'll find out someday."

But Jacinth's older sister, Noa, who was fourteen and jealous of Jacinth's weavings, grinned wickedly and said, "No you won't. You'll never find out, old one-eye, because you're ugly, and nobody will ever want to bring *you* a lily!"

Jacinth ran her fingers across the familiar smooth skin where her left eye should have been. She remembered how her own reflection had made her run screaming from the still water of the millpond the first time she had seen it. And she knew Noa was right. She was ugly, and all the best things in the world, even flowers, were reserved for the beautiful. She bolted, covering her terrible face with her arms, heedless of her mother and Wynna as they cried, "Come back! Noa didn't mean it."

Jacinth ran alone through the deserted streets. The tears in her single eye dimmed the sun. The world, so bright with possibilities a moment before, seemed dark and frightening now. Rounding a corner, she lost her footing and hit the ground in a shower of dirt. Over and over she rolled, until she came to rest against a stone doorstep. There she lay weeping. Dust stung her nose and throat. Her knees and elbows throbbed where she had scraped them in her fall. But the greatest pain of all lodged in her heart, where Noa's words repeated themselves insistently.

Just then, she heard a voice above her.

"Are you all right?"

Jacinth raised her head. From between the dusty strands of her hair, she saw a well-made shoe and the tips of two wooden crutches. Raising her head a bit further, she saw that the shoe fit a foot that was attached to a sturdy leg that was attached to a boy. The boy was clothed in brown wool—coarse, patched, and poorly spun, but clean. He had only one leg. Still, he was tall, and Jacinth could see that he was older than she, perhaps Noa's age.

"Are you all right?" he asked again.

She sat up and brushed her hair away from her face, waiting for his eyes to widen when he realized that she didn't look like other people. But his expression stayed the same. His pale brow was slightly furrowed, and his clear hazel eyes shone bright with concern.

With the back of her hand, she wiped the tears away. "Don't I scare you?" she said.

The boy looked surprised. "Well, I was afraid you had hurt yourself."

"Oh, I *did*," said Jacinth, proudly displaying her bloody elbows.

The boy pursed his lips, which made him look much more grown up than he really was. "Wait here," he said. "I'll get some water and a cloth. My master says it's bad to leave dirt in a scrape."

He turned and hobbled off into the house, which she now recognized as the shop of Bot the cobbler. A few minutes later, he returned with a crockery bowl of cool water and a scrap of soft cloth. He stacked his crutches and, with surprisingly little trouble, sat down beside her on the doorstep. Gently, he took one of her elbows in his slender hands and began to clean the bits of gravel and blood from it.

"You're Jacinth, the miller's daughter, aren't you?" he said. "I've seen you before, and I've heard my master talk about your weavings."

Jacinth nodded, suddenly afraid to speak for fear the tears would start again. If he had seen her before, that explained why her face hadn't frightened him.

"My name is Joth," he said. "I . . . I'm the cobbler's apprentice." Color rose suddenly in his cheeks and he looked away from her, giving more attention to her elbow than it required.

She watched him silently, wondering at his strange behavior.

Joth dipped the cloth in the water and looked up again. "You didn't laugh," he said.

"Why should I laugh?"

Joth shrugged. "Most people think it's funny that a boy with only one foot makes shoes."

Something about Joth's words gave Jacinth a soft, warm feeling, as if a meadow full of buttercups had bloomed inside her. She looked at him, wondering if she could find some hint of a lie or a trick meant to make her trust him when she shouldn't. But his clear eyes seemed kind and honest.

At last she said, "I know. People think it's funny that a girl with only one eye should weave tapestries, or go to see the lily hunt begin, too." She looked off toward the center of Aranho, where she knew the handsome young men must still be striding through the street on their way to the lilies that grew in the faraway forests. When she looked at Joth again, he was resting his chin in his hands and staring sadly away in the same direction.

Jacinth felt the tide of tears rising in her once more. "My sister says that no one will ever bring me a lily. She says I'm too ugly."

Joth sat up straight and smiled at her as softly as the last light of dusk. "I don't think you're ugly," he said. "I would bring you a lily if I had two good legs."

The strongest dike ever built could not have held back Jacinth's tears then. The hot salty stream of them poured down her cheek as she stumbled up from the doorstep. She didn't know whether to hug Joth or run. She wanted to believe him. But no one had ever said such a thing to her before. What if he were lying? What if this were his way of making fun of her?

"Don't cry, Jacinth. Please don't," said Joth.

But she couldn't stop, and not knowing what else to do, she fled down the steps and into the street.

"It's true, Jacinth. You're not ugly," Joth called after her.

"I don't believe you!" she cried, without looking back.

Barely a week had passed when the first of the young men returned to Aranho, scruffy and mud-smeared but triumphant, bearing orange and yellow lilies like torches in their hands. That very evening, there was a proud, firm knock at the miller's door. Jacinth ran after Wynna as she hurried to answer it. There stood Sten, tall as clouds, the first stars strung like diamonds in the violet sky behind him. He smiled as he held out a flower on a leafy stem. Even the twilight could not rob the lily of its amber brilliance.

"Yes. Oh, yes," whispered Wynna as she took it from him.

Jacinth watched as they walked arm-in-arm down the stone path to the gate, their bodies swaying together like stalks of wheat in the wind, and their faces aglow with mysterious joy. She thought of the scene in her tapestry—her father at his mill, the streets and the white cottages, the tall men with their knives and bows. She thought of Joth, and of what he had said to her. And for the first time, the deep winter coldness that would someday become old and familiar settled over her heart. For the first time, it occurred to her that perhaps there was no place at all in the tapestry for a boy with one leg, no place for a girl with one eye.

Soon enough, autumn came, and the citizens of Aranho prepared for the Great Wedding. The men stalked the fields in search of tender young deer, and the fattest pigs in the village were slaughtered. The women gossiped amiably among themselves as they sewed wedding costumes and cooked spicy dishes of squash, grain, and apples. Even the children ran errands and gathered branches laden with bright leaves for the marriage beds. Many of the men who had returned from the hunt with lilies that year were to be married. Sten and Wynna were among the new couples who danced in the wedding circle and drank from the high elder's cup of secret wine.

After the wedding, Sten took Wynna away to the cottage he had built for them. The miller waved good-bye, his shoulders square and a smile of pride on his face. His wife wept, though she could not say why. And Noa ran at the newlyweds' heels like a puppy, begging them to invite her often to the new house.

But Jacinth went off by herself and climbed quietly to her loft in the rafters above the millstones. She cut the unfinished tapestry from her loom, rolled it up, tied it carefully with strong twine, and carried it to a dark corner where it stood untouched for many years thereafter.

◆◆◆

Summer followed summer, and Jacinth watched the passage of many lily hunts, many triumphant returns, and many weddings. Three years after Wynna's marriage, there was another knock at the door one midsummer's dusk, and then Noa was gone, too, off into the world with a lily in her hand and a man beside her. With each year, Jacinth felt herself changing into a woman, cherishing a woman's hopes and desires. But each year the chill in her heart grew a little deeper, and the anger and energy with which she faced the world grew a little stronger.

At last, the time for her own lily went by, as she had feared it would, without event. After the Great Wedding that year, she trudged back toward her father's mill alone, tearing the garlands from her long hair and wishing she could tear away the maiden's gown she wore as well. As it happened, she passed the cobbler's shop on her way, and there stood Joth on the doorstep. He had grown taller in the time that had passed, and his kind hazel eyes were set in a leaner face, with a jaw more firm and knowing than she remembered. His crutches were propped beneath his arms and he held a jar of dark ale in his hands. He was smiling.

"Hello, Jacinth. It was a fine day for the wedding, wasn't it?" he said.

"If you like that sort of thing," she replied.

Joth held out his jar. "Will you have a drink of ale with me, to wish the newlyweds well?"

But Jacinth's frustrations swept over her head like angry water, and she shouted, "How can you be so gay about it? Don't you see that there's no place for us here? Half the roads in the world are closed to us for no good reason at all!"

She started to run, her head awhirl with her own cares. But the clash of breaking crockery in the road behind her made her stop. She turned.

There lay the ale jar, a heap of shattered fragments in a dark brown pool. Joth's eyes were wet and bright, and his body as taut as a bowstring. "Then what are we to do?" he cried. "Lie down and die? I would rather make my own roads!"

He spun on his one leg and disappeared into the cobbler's shop.

All through the smoky autumn and the winter, Jacinth spent her days alone in the meads and thickets, foraging for bark and stones and roots with which to dye her yarns. At night, she lit candles in the chilly loft and sat at her loom while the wind rushed across the meadows and through the brittle trees outside. She worked as if a demon lived inside her. Her fingers grew stiff and raw, and thin lines creased her forehead from the effort of peering at close work with her single eye. Only when the sun rose and the candles had turned to stubs did she ever give in to sleep, for she hated the dreams that came to her, and awoke from them weeping.

The tapestries she wove in that long, dark season became her only respite. When her heart thrashed like a desperate bird, when she could not face her lonely bed, she wove tapestries, and they were like no others.

They were filled with all the power, beauty, and pain that had no other way of escaping from her. She spun fabulous worlds, told impossible tales, and the people she wove danced and wept as if they were alive.

When the weather began to soften and the air to grow rich with the smells of green buds, a merchant came to the miller's door. He said that in his village, which lay two days' ride to the west, he had heard rumors of the one-eyed weaver of Aranho. He asked to see the tapestries, and when Jacinth showed them to him, he bought several, paying her well for them.

The next afternoon, Jacinth sat in the dappled sunlight beneath a willow tree and bounced Wynna's children on her knee. They were used to her, and thought nothing of the fact that their aunt had an eyeless cheek. They spoke to her and laughed as if she were anyone else. Jacinth felt the fragrant spring breeze touch her. She thought of her good fortune with the merchant, and of the places and futures she had woven into the tapestries. It came to her that perhaps Joth was right. Perhaps even a woman with one eye, if she were strong enough, could make her own roads.

That summer, Jacinth watched a man build a new cottage. As she observed him, she took careful stock of the money she had made from the sale of her tapestries. When the man was finished and she had learned all she could from watching him, she set about making a cottage for herself. She chose a small piece of land near a creek on the outskirts of Aranho, and she bought a few tools. From a glazier who lived nearby, she purchased six round pats of thick, bubbly glass with which to make a window.

The work of building a house was not easy. The sun reddened her skin, and the tools slipped sometimes and bit into her weary hands. She made mistakes, for she had to learn as she went along. At first, the villagers laughed and jeered at her because it was unheard-of for a woman to build her own house. They said that Jacinth must wish she were a man. Noa ordered her to stop, for her actions were unseemly and embarrassing. But Jacinth only smiled and went on.

When it became clear that her project would succeed, the villagers stopped laughing and grew sullen. Still she worked, and before the summer ended, she moved her loom from the loft above the millstones to her own snug cottage with its thick window, straw roof, and warm hearth. In a corner by the fire, she propped the unfinished tapestry she had cut from the loom so many years before. There it stood, where she could always see it.

By the time the leaves changed color, the world seemed a different place to Jacinth. Her senses, which had for so long been deadened by her sorrow, began to awaken again. When she wandered in the groves and fields in search of dyestuffs, the songs of hidden birds swept over her like wind, and the autumn sun made her body tingle with pleasure. The smells of soil and ripe fruit and leaf mold no longer made her think of wintry death. Instead, they seemed a part of something wonderful and vast, a ritual of the earth much larger and more lasting than those of men. She gathered berries and insects and flowers that she had never noticed before, and the dyes they yielded gave her a palette like that of no other weaver in the land. When winter came, all the corners and nooks of her house were stuffed with skeins of yarn in every color, ready to be threaded into warp and weft and woven into the images of Jacinth's heart.

While the snow fell and the sharp wind blew it into drifts, Jacinth sat at her loom. She worked long hours every day, stopping only when she needed firewood or food, or when her eye grew too tired to decipher the threads before her. In the cheerful warmth of the cottage, her fingers stayed supple much longer than they had in the drafty mill loft. From dawn till dusk, the well-made window let in winter's pale light, which served her much better than the flames of tallow candles had. Jacinth finished tapestry after tapestry, each one alive and powerful in its own right, each one an improvement on the last.

When the ice and snow began to melt and the first green shoots of grass pushed up from the muddy fields, three men came to Aranho asking for the one-eyed weaver. Two of the men were ordinary merchants who had driven donkey carts from villages in the nearby countryside. But the third man wore rich clothes and rode a glossy black horse.

"I am here in the service of a wealthy nobleman," he said. "My master asked me to pay you for some tapestries to warm the stone walls of his house."

Jacinth shrugged and spread her winter's work in the sun for the men to see. Then she watched with her arms crossed and her lips pressed tightly together as they argued and compromised with one another over who was to get which of the pieces. A part of her felt elated and triumphant at this evidence of her success. But the old bitterness still lay inside her like a small, sharp jewel. And the part of her which cherished it could not forget that although men might desire her tapestries, they had never desired the woman who wove them.

The next week, Jacinth took her dye pot to a sunny glade near the creek. She filled the pot with water and set it to boil over an open fire, then went about gathering enough meadow flowers to make a good yellow dye. As she stopped to pick a handful of wild mustard, she heard someone whistling in a tuneless and preoccupied way among the linden trees that grew by the water. She stood up to see who it could be, and the whistling stopped.

"Jacinth, is that you?" someone called.

She recognized Joth hobbling toward her over the muddy spring soil. She sighed, for in a small, mean way, she resented the fact that no one except another cripple ever took the trouble to greet her with such kindness. Nevertheless, the air was so sweet and warm and the songs of the robins so bright that she made up her mind to be friendly in return.

"Hello," she said. "What brings you to the creek today?"

"Cobbler's reeds," he said, standing still before her with the sun in his hair. "Old Bot sent me to see if there will be enough cobbler's reeds this year to make shoes for those who can't afford leather."

Jacinth dropped the mustard flowers into her basket, and she and Joth wandered toward the waiting dye pot. "And what will you tell him? Will there be enough reeds?"

Joth nodded. "A sizable crop. And what brings you to the creek?"

"Yellow dye." Jacinth motioned toward the flowers that lay in her basket like a mound of captured sunlight, bees whirring above them in a single-minded search for pollen.

When they reached the dye pot, Jacinth shooed the bees away and tipped the basket up. Joth, with his crutches tucked under his arms, scooped the fragrant harvest into the boiling water for her. He lay down in the grass and, chewing on a single leafy blade, watched her stir the dye with a stick and carefully add unspun flax to it. The water hissed and bubbled.

In the drowsy afternoon, Joth began to talk, slowly and idly, laughing now and then, about leather and lasts and awls, and about his childhood in the house of Bot the cobbler. Much to her astonishment, Jacinth found herself speaking in return. She told him about the little round beetles from which she made her best blue dye, and about the long winter of weaving and the light that came through her window.

Shadows were thin and the air had grown chilly when Joth looked down at his hands and said, "I'm sorry. You must think I'm a silly fool to lie in the grass all day and bother you when you are busy with your work."

Jacinth glanced at him and smiled, for his solemn frown looked out of place beside the foxtails that rode here and there among the strands of his shining hair.

"Not at all," she said. "No one has ever spoken to me that way before. And I've never spoken to anyone as I have to you just now, except perhaps in dreams." She felt her cheeks redden, and she brushed her face with the full sleeve of her blouse, as if to wipe away steam from the dye pot.

Joth reached for his crutches and began the slow process of standing up. Jacinth offered him her arm, and he leaned against her as he rose. She felt the warmth of his strong hands on her shoulder, and remembered how gently he had cleaned the gravel from her elbows when they were children.

"I'll be back a week from today," he said, "to check the reeds again. Perhaps I'll see you."

"Perhaps," said Jacinth, and she waved to him as he started across the field toward Aranho. When he had dwindled to a small, limping figure in the distance, she sat down by the fire and picked up a stick. Staring after him, she stirred the ruddy embers beneath the dye pot into a confusion of hungry flames.

They met many times in the field beside the creek that spring. Joth came more and more often to check the reeds, and Jacinth found reasons, no matter how small, to gather whatever flowers were blooming in the meadow. In the long afternoons, only the birds and the buzzing insects heard the murmur of two human voices in the glens and linden groves. As spring turned into summer, Joth and Jacinth spoke to each other first like gregarious children, then like old friends. By and by, they spoke almost without words.

The first month of summer was nearly through when Jacinth recognized the longing that welled up in them both. They lay beside the creek, propped on their elbows, facing each other. Joth tickled her lips with a long blade of timothy. Then softly, with his finger tips, he stroked her hair and her cheek and the smooth hollow above it, which no one but Jacinth had ever touched before. She closed her eye, and felt the large wetness of tears forming there, and did not know whether joy brought them, or confusion, or knowledge that the time was not yet right.

Jacinth caught his hand and wove her fingers through his. "Though I wish it were otherwise," she said, "we must be patient a while longer."

A shadow fell across Joth's face, and his eyes grew dark for a moment. "Have I overstepped myself?" he asked. The question seemed simple, but in the sound of his voice and the way he held his head, Jacinth saw that he had left much unasked. She held his hand tighter.

"No, dear Joth," she said. "You are like the sun to me. No day seems whole without you anymore. No task seems meaningful. But there is something I must do first." She gazed at him, thinking of the tapestry, of the lily she had never received, and of the bitterness that lingered in spite of her love for Joth. From a thicket across the stream came the hollow cry of a short-eared owl.

So it came to pass that in the early summer Jacinth prepared to join the lily hunt. She told no one the exact nature of her plan, not even Joth, though she was sometimes certain he had guessed it. She made herself a pair of stout, coarse trousers and a sturdy jerkin the color of thick forests. The smith of Aranho gazed at her quizzically when she bought a tempered dirk from him; the fletcher frowned at her request for a bow and a quiver of ashwood arrows. But in the end, her gold was as good as anyone else's, and they accepted her money though she offered no explanations. Last of all, she straightened her back and strode into the shop of Bot the cobbler, as if she were any other customer.

Bot was old, and his hands too gnarled for proper cobbling, so Joth did the fine work while Bot cut leather and cajoled his customers. Jacinth ordered a pair of tall leather boots from him, finished with beeswax to keep out the cold and damp.

"I'll be walking a long way," she said as Bob measured her. "Sometimes through deep mud, and sometimes over rocks."

She looked up and saw Joth watching her as he worked at his last, one eyebrow raised. Her heart quickened with fear and excitement at the thought of the task she was about to undertake.

At last the appointed morning arrived. In the chill light of dawn, Jacinth dressed carefully, as she imagined a knight might dress before battle, pale and filled with the need to trust something larger than herself, a set of rules, a ritual made right by centuries of practice. She tugged the new boots over her calves, slipped the dirk through her belt and the quiver over her shoulders. Then she knotted a bag of journey bread at her hip, took up her bow, and started down the road to Aranho, looking neither right nor left.

By the time she reached the village, a crowd of young men had already gathered in the square, all laughter and nerves in the first copper light of the sun. As she approached, a hush fell over them. The muscles of her stomach tightened as she waited to see what would happen.

"What are you doing here, one-eye, dressed up as if you were a man?" asked one of them.

Jacinth fought the old fury and pain as she replied quietly, "I am walking with you to the forest."

Several of the young men cried out at once. "But you can't!" . . . "But you're a woman!" . . . "You have no right to join in the lily hunt!"

Jacinth laid her hand on her dirk. "I have a right to walk wherever I please, whenever I choose. And if any of you think otherwise, then I invite you to stop me, at the expense of your own blood or mine."

A low muttering rippled through the crowd, and Jacinth tightened her grip on the dirk.

At that moment, a clear voice cut across the morning air, as sharp as the cry of a meadow lark. There stood the high elder of Aranho, a man who was old long before Jacinth or the lily hunters had been born. He rested withered hands on thin hips and said, "Who among you ever offered her a lily?"

Silence fell on the crowd once more as men looked away across the fields or watched their own feet shuffling uneasily in the dust. No one answered.

"Then none of you has the right to stop her," he said, standing squarely, like a battle-scarred hound who is well aware of his own strength. After a moment, he squinted at Jacinth and smiled through his wrinkles. She nodded her thanks.

Without another word, the young men made way for her and she took her place among them. She stood as straight and tall as she could, resisting the urge to paw the ground like a nervous horse as she waited for the procession to begin. Neither did she turn her head, searching for particular faces in the growing crowd of spectators, as some did. Her cheeks burned, for she knew how she must stand out among the sturdy hunters. She imagined the citizens of Aranho whispering about her, snickering behind their hands, as they had done so many times before.

Though it seemed to her that hours passed, the sun was still low in the sky when the march began at last. They headed east, toward the sea and the deep forests.

As they approached the last stone cottage before the village gates, she heard someone call her name. From the grassy verge beside the road, her sister Wynna waved, children clinging to her skirts as Jacinth had clung to her own mother's skirts long years before. Beside her stood Joth, looking tall and strong in spite of the crutches tucked under his arms. Jacinth slowed her vigorous pace and blinked, for in all the years she had known him, Joth had never gone to watch a lily hunt begin.

"Good luck!" called Wynna.

Jacinth raised her hand to return Wynna's greeting, but her gaze never left Joth's face. He was smiling, and the smile illuminated him as if the day's soft yellow sun had risen from the horizon of his own heart. Its light crept into every corner of her, no matter how deep the shadows, and courage came with it.

"I'll be back soon," she cried. "I promise you!"

Then the tide of marching hunters swept her up, and the journey began in earnest.

They followed the road toward the east, traveling across grassy plains that ran unbroken for miles and miles. For two nights, Jacinth camped alone, ahead of the others. They would have nothing to do with her once the high elder had been safely left in the distance. On the first day's march, some of them made a game of throwing pebbles at her, so that she was forced to choose between endless small bruises and solitude. In her pride and pain, she took advantage of the fine boots Joth had made for her, and strode ahead smiling grimly while the strong young men of Aranho trudged along on tired and blistered feet. A bitter satisfaction filled her, for she had been forced to accept solitude many times over in her life. It was nothing new to her. No matter, she thought, as she lay beside her small fire. She tried to dream only of Joth and the lilies, but the night songs of toads and owls pounded down on her like cold, lonely rain, and she cried in her sleep, her fingers clenched white around the handle of her dirk. For it did matter. It mattered as much as it always had.

Jacinth knew nothing specific about where the lilies might be found. She suspected that some of the other hunters had received instructions from those who had gone before. But even if that were true, none of them would have shared such manly secrets with a woman—particularly one so proud and hideous. She knew only that lilies favored damp, shady places, loamy ground near bogs or the margins of deep forest ponds. She knew also that the forests lay in the low hills that separated the meadowlands from the eastern sea. When the hunters began their march from Aranho, the wooded coastal hills lay far off in the blue distance. But every day they grew closer, until on the third morning the faint smells of leaf mold and pitch and the vast wet sea awakened Jacinth from her troubled sleep.

She sat up at once, sniffing the air. The sun had just risen. Birds twittered sleepily, and somewhere in the shadowy grass a cricket still chirped. She looked into the windless sky, and eagerness surged through her as she realized that before this day was over she might well be holding a lily in her own hands. She scramble into her boots, picked up her weapons, and started down the road.

Before noon, the road had become a narrow path among tall, leafy trees. Jacinth sat down to rest a moment. She wondered whether to follow the road until it disappeared entirely, or strike out on her own. The thought of leaving the traveled way frightened her, for she had never been in a real forest before. Strange, bright flowers pushed up through the carpet of fallen leaves and needles; shining beetles crept over the rocks. She did not know what animals might lurk among the trees.

Suddenly, as if fierce bears and wild pigs had leapt from her mind into the woods, she heard the sharp snap of a dry twig.

She jumped up, drawing her dirk, and found herself staring into the grimy face of a lily hunter. His fair hair stood up in dusty spikes, and the lines of dirt around his mouth flowed into an arrogant grin.

"You slept too late, one-eye," he said, hooking his thumbs into his belt. "My friends and I will take all the lilies, and we'll be on our way back to Aranho before you even know where to look. Then maybe you'll understand your place in the world."

Jacinth's heart sank like a rock tossed carelessly into an icy stream. The long winters of lonely weaving washed over her, and she thought of the unfinished tapestry, of returning to Joth empty-handed and broken beyond saving.

The young hunter must have seen the terror in her face, for he leaned back and roared with ugly laughter. "That's what you get!" he shouted jubilantly. "That's what you get for trampling the old laws!"

She stared at the dirk in her hands, its cool blade gleaming in the sunlight. *The old laws!* a voice inside her screamed. *The laws that say there is no place for a one-eyed weaver or a cobbler with one leg!* In her fury she grasped the blade and crushed it until she felt the metal bite through her palm. Blood ran in scarlet rivulets down her wrist.

Through a haze of pain and passion, Jacinth watched the young hunter turn and swagger off down the path, his shoulders still jumping with laughter.

"I make my own roads!" she cried. "I make my own roads!"

But if he heard her at all, he gave no sign of it.

She sat down on a flat stone and bound her hand as well as she could with a strip she tore from the hem of her shirt. After a time, the anger and trembling left her. A cold, desperate courage replaced it. Let the menfolk of Aranho seek lilies where they always had! The woods were thick and huge and full of places where no human being had ever walked before. She would find her own lilies, or she would die in the attempt. She stood up, straightened her back, and plunged into the forest.

She followed the contours of the land ever upward, leaving a trail for herself by cutting notches into the tree trunks at regular intervals. The further she went into the woods, the larger the trees became, and the thicker the undergrowth. Spiral ferns snatched at her arms and legs, and bloated insects stung her face. She tripped over roots and waded through thick, slimy mud. She tried not to notice the eerie cries and thrashings of the unknown creatures around her, tried to ignore the swollen fungi that sprang up in rank profusion on the damp forest floor.

Late in the afternoon, when dusk had already descended around her, she came to a place where the land sloped down in all directions. She stood at the base of an ancient maple tree and turned slowly. She had arrived at the crest of a hill. Yet the trees were so tall and closely spaced that she could see nothing, so she laid down her bow and set about climbing the maple.

Its trunk was almost as big around as her father's largest millstone, and the branches hung far above her head. But the maple had stood in the forest for many long years, and its bark was thick and full of ridges. By stretching and straining and planting her supple boots carefully in these small footholds, she gained the lowest branch. Higher and higher she climbed until at last she stood erect in leafy sunlight far above the other trees. She clung to the branches for a moment, giddy with the view that spread below her. As the sun sank lower and the land cooled, a spicy wind flowed out of the forest toward the sea, which lay like a bolt of blue-gray satin on the eastern horizon. The trees marched down to it, thronging over the hills until they reached the broad white shore.

A valley lay at the southeastern foot of her vantage point. The valley cradled just what Jacinth had hoped to find—a small glassy lake, fringed on one side by a marsh. Loons flew above it in profusion, making ready for the night. Their laughing cries floated up whenever the wind dropped. Jacinth's blood sang like the strings of a well-tuned harp. The land, the sea, the wind spoke to her like old friends and she knew deep within her that if she could reach that lake, she would find the key to a new life for herself and Joth; she would finish the tapestry and pluck it from her loom in jubilation at last. She took one last worried glance at the sinking sun, then scurried down the tree and trotted off through the dusky undergrowth toward the southeast.

She knew full well that she shouldn't travel at night, but she was loath to camp in the closeness of the forest, which clung to her and made her feel as if she walked through invisible cobwebs. She ached to reach the lake and the wide sky above it. As the light waned, color seeped out of the woods until at last Jacinth saw only gray shapes everywhere, some deeper in shadow than others. Huge dusty moths flew out of the ferns as she passed. Mist hovered near the ground. She stumbled frequently, splashed through hidden puddles, and stirred up ashlike swarms of stinging insects. At first she slapped at them, but there were far too many. Before long, her face was swollen and tender from their venom. Still, she pushed on with as much speed as she dared, stopping only to cut marker notches in the trees, for there were noises everywhere in the brooding darkness around her. Wherever the forest drew back enough to admit the sky, she saw the first stars twinkling. Sometimes she heard the calls of the loons as they flapped across the violet evening to the safety of the lake. Just a little further, she thought. And she forced herself onward.

Though she could not yet see the lake, she could already smell its rank dampness, hear the splash of fish and loons on its wide surface, when she realized that something was tracking her. She stood still and listened. In the underbrush to her right, leaves crackled for an instant, then stopped. Jacinth felt her blood, like hot oil, surging through her knees and wrists, boiling in her throat and in the knife cuts on her hand. She took the bow from her shoulders and nocked an arrow slowly, as if she moved in a long, disturbing dream. She squinted into the darkness, straining to discern the creature that must be lurking there. With only one eye, she was not certain that she could hit her target even if she could see it. Images of huge black bears and slavering wolves leapt through her mind. The bow and the ashwood arrow trembled in her hands as if they had nerves of their own. The woods seemed choked with the silence of waiting. Then she heard it again—the crackle of dead leaves under the weight of something large.

She whirled blindly toward the sound. Almost with surprise, she heard the twang of her bowstring, felt the sting of the wobbly arrow as its shaft and stiff feathers rushed past her left wrist. With a sharp *thunk* the arrow hit something substantial—either tree trunk or bone. It shivered musically in its unseen mark.

From the deep shadows came a cry of indrawn breath, and an instant later a quavering voice called, "Don't! Don't kill me! I'm alone."

Jacinth lowered her bow in astonishment. "Show yourself," she shouted into the gloom, half relieved and half furious.

With great crashing and crackling, a man emerged from among the trees. By the light of the stars and the rising moon, she could see that he held his hands out at his sides, palms up and empty. When he stood within a few steps of her, she recognized him as the arrogant lily hunter who had confronted her on the road. He had no arrow in him.

"I'm . . . I'm sorry," he stammered. "I . . . we've found hardly any lilies where the elders told us to look. Only two or three. There's not enough food. The hunting's been bad, and today a bear killed the baker's son. It was my idea to follow you. Because of what you said . . . that you make your own roads. I thought . . . I thought you might . . ."

His voice trailed off into self-conscious silence. By the faint, cold light of the moon, she saw that he was nearly weeping with fatigue. His face and hands were covered with dark scratches, and mud smeared his clothes.

Jacinth stared at him dumbfounded. She felt as she had when, as a child, Noa had blindfolded her and forced her to walk across a narrow, bouncing plank. They were playing in the rafters of the mill. Noa told her that the plank stretched high above the grinding stones, and that if Jacinth slipped, she would fall to a grisly death. Jacinth had started across the plank, her knees quaking and fear clawing at her insides like a wild animal.

Midway she had fallen, and in the moments after she realized that Noa had lied, that the plank was only a few hands above the floor, she had felt just as she did now—betrayed, foolish, and ashamed of her gullibility.

All her life she had revered the lily hunt, connecting it with the mystery of that summer dusk when Sten had come for Wynna, attributing to it all the magic of hard-earned passage from a child's thralldom into the independence of maturity. But now the blindfold was ripped away. So *this* was the lily hunt! The old men of the village told the young men exactly where the prizes were to be found and what to expect along the way. If it had ever been a true test of courage and resourcefulness, it was no longer. The brave lily hunter who stood before her was just a boy, whining because he'd had an unexpected taste of manhood and didn't like the flavor. If he found a lily tomorrow, he would think of it as something he deserved, and probably sulk because it hadn't come more easily. If he ever became a man, what happened in these woods would have precious little to do with it.

Like a cave dweller who has climbed up through bleak caverns and seen the sun for the first time rising at her door, Jacinth now realized that the thing she sought had been there all along. She had convinced herself that without the flower talisman, she could never be a woman. She had spent her life in bitter longing because her peers had judged her by her eyeless cheek and found her wanting, and so, she thought, withheld from her the thing she desired most. All along, the lily had been inside her. And Joth, dear Joth, who had always known, waited patiently while she found her own road to it.

In the forest night, Jacinth threw back her head and laughed, more freely and joyously than she ever had before. The lily hunter shuffled his feet and watched her nervously as if she had gone mad, which only made her laugh even more. Her ribs ached and her voice was hoarse by the time she stopped.

She smiled at the disheveled young man and shook her head. "All right then. If you'd like, we can share a fire tonight," she said, wiping the tears of mirth from her eye.

She looked up into the starry sky. "Do you see those loons?" she asked. "They live on the lake that lies just ahead of us. Stand still a moment and you can hear the water lapping at its banks. It's the kind of place where lillies are likely to grow. I plan to camp there."

Without another word, she turned and started through the dark woods again. The young hunter breathed deeply, dragged the back of his hand across his forehead, and trotted after her.

Before another hour had passed, the trees suddenly gave way to open meadow. Jacinth stood at the edge of the clearing, silenced by its beauty. The stars and the full moon hung like pearls in the deep sky. The surface of the lake shivered with cool light. Loons laughed softly from the safety of the cattails, and frogs and crickets warmed the night with their songs. But most wonderful of all were the lilies.

Mingled with the grasses, the lilies grew in rich abundance, their blossoms waving in the soft breeze like the bright faces of a throng.

"Silver!" the young man murmured beside her. "They're silver!"

And indeed it was true. Even in the moon's chilly light, Jacinth could see that the graceful lily trumpets bore no hint of orange or yellow. She laughed once more, softly this time, with wonder. She had made her own roads indeed. And they led to lilies such as no one in Aranho had ever seen before.

Jacinth and the young hunter made a fire, caught fish, and roasted them without speaking, for the lake and the lilies and the light of the moon cast a spell that words would have broken. When the fire had died to red coals and the hunter lay beside it, twitching in his sleep, Jacinth rested in the soft grass and looked up at the stars. Dearest Joth, she thought. I will be home soon, and I will bring with me greater treasure than I had ever hoped to find.

In the morning, Jacinth left the hunter where he slept. She broke off a piece of journey bread and laid it in the grass beside him, as a sign of goodwill. Then she went about the happy business at hand. First she wove a basket from cattails. Root and all, she dug a single silver lily decked with two blossoms and several buds. This she planted in the basket with good loamy earth and water from the lake. With her bow slung across her shoulders and the lily cradled in one arm, she set off through the forest again, back the way she had come, following the notches she had cut into the trees.

By afternoon, she reached the main road. Her heart was light as thistledown as she strode along, humming a tune and wondering idly what kinds of dyes could be made from the unfamiliar flowers she passed.

Once, she heard voices. She crouched behind a boulder as two lily hunters trudged up the road toward the forest.

"Yes," she heard one tell the other. "He said there's a lake up there in the woods. The lily he showed me was beautiful—white like a pearl. He says there are hundreds of them."

"Do you know the way?" asked the other.

"He said there's a trail—notches cut into the trees. He said . . . he said it was the one-eyed weaver who found the way to them."

Jacinth grinned and kept silent until they had passed. Then she continued toward home, whistling.

She reached Aranho on the evening of the eighth day. Though she was tired and hungry and her body ached, she stepped proudly along the main street. The lily, snug in its basket of soft, moist earth, glowed softly in the dusk, still as fresh as it had been on the morning when she dug it. As she passed, curious citizens thrust their heads from windows or walked out onto their doorsteps to whisper with their neighbors. It was not the usual greeting reserved for the first returnee from the lily hunt. Nevertheless, she noticed the onlookers much less than she noticed the familiar stone houses and straw roofs. Whatever its shortcomings, Aranho was her home, and she was glad to be back.

Through the purple twilight she marched to the door of the cobbler's shop. Joth opened it as she raised her hand to knock. His face was as luminous as the lily.

"I'll tell you a story," he said as they stepped into the street on their way to Jacinth's cottage. "About a lame cobbler who fell in love with a one-eyed weaver."

She laughed. "I already know that one. I'll tell you one even better. About a weaver who traveled all the way to the sea and back just to find out that all she really wanted was to marry a cobbler and live the rest of her life in the town where she was born."

Joth gazed at her merrily as he swung along on his crutches, his eyebrows arched in mock surprise. "All the way to the sea?"

"Oh, yes, it took that great a distance," she replied.

And they laughed and sighed together as Jacinth began to tell him all that she had seen.

Later, they lay together on the soft straw of her pallet before a small fire in the house she had built with her own hands. She held Joth close to her as he slept. She gazed drowsily at her warm, familiar room. There was the loom, and the thick window above it, and the baskets of many-colored yarn. There was the lily. She would plant it tomorrow, in the cool sheltered light on the east side of the cottage. In a shadowy corner, the unfinished tapestry stood waiting, as if today were no different from any other.

Quietly, she rose and began to thread it back onto the loom.

# Silvershod

## Ellen Steiber

♦

In the north country
beneath a winter moon
a small gray stag with a silver hoof
speaks with a red-brown cat.

In the north country
in a darkened hut
a hunter watches over
an orphan child
and the red-brown cat
who is all that the child has left of her home.

She has changed his evenings.
He used to return to an empty hut
to eat, sleep,
then rise again at dawn.
Now he returns to a child laughing.
It is still a wonder to him.
Now he feeds wood to the stove,
eats the simple meals
she's so eagerly prepared,
and tells her of the five-point buck
he has never seen
and will never hunt.

Sixty winters he's followed the herds.
He knows every ridge, every trail, every tree.
He never comes home without a deer,
he finds them even in blinding snow.
She cannot understand
why he has never glimpsed
the one they call Silvershod.

*He can only tell her*
*what he has known since he was a boy:*
*You can wait a lifetime to see the stag.*

*"He is small for a buck,*
*his pale gray coat*
*nearly bright as his hoof,*
*his eyes like amber.*
*And when he strikes the ground*
*with his silver hoof*
*colored sparks fly through the night air*
*and turn to colored gems.*
*Rubies cut like roses,*
*crystal drops like tears,*
*emeralds like the heart of spring . . ."*
*The hunter stops his tale*
*for he has never known*
*if it is true.*

*It is the child's sixth winter.*
*She listens to the stories*
*as a bride listens to her wedding vows,*
*breathless, hoping,*
*knowing that to see the stag*
*will forever change her life.*

*Each night she dreams of Silvershod*
*racing across a road of white starlight*
*sending topaz and sapphires and diamonds*
*tumbling through the night sky.*
*Pearls hover on the tips of trees.*
*Opals and citrine blaze fire*
*as they ring the wide frozen lake.*
*And then it's the stars themselves that turn to gems,*
*falling red and green, purple and blue from the sky.*
*In the dreams she reaches out*
*and catches the stones*
*and cannot understand why*
*when she wakes*
*they are no longer in her hands.*

*By day she cleans the hut:*
*a rough table*
*two chairs, two sleeping pallets*
*a basin for washing*
*and the blackened wood stove.*

*"I will find Silvershod,"*
*she tells the hunter.*
*"And then we will have a tall, gabled house*
*with crystal plates and goose-feather beds.*
*I will wear fine wool frocks and soft leather shoes*
*and you will no longer go out into the storms to hunt."*

*Each day she searches the slopes,*
*reads the marks in the snow.*
*She trails birds and squirrels,*
*rabbit and fox*
*and once the prints of her own dear cat.*
*She finds no trace of the stag.*
*In the hut she weaves a cord of silver thread;*
*when she sees Silvershod*
*she will catch him*
*and bring him home to be her friend.*

*Each day at dusk*
*the hunter returns*
*pulling a sled piled high with pelts.*
*And each night*
*beside the blackened stove*
*the child listens*
*to the story of the stag.*
*But the cat listens even more closely,*
*and somewhere in the snow-filled skies*
*the stag listens, too.*

*At last there are are too many pelts to store.*
*The hunter takes them to the village*
*and leaves the child alone.*
*She sits by the window*
*as sunset colors the slopes blood red.*
*A quick shape darts from the trees,*
*quicker than the wind across the frozen lake.*
*Her heart skips a beat*
*as she glimpses*
*the small gray stag.*
*She grabs the silver cord,*
*races for the door,*
*but long before she reaches it,*
*the stag is gone,*
*leaving no trace in the snow.*

*Darkness falls, and the orange glow of the stove*
*lights the hut.*

*The child steps out into the night*
*where even starlight is ice.*
*She clears snow from a wooden bench,*
*sets the cat on her lap,*
*and gazes up at the stars.*
*Surely, even they*
*cannot move through the frozen sky.*

*And, indeed, the stars are fixed,*
*waiting*
*until, half-frozen, the child returns*
*to the warmth of the stove.*
*The cat follows,*
*touches a cold nose to her neck*
*and curls sleeping in her arms.*
*The stars are patient.*
*They wait until the child dreams*
*until the cat stretches,*
*and slips out out the window.*
*As if she understood the clear, bright song of the stars,*
*as if the roof were no higher than a chair,*
*the cat leaps to the top of the hut*
*and greets the silver-hoofed stag.*

*All here is known.*
*Cat and stag and stars,*
*they have all been calling to each other*
*for a very long time.*

*When the sun catches on the tops of the pines*
*the child wakes.*
*The hut is empty of all life but her own.*
*The cat has gone missing.*

*All that day*
*the child searches for the cat.*
*It is not until the moon blazes silver on the snow*
*and the stars burn fixed in the frozen night*
*that she finds her cat*
*sitting atop a round white hill*
*conversing with a small gray stag.*
*Carefully, the child counts five points on each antler,*
*and checks to find the one silver hoof.*
*Then she cries out, and mortal that she is, stumbles*
*knee-deep in thick wet snow*
*only to watch the cat dart away*

*and the stag after her*
*until it's the cat's turn*
*to give chase.*
*Never once do they break the surface.*
*They skim across the snow*
*like ghosts*
*casting no shadow beneath the moon.*
*And the child watches the wild dance*
*beneath fixed stars*
*until it slows enough for her to follow them*
*back to the hut.*

*There the cat waits on the bench,*
*as if she'd never left,*
*amber eyes gazing at the roof*
*where the stag strikes with his silver hoof.*
*It is all the child hoped for.*
*The stag strikes fire into the winter night,*
*and the night freezes that fire*
*into gems.*
*Blue sparks leap into the air*
*and sapphires fall to earth.*
*Red sparks fly into the black night*
*and rubies sink into the snow.*
*Green sparks to emeralds,*
*pink to tourmalines.*
*Amethysts like a rain of wild violets.*
*The stag's silver hoof strikes and strikes*
*until even the roof thinks itself a tinderbox of jewels.*
*It is a blaze of color,*
*a flowering of light.*
*The child will never know another night*
*like this one.*

*Silvershod stops*
*only when the child closes her hands*
*laughing*
*as gems pour through her fingers.*
*There are so many,*
*they are so big,*
*no one could hold them all.*
*She does not hear the cat cry out*
*or see her leap to the roof.*
*She does not hear the stag laugh*
*as he and the cat beside him*
*soar toward the blazing stars*

*that once again*
*wheel through the night skies.*

*The hunter returns*
*to find that the child has learned to juggle.*
*She stands in the moonlight*
*charmed*
*beneath a spinning arc of colored stones.*
*And still more spill from the roof.*
*He can barely find his hut*
*under the rain of precious gems.*
*He kneels in the snow*
*pulls his hat from his head*
*and fills it with jewels.*
*"Leave the rest!" the child tells him.*
*"Think how they'll sparkle in the sun!"*
*That night the snow drifts down from the stars*
*soft and silent and deep.*

*The sun has barely risen*
*when hunter and child*
*dig through the snow.*
*They dig until they reach*
*bare, frozen earth.*
*The gems are gone*
*as if they'd never been.*
*They have only the hat.*
*"It is enough," he tells the sobbing child.*
*"You will have your house and frocks and shoes.*
*It is is enough to last a lifetime."*

*In the north country*
*a child wakes in a soft feather bed*
*and remembers*
*a red-brown cat*
*whose nose was cold against her neck.*

*In the north country*
*a child sits in a tall, gabled house*
*and remembers a pale gray stag*
*with a silver hoof*
*who gave and took*
*what was most precious.*

*In the north country*
*a child finds her dreams unchanged:*

*Each morning she wakes*
*and cannot understand why*
*what mattered most*
*is gone from her hands.*

Too many of the modern, watered-down versions of fairy tales have given us passive heroines and insipid heroes. In the following story (reminiscent of "Bluecrest," "Beauty and the Beast" and other classics) the protagonist is brave, quick-witted and resourceful. The household she comes from is not a troubled or unhappy one. But our heroine is simply different from everyone else in her family, and therein lies her problem. It is an adult fairy tale, asking us: How much can love stand?

# The Lion and the Lark
### ✦ Patricia A. McKillip ✦

There was once a merchant who lived in an ancient and magical city with his three daughters. They were all very fond of each other, and as happy as those with love and leisure and wealth can afford to be. The eldest, named Pearl, pretended domesticity. She made bread and forgot to let it rise before she baked it; she pricked her fingers sewing black satin garters; she inflicted such oddities as eggplant soup and barley muffins on her long-suffering family. She was very beautiful, though a trifle awkward and absent-minded, and she had suitors who risked their teeth on her hard, flat bread as boldly as knights of old slew dragons for the heart's sake. The second daughter, named Diamond, wore delicate, gold-rimmed spectacles, and was never without a book or a crossword puzzle at hand. She discoursed learnedly on the origins of the phoenix and the conjunctions of various astrological signs. She had an answer for everything, and was considered by all her suitors to be wondrously wise.

The youngest daughter, called Lark, sang a great deal but never spoke much. Because her voice was so like her mother's, her father doted on her. She was by no means the fairest of the three daughters; she did not shine with beauty or wit. She was pale and slight, with dark eyes, straight, serious brows, and dark braided hair. She had a loving and sensible heart, and she adored her family, though they worried her with their extravagances and foolishness. She wore Pearl's crooked garters, helped Diamond with her crossword puzzles, and heard odd questions arise from deep in her mind when she sang. "What is life?" she would wonder. "What is love? What is man?" This last gave her a good deal to ponder, as she watched her father shower his daughters with chocolates and taffeta gowns and gold bracelets. The young gentlemen who came calling seemed especially puzzling. They sat in their velvet shirts and their leather boots, nibbling burnt cakes and praising Diamond's mind, and all the while their eyes said other things. Now, their eyes said: Now. Then: Patience, patience. You are flowers, their mouths said, you are jewels, you are golden dreams. Their eyes said: I eat flowers, I burn with dreams, I have a tower without a door in my heart and I will keep you there . . .

Her sisters seemed fearless in the face of this power—whether from innocence or design, Lark was uncertain. Since she was wary of men, and seldom spoke to them, she felt herself safe. She spoke mostly to her father, who only had a foolish, doting look in his eyes, and who of all men could make her smile.

One day their father left on a long journey to a distant city where he had lucrative business dealings. Before he left, he promised to bring his daughters whatever they asked for. Diamond, in a riddling mood, said merrily, "Bring us our names!"

"Oh, yes," Pearl pleaded, kissing his balding pate. "I do love pearls." She was wearing as many as she had, on her wrists, in her hair, on her shoes. "I always want more."

"But," their father said with an anxious glance at his youngest, who was listening with her grave, slightly perplexed expression, "does Lark love larks?"

Her face changed instantly, growing so bright she looked almost beautiful. "Oh, yes. Bring me my singing name, Father. I would rather have that than all the lifeless, deathless jewels in the world."

Her sisters laughed; they petted her and kissed her, and told her that she was still a child to hunger after worthless presents. Someday she would learn to ask for gifts that would outlast love, for when love had ceased, she would still possess what it had once been worth.

"But what is love?" she asked, confused. "Can it be bought like yardage?" But they only laughed harder and gave her no answers.

She was still puzzling ten days later when their father returned. Pearl was in the kitchen baking spinach tea cakes, and Diamond in the library, dozing over the philosophical writings of Lord Thiggut Moselby. Lark heard a knock at the door, and then the lovely, liquid singing of a lark. Laughing, she ran down the hall before the servants could come, and swung open the door to greet their father.

He stared at her. In his hands he held a little silver cage. Within the cage, the lark sang constantly, desperately, each note more beautiful than the last, as if, coaxing the rarest, finest song from itself, it might buy its freedom. As Lark reached for it, she saw the dark blood mount in her father's face, the veins throb in his temples. Before she could touch the cage, he lifted it high over his head, dashed it with all his might to the stone steps.

"No!" he shouted. The lark fluttered within the bent silver; his boot lifted over cage and bird, crushed both into the stones. "No!"

"No!" Lark screamed. And then she put both fists to her mouth and said nothing more, retreating as far as she could without moving from the sudden, incomprehensible violence. Dimly, she heard her father sobbing. He was on his knees, his face buried in her skirt. She moved finally, unclenched one hand, allowed it to touch his hair.

"What is it, Father?" she whispered. "Why have you killed the lark?"

He made a great, hollow sound, like the groan of a tree split to its heart. "Because I have killed you."

In the kitchen, Pearl arranged burnt tea cakes on a pretty plate. The maid who should have opened the door hummed as she dusted the parlor, and thought of the carriage driver's son. Upstairs, Diamond woke herself up mid-snore, and stared dazedly at Lord Moselby's famous words and wondered, for just an instant, why they sounded so empty. That has nothing to do with life, she protested, and then went back to sleep. Lark sat down on the steps beside the mess of feathers and silver and blood, and listened to her father's broken words.

"On the way back . . . we drove through a wood . . . just today, it was . . . I had not found you a lark. I heard one singing. I sent the post boy looking one way, I searched another. I followed the lark's song, and saw it finally, resting on the head of a great stone lion." His face wrinkled and fought itself; words fell like stones, like the tread of a stone beast. "A long line of lions stretched up the steps of a huge castle. Vines covered it so thickly it seemed no light could pass through the windows. It looked abandoned. I gave it no thought. The lark had all my attention. I took off my hat and crept up to it. I had it, I had it . . . singing in my hat and trying to fly . . . And then the lion turned its head to look at me."

Lark shuddered; she could not speak. She felt her father shudder.

"It said, 'You have stolen my lark.' Its tail began to twitch. It opened its stone mouth wide to show me its teeth. 'I will kill you for that.' And it gathered its body into a crouch. I babbled—I made promises—I am not a young man to run from lions. My heart nearly burst with fear. I wish it had . . . I promised—"

"What," she whispered, "did you promise?"

"Anything it wanted."

"And what did it want?"

"The first thing that met me when I arrived home from my journey." He hid his face against her, shaking her with his sobs. "I thought it would be the cat! It always suns itself at the gate! Or Columbine at worst—she always wants an excuse to leave her work. Why did you answer the door? Why?"

Her eyes filled with sudden tears. "Because I heard the lark."

Her father lifted his head. "You shall not go," he said fiercely. "I'll bar the doors. The lion will never find you. If it does, I'll shoot it, burn it—"

"How can you harm a stone lion? It could crash through the door and drag me into the street whenever it chooses." She stopped abruptly, for an odd, confused violence tangled her thoughts. She wanted to make sounds she had never heard from herself before. *You killed me for a bird!* she wanted to shout. *A father is nothing but a foolish old man!* Then she thought more calmly, *But I always knew that.* She stood up, gently pried his fingers from her skirt. "I'll go now. Perhaps I can make a bargain with this lion. If it's a lark it wants, I'll sing to it. Perhaps I can go and come home so quickly my sisters will not even know."

"They will never forgive me."

"Of course they will." She stepped over the crushed cage, started down the path without looking back. "I have."

But the sun had begun to set before she found the castle deep in the forest beyond the city. Even Pearl, gaily proffering tea cakes, must notice an insufficiency of Lark, and down in the pantry, Columbine would be whispering of the strange, bloody smear she had to clean off the porch. . . . The stone lion, of pale marble, snarling a warning on its pedestal, seemed to leap into her sight between the dark trees. To her horror, she saw behind it a long line of stone lions, one at each broad step leading up to the massive, barred doors of the castle.

"Oh," she breathed, cold with terror, and the first lion turned its ponderous head. A final ray of sunlight gilded its eye. It stared at her until the light faded. She heard it whisper,

"Who are you?"

"I am the lark," she said tremulously, "my father sent to replace the one he stole."

"Can you sing?"

She sang, blind and trembling, while the dark wood rustled around her, grew close. A hand slid over her mouth, a voice spoke into her ear. "Not very well, it seems."

She felt rough stubbled skin against her cheek, arms tense with muscle; the voice, husky and pleasant, murmured against her hair. She turned, amazed, alarmed for different reasons. "Not when I am so frightened," she said to the shadowy face above hers. "I expected to be eaten."

She saw a sudden glint of teeth. "If you wish."

"I would rather not be."

"Then I will leave that open to negotiation. You are very brave. And very honest to come here. I expected your father to send along the family cat or some little yapping powder puff of a dog."

"Why did you terrify him so?"

"He took my lark. Being stone by day, I have so few pleasures."

"Are you bewitched?"

He nodded at the castle. Candles and torches appeared on steps now. A row of men stood where the lions had been, waiting, while a line of pages carrying light trooped down the steps to guide them. "That is my castle. I have been under a spell so long I scarcely remember why. My memory has been turning to stone for some time, now . . . I am only human at night, and sunlight is dangerous to me." He touched her cheek with his hand; unused to being touched, she started. Then, unused to being touched, she took a step toward him. He was tall and lean, and if the mingling of fire and moonlight did not lie, his face was neither foolish nor cruel. He was unlike her sisters' suitors; there was a certain sadness in his voice, a hesitancy and humor that made her want to hear him speak. He did not touch her again when she drew closer, but she heard the pleased smile in his voice. "Will you have supper with me?" he asked. "And tell me the story of your life?"

"It has no story yet."

"You are here. There is a story in that." He took her hand, then, and drew it under his arm. He led her past the pages and the armed men, up the stairs to the open doors. His face, she found, was quite easy to look at. He had tawny hair and eyes, and rough, strong, graceful features that were young in expression and happier than their experience.

"Tell me your name," he asked, as she crossed his threshold.

"Lark," she answered, and he laughed.

His name, she discovered over asparagus soup, was Perrin. Over salmon and partridge and salad, she discovered that he was gentle and courteous to his servants, had an ear for his musicians' playing, and had lean, strong hands that moved easily among the jeweled goblets and gold-rimmed plates. Over port and nuts, she discovered that his hands, choosing walnuts and enclosing them to crack them, made her mouth go dry and her heart beat. When he opened her palm to put a nut into it, she felt something melt through her from throat to thigh, and for the first time in her life she wished she were beautiful. Over candlelight, as he led her to her room, she saw herself in his eyes. In his bed, astonished, she thought she discovered how simple life was.

And so they were married, under moonlight, by a priest who was bewitched by day and pontifical by night. Lark slept until dusk and sang until morning. She was, she wrote her sisters and her father, entirely happy. Divinely happy. No one could believe how happy. When wistful questions rose to the surface of her mind, she pushed them under again ruthlessly. Still they came—words bubbling up—stubborn, half-coherent: Who cast this spell and is my love still in danger? How long can I so blissfully ignore the fact that by day I am married to a stone, and by night to a man who cannot bear the touch of sunlight? Should we not do something to break the spell? Why is even the priest, who preaches endlessly about the light of grace, content to live only in the dark? "We are used to it," Perrin said lightly, when she ventured these questions, and then he made her laugh, in the ways he had, so that she forgot to ask if living in the dark, and in a paradox, was something men inherently found more comfortable than women.

One day she received letters from both sisters saying that they were to be married in the same ceremony; and she must come, she could not refuse them, they absolutely refused to be married without her; and if their bridegrooms cast themselves disconsolately into a dozen mill ponds, or hung themselves from a hundred pear trees, not even that would move them to marry without her presence.

"I see I must go," she said with delight. She flung her arms around Perrin's neck. "Please come," she pleaded. "I don't want to leave you. Not for a night, nor for a single hour. You'll like my sisters—they're funny and foolish, and wiser, in their ways, than I am."

"I cannot," he whispered, loath to refuse her anything.

"Please."

"I dare not."

"Please."

"If I am touched by light as fine as thread, you will not see me again for seven years except in the shape of a dove."

"Seven years," she said numbly, terrified. Then she thought of lovely, clumsy Pearl and her burnt tea cakes, and of Diamond and her puzzles and earnest discourses on the similarities between the moon and a dragon's egg. She pushed her face against Perrin, torn between her various loves, gripping him in anguish. "Please," she begged. "I must see them. But I cannot leave you. But I must go to them. I promise: no light will find you, my night-love. No light, ever."

So her father sealed a room in his house so completely that by day it was dark as night, and by night as dark as death. By chance, or perhaps because, deep in the most secret regions of his mind he thought to free Lark from her strange, enchanted husband, and bring her back to light and into his life, he used a piece of unseasoned wood to make a shutter. While Lark busied herself hanging pearls on Pearl, diamonds on Diamond, and swathing them both in yards of lace, Sun opened a hair-fine crack in the green wood where Perrin waited.

The wedding was a sumptuous, decadent affair. Both brides were dressed in cloth-of-gold, and they carried huge languorous bouquets of calla lilies. So many lilies and white irises and white roses crowded the sides of the church that, in their windows and on their pedestals, the faces of the saints were hidden. Even the sun, which had so easily found Perrin in his darkness, had trouble finding its way into the church. But the guests, holding fat candles of bees' wax, lit the church with stars instead. The bridegrooms wore suits of white and midnight blue; one wore pearl buttons and studs and buckles, the other diamonds. To Lark they looked very much alike, both tall and handsome, tweaking their mustaches straight, and dutifully assuming a serious expression as they listened to the priest, while their eyes said: At last, at last, I have waited so long, the trap is closing, the night is coming. . . . But their faces were at once so vain and tender and foolish that Lark's heart warmed to them. They did not seem to realize that one had been an ingredient in Pearl's recipes that she had stirred into her life, and the other a three-letter solution in Diamond's crossword puzzle. At the end of the ceremony, when the bridegrooms had searched through cascades of heavy lace to kiss their brides' faces, the guests blew out their candles.

In the sudden darkness a single hair-fine thread of light shone between two rose petals.

Lark dropped her candle. Panicked without knowing why, she stumbled through the church, out into light, where she forced a carriage driver to gallop madly through the streets of the city to her father's house. Not daring to let light through Perrin's door, she pounded on it.

She heard a gentle, mournful word she did not understand.

She pounded again. Again the sad voice spoke a single word.

The third time she pounded, she recognized the voice.

She flung open the door. A white dove sitting in a hair-fine thread of light fluttered into the air, and flew out the door.

"Oh, my love," she whispered, stunned. She felt something warm on her cheek that was not a tear, and touched it: a drop of blood. A small white feather floated out of the air, caught on the lace above her heart. "Oh," she said again, too grieved for tears, staring into the empty room, her empty life, and then down the empty hall, her empty future.

"Oh, why," she cried, wild with sorrow, "have I chosen to love a lion, a dove, an enchantment, instead of a fond foolish man with waxed mustaches whom nothing, neither light nor dark, can ever change? Someone who could never be snatched away by magic? Oh, my sweet dove, will I ever see you? How will I find you?"

Sunlight glittered at the end of the hall in a bright and ominous jewel. She went toward it thoughtlessly, trembling, barely able to walk. A drop of blood had fallen on the floor, and into the blood, a small white feather.

She heard Perrin's voice, as in a dream: *Seven years.* Beyond the open window on the flagstones another crimson jewel gleamed. Another feather fluttered, caught in it. On the garden wall she saw the dove turned to look at her.

*Seven years.*

This, its eyes said. Or your father's house, where you are loved, and where there is no mystery in day or night. Stay. Or follow.

*Seven years.*

By the end of the second year, she had learned to speak to animals and understand the mute, fleeting language of the butterflies. By the end of the third year, she had walked everywhere in the world. She had made herself a gown of soft white feathers stained with blood that grew longer and longer as she followed the dove. By the end of the fifth year, her face had grown familiar to the stars, and the moon kept its eye on her. By the end of the sixth year, the gown of feathers and her hair swept behind her, mingling light and dark, and she had become, to the world's eye, a figure of mystery and enchantment. In her own eyes she was simply Lark, who loved Perrin; all the enchantment lay in him.

At the end of the seventh year she lost him.

The jeweled path of blood, the moon-white feathers stopped. It left her stranded, bewildered, on a mountainside in some lonely part of the world. In disbelief, she searched frantically: stones, tree boughs, earth. Nothing told her which direction to go. One direction was as likely as another, and all, to her despairing heart, went nowhere. She threw herself on the ground finally and wept for the first time since her father had killed the lark.

"So close," she cried, pounding the earth in fury and sorrow. "So close—another step, another drop of blood— Oh, but perhaps he is dead, my Perrin, after losing so much blood to show me the way. So many years, so much blood, so much silence, so much, too much, too much . . ." She fell silent finally, dazed and exhausted with grief. The wind whispered to her, comforting; the trees sighed for her, weeping leaves that caressed her face. Birds spoke.

*Maybe the dove is not dead,* they said. *We saw none of ours fall dying from the sky. Enchantments do not die, they are transformed. . . . Light sees everything. Ask the sun. Who knows him better than the sun who changed him into a dove?*

"Do you know?" she whispered to the sun, and for an instant saw its face among the clouds.

*No,* it said in words of fire, and with fire, shaped something out of itself. *It's you I have watched, for seven years, as constant and faithful to your love as I am to the world. Take this. Open it when your need is greatest.*

She felt warm light in her hand. The light hardened into a tiny box with jeweled hinges and the sun's face on its lid. She turned her face away disconsolately; a box was not a bird. But she held it, and it kept her warm through dusk and nightfall as she lay unmoving on the cold ground.

She asked the full moon when it rose above the mountain, "Have you seen my white dove? For seven years you showed me each drop of blood, each white feather, even on the darkest night."

*It was you I watched,* the moon said. *More constant than the moon on the darkest night, for I hid then and you never faltered in your journey. I have not seen your dove.*

"Do you know," she whispered to the Wind, and heard it question its four messengers, who blew everywhere in the world. *No,* they said, and *No,* and *No,* And then the sweet South Wind blew against her cheek, smelling of roses and warm seas and endless summers. "Yes."

She lifted her face from the ground. Twigs and dirt clung to her. Her long hair was full of leaves and spiders and the grandchildren of spiders. Full of webs, it looked as filmy as a bridal veil. Her face was moon pale; moonlight could have traced the bones through it. Her eyes were fiery with tears.

"My dove."

"He has become a lion again. The seven years are over. But the dove changed shape under the eyes of an enchanted dragon, and when the dragon saw lion, battle sparked. He is still fighting."

Lark sat up. "Where?"

"In a distant land, beside a southern sea. I brought you a nut from one of the trees there. It is no ordinary nut. Now listen. This is what you must do . . ."

So she followed the South Wind to the land beside the southern sea, where the sky flashed red with dragon fire, and its fierce roars blew down trees and tore the sails from every passing ⌐hip. The lion, no longer stone by daylight, was golden and as flecked with blood as Lark's gown of feathers. Lark never questioned the wind's advice, for she was desperate beyond the advice of mortals. She went to the seashore and found reeds broken in the battle, each singing a different, haunting note through its hollow throat. She counted. She picked the eleventh reed and waited. When the dragon bent low, curling around itself to roar rage and fire at the lion gnawing at its wing, she ran forward quickly, struck its throat with the reed.

Smoke hissed from its scales, as if the reed had seared it. It tried to roar; no sound came out, no fire. Its great neck sagged; scales darkened with blood and smoke. One eye closed. The lion leaped for its throat.

There was a flash, as if the sun had struck the earth. Lark crouched, covering her face. The world was suddenly very quiet. She heard bullfrogs among the reeds, the warm, slow waves fanning across the sand. She opened her eyes.

The dragon had fallen on its back, with the lion sprawled on top of it. A woman lay on her back, with Perrin on top of her. His eyes were closed, his face bloody; he drew deep, ragged breaths, one hand clutching the woman's shoulder, his open mouth against her neck. The woman's weary face, upturned to the sky above Perrin's shoulder, was also bloodstained; her free hand lifted weakly, fell again across Perrin's back. Her hair was as gold as the sun's little box; her face as pale and perfect as the moon's face. Lark stared. The waves grew full again, spilled with a languorous sigh across the sand. The woman drew a deep breath. Her eyes flickered open; they were as blue as the sky.

She turned her head, looked at Perrin. She lifted her hand from his back, touched her eyes delicately, her brows rising in silent question. Then she looked again at the blood on his face.

She stiffened, began pushing at him and talking at the same time. "I remember. I remember now. You were that monstrous lion that kept nipping at my wings." Her voice was low and sweet, amused as she tugged at Perrin. "You must get up. What if someone should see us? Oh, dear. You must be hurt." She shifted out from under him, made a hasty adjustment to her bodice, and caught sight of Lark. "Oh, my dear," she cried, "it's not what you think."

"I know," Lark whispered, still amazed at the woman's beauty, and at

the sight of Perrin, whom she had not seen in seven yeras, and never in
the light, lying golden-haired and slack against another woman's body.
The woman bent over Perrin, turned him on his back.

"He is hurt. Is there water?" She glanced around vaguely, as if she
expected a bullfrog to emerge in tie and tails, with water on a tray. But
Lark had already fetched it in her hands, from a little rill of fresh water.

She moistened Perrin's face with it, let his lips wander over her hands,
searching for more. The woman was gazing at Lark.

"You must be an enchantress or a witch," she exclaimed. "That ex-
plains your—unusual appearance. And the way we suddenly became ourselves again. I am—we are most grateful to you. My father is King of this
desert, and he will reward you richly if you come to his court." She took a
tattered piece of her hem, wiped a corner of Perrin's lips, then, in after-
thought, her own.

"My name is Lark. This man is—"

"Yes," the princess said, musing. Her eyes were very wide, very blue;
she was not listening to Lark. "He is, isn't he? Do you know, I think there
was a kind of prophecy when I was born that I would marry a lion. I'm
sure there was. Of course they kept it secret all these years, for fear I
might actually meet a lion, but—here it is. He. A lion among men. Do you
think I should explain to my father what he was, or do you think I should
just—not exactly lie, but omit that part of his past? What do you think?
Witches know these things."

"I think," Lark said unsteadily, brushing sand out of Perrin's hair,
"that you are mistaken. I am—"

"So I should tell my father. Will you help me raise him? There is a
griffin just beyond those rocks. Very nice; in fact we became friends
before I had to fight the lion. I had no one else to talk to except bullfrogs.
And you know what frogs are like. Very little small talk, and that they repeat incessantly." She hoisted Perrin up, brushing sand off his shoulders,
his chest, his thighs. "I don't think my father will mind at all. About the
lion part. Do you?" She put her fingers to her lips suddenly and gave a
piercing whistle that silenced the frogs and brought the griffin, huge and
flaming red, up over the rocks. "Come," she said to it. Lark clung to Perrin's arm.

"Wait," she said desperately, words coming slowly, clumsily, for she
had scarcely spoken to mortals in seven years. "You don't understand.
Wait until he wakes. I have been following him for seven years."

"Then how wonderful that you have found him. The griffin will fly us
to my father's palace. It's the only one for miles, in the desert. You'll find it
easily." She laid her hand on Lark's. "Please come. I'd take you with us,
but it would tire the griffin—"

"But I have a magic nut for it to rest on, while we cross the sea—"

"But you see we are going across the desert, and anyway I think a nut
might be a little small." She smiled brightly, but very wearily at Lark. "I

feel I will never be able to thank you enough." She pushed the upright Perrin against the griffin's back, and he toppled face down between the bright, uplifted wings.

"Perrin!" Lark cried desperately, and the princess, clinging to the griffin's neck, looked down at her, startled, uncertain. But the thrust of the griffin's great wings tangled wind and sand together and choked Lark's voice. She coughed and spat sand while the princess, cheerful again, waved one hand and held Perrin tightly with the other.

"Good-bye . . ."

"No!" Lark screamed. No one heard her but the frogs.

She sat awake all night, a dove in speckled plumage, mourning with the singing reeds. When the sun rose, it barely recognized her, so pale and wild was her face, so blank with grief her eyes. Light touched her gently. She stirred finally, sighed, watching the glittering net of gold the sun cast across the sea. They should have been waking in a great tree growing out of the sea, she and Perrin and the griffin, a wondrous sight that passing sailors might have spun into tales for their grandchildren. Instead, here she was, abandoned among the bullfrogs, while her true love had flown away with the princess. What would he think when he woke and saw her golden hair, heard her sweet, amused voice telling him that she had been the dragon he had fought, and that at the battle's end, she had awakened in his arms? An enchantress—a strange, startling woman who wore a gown of bloodstained feathers, whose long black hair was bound with cobweb, whose face and eyes seemed more of a wild creature's than a human's—had wandered by at the right moment and freed them from their spells.

And so. And therefore. And of course what all this must mean was, beyond doubt, their destiny: the marriage of the dragon and the lion. And if they were very lucky—wouldn't it be splendid—the enchantress might come to see them married.

"Will he remember me?" Lark murmured to the bullfrogs. "If he saw me now, would he even recognize me?" She tried to see her face reflected in the waves—but of the faces gliding and breaking across the sand, none seemed to belong to her, and she asked desperately, "How will he recognize me if I cannot recognize myself?"

She stood up then, her hands to her mouth, staring at her faceless shadow in the sand. She whispered, her throat aching with grief, "What must I do? Where can I begin? To find my lost love and myself?"

"You know where he is," the sea murmured. "Go there."

"But she is so beautiful—and I have become so—"

"He is not here," the reeds sang in their soft, hollow voices. "Find him. He is again enchanted."

"Again! First a stone lion, and then a dove, and then a real lion—now what is he?"

"He is enchanted by his human form."

She was silent, still gazing at her morning shadow. "I never knew him fully human," she said at last. "And he never knew me. If we meet now by daylight, who is to say whether he will recognize Lark, or I will recognize Perrin? Those were names we left behind long ago."

"Love recognizes love," the reeds murmured. Her shadow whispered, "I will guide you."

So she set her back to the sun and followed her shadow across the desert.

By day the sun was a roaring lion, by night the moon a pure white dove. Lion and dove accompanied her, showed her hidden springs of cool water among the barren stones, and trees that shook down dates and figs and nuts into her hands. Finally, climbing a rocky hill, she saw an enormous and beautiful palace, whose immense gates of bronze and gold lay open to welcome the richly dressed people riding horses and dromedaries and elegant palanquins into it.

She hurried to join them before the sun set and the gates were closed. Her bare feet were scraped and raw; she limped a little. Her feathers had grown frayed; her face was gaunt, streaked with dust and sorrow. She looked like a begger, she knew, but the people spoke to her kindly, and even tossed her a coin or two.

"We have come for the wedding of our princess and the Lion of the Desert, whom it is her destiny to wed."

"Who foretold such a destiny?" Lark asked, her voice trembling.

"Someone," they assured her. "The King's astrologer. A great sorceress disguised as a beggar, not unlike yourself. A bullfrog, who spoke with a human tongue at her birth. Her mother was frightened by a lion just before childbirth, and dreamed it. No one exactly remembers who, but someone did. Destiny or no, they will marry in three days, and never was there a more splendid couple than the princess and her lion."

Lark crept into the shadow of the gate. "Now what shall I do?" she murmured, her eyes wide, dark with urgency. "With his eyes full of her, he will never notice a beggar."

Sun slid a last gleam down the gold edge of the gate. She remembered its gift then and drew the little gold box out of her pocket. She opened it.

A light sprang out of it, swirled around her like a storm of gold dust, glittering, shimmering. It settled on her, turned the feathers into the finest silk and cloth of gold. It turned the cobwebs in her hair into a long sparkling net of diamonds and pearls. It turned the dust on her feet into soft golden leather and pearls. Light played over her face, hiding shadows of grief and despair. Seeing the wonderful dress, she laughed for the first time in seven years, and with wonder, she recognized Lark's voice.

As she walked down the streets, people stared at her, marveling. They made way for her. A man offered her his palanquin, a woman her sunshade. She shook her head at both, laughing again. "I will not be shut up in a box, nor will I shut out the sun." So she walked, and all the wedding guests slowed to accompany her to the inner courtyard.

Word of her had passed into the palace long before she did. The princess, dressed in fine flowing silks the color of her eyes, came out to meet the stranger who rivaled the sun. She saw the dress before she saw Lark's face.

"Oh, my dear," she breathed, hurrying down the steps. "Say this is a wedding gift for me. You cannot possibly wear this to my wedding—no one will look at me! Say you brought it for me. Or tell me what I can give you in return for it." She stepped back, half-laughing, still staring at the sun's creation. "Where are my manners? You came all the way from—from—and here all I can do is— Where are you from, anyway? Who in the world are you?" She looked finally into Lark's eyes. She clapped her hands, laughing again, with a touch of relief in her voice. "Oh, it is the witch! You have come! Perrin will be so pleased to meet you. He is sleeping now; he is still weak from his wounds." She took Lark's hand in hers and led her up the steps. "Now tell me how I can persuade you to let me have that dress. Look how everyone stares at you. It will make me the most beautiful woman in the world on my wedding day. And you're a witch, you don't care how you look. Anyway, it's not necessary for you to look like this. People will think you're only human."

Lark, who had been thinking while the princess chattered, answered, "I will give you the dress for a price."

"Anything!"

Lark stopped short. "No—you must not say that!" she cried fiercely. "Ever! You could pay far more than you ever imagined for something as trivial as this dress!"

"All right," the princess said gently, patting her hand. "I will not give you just anything. Though I'd hardly call this dress trivial. But tell me what you want."

"I want a night alone with your bridegroom."

The princess's brows rose. She glanced around hastily to see if anyone were listening, then she took Lark's other hand. "We must observe a few proprieties," she said softly, smiling. "Not even I have had a whole night in my lion's bed—he has been too ill. I would not grant this to any woman. But you are a witch, and you helped us before, and I know you mean no harm. I assume you wish to tend him during the night with magic arts so that he can heal faster."

"If I can do that, I will. But—"

"Then you may. But I must have the dress first."

Lark was silent. So was the princess, who held her eyes until Lark bowed her head. *Then I have lost,* she thought, *for he will never even look at me without this dress.*

The princess said lightly, "You were gracious to refuse my first impulse to give you anything. I trust you, but in that dress you are very beautiful, and you know how men are. Or perhaps, being a witch, you don't. Anyway, there is no need at all for you to appear to him like this. And how can I surprise him on our wedding day with this dress if he sees you in it first?"

*You are like my sisters,* Lark thought. *Foolish and wiser than I am.*
She yielded, knowing she wanted to see Perrin with all her heart, and the
princess only wanted what dazzled her eyes. "You are right," she said.
"You may tell people that I will stay with Perrin to heal him if I can. And
that I brought the dress for you."

The princess kissed her cheek. "Thank you. I will find you something
else to wear, and show you his room. I'm not insensitive—I fell in love
with him myself the moment I looked at him. So I can hardly blame you
for—and of course he is in love with me. But we hardly know each other,
and I don't want to confuse him with possibilities at this delicate time. You
understand."

"Perfectly."

"Good."

She took Lark to her own sumptuous rooms and had her maid dress
Lark in something she called "refreshingly simple" but which Lark called
"drab," and knew it belonged not even to the maid, but to someone much
farther down the social strata, who stayed in shadows and was not allowed
to wear lace.

*I am more wren or sparrow than Lark,* she thought sadly, as the princess brought her to Perrin's room.

"Till sunrise," she said; the tone of her voice added, *And not a moment
after.*

"Yes," Lark said absently, gazing at her sleeping love. At last the puzzled princess closed the door, left Lark in the twilight.

Lark approached the bed. She saw Perrin's face in the light of a single
candle beside the bed. It was bruised and scratched; there was a long weal
from a dragon's claw down one bare shoulder. He looked older, weath-
ered, his pale skin burned by the sun, which had scarcely touched it in
years. The candlelight picked out a thread of silver here and there among
the lion's gold of his hair. She reached out impulsively, touched the silver.
"My poor Perrin," she said softly. "At least, as a dove, for seven years, you
were faithful to me. You shed blood at every seventh step I took. And I
took seven steps for every drop you shed. How strange to find you naked
in this bed, waiting for a swan instead of Lark. At least I had you for a little
while, and at long last you are unbewitched."

She bent over him, kissed his lips gently. He opened his eyes.

She turned away quickly before the loving expression in them
changed to disappointment. But he moved more swiftly, reaching out to
catch her hand before she left.

"Lark?" He gave a deep sigh as she turned again, and eased back into
the pillows. "I heard your sweet voice in my dream . . . I didn't want to
wake and end the dream. But you kissed me awake. You are real, aren't
you?" he asked anxiously, as she lingered in the shadows, and he pulled
her out of darkness into light.

He looked at her for a long time, silently, until her eyes filled with
tears. "I've changed," she said.

"Yes," he said. "You have been enchanted, too."

"And so have you, once again."

He shook his head. "You have set me free."

"And I will set you free again," she said softly, "to marry whom you choose."

He moved again, too abruptly, and winced. His hold tightened on her hand. "Have I lost all enchantment?" he asked sadly. "Did you love the spellbound man more than you can love the ordinary mortal? Is that why you left me?"

She stared at him. "I never left you—"

"You disappeared," he said wearily. "After seven long years of flying around in the shape of a dove, due to your father's appalling carelessness, I finally turned back into a lion, and you were gone. I thought you could not bear to stay with me through yet another enchantment. I didn't blame you. But it grieved me badly—I was glad when the dragon attacked me, because I thought it might kill me. Then I woke up in my own body, in a strange bed, with a princess beside me explaining that we were destined to be married."

"Did you tell her you were married?"

He sighed. "I thought it was just another way of being enchanted. A lion, a dove, marriage to a beautiful princess I don't love— What difference did anything make? You were gone. I didn't care any longer what happened to me." She swallowed, but could not speak. "Are you about to leave me again?" he asked painfully. "Is that why you'll come no closer?"

"No," she whispered. "I thought—I didn't think you still remembered me."

He closed his eyes. "For seven years I left you my heart's blood to follow . . ."

"And for seven years I followed. And then on the last day of the seventh year, you disappeared. I couldn't find you anywhere. I asked the sun, the moon, the wind. I followed the South Wind to find you. It told me how to break the spell over you. So I did—"

His eyes opened again. "You. You are the enchantress the princess talks about. You rescued both of us. And then—"

"She took you away from me before I could tell her—I tried—"

His face was growing peaceful in the candlelight. "She doesn't listen very well. But why did you think I had forgotten you?"

"I thought—she was so beautiful, I thought—and I have grown so worn, so strange—"

For the first time in seven years, she saw him smile. "You have walked the world, and spoken to the sun and wind . . . I have only been enchanted. You have become the enchantress." He pulled her closer, kissed her hand, and then her wrist. He added, as she began to smile, "What a poor opinion you must have of my human shape to think that after all these years I would prefer the peacock to the Lark."

He pulled her closer, kissed the crook of her elbow, and then her breast. And then she caught his lips and kissed him, one hand in his hair, the other in his hand.

And thus the princess found them, as she opened the door, speaking softly, "My dear, I forgot, if he wakes you must give him this potion—I mean, this tea of mild herbs to ease his pain a little—" She kicked the door shut and saw their surprised faces. "Well," she said frostily. "Really."

"This is my wife," Perrin said.

"Well, really." She flung the sleeping potion out the window, and folded her arms. "You might have told me."

"I never thought I would see her again."

"How extraordinarily careless of you both." She tapped her foot furiously for a moment, and then said, slowly, her face clearing a little, "That's why you were there to rescue us! Now I understand. And I snatched him away from you without even thinking—and after you had searched for him so long, I made you search—oh, my dear." She clasped her hands tightly. "What I said. About not spending a full night here. You must not think—"

"I understand."

"No, but really—tell her, Perrin."

"It doesn't matter," Perrin said gently. "You were kind to me. That's what Lark will remember."

But she remembered everything, as they flew on the griffin's back across the sea: her father's foolish bargain, the fearsome stone lion, the seven years when she followed a white dove beyond any human life, the battle between dragon and lion, and then the hopeless loss of him again. She turned the nut in her palm, and questions rose in her head: Can I truly stand more mysteries, the possibilities of more hardships, more enchanting princesses between us? Would it be better just to crack the nut and eat it? Then we would all fall into the sea, in this moment when our love is finally intact. He seems to live from spell to spell. Is it better to die now, before something worse can happen to him? How much can love stand?

Perrin caught her eyes and smiled at her. She heard the griffin's labored breathing, felt the weary catch in its mighty wings. She tossed the nut high into the air and watched it fall a long, long way before it hit the water. And then the great tree grew out of the sea, to the astonishment of passing sailors, who remembered it all their lives, and told their incredulous grandchildren of watching a griffin red as fire drop out of the blue to rest among its boughs.

# The Iron Shoes

Johnny Clewell

♦

Seven long years I looked for you.
I wore seven pairs of iron shoes.
I ate seven loaves of iron bread.
I climbed seven iron mountains
until I reached this shore.

Here, it is always summer.
Here, the grass is soft underfoot, plums
and peaches fall sweet and ripe
right into our outstretched hands.
We lie at night on sheets edged with lace.

Why is it I cannot sleep?
I lie on the royal pillows,
the wind of your breath rises and falls,
a sliver of moon travels over the hills,
and I wait for sleep to come.

When I dream, I am on that road once more.
I follow a trail of purpose and will,
my legs are strong, and you
my dear are the moon
on the distant horizon.

I know iron. I know its weight. Its taste.
The rise and fall
of black, black hills.
Seven long years I looked for you.
Now I'm lost in this gentle green land.

"The Green Children" is a English fairy story recorded as historical fact in the medieval chronicles of both Ralph of Coggeshall and William of Newbridge. According to these accounts, during the reign of King Stephen, two green children were found at St. Mary's of the Wolf-pits in Suffolk, and were taken as curiosities to the house of a certain knight, Sir Richard de Calne, where they spoke in a strange language and would eat nothing but raw beans. The following story sets the tale in the Arizona desert.

# The Green Children

### ✦ Terri Windling ✦

Back around '63, I think it was, my mother was running from the law. I remember us kids sweating on the slick vinyl seats of her old green station wagon: Frisbee, Butch, and Tot in back and me the oldest up front with the map telling the rest to shut up now, Mom was driving. We played the alphabet game, looking for letters on the highway signs, names that still hold that desperate bright magic when I hear them: Louisville, Tulsa, Amarillo, Phoenix. Then went south and hit the border at Nogales and my mother she stopped the car.

She looked at me, confused, like she'd forgotten she had a daughter. Like she didn't know how she'd gotten there to that sunbaked land with big cactus standing up by the roadside waving their prickly green hands. We were on the highway running south on down to Mexico and I gave Tot his bottle to keep him quiet while that look was on my mother's face like a jackrabbit caught in the headlights. "Am I crazy?" she said, talking to herself again. "Four kids and me and I don't even speak Spanish." So she turned from the border and drove till we come to a town she liked the look of and that town was home, she said, and the littler kids believed her. "We're home," Butch said to Frisbee and Frisbee said to Tot and Tot said to his pup with the stuffing falling out of it.

Now a long time home was that same car, parked in the lot out back of Bubba's Arizona Cow Palace where my mother served burgers and kissed the fry man and us kids stayed quiet. After that come a tent on flat scrub desert land back of the Tucson Mountains in a RV park where everybody but us came and went. Then my mother got it into her head me and Butch we should go to school and for that we needed an address.

She found an address clear on the other side of the valley in mountains that had always looked to me no bigger than Tot's baby teeth, where the sun got up red-faced and grumpy in the morning. We drove east around the town and straight into the mountains and they got bigger and bigger around us till they were giants standing over the desert, looking down at us with their hands on their hips. We were the sun's next-door neighbors in a trailer on a piece of land at the edge of Pima County School District. My mother told them I was a year younger than I was and she told them Butch was a year older than he was and that's how come we were in the first grade together.

Now this trailer it looked like the place we'd lived up north before Momma killed a man and so I didn't like it, but the littler kids thought it was heaven on earth because they never remembered much that happened before. They thought all the world was made of pecan trees and cactus-to-be-careful-of but I remembered my grandmother's house with real stairs and toboggans and the taste of snow and that made me different. That made me like my mother.

I didn't like the trailer and I didn't like the school but what I did like were the mountain foothills on this side of the valley where pecan trees and mesquite and cottonwood were on friendly terms with the cactus, sharing the heavier rainfall between them and turning the dry land green. The Rincon Mountains rose steep out of the rocks behind our trailer and when the storms came drumming rain on our roof down in the valley, up yonder the mountain giants were tasting snow. The Tanque Verde Wash was a magic river that somedays was there, running broad and strong, and somedays was gone, vanishing in the white sun and leaving a dry bed where us kids hunted for snakes and lizards.

Up back of our house was a dirt track that wound through the pass between the Catalinas and the Rincon, and on a Sunday my mother would pile us in the old car and drive slow up the rutted road, the valley dropping down far below as we climbed up into the clouds. She said on a Sunday a body should be close to God and up on that mountain we were surely in shoutin' distance.

There came a place where she parked the car and we all had to walk except for Tot my Momma carried. A foot trail hugged the mountainside guarded by tall saguaro cactus who saluted us as we passed by, and Butch and me, we saluted them back. I liked thinking of them looking after us because we needed looking after, my mother particular. The trail was steep over rocky land bright with wildflowers like orange mallow Frisbee picked for my mother and Indian paintbrushes splashing red against the cactus green. At the end of the trail was water that had tumbled so hard down the mountainside that it broke at the bottom and splintered into many little falls dropping into quiet orange pools and sandy-bottomed creeks. Now this is where the story I want to tell you really begins and I've got to apologize for all the rest, but you know how it is when you start dipping into memories and you think it's a shallow wash and it's flood water instead.

On this day it was February or March, the sun shining hot like it does in this country and fairy dusters turning the mountainside pink and smelling as sweet as candy. The rain it run so heavy that year and the snow was coming down off the mountain filling the creek till it roared over orange rocks and colored stones and the big slabs of boulders bleached white by the sun. It roared so loud you couldn't hear your own voice when you spoke and us kids could whoop and holler and not bother my mother smoking her cigarette and having some peace for a change. My mother was a woman born tired she always said and every day driving cross the valley to Bubba's didn't help none, getting home so late I'd have the littler ones in bed already. Come morning, Butch and me we were up early for the school bus and now Butch who's a grown man working at a garage says he doesn't much remember our mother. But I do, and this is one of the things I remember best.

On that Sunday she was tired particular, up all night crying like she did sometimes and I know she's thinking about That Man again and praying the law don't find us. She's got that rabbit look, sitting by the falls with her cigarette talking to God. I was watching the littler kids playing in the streambed and that's how come I wasn't watching when the green children came.

My mother says they climbed out from under the earth through the cracks in the rocks behind the falls. Only sometimes when my mother talks you don't always know what's true and what's not and it's not that she's a liar, my mother, only she does like a good story. Now these children, there were two of them, and they were wet and they were green. Green like the color of a prickly pear cactus, like the leaves on the acacia after a hot summer day, like the feathery fingers of desert broom waving against the trailer on a cool desert evening. The girl was small like Frisbee only skinnier and the boy was big like me and skinny too, all arms and legs and long green fingers and his eyelashes green as new grass against his cheek. Their clothes were brown and soft as brushed leather, the trousers and the shirts cut into lots of little jagged scraps and then sewn up again with leather thongs like piecing together a jigsaw puzzle. The girl wore a cap stuck through with cactus spines and the boy's hair was long as hers and braided with stones and feathers in it. Their faces were narrow with red blood in the cheeks like the kiss of red on a green apple from the market. Their eyes were as wide and dark as a deer's and Butch said later he figured them for Indian children but I know the Indians that live around these parts, the 'Pache and the Papago and the ones come up from Mexico way, and their faces are round and none of them are green.

These green children were crying, not the hollering the little kids make when they stub their toe or run into a cactus but that rabbit scared look with tears raining on their chins. My mother was talking to them gentle like she did when I woke up at night shaking. I couldn't hear her words and probably neither could they but her face was kind and she was smiling, she was sitting still not to scare them and that green girl she takes my mother's hand and that was it. Now there were six of us kids in the family. Weren't no different from how we got Butch, when my Uncle Bill up and left him behind.

So we climbed back to the car, the saguaro behind us waving goodbye, and them green children had never seen anything like my mother's big station wagon, all beat up and rusted from winters up north. The girl was hanging on to my mother's hand and the boy was scared to get into it, saying something we didn't understand. Butch showed him how to do it, and when us kids were in there and the green girl was sitting squeezed up against my mother, then he thought maybe we'd leave him behind and he got in quick, his green hands shaking. We drove down the mountain and his eyes got darker and wider, looking at the city spreading across the valley and clouds like banners across the blue sky.

We got home and my mother said first thing you kids must be hungry and she told me to fetch the peanut butter and the bread for the littler kids as I got to eat food from Bubba's like she did. I made five sandwiches and put them on plates while the green children sat careful on the plastic kitchen seats like they were wild things we'd brought down from the mountain and they weren't sure they wanted to be tamed.

We're all quiet like the green children, and this is strange in our family. We commenced to eat and the green boy poked at his sandwich curious and the green girl looked at hers and looked at us all eating and she began to cry. Maybe she didn't know what peanut butter was or maybe she didn't like it any, but she wasn't going to eat it and she was hungry, you could tell. My mother looked stern 'cause it's a rule in our family that you eat what's put in front of you. Only the green children were new here so she decided to make allowance. She thought maybe they wanted a burger like me and her, only when that's put in front of them even the boy began to cry and he was a big kid like I was.

There was nothing she gave them they wanted to eat and they were skinny things with no meat on their bones. So my mother took them over to the icebox and said well look for yourselves and the green boy touched it, surprised by the cold, 'cause he was always the more curious. Then the girl made a happy sound, looking at the beans lying shelled in a bowl and soaking for dinner. She and the green boy they ate those beans raw and me and my mother we were shaking our heads with wonder.

Now the green boy, he never ate anything else his whole life but the girl, she learned to eat what the rest of us ate and you know after a while she didn't even look so green no more. She learned our language quick for a baby, but the boy, he liked best to talk with her in theirs. She told us their names which were long and strange so we called them something else like we do in our family anyway, and who even remembers anymore that my Christian name is Emily? We called her Fern for the color she was when she came to us and we called him Kit like the fox that lived in our hills. And my mother said they were our brother and sister now only Kit never went to school like the rest of us because he was too wild a thing and because he was so green.

I could never think of Kit like a brother. Brothers were like Frisbee and Butch, loud and rough and inclined to trouble. Kit was quiet as a girl, as the mule-eared deer that lived in the hills, and I liked him best of our whole family. Nights when my mother was at Bubba's and the littler kids were sleeping, we'd climb the rocky mountain slopes and sit quiet watching the moon together. In the trailer Kit looked small and pale but on the mountain there wasn't anything he was afeared of and nothing was afeared of him either. Jackrabbits came up close to his hand, and the small wild deer stepping long-legged through the cactus. Only the coyotes kept their distance, sitting and watching us from up the hill, singing in the cottonwoods when we went back to the trailer to sleep and I'd sit up listening to them, wondering what they were saying to Kit.

The green boy didn't talk much but he would show me things, stopping me with a touch on my hand and smiling, sharp teeth white in his pale green face. He'd show me a cluster of flowers, or the marks of javelina teeth on a prickly pear cactus, or a Gambel's quail running cross the yard with its mate. Everything I know about those mountains I know from the green boy Kit and it don't matter that I learned it without language because I know it deep inside my bones. There are things you have to learn without words because words will make them scurry away like lizards hearing the sound of a human step. I knew Kit without words and Kit knew me, and no one has known me so well since.

Now Butch, he needs things explained in words. He wanted to know where those green children came from but Kit wasn't talking and Fern didn't remember any more than Butch remembers Uncle Bill or the trailers up north. Fern said, we come from a place like this, only there weren't no city and there weren't no sun and everything was green like them. The green children were out with their momma, walking on the hills with the big desert sheep, and the next thing was they had fallen asleep and woke up here.

Now I can picture easy this place of people with stones braided in their hair, shy like Fern and gentle like Kit, but Butch, he wanted to know why their momma didn't come after them and that was like to make little Fern cry only my mother said, Maybe their momma wanted them to come to us. Maybe their momma thought this was a better place for them. I thought about Butch and Uncle Bill and I thought about That Man my mother killed and I think maybe she was right. In the RV park I once saw a momma cat starving with her litter of kittens. She took one of those kittens in her mouth and set it down where people were walking and then she went and she hid and soon some people come by and said, Look, this here kitten is abandoned so we better take him and take care of him. Soon as they left the momma cat put out the next one and she did that till all her young'uns were gone and living life in style in RV campers headed north to the Grand Canyon. I fed that momma cat myself and she's living with me still, old now and blind in one eye and sleeping on that pillow yonder.

So Fern, she grew up and looked same as any one of us. She dropped out of school like Frisbee and Butch and now she's working as a housemaid and this spring she's set to be married. She don't talk about the green country no more and she acts like I really am her big sister, getting old now myself, nineteen come April. But Kit, he would have gone back to that place if only he could. Come Sundays we'd go to the falls and he'd be searching every crack and crevice and then he'd come and sit and hold my hand, looking sad as my mother and just as tired.

He was green as an apple till the day he died, the year I turned twelve and fire broke out on the mountainside. Every year he was thinner and paler until he was just a green shadow on the dry wash bed, and then he was gone and it was me and the coyotes, howling on the hillside and missing him.

My mother faded out kind of the same way, died a couple years back, cancer turning her lungs to shredded paper. Law never did catch up with her. Went after Frisbee instead, caught him running drugs across the border. The state took Tot, said I'm not old enough to raise him as if I haven't been doing it my life entire. Me, I got a job at Bubba's but I'm not so much like my mother after all. Nights I'm planning on getting an education down at Community College, put a name to some of those things Kit taught me. Not all of them, mind, cause some things you just got to let be; God needs secrets just like you and me.

Those fry men at Bubba's, they haven't changed none. They still liked to kiss all the waitresses, only I don't let those ol' boys kiss me. I'm not the marrying kind, I told Butch and Fern just yesterday. I'm happy in the old trailer back of the Rincon Mountains. When I wake up shaking, my bed full of sweat, I like to wake up alone, now that Momma's not there to talk gentle to me. I like knowing That Man can never touch me again because my Momma killed him and and even if she didn't mean to all the same dead is dead and she did it for me. No, I don't reckon I'm ever going to let any man into my bed to kiss me. Except sometimes when I get lonesome I think maybe it would be okay if that man was green.

Come Sundays I drive up the old rutted track, climbing to the clouds to be closer to God. I like to sit on the rocks by the falls, talking out loud like my momma used to do. Maybe someday somebody in that green country will hear me. Maybe someday somebody will let me in.

# Guardian Neighbor

Lynda Barry

♦

When I was growing up, my mother was a janitor in a Catholic hospital and when they were tearing down a wing where the nuns used to live they tossed out some pictures in frames. Mom brought one home, a print of a boy and a girl barefoot and frightened and crossing a bridge at night. Behind them flew an incredibly gorgeous angel looking exactly like Inger Stevens with huge wings and a different hairdo and the most understanding look on her face. My brother and I couldn't believe it! Our own picture of the guardian angel formerly owned by actual nuns!

The idea of protection was a big deal to us. Michael needed her to balance out his taped-up picture of Alfred E. Neuman, from Mad magazine, whom he worshiped but never really trusted since the day he got a high fever and saw Alfred's lips moving. I wanted protection because things hadn't been going so well in our house lately. My father made a bedroom for himself in the basement. I knew it meant something and I knew that it wasn't good.

We heard a a lot about guardian angels from our Auntie Elizabeth who was from the Philippines and knew a tremendous amount about the social structure of heaven and also about the lives of movie stars, the virtues of nail polish, and the tricky ways of the wild Filipino vampires who could make blood suddenly shoot out of anything. As far as I could tell, my guardian angel never hated me once for being bad. She couldn't afford to because she was stuck with me for life.

When I got into trouble, I imagined she could explain my side of a story to God, who was usually so busy that he only showed up when something really bad happened, like when my brother broke his collarbone after I pushed his Go Kart a little too hard. "Oh now Lord, she's just a kid. I mean, haven't you ever pushed a Go Kart too hard by accident? Shoot. I know I have." And the night my father didn't come home and my mother cried in the kitchen until morning, I believed my guardian angel could explain God's side of *the story to me. "Don't even worry because God may be busy, but he's not cruddy and something is bound to happen that will make everything okay."*

*I grew up on the last street before a garbage ravine where people from other places drove up to dump old refrigerators and mattresses and bodies of dogs and other trash. My parents needed a place quick and a real-estate man directed us to a run-down house with broken windows in a yard full of sticker bushes. I remember our first night perfectly. My brother and I screamed when we turned on the faucet because the water came out thick with rust and we were sure it was blood. The sign of the wild Filipino vampires!*

*You can bet that, like most kids in disintegrating situations, we needed a guardian angel. She came knocking on our back door the next morning, Mrs. Yvonne Taylor with a welcome cake in her hands and her sons, J.J. and Sammy, peeking at us from behind her legs. She had dark hair in a bun and pointed glasses and she was married to a Negro man. A white woman married to a Negro man! With two kids to prove they really meant business!*

*I knew right away there was something different about her. It was a look she had when you talked to her that we had hardly ever seen on an adult. She looked like she was actually paying attention. I soon followed the lead of other kids who had a ritual for visiting Mrs. Taylor. First you stole flowers from someone's yard. Then you hid them behind your back, walked into Mrs. Taylor's and stood around like you weren't doing anything big. When you whipped out the flowers, she acted like she had never seen anything so beautiful in all her life. Even if you were handing her yanked-up plants with dirt clouds hanging off them, she still said, "Well, God bless you!" And then she put her arms around you and held you tight.*

*Most of the kids on my street saw things like this on TV or read about it at school, but for the most part it seemed like a lost practice from an ancient tribe. Almost all of us had parents who were deep in various sorts of trouble and they just could not remember how to do this anymore. Mrs. Taylor was about the only remaining evidence of purely affectionate contact for no good reason between adult and child, and I have no doubt that a lot of credit for the sanity of the kids who grew up in my neighborhood is due to her.*

*One day I asked Mrs. Taylor if I could go with her to her church. Morning Star Congregational was a Baptist church in an old store. I couldn't believe it was even a church because of the hanging light bulbs and beat-up chairs and actual Scotch tape on the picture of Jesus. Also, people were talking pretty loud and laughing.*

*Then the service began. The choir I had felt sorry for because it*

*had only nine people and their robes didn't match started singing
and moving sideways back and forth. Then a regular-looking teenager with a blue plastic headband stepped forward and the whole
congregation started shouting, "Yes! Tell us about it!" She looked
so normal and this voice as good as a record was coming out of her
mouth. She started going faster and faster until she jumped and
pure music shot out her mouth like a light, like wild electricity
jumping free of the wires and shooting into people who leapt up
shouting, "Thank you! Thank you! Yes!" And tears were coming
down their faces and suddenly it got me! It got me! Lifting and
holding and shaking me in the most powerful, beautiful, terrifying
way. I didn't know what happened but for years after that I could
not sing or listen to live singing without crying, even if it was
"Farmer in the Dell." No music ever sounded the same after that
because I could always feel it like it was touching me.*

*We invented a game called "Church" in Mrs. Taylor's front
room. We dragged out her huge Bible and took turns playing the
preacher, the lead singer and the lady whose wig was on crooked
by the end of the song. And the greatest part was Mrs. Taylor leaning out of the kitchen to tell us that our sins had been washed off us
and they were laying all over the rug so would one of us please
vacuum.*

*I loved going to her house so much that one day I sneaked over
at dawn. I stood on her porch knocking and knocking and knocking, weighing how much of a bother I was becoming against how
badly I needed to see her. Finally the door opened. Mr. Taylor in
his bathrobe looked down at me and said, "Now, girl, what are you
doing here?"*

*"Who is it, John?" Mrs. Taylor stepped out from behind him
with her robe on and for the first time ever I saw her long hair
down. The whole picture of it made me unable to speak.*

*Mr. Taylor was getting up for work anyway and Mrs. Taylor
was making him breakfast. When I told her my mom said I could
eat with them, she laughed and pushed open the screen door. I'll
never forget that morning, sitting at their table eating eggs and
toast, watching them talk to each other and smile. How Mr. Taylor
made a joke and Mrs. Taylor laughed. How she put her hand on his
shoulder as she poured coffee and how he leaned his face down to
kiss it. And that was all I needed to see. I only needed to see it once
to be able to believe for the rest of my life that happiness between
two people can exist.*

*And I remember Sammy walking in and crawling up onto his
father's lap, leaning his head into his dad's green coveralls like
doing that was the most ordinary thing in the world. Even if it
wasn't happening in my house, I knew that just being near it*

*counted for something. When I got back home my mother told me she was ready to wring my neck. She couldn't figure out why in the world I kept going over there to bother those people.*

*When Morning Star needed a new sign it was Mrs. Taylor who painted it. I watched her leaning with a brush over the painted plywood, drawing the shining lines of light around the crosses. By then I already knew her secret. "I need to tell you something about Mrs. Taylor," my mom said one day in a serious voice. "But first you have to promise never to tell anyone. Okay?" I nodded. "Mrs. Taylor," my mother said, "is an artist." I could tell from the way she said the word it was supposed to be pretty bad news but I just couldn't figure out how.*

*After that I looked at the different pictures on Mrs. Taylor's walls, thinking, "That one of the mill by the river. She painted that. That one of all those guys eating with Jesus. I bet she did that one, too." As I watched her letter that sign so perfectly, I remember thinking that word. Artist. And when she let me make one of the shining lines off the cross I made a vow in my head that that was what I was going to be. I vowed that I was going to grow up and be great at it. I was going to do something like make an incredibly gorgeous picture of her to hang where everyone in the world could see it so they could know how great she was.*

*I never did tell anyone her secret. For twenty-seven years I didn't breathe a word. But now I think it's finally okay to go ahead and spill the beans.*

The rag-taggle child who appears from nowhere is a figure found in many tales and legends. Sometimes she is a princess in disguise, sometimes a ghost from the past, sometimes a faerie creature wandering dazed through the human world. There is not much more I can say about the tale that follows without giving its plot away, except that I think it is one of the finest stories about childhood I have ever read.

# The Little Dirty Girl

## ✦ Joanna Russ ✦

Dear ——————

Do you like cats? I never asked you. There are all sorts of cats: elegant, sinuous cats, clunky, heavy-breathing cats, skinny, desperate cats, meatloaf-shaped cats, waddling, dumb cats, big slobs of cats who step heavily and groan whenever they try to fit themselves (and they never do fit) under something or in between something or past something.

I'm allergic to all of them. You'd think they'd know it. But as I take my therapeutic walks around the neighborhood (still aching and effortful after ten months, though when questioned, my doctor replies, with the blank, baffled innocence of those Martian children so abstractedly brilliant they've never learned to communicate about merely human matters with anyone, that *my back will get better*), cats venture from alleyways, slip out from under parked cars, bound up cellar steps, prick up their ears and flash out of gardens, all lifting up their little faces, wreathing themselves around my feet, crying *Dependency! Dependency!* and showing their elegantly needly little teeth, which they never use save in yearning appeal to my goodness. They have perfect confidence in me. If I try to startle them by hissing, making loud noises, or clapping my hands sharply, they merely stare in interested fashion and scratch themselves with their hind legs: how nice. I've perfected a method of lifting kitties on the toe of my shoe and giving them a short ride through the air (this is supposed to be alarming); they merely come running back for more.

And the children! I don't dislike children. Yes I do. No I don't, but I feel horribly awkward with them. So of course I keep meeting them on my walks this summer: alabaster little boys with angelic fair hair and sky-colored eyes (this section of Seattle is Scandinavian and the Northwest gets very little sun) come up to me and volunteer such compelling information as:

"*I'm* going to my friend's house."

"I'm going to the store."

"My name is Markie."

"I wasn't really scared of that big dog; I was just *startled.*"

"People leave a lot of broken glass around here."

The littler ones confide; the bigger ones warn of the world's dangers: dogs, cuts, blackberry bushes that might've been sprayed. One came up to me once—what do they see in a tall, shuffling, professional, intellectual woman of forty?—and said, after a moment's thought:

"Do you like frogs?"

What could I do? I said yes, so a shirt-pocket that jumped and said *rivit* was opened to disclose Mervyn, an exquisite little being the color of wet, mottled sea-sand, all webbed feet and amber eyes, who was then transferred to my palm where he sat and blinked. Mervyn was a toad, actually; he's barely an inch long and can be found all over Seattle, usually upside down under a rock. I'm sure he (or she) is the Beloved Toad and Todkins and Todlekrancz Virginia Woolf used in her letters to Emma Vaughan.

And the girls? O they don't approach tall, middle-aged women. Little girls are told not to talk to strangers. And the little girls of Seattle (at least in my neighborhood) are as obedient and feminine as any in the world; to the jeans and T-shirts of Liberation they (or more likely their parents) add hair-ribbons, baby-sized pocketbooks, fancy pins, pink shoes, even toe polish.

The liveliest of them I ever saw was a little person of five, coasting downhill in a red wagon, her cheeks pink with excitement, one ponytail of yellow hair undone, her white T-shirt askew, who gave a decorous little squeak of joy at the sheer speed of it. I saw and smiled; pink-cheeks saw and shrieked again, more loudly and confidently this time, then looked away, embarrassed, jumped quickly out of her wagon, and hauled it energetically up the hill.

Except for the very littlest, how neat, how clean, how carefully dressed they are! with long, straight hair that the older ones (I know this) still iron under waxed paper.

The little, dirty girl was different.

She came up to me in the supermarket. I've hired someone to do most of my shopping, as I can't carry much, but I'd gone in for some little thing, as I often do. It's a relief to get off the hard bed and away from the standing desk or the abbreviated kitchen stools I've scattered around the house (one foot up and one foot down); in fact it's simply such a relief—

Well, the little, dirty girl *was* dirty; she was the dirtiest eight-year-old I've ever seen. Her black hair was a long tangle. Her shoes were down-at-heel, the laces broken, her white (or rather gray) socks belling limply out over her ankles. Her nose was running. Her pink dress, so ancient that it showed her knees, was limp and wrinkled and the knees themselves had been recently skinned. She looked as if she had slid halfway down Volunteer Park's steepest, dirtiest hill on her panties and then rolled end-over-end the rest of the way. Besides all this, there were snot-and-tear-marks on her face (which was reddened and sallow and looked as if she'd been crying) and she looked—well, what can I say? *Neglected.* Not poor, though someone had dressed her rather eccentrically, not physically unhealthy or underfed, but messy, left alone, ignored, kicked out, bedraggled, like a cat caught in a thunderstorm.

She looked (as I said) tear-stained, and yet came up to my shopping cart with perfect composure and kept me calm company for a minute or so. Then she pointed to a box of Milky Way candy bars on a shelf above my head, saying "I like those," in a deep, gravelly voice that suggested a bad cold.

I ignored the hint. No, that's wrong; it wasn't a hint; it was merely a social, adult remark, self-contained and perfectly emotionless, as if she had long ago given up expecting that telling anyone she wanted something would result in getting it. Since my illness I have developed a fascination with the sheer, elastic wealth of children's bodies, the exhaustless, energetic health they don't know they have and which I so acutely and utterly miss, but I wasn't for an instant tempted to feel this way about the Little Dirty Girl. She had been through too much. She had Resources. If she showed no fear of me, it wasn't because she trusted me but because she trusted nothing. She had no expectations and no hopes. Nonetheless she attached herself to me and my shopping cart and accompanied me down two more aisles, and there seemed to be hope in that. So I made the opening, social, adult remark:

"What's your name?"

"A. R." Those are the initials on my handbag. I looked at her sharply but she stared levelly back, unembarrassed, self-contained, unexpressive.

"I don't believe that," I said finally.

"I could tell you lots of things you wouldn't believe," said the Little Dirty Girl.

She followed me up to the cashier and as I was putting out my small packages one by one by one, I saw her lay out on the counter a Milky Way bar and a nickel, the latter fetched from somewhere in that short-skirted, cap-sleeved dress. The cashier, a middle-aged woman, looked at me and I back at her; I laid out two dimes next to the nickel. She really did want it!

As I was going into the logistics of How Many Short Trips From The Cart To The Car And How Many Long Ones From The Car To The Kitchen, the Little Dirty Girl spoke: "I can carry that." (Gravelly and solemn.)

She added hoarsely, "I bet I live near you."

"Well, *I* bet you don't," I said.

She didn't answer, but followed me to the parking lot, one proprietary hand on the cart, and when I unlocked my car door, she darted past me and started carrying packages from the cart to the front seat. I can't move fast enough to escape these children. She sat there calmly as I got in. Then she said, wiping her nose on the back of her hand:

"I'll help you take your stuff out when you get home."

Now I know that sort of needy offer and I don't like it. Here was the Little Dirty Girl offering to help me, and smelling in close quarters as if she hadn't changed her underwear for days: demandingness, neediness, more annoyance. Then she said in her flat, crow's voice: "I'll do it and go away. I won't bother you."

Well, what can you do? My heart misgave me. I started the car and we drove the five minutes to my house in silence, whereupon she grabbed all the packages at once (to be useful) and some slipped back on the car seat; I think this embarrassed her. But she got my things up the stairs to the porch in only two trips and put them on the unpainted porch rocker, from where I could pick them up one by one, and there we stood.

Why speechless? Was it honesty? I wanted to thank her, to act decent, to make that sallow face smile. I wanted to tell her to go away, that I wouldn't let her in, that I'd lock the door. But all I could think of to say was, "What's your name, really?" and the wild thing said stubbornly, "A. R." and when I said, "No, really," she cried *"A. R.!"* and facing me with her eyes screwed up, shouted something unintelligible, passionate and resentful, and was off up the street. I saw her small figure turning down one of the cross streets that meets mine at the top of the hill. Seattle is gray and against the massed storm clouds to the north her pink dress stood out vividly. She was going to get rained on. Of course.

I turned to unlock my front door and a chunky, slow, old cat, a black-and-white Tom called Williamson who lives two houses down, came stiffly out from behind an azalea bush, looked slit-eyed (bored) about him, noticed me (his pupils dilated with instant interest) and bounded across the parking strip to my feet. Williamson is a banker-cat, not really portly or dignified but simply too lazy and unwieldy to bother about anything much. Either something scares him and he huffs under the nearest car or he scrounges. Like all kitties he bumbled around my ankles, making steam-engine noises. I never feed him. I don't pet him or talk to him. I even try not to look at him. I shoved him aside with one foot and opened the front door; Williamson backed off, raised his fat, jowled face and began the old cry: *Mrawr! Mrawr!* I booted him urgently off the porch before he could trot into my house with me, and as he slowly prepared to attack the steps (he never quite makes it) locked myself in. And the Little Dirty Girl's last words came suddenly clear:

*I'll be back.*

Another cat. There are too many in this story but I can't help it. The Little Dirty Girl was trying to coax the neighbor's superbly elegant half-Siamese out from under my car a few days later, an animal tiger-marked on paws and tail and as haughty-and-mysterious-looking as all cats are supposed to be, though it's really only the long Siamese body and small head. Ma'amselle (her name) still occasionally leaps on to my dining room windowsill and stares in (the people who lived here before me used to feed her). I was coming back from a walk, the Little Dirty Girl was on her knees, and Ma'amselle was under the car; when the Little Dirty Girl saw me she stood up, and Ma'amselle flashed Egyptianly through the laurel hedge and was gone. Someone had washed the Little Dirty Girl's pink dress (though a few days back, I'm afraid) and made a half-hearted attempt to braid her hair: there were barrettes and elastic somewhere in the tangle. Her cold seemed better. When it rains in August our summer can change very suddenly to early fall, and this was a chilly day; the Little Dirty Girl had nothing but her mud-puddle-marked dress between her thin skin and the Seattle air. Her cold seemed better, though, and her cheeks were pink with stooping. She said, in the voice of a little girl this time and not a raven, "She had *blue* eyes."

"She's Siamese," I said. "What's your name?"

"A. R."

"Now look, I don't—"

"*It's A. R.!*" She was getting loud and stolid again. She stood there with her skinny, scabbed knees showing from under her dress and shivered in the unconscious way kids do who are used to it; I've seen children do it on the Lower East Side in New York because they had no winter coat (in January). I said, "You come in." She followed me up the steps—warily, I think—but when we got inside her expression changed, it changed utterly; she clasped her hands and said with radiant joy, "Oh, they're *beautiful!*"

These were my astronomical photographs. I gave her my book of microphotographs (cells, crystals, hailstones) and went into the kitchen to put up water for tea; when I got back she'd dropped the book on my old brown-leather couch and was walking about with her hands clasped in front of her and that same look of radiant joy on her face. I live in an ordinary, shabby frame house that has four rooms and a finished attic; the only unusual thing about it is the number of books and pictures crammed in every which way among the (mostly second-hand) furniture. There are Woolworth frames for the pictures and cement-block bookcases for the books; nonetheless the Little Dirty Girl was as awed as if she'd found Aladdin's Cave.

She said, "It's so . . . sophisticated!"

Well, there's no withstanding that. Even if you think: what do kids know? She followed me into the kitchen where I gave her a glass of milk and a peach (she sipped and nibbled). She thought the few straggling rose bushes she could see in the back garden were wonderful. She loved my old brown refrigerator; she said, "It's so big! And such a color!" Then she said anxiously, "Can I see the upstairs?" and got excited over the attic eaves which were also "so big" (wallboard and dirty pink paint) to the point that she had to run and stand under one side and then run across the attic and stand under the other. She liked the "view" from the bedroom (the neighbor's laurel hedge and a glimpse of someone else's roof) but my study (books, a desk, a glimpse of the water) moved her so deeply and painfully that she only stood still in the center of the room, struggling with emotion, her hands again clasped in front of her. Finally she burst out, "It's so . . . *swanky!*" Here my kettle screamed and when I got back she had gotten bold enough to touch the electric typewriter (she jumped when it turned itself on) and then walked about slowly, touching the books with the tips of her fingers. She was brave and pushed the tabs on the desk lamp (though not hard enough to turn it on) and boldly picked up my little mailing scale. As she did so, I saw that there were buttons missing from the back of her dress; I said, "A. R., come here."

She dropped the scale with a crash. "I didn't mean it!" Sulky again.

"It's not that, it's your buttons," I said, and hauled her to the study closet where I keep a Band-Aid box full of extras; two were a reasonable match: little, flat-topped, pearlized, pink things you can hardly find anymore. I sewed them on to her, not that it helped much, and the tangles of her hair kept falling back and catching. What a forest of lost barrettes and snarls of old rubber bands! I lifted it all a little grimly, remembering the pain of combing out. She sat flatly, all adoration gone:

"You can't comb my hair against my will; you're too weak."

"I wasn't going to," I said.

"That's what *you* say," the L.D.G. pointed out.

"If I try, you can stop me," I said. After a moment she turned around, flopped down on my typing chair, and bent her head. So I fetched my old hairbrush (which I haven't used for years) and did what I could with the upper layers, managing even to smooth out some of the lower ones, though there were places near her neck nearly as matted and tangled as felt; I finally had to cut some pieces out with my nail scissors.

L.D.G. didn't shriek (as I used to, insisting my cries were far more artistic than those of the opera singers on the radio on Sundays) but finally asked for the comb herself and winced silently until she was decently braided, with rubber bands on the ends. We put the rescued barrettes in her shirt pocket. Without that cloud of hair her sallow face and pitch-ball eyes looked bigger, and oddly enough, younger; she was no more a wandering Fury with the voice of a Northwest-coast raven but a reasonably human (though draggly) little girl.

I said, "You look nice."

She got up, went into the bathroom, and looked at herself in the mirror. Then she said calmly, "No, I don't. I look conventional."

"Conventional?" said I. She came out of the bathroom, flipping back her new braids.

"Yes, I must go."

And as I was wondering at her tact (for anything after this would have been an anticlimax):

"But I shall return."

"That's fine," I said, "but I want to have grown-up manners with you, A. R. Don't ever come before ten in the morning or if my car isn't here or if you can hear my typewriter going. In fact, I think you had better call me on the telephone first, the way other people do."

She shook her head sweetly. She was at the front door before I could follow her, peering out. It was raining again. I saw that she was about to step out into it and cried, "Wait, A. R.!" hurrying as fast as I could down the cellar steps to the garage, from where I could get easily to my car. I got from the backseat the green plastic poncho I always keep there and she didn't protest when I dumped it over her and put the hood over her head, though the poncho was much too big and even dragged on the ground in the front and back. She said only, "Oh, it's swanky. Is it from the Army?" So I had the satisfaction of seeing her move up the hill as a small, green tent instead of a wet, pink draggle. Though with her tea-party manners she hadn't really eaten anything; the milk and peach were untouched. Was it wariness? Or did she just not like milk and peaches? Remembering our first encounter, I wrote on the pad by the telephone, which is my shopping list:

*Milky Way Bars*
And then:
*1 doz.*

She came back. She never did telephone in advance. It was all right, though; she had the happy faculty of somehow turning up when I wasn't working and wasn't busy and was thinking of her. But how often is an invalid busy or working? We went on walks or stayed home and on these occasions the business about the Milky Ways turned out to be a brilliant guess, for never have I met a child with such a passion for junk food. A. R.'s formal, disciplined politeness in front of milk or fruit was like a cat's in front of the mass-produced stuff; faced with jam, honey, or marmalade, the very ends of her braids crisped and she attacked like a cat flinging itself on a fish; I finally had to hide my own supplies in self-defense. Then on relatively good days it was ice cream or Sara Lee cake, and on bad ones Twinkies or Mallomars, Hostess Cupcakes, Three Musketeers bars, marshmallow cream, maraschino chocolates, Turkish taffy, saltwater taffy, or—somewhat less horribly—Doritos, reconstituted potato chips, corn chips, pretzels (fat or thin), barbecued corn chips, or onion-flavored corn chips, anything like that. She refused nuts and hated peanut butter. She also talked continuously while eating, largely in poly-syllables, which made me nervous as I perpetually expected her to choke, but she never did. She got no fatter. To get her out of the house and so away from food, I took her to an old-fashioned five-and-ten nearby and bought her shoelaces. Then I took her down to watch the local ship-canal bridge open up (to let a sailboat through) and we cheered. I took her to a department store (just to look; "I know consumerism is against your prin-ciples," she said with priggish and mystifying accuracy) and bought her a pin shaped like a ladybug. She refused to go to the zoo ("An animal jail!") but allowed as the rose gardens ("A plant *hotel*") were both pleasant and educational. A ride on the zoo merry-go-round excited her to the point of screaming and running around dizzily in circles for half an hour after-wards, which embarrassed me—but then no one paid the slightest atten-tion; I suppose shrieky little girls had happened there before, though the feminine youth of Seattle, in its Mary Jane shoes and pink pocketbooks, rather pointedly ignored her. The waterfall in the downtown park, on the contrary, sobered her up; this is a park built right on top of a crossing over one of the city's highways and is usually full of office workers; a walkway leads not only up to but actually behind the waterfall. A. R. wandered among the beds of bright flowers and passed stopping, behind the water, trying to stick her hand in the falls; she came out saying:

"It looks like an old man's beard," (pointing to one of the ragged Skid Row men who was sleeping on the grass in the rare, northern sunlight). Then she said, "No, it looks like a lady's dress without any seams."

Once, feeling we had become friends enough for it, I ran her a bath and put her clothes through the basement washer-dryer; her splashing and yellings in the bathroom were terrific and afterwards she flashed nude about the house, hanging out of windows, embellishing her strange, raucous shouts with violent jerkings and boundings-about that I think were meant for dancing. She even ran out the back door naked and had circled the house before I—voiceless with calling, *"A. R., come back here!"*—had presence of mind enough to lock both the front and back doors after she had dashed in and before she could get out again to make the entire *tour de Seattle* in her jaybird suit. Then I had to get her back into that tired pink dress, which (when I ironed it) had finally given up completely, despite the dryer, and sagged into two sizes too big for her.

Unless A. R. was youthifying.

I got her into her too-large pink dress, her baggy underwear, her too-large shoes, her new pink socks (which I had bought for her), and said:

"A. R., where do you live?"

Crisp and shining, the Little Clean Girl replied, "My dear, you always ask me that."

"And you never answer," said I.

"O yes I do," said the Little Clean Girl. "I live up the hill and under the hill and over the hill and behind the hill."

"That's no answer," said I.

"Wupf merble," said she (through a Mars Bar) and then, more intelligibly, "If you knew, you wouldn't want me."

"I would so!" I said.

L.D.G.—now L.C.G.—regarded me thoughtfully. She scratched her ear, getting, I noticed, chocolate in her hair. (She was a fast worker.) She said, "You want to know. You think you ought to know. You think you have a right. When I leave you'll wait until I'm out of sight and then you'll follow me in the car. You'll sneak by the curb way behind me so I won't notice you. You'll wait until I climb the steps of a house—like that big yellow house with the fuchsias in the yard where you think I live—and you'll watch me go in. And then you'll ring the bell and when the lady comes to the door you'll say, 'Your little daughter and I have become friends,' but the lady will say, 'I haven't got any little daughter,' and then you'll know I fooled you. And you'll get scared. So don't try."

Well, she had me dead to rights. Something very like that had been in my head. Her face was preternaturally grave. She said, "You think I'm too small. I'm not.

"You think I'll get sick if I keep on eating like this. I won't.

"You think if you bought a whole department store for me, it would be enough. It wouldn't."

"I won't—well, I can't get a whole department store for you," I said. She said, "I know." Then she got up and tucked the box of Mars Bars under one arm, throwing over the other my green plastic poncho, which she always carried about with her now.

"I'll get you anything you want," I said; "No, not what you want, A. R., but anything you really, truly need."

"You can't," said the Little Dirty Girl.

"I'll try."

She crossed the living room to the front door, dragging the poncho across the rug, not paying the slightest attention to the astronomical photographs that had so enchanted her before. Too young now, I suppose. I said, "A. R., I'll try. Truly I will." She seemed to consider it a moment, her small head to one side. Then she said briskly, "I'll be back," and was out the front door.

And I did not—would not—could not—did not dare to follow her.

Was this the moment I decided I was dealing with a ghost? No, long before. Little by little, I suppose. Her clothes were a dead giveaway, for one thing: always the same and the kind no child had worn since the end of the Second World War. Then there was the book I had given her on her first visit, which had somehow closed and straightened itself on the coffee table, another I had lent her later (the poems of Edna Millay) which had mysteriously been there a day afterwards, the eerie invisibility of a naked little girl hanging out of my windows and yelling; the inconspicuousness of a little twirling girl nobody noticed spinning round and shrieking outside the merry-go-round, a dozen half-conscious glimpses I'd had, every time

I'd got in or out of my car, of the poncho lying on the backseat where I always keep it, folded as always, the very dust on it undisturbed. And her unchildlike cleverness in never revealing either her name or where she lived. And as surely as A. R. had been a biggish eight when we had met, weeks ago, just as surely she was now a smallish, very unmistakable, unnaturally knowledgeable five.

But she was such a *nice* little ghost. And so solid! Ghosts don't run up your grocery bills, do they? Or trample Cheez Doodles into your carpet or leave gum under your kitchen chair, large smears of chocolate on the surface of the table (A. R. had) and an exceptionally dirty ring around the inside of the bathtub? Along with three (count 'em, three) large, dirty, sopping-wet bath towels on the bathroom floor? If A. R's social and intellectual life had a tendency to become intangible when looked at carefully, everything connected with her digestive system and her bodily dirt stuck around amazingly; there was the state of the bathroom, the dishes in the sink (many more than mine), and the ironing board still up in the study for the ironing of A. R.'s dress (with the spray starch container still set up on one end and the scorch mark where she'd decided to play with the iron). If she was a ghost, she was a good one and I liked her and wanted her back. Whatever help she needed from me in resolving her ancient Seattle tragedy (ancient ever since nineteen-forty-two) she could have. I wondered for a moment if she were connected with the house, but the people before me—the original owners—hadn't had children. And the house itself hadn't even been built until the mid-fifties; nothing in the neighborhood had. Unless both they and I were being haunted by the children we hadn't had; could I write them a psychotherapeutic letter about it? ("Dear Mrs. X, How is your inner space?") I went into the bathroom and discovered that A. R. had relieved herself interestingly in the toilet and had then not flushed it, hardly what I would call poetical behavior on the part of somebody's unconscious. So *I* flushed it. I picked up the towels one by one and dragged them to the laundry basket in the bedroom. If the Little Dirty Girl was a ghost, she was obviously a bodily-dirt-and-needs ghost traumatized in life by never having been given a proper bath or allowed to eat marshmallows until she got sick. Maybe this was it and now she could rest (scrubbed and full of Mars Bars) in peace. But I hoped not. I was nervous; I had made a promise ("I'll give you what you need") that few of us can make to anyone, a frightening promise to make to anyone. Still, I hoped. And she was a businesslike little ghost. She would come back.

For she, too, had promised.

Autumn came. I didn't see the Little Dirty Girl. School started and I spent days trying to teach freshmen and freshwomen not to write like Rod McKuen (neither of us really knowing why they shouldn't actually) while advanced students pursued me down the halls with thousand-page trilogies, demands for independent study, and other unspeakables. As a friend of ours said once, everyone will continue to pile responsibility on a woman and everything and everyone must be served except oneself; I've been a flogged horse professionally long enough to know that, and meanwhile the dishes stay in the sink and the kindly wife-elves do *not* come out of the woodwork at night and do them. I was exercising two hours a day and sleeping ten; the Little Dirty Girl seemed to have vanished with the summer.

Then one day there was a freak spell of summer weather and that evening a thunderstorm. This is a very rare thing in Seattle. The storm didn't last, of course, but it seemed to bring right after it the first of the winter rains: cold, drenching, ominous. I was grading papers that evening when someone knocked at my door; I thought I'd left the garage light on and my neighbor'd come out to tell me, so I yelled "Just a minute, please!", dropped my pen, wondered whether I should pick it up, decided the hell with it, and went (exasperated) to the door.

It was the Little Dirty Girl. She was as wet as I've ever seen a human being be and had a bad cough (my poncho must've gone heaven knows where) and water squelching in her shoes. She was shivering violently and her fingers were blue—it could not have been more than fifty degrees out—and her long, baggy dress clung to her with water running off it; there was a puddle already forming around her feet on the rug. Her teeth were chattering. She stood there shivering and glowering miserably at me, from time to time emitting that deep, painful chest cough you sometimes hear in adults who smoke too much. I thought of hot baths, towels, electric blankets, aspirin—can ghosts get pneumonia? "For God's sake, get your clothes off!" I said, but A. R. stepped back against the door, shivering, and wrapped her starved arms in her long, wet skirt.

"No!" she said, in a deep voice more like a crow's than ever. "Like this!"

"Like what?" said I helplessly, thinking of my back and how incapable I was of dragging a resistant five-year-old anywhere.

"You hate me!" croaked A. R. venomously. "You starve me! You do! You won't let me eat anything!"

Then she edged past me, still coughing, her dark eyes ringed with blue, her skin mottled with bruises, and her whole body shaking with cold and anger, like a little mask of Medusa. She screamed:

"You want to clean me up because you don't like me!

"You like me clean because you don't like me dirty!

"You hate me so you won't give me what I need!

"You won't give me what I need and I'm dying!"

"I'm dying! I'm dying!

"I'M DYING!"

She was interrupted by coughing. I said "A. R.—" and she screamed again, her whole body bending convulsively, the cords in her neck standing out. Her scream was choked by phlegm and she beat herself with her fists, then wrapping her arms in her wet skirt through another bout of coughing, she said in gasps:

"I couldn't get into your house to use the bathroom, so I had to shit in my pants.

"I had to stay out in the rain; I got cold.

"All I can get is from you and you won't give it."

"Then tell me what you need!" I said, and A. R. raised her horrid little face to mine, a picture of venomous, uncontrolled misery, of sheer, demanding starvation.

"You," she whispered.

So that was it. I thought of the pleading cats, whose open mouths (*Dependency! Dependency!*) reveal needle teeth which can rip off your thumb; I imagined the Little Dirty Girl sinking her teeth into my chest if I so much as touched her. Not touched for bathing or combing or putting on shoelaces, you understand, but for touching only. I saw—I don't know what; her skin ash-gray, the bones of her little skull coming through her skin worse and worse every moment—and I knew she would kill me if she didn't get what she wanted, though she was suffering far worse than I was and was more innocent—a demon child is still a child, with a child's needs, after all. I got down on one knee, so as to be nearer her size, and saying only, "My back—be careful of my back," held out my arms so that the terror of the ages could walk into them. She was truly gray now, her bones very prominent. She was starving to death. She was dying. She gave the cough of a cadaver breathing its last, a phlegmy wheeze with a dreadful rattle in it, and then the Little Dirty Girl walked right into my arms.

And began to cry. I felt her crying right up from her belly. She was cold and stinky and extremely dirty and afflicted with the most surprising hiccough. I rocked her back and forth and mumbled I don't know what, but what I meant was that I thought she was fine, that all of her was fine: her shit, her piss, her sweat, her tears, her scabby knees, the snot on her face, her cough, her dirty panties, her bruises, her desperation, her anger, her whims—all of her was wonderful, I loved all of her, and I would do my best to take good care of her, all of her, forever and forever and then a day.

She bawled. She howled. She pinched me hard. She yelled, "Why did it take you so long!" She fussed violently over her panties and said she had been humiliated, though it turned out, when I got her to the bathroom, that she was making an awfully big fuss over a very little brown stain. I put the panties to soak in the kitchen sink and the Little Dirty Girl likewise in a hot tub with vast mounds of rose-scented bubble bath which turned up from somewhere, though I knew perfectly well I hadn't bought any in years. We had a shrieky, tickly, soapy, toe-grabby sort of a bath, a *very* wet one during which I got soaked. (I told her about my back and she was careful.) We sang to the loofah. We threw water at the bathroom tiles. We lost the soap. We came out warm in a huge towel (I'd swear mine aren't that big) and screamed gaily again, to exercise our lungs, from which the last bit of cough had disappeared. We said, "Oh, floof! there goes the soap." We speculated loudly (and at length) on the possible subjective emotional life of the porcelain sink, American variety, and (rather to my surprise) sang snatches of *The Messiah* as follows:

> *Every malted*
> *Shall be exalted!*

and:

> *Behold and see*
> *Behold and see*
> *If there were e'er pajama*
> *Like to this pajama!*

and so on.

My last memory of the evening is of tucking the Little Dirty Girl into one side of my bed (in my pajamas, which had to be rolled up and pinned even to stay on her) and then climbing into the other side myself. The bed was wider than usual, I suppose. She said sleepily, "Can I stay?" and I (also sleepily) "Forever."

But in the morning she was gone.

Her clothes lasted a little longer, which worried me, as I had visions of A. R. committing flashery around and about the neighborhood, but in a few days they too had faded into mist or the elemental particles of time or whatever ghosts and ghost-clothes are made of. The last thing I saw of hers was a shoe with a new heel (oh yes, I had gotten them fixed) which rolled out from under the couch and lasted a whole day before it became—I forget what, the shadow of one of the ornamental teacups on the mantel, I think.

And so there was no more five-year-old A. R. beating on the door and demanding to be let in on rainy nights. But that's not the end of the story.

As you know, I've never gotten along with my mother. I've always supposed that neither of us knew why. In my childhood she had vague, long-drawn-out symptoms which I associated with early menopause (I was a late baby); then she put me through school, which was a strain on her librarian's budget and a strain on my sense of independence and my sense of guilt, and always there was her timidity, her fears of everything under the sun, her terrified, preoccupied air of always being somewhere else, and what I can only call her furtiveness, the feeling I've always had of some secret life going on in her which I could never ask about or share. Add to this my father's death somewhere in pre-history (I was two) and then that ghastly behavior psychologists call The Game of Happy Families—I mean the perpetual, absolute insistence on How Happy We All Were that even aunts, uncles, and cousins rushed to heap on my already bitter and most unhappy shoulders, and you'll have some idea of what's been going on for the last I-don't-know-how-many years.

Well, this is the woman who came to visit a few weeks later. I wanted to dodge her. I had been dodging academic committees and students and proper bedtimes; why couldn't I dodge my mother? So I decided that *this time I would be openly angry* (I'd been doing that in school, too).

Only there was nothing to be angry about, this time.

Maybe it was the weather. It was one of those clear, still times we sometimes have in October: warm, the leaves not down yet, that in-and-out sunshine coming through the clouds, and the northern sun so low that the masses of orange pyracantha berries on people's brick walls and the walls themselves, or anything that color, f' ɪme indescribably. My mother got in from the airport in a taxi (I still can't drive far) and we walked about a bit, and then I took her to Kent and Hallby's downtown, that expensive, old-fashioned place that's all mirrors and sawdust floors and old-fashioned white tablecloths and waiters (also waitresses now) with floor-length aprons. It was very self-indulgent of me. But she had been so much better—or I had been—it doesn't matter. She was seventy and if she wanted to be fussy and furtive and act like a thin, old guinea-hen with secret dispatches from the CIA (I've called her worse things), I felt she had the right. Besides, that was no worse than my flogging myself through five women's work and endless depressions, beating the old plough horse day after day for weeks and months and years—no, for decades—until her back broke and she foundered and went down and all I could do was curse at her helplessly and beat her the more.

All this came to me in Kent and Hallby's. Luckily my mother squeaked as we sat down. There's a reason; if you sit at a corner table in Kent and Hallby's and see your face where the mirrored walls come to-gether—well, it's complicated, but briefly, you can see yourself (for the only time in your life) as you look to other people. An ordinary mirror reverses the right and left sides of your face but this odd arrangement re-reflects them so they're back in place. People are shocked when they see themselves; I had planned to warn her.

She said, bewildered, "What's that?" But rather intrigued too, I think. Picture a small, thin, white-haired, extremely prim ex-librarian, worn to her fine bones but still ready to take alarm and run away at a moment's notice; that's my mother. I explained about the mirrors and then I said:

"People don't really know what they look like. It's only an idea people have that you'd recognize yourself if you saw yourself across the room. Any more than we can hear our own voices; you know, it's because longer frequencies travel so much better through the bones of your head than they can through the air; that's why a tape recording of your voice sounds higher than—"

I stopped. Something was going to happen. A hurricane was going to smash Kent and Hallby's flat. I had spent almost a whole day with my mother, walking around my neighborhood, showing her the University, showing her my house, and nothing in particular had happened; why should anything happen now?

She said, looking me straight in the eye, "You've changed."

I waited.

She said, "I'm afraid that we—like you and I were not—are not—a happy family."

I said nothing. I would have, a year ago. It occurred to me that I might, for years, have confused my mother's primness with my mother's self-control. She went on. She said:

"When you were five, I had cancer."

I said, *"What? You had what?"*

"Cancer," said my mother calmly, in a voice still as low and decorous as if she had been discussing her new beige handbag or Kent and Hallby's long, fancy menu (which lay open on the table between us). "I kept it from you. I didn't want to burden you."

*Burden.*

"I've often wondered—" she went on, a little flustered, "they say now—but of course no one thought that way then." She went on, more formally, "It takes years to know if it has spread or will come back, even now, and the doctors knew very little then. I was all right eventually, of course, but by that time you were almost grown up and had become a very capable and self-sufficient little girl. And then later on you were so successful."

She added, "You didn't seem to want me."

Want her! Of course not. What would you feel about a mother who disappeared like that? Would you trust her? Would you accept anything from her? All those years of terror and secrecy; maybe she'd thought she was being punished by having cancer. Maybe she'd thought she was going to die. Too scared to give anything and everyone being loudly secretive and then being faced with a daughter who wouldn't be questioned, wouldn't be kissed, wouldn't be touched, who kept her room immaculate, who didn't want her mother and made no bones about it, and who kept her fury and betrayal and her misery to herself, and her schoolwork excellent. I could say only the silliest thing, right out of the movies:

"Why are you telling me all this?"

She said simply, "Why not?"

I wish I could go on to describe a scene of intense and affectionate reconciliation between my mother and myself, but that did not happen—quite. She put her hand on the table and I took it, feeling I don't know what; for a moment she squeezed my hand and smiled. I got up then and she stood too, and we embraced, not at all as I had embraced the Little Dirty Girl, though with the same pain at heart, but awkwardly and only for a moment, as such things really happen. I said to myself: *Not yet. Not so fast. Not right now,* wondering if we looked—in Kent and Hallby's mirrors—the way we really were. We were both embarrassed, I think, but that too was all right. We sat down: *Soon. Sometime. Not quite yet.*

The dinner was nice. The next day I took her for breakfast to the restaurant that goes around and gives you a view of the whole city and then to the public market and then on a ferry. We had a pleasant, affectionate quiet two days and then she went back East.

We've been writing each other lately—for the first time in years more than the obligatory birthday and holiday cards and a few remarks about the weather—and she sent me old family photographs, talked about being a widow, and being misdiagnosed for years (that's what it seems now) and about all sorts of old things: my father, my being in the school play in second grade, going to summer camp, getting moths to sit on her finger, all sorts of things.

And the Little Dirty Girl? Enclosed is her photograph. We were passing a photographer's studio near the University the other day and she was seized with a passionate fancy to have her picture taken (I suspect the Tarot cards and the live owl in the window had something to do with it), so in we went. She clamors for a lot lately and I try to provide it: flattens her nose against a bakery window and we argue about whether she'll settle for a currant bun instead of a doughnut, wants to stay up late and read and sing to herself so we do, screams for parties so we find them, and *at* parties impels me toward people I would probably not have noticed or (if I had) liked a year ago. She's a surprisingly generous and good little soul and I'd be lost without her, so it's turned out all right in the end. Besides, one ignores her at one's peril. I try not to.

Mind you, she has taken some odd, good things out of my life. Little boys seldom walk with me now. And I've perfected—though regretfully—a more emphatic method of kitty-booting which they seem to understand; at least one of them turned to me yesterday with a look of disgust that said clearer than words: "Good Heavens, how you've degenerated! Don't you know there's nothing in life more important than taking care of Me?"

About the picture: you may think it odd. You may even think it's not her. (You're wrong.) The pitch-ball eyes and thin face are there, all right, but what about the bags under her eyes, the deep, downward lines about her mouth, the strange color of her short-cut hair (it's gray)? What about her astonishing air of being so much older, so much more intellectual, so much more professional, so much more—well, competent—than any Little Dirty Girl could possibly be?

Well, faces change when forty-odd years fall into the developing fluid.

And you have always said that you wanted, that you must have, that you commanded, that you begged, and so on and so on in your interminable, circumlocutory style, that the one thing you desired most in the world was a photograph, a photograph, your kingdom for a photograph—of me.

# Donkeyskin
## Terri Windling

♦

### The Godmother Finds the Princess Weeping
Her Godmother found the Princess weeping. "Don't cry, child," she said, "misery can turn to joy if you are brave. Wrap up in the donkyskin. Leave here and walk until you can walk no more. If you give up everything for virtue's sake, heaven will reward you richly."

### The Moon is Bright upon the Hills
The road carries her to the Land of Enchantment. The moon is bright upon the hills. Maria walks on the shoulder of the highway; she has walked until she can walk no more. A truck stop is her salvation, hunkered low on the bones of the land.

### Once Upon a Time
Once upon a time there was a fortunate King. His subjects loved him; his neighbors respected him; his wife was as beautiful as she was good, and gave him a daughter just as lovely. Their palace was grand and their stables housed six dozen of the world's best horses. The marvel of the stables, however, was not a horse at all, but a magic donkey who soiled his straw with the bright gold of new-minted coins.

### Have You Seen This Child?
Donna Maria Alvarez. Fifteen years old. Brown hair, brown eyes, 5'2" tall. Last seen February 15th in Boise, Idaho. Have you seen this child? Her family is very concerned about her whereabouts. If you have any information, please call the National Hotline for Missing and Exploited Children: 800-572-9054. All information confidential.

### She Asks for a Dress the Color of the Sun
"I will do as you wish, Father," she said, "if you can find me a

*dress the color of the Sun." The King roared, "But that is impossible!" Yet he ordered the finest weavers and tailors to make him a dress the color of the Sun; and when they had done so he laid the radiant garment before his daughter. She took the dress, fled to her room, and said, "Oh Godmother, what shall I do now?"*

### She Comes to a Room That Is Bright and Warm
Maria leans her head against the bathroom mirror and thinks, "Oh Godmother, what shall I do now?" The truck stop's bathroom is bright and warm, and water from the tap eases her thirst. She has not eaten in a day and a half and the smell of charcoal broil makes her feel faint. Someone is knocking on the bathroom door and she cannot sit here any longer.

### She Asks for a Dress the Color of the Moon
*"I will do as you wish, Father," she said, "if you can find me a dress the color of the Moon." The King roared, "That will be difficult!" But when he laid the dress before the Princess, it glowed with a pure and silver light, and stars were captured in the folds of its cloth. She took the dress, fled to her room, and said, "Oh Godmother, what shall I do now?"*

### She Has No Gold Coins to Offer
Maria passes by the truck stop bulletin board with its notices full of goods bought and good sold, men wanted and women and children misplaced. She is drawn to the kitchen by black coffee smells, the clatter of dishes, the voices and lights; but her pockets are empty of magic and jewels and she has no gold coins to offer. The cook is dark-haired and dark of skin; she can see him through a little window. She prays he will give her a break and a job, for he looks like a man acquainted with hunger.

### She asks for a Dress the Color of the Weather
*"I will do as you wish, Father," she said, "if you can find me a dress the color of the weather." The tailors whispered it couldn't be done, but the King roared, "You shall have it tomorrow!" The dress he brought her was sewn with jewels whose colors changed with the changeable sky; the sumptuous cloth was blue and then gray, fickle as a summer storm. She took the dress, fled to her room, and said, "Oh Godmother, what shall I do now?"*

### She Reminds Him of His Sister
*"That girl at the counter, sixteen if she's a day, mebbe younger. Lookit how she struts her little ass—you know exactly what she's looking for, and I've a mind to give it to her." But the other trucker*

*shakes his head; hell, the kid reminds him of his sister back in El
Paso. A girl that age out on her own, she was probably running
away from trouble; she wasn't out here looking for it. He wishes
Joe would leave the poor kid alone. "We've got work to do, man.
You comin'?"*

### She Asks for One Thing More
*"You must ask for one thing more," said her Godmother; "some-
thing he cannot give you. You must ask for the skin of the donkey
in the stable, the source of your father's wealth." But the King had
the bloody hide brought to her and said, "I have done your bid-
ding, Daughter; and now you must do mine." She took the hide,
fled to her room, fell to her knees and wept.*

### Time Passes
*Time passes, now quick, now slow, and the job has become familiar
to Maria, and the tired come-on lines of the truckers, and the
whine of traffic on the highway between Gallup and Santa Fe. The
bruise on her face has faded to yellow and she walks without limping now except when she's tired. She has a room all to herself out
back, with a mattress, a table, two mended wood chairs, and six
paperback books lined up in a neat row. She's never had a room to
herself and she is giddy with space and possession. She locks the
door behind her at night, turning the key with satisfaction.*

### The King Makes a Promise
*But one day the Queen fell ill, and she knew that she was dying.
She called the King to her bedside and said, "My dear, you must
make me a promise. You must promise you will not remarry unless
you find a wife who is better than me." For she worried about her
young daughter, and tales of stepmothers evil and cruel. The King
promised he would not marry unless it was to a maid even better
than she, and so she died content.*

### Next Time She's Going to Fly
*Suzanne smooths the creases out of her silk trousers before she sits
down carefully on the taped vinyl seat. She hates these tacky highway dives, but it is the only place open this late for miles and Barb
claims to be amused by the place, in a campy Roadside America
kind of way. It was madness to let Barbra convince her to drive all
the way to Santa Fe from Los Angeles. She grimaces at the menu
while her companion goes into raptures about the Local Color: the
good ol' boy truckers, the old Hispanic men propping up the
counter, the rabbity teenage waitress with a shiner fading beneath
one eye. . . . Next time Suzanne's going to fly.*

### She Begs Him to Forget This Idea

For some time the King mourned his wife, but then the grief passed and he wished to marry. Yet he was bound by his promise—and there was no maid to be found better than the Queen, unless it was their own daughter. He looked upon his daughter and he saw that she was beautiful indeed. He told the Princess he would marry her, and instructed her to set the date for their wedding. She begged and begged him to forget this idea, but he was mad with desire and would not.

### She Has Come a Long Way

She has come a long way to this vast, empty land; she doesn't think they will find her here. She has begun to relax, even to smile, to sass back the truckers at the counter. One day a dark, heavy man comes in; Maria turns and feels her heart twisting, lodging there like a stone in her breast, a knife blade pressed against hot skin. Until she sees that it's not her father at all, just a stranger looking for the phone.

### The Princess Gives Up Everthing

"If you give up everything for virtue's sake, heaven will reward you richly. Now go, quickly, before your father comes and claims what belongs to him." The Princess wrapped herself in the don-keyskin, her gold hair hidden beneath dirt and soot. And she walked until she could walk no more, until she reached the Enchanted Lands.

### She Likes to Walk the Hills by Night

Maria likes to walk the hills by night when she finishes up the late-night shift and the starlight fills the vast desert sky, turning the red mesas to silver. She says as she walks, "Underneath this skin I am regal, tall, soft as silk and bright as gold. My song is a melancholy one yet my voice is beautiful beyond compare." In fact she is small, sturdy, and dark but she walks in the Land of Enchantment none-theless. She cups moonlight in her strong chapped hands and be-gins to weave herself a dress: the color of the sun, the moon, the weather, with starlight captured in the cloth.

### He Likes to Listen to Her Songs

Now one day the Prince of the Enchanted Lands was strolling past the pig-keeper's hut. The pig-keeper was called Donkeyskin, a strange foreign girl, filthy and rough, yet he loved to listen to the beautiful melancholy songs she sang as she worked. Instead of knocking, he put his eye down to the keyhole and peered inside the room. And there was the loveliest girl he'd ever seen, wearing a dress the color of the Sun, and he promptly lost his heart to her.

### He Stops for a Cup of Coffee

*If Billy doesn't get a cup of java soon, he is going to fall asleep behind the wheel. He stops at an all-night roadside joint, propping his guitar and his University of New Mexico duffel bag against the counter beside him. The waitress is a smallish girl, plain and serious-looking; yet there is something in her that makes him stare at the girl when she turns away. It is something bright and dark; something gay and sad; something golden-hued and fierce and fine. So he orders a second coffee he doesn't want and lingers at the counter. When he teases a smile from her at last, he is stunned by how beautiful she is after all. He leaves with regret five cups later; but his parents will worry if he's late.*

### The Moon Is Bright Upon the Hills

*Maria stands at the window and watches him go. The moon is bright upon the hills. She collects his empty cup and spoon, squeezing quickly past the big red-faced trucker who always tries to pinch her ass; past the booth where the golden women sit, laughing like bells, shining like jewels. She pulls the donkeyskin back around her shoulders, taking comfort in the soft, familiar fur. She knows one day she will have to learn to live without it. She knows one day the Prince will return, the one who can see beneath the fur. The highway will bring him back to her; next week, next month, or maybe next year. She knows he'll come because he's lost his heart; it's there on the counter, beside the tip.*

### The Godmother Finds the Princess Weeping

*Her godmother found the Princess weeping. "Don't cry, child," she said. "Misery can turn to joy if you are brave. Wrap up in the donkeyskin. Leave here and walk until you can walk no more." The Princess put on the donkeyskin. She walked until she could walk no more and she found herself on a long, straight road where a sign said* WELCOME TO NEW MEXICO: THE LAND OF ENCHANTMENT *in bold black script. The past stretched out behind her. The future stretched out before her. And she knew which way she had to go.*

"Brother and Sister" is a German tale from Grimms' that can be found in variations around the world, including Native American stories in our own country. The theme of shape-changing, turning from human to animal form, is a particularly evocative one, connecting us to the untamed wild inside ourselves. In the following modern version, the boy and the girl are not actually siblings, but are nonetheless drawn together in the realm that lies on the other side of midnight.

# In the Night Country

## ♦ Ellen Steiber ♦

*"We're the people who see the colors. We've been around forever."*
*—RuPaul*

He was the unruly child. She remembered him from fourth grade when his family had lived down the street from hers. He was the one who started all the fights; who in a rage threw a blue glass vase against a school window, shattering both; who twisted Greta Kreske's arm behind her back till she cried. Their teacher had written a note to his mother. He'd shown it to all the boys. It began, "I'm sorry to have to tell you that Devon is an unruly child. . . ."

Like most of the others in her class, Cilla had felt a sense of profound relief when their teacher quite suddenly announced that the McKennas had moved upstate. She never knew where, she never cared. There were miles between them. The classroom was a safer place.

And now eight years later he was sitting across from her under the fluorescent lights of Vic's All-Night Diner at just past one on a Wednesday morning. Cilla did not often frequent Vic's at this hour. It was, in fact, the first time she'd been out this late on her own. Seventeen years old, and sitting in the local diner seemed an extremely daring thing to do. She had no choice, she told herself. Tonight she wouldn't stay in that house. And Vic's was the only place open. She'd ordered black coffee because she thought that's what one did in all-night diners. She sat staring into her third cup, feeling the caffeine speed through her, trying to pretend she didn't see Devon McKenna.

He was wearing a black leather jacket, its left arm ripped shoulder to elbow. His hair was longer now, straight deep red hair that fell to his shoulders. A small silver skull hung from his left ear. He was still good-looking, with long, narrow eyes that seemed to measure everything they took in. He was smoking a cigarette, and slowly, deliberately, harassing the hell out of the waitress—first telling her his doughnut was stale, insisting she exchange it for another and another after that, then complaining that the coffee was piss poor. The waitress was growing increasingly annoyed, and yet she brought him three different doughnuts, put up a new pot of cofee. She did what he wanted, and Cilla knew why.

His eyes came to rest on her and lit with recognition, as if to say, "Look what's come round again." She began earnestly reading a packet of sugar, but it was too late.

He was standing up, looking at her hard and long, and now made his way through the tables to the back of the diner. The unruly child was coming straight toward her. As he had when he was nine, he scared her to death.

"As I live and breathe . . ." Devon spoke with a decidedly Texan twang. "If isn't Prissss-cilla Biehler."

"It isn't," she wanted to say. She said nothing, just stared at the imitation-marble Formica tabletop.

"Where you been keepin' yourself, girl?" The accent went beyond Texan. It parodied an imaginary maiden aunt who'd survived the Alamo.

Maybe if she stared at the table long enough, he would get the message and go away.

"Musta been doin' *something* since the fourth grade." He sat down across from her in the red vinyl booth, reached out and grabbed her hand. "I asked you a question," he said, and the country twang and the mockery were gone from his voice. His tone was quiet and low and surprisingly gentle.

"I—"

"You," he prompted. She could almost believe he was interested.

"I was drinking some coffee," she said.

"Since the fourth grade?" The twang was back. "Must be quite a cup of coffee there."

"Stop talking like you're from Texas or something," she snapped, startling them both. "Where'd you pick up that stupid accent, anyway?"

He laughed. "You've gotten grouchy since the fourth grade."

He was still holding her wrist. She jerked it back, but her hand didn't move. He had pinned it to the table.

"Let go of me."

Devon shook his head slowly. "Not until you tell me what you're doing here. You got me curious, Ms. Biehler."

"I'll tell the waitress you're bothering me."

He gave an elaborate shrug and reverted to the Texan twang. "I'll tell *you* a secret," he offered. "That waitress there isn't going to help you. Hell, she can't even make coffee. She's just plain relieved it's you I'm botherin' and not her."

Cilla stole a look at the round black-and-white clock: one twenty-three. How many minutes would it be before he left her alone? And then what? Would she remain in the diner, waiting for the next psychopath to notice her? Home almost seemed a welcome alternative. Almost. She'd find somewhere else to wait out the night, even if meant walking seven miles to the next town. "Let me go," she repeated.

He did as she asked. She stood up, snatched the check from the table, left a fifty-cent tip, and without looking at him marched straight to the cash register at the front of the diner. "I want to pay," she announced loudly. She pretended not to notice as Devon crossed the floor of the diner and and came to stand directly behind her.

The waitress was at the other end of the counter, wiping it down with a dirt-smeared rag. She looked up. "Be right with you, honey."

"Honey." Devon stood close behind, whispering in her ear. "Betcha not too many people call you honey."

She ignored him.

"C'mon, honey, I'm not so bad. Why don't you give me a chance? Why don't you take a risk?" He snaked around to her other side. "You *ever* take a risk?" he asked, sounding genuinely curious.

She whirled to face him. "Are you going to follow me out of here?"

He studied her, as if the idea had only just occurred to him, and she cursed herself for bringing it up.

"Why won't you give me a chance?" he asked in the voice without mockery.

Cilla decided to try honesty. "Because you scare me. Because you *want* to scare me."

"I see." He sat down on one of the stools at the counter, spinning himself toward her then away. "Do you run from everything that scares you?"

The waitress took her money, handed back her change, and told her to have a good day.

"I—I don't have to tell you anything."

"No," he agreed reasonably, "but I'll keep asking till you do. If you want to get rid of me, you're going to have to give me a straight answer."

"All right, then," she said. "Yes. I run from everything that scares me. Are you satisfied?"

"Uh-huh," he said, exactly the way the school shrink said uh-huh every time she told him what was going on at home.

"So where are you headed?" Devon asked abruptly.

She had no idea of where she was going. She only knew she wasn't going to take any more of this. "I gave you your straight answer," she told him. "No more."

"You don't have a car," he stated with maddening surety. "Why don't you let me run you home? It's kind of late for you to be walking."

"I'm not going home."

He reached for her arm and drew her toward him. "Now that," he told her, "is the first interesting thing you've said."

She was aware of being close to him, of being drawn into his radius. It made her keenly aware of her baggy brown corduroy pants, her faded green cotton turtleneck, her ratty black hightops, and her straight brown hair cut in layers that had grown out six weeks ago. He made her aware of how just how plain she was.

"So what do you want to do tonight?" he asked casually, as if they went out all the time.

She wanted to go home. Or rather, she wanted to go to a place where there was a warm, comfortable bed she could sink into. A place where she would be safe. Such a place, as far as she knew, had never existed.

"I want you to stop bothering me," she answered.

"And leave you all by your lonesome? In this end of town?"

He'd let go of her. She edged away from him, balanced herself on the end of the next counter stool. "I've changed my mind. I think I'll have another cup of coffee." She looked for the waitress, who had disappeared.

"You're stalling," he said. "You know you have to walk out of here sometime tonight. And"—he gave a huge yawn—"deep down in your heart of hearts you know you want to go with me."

"You're an egomaniac."

Devon grinned, held out his hand. "An egomaniac with a car who'll get you out of this lousy diner. Could be worse."

Cilla looked again for the waitress who was nowhere to be seen.

"I'll buy you that cup of coffee," he offered. "For the road."

"No." She was going to end this now. She stood up and walked out of the diner into the cold night air. It was February and the streets were covered with a thin film of ice. She was wearing a cheap down jacket that must have had all of forty feathers left. Even brand new, three years ago, it had never kept her warm. She hugged it tightly around her. There was no one on the streets. Maybe she could walk for a while and then go back to the diner. Devon McKenna would have gotten bored and left. Or maybe she'd walk the seven miles to the next town. Maybe she'd just freeze to death and not have to deal with any of this.

She felt the old sensation along her shoulder blades. The shrink had named it and dismissed it, said, "It's understandable. You don't feel you can cover your back." It was much worse than that. It felt as if her skin had been stripped clean, leaving the nerve endings exposed. And the nerves sensed the dark behind her, waited for something to manifest itself in that emptiness. What it would be was no mystery. One crazy day, or night, something would be there. And she'd always known that when the emptiness was filled, there would be an attacker in that space. She was sure of it. That's where her death would come from.

"Well, at least you're goin' in the right direction."

He was right beside her. She hadn't heard him follow her out of the diner, hadn't seen his shadow under the street lights.

"My car's down the street."

"Wonderful," she said. "I'm so excited."

"Lotta girls like riding with me," he informed her. It was said without vanity, a simple fact.

He walked with a rock-star strut, canted forward, boot heels coming down hard against the icy pavement. It was a walk that was both promise and warning, said as clear as words, "Gonna lay you down and fuck you all night long." It made her wonder if what he said was true. Did lots of girls like riding with him? Did he have girlfriends? One girl? She glanced up at him and saw the planes of his face made sharper by the shadows.

A thin cat darted out from between two brick buildings and cut in front of them.

"Black cat cross your path, bad luck," Devon said lightly.

Cilla hadn't even noticed the cat was black. She'd always wanted a cat. In the second she'd seen it she'd wished this one were hers.

"So." He grabbed her arm again, bringing her to an abrupt halt. "I'd say it's your bad luck you happened to run into me tonight. But I'll tell you what I've figured out about bad luck. Once it's got you, you can't fight it. You just gotta ride it out."

"Gee, that's profound." She watched his face to see if sarcasm worked against him, and saw only a glint of what might have been reproof in the long, narrow eyes.

"Don't pretend it doesn't have you," he chided her softly. "Girl, you got back luck wrapped around you so thick, it's a wonder you can walk." Somehow those words frightened her worse than anything else that had happened that night. They frightened her because the second he said them she knew they were true.

"It's not going to let you go." He was taunting her now. "Not until it's done with you."

"That's not luck. That's you."

"Comes down to the same thing now, don't it?"

She heard voices and saw a couple walking on the other side of the street, a middle-aged man in a bulky coat and a woman with long, dark hair. "I'll scream," she threatened.

"Go ahead."

Instead she darted past him, toward them. He reached out, caught the collar of her jacket, and reeled her back in. She began shouting in earnest, unnerved by the terror in her own voice.

The couple slowed and the man called out an unintelligible reply.

Devon's laughter cut through the night. "This just ain't your night, Priscilla. Who'd've thought we'd get Japanese tourists in this end of town?"

She twisted away violently and again found she couldn't break free. She could still scream. Even if the couple didn't understand English, they'd understand that she was in trouble. "Please," she cried, "I need—"

Devon turned her toward her him. He ran one hand gently down the side of her face, cutting off her cry. "What *do* you need?" he asked, all menace gone. He grinned at her, rubbed her shoulders briskly. "A blanket for starters. You're freezing to death."

She stood shaking, unable to scream, unable to answer. The caffeine was still speeding through her, converting adrenaline to fear at a lightning rate. Everything was going too fast, and everything was constricted. She fought a wave of dizziness, as if she'd suddenly become unmoored. His terrorizing her, she expected; the flash of kindness nearly undid her. She desperately wanted to believe it was real, a lifeline out of a long, slow drowning.

On the other side of the street the couple kept walking and turned the corner, and Cilla knew with sudden certainty that what Devon was holding out was not a lifeline at all, but the hand that was going to take her down.

"Come on," he said. He was walking at her side, hemming her in against the buildings. He steered her two blocks south and then up against the dented fender of an early '70s Trans Am. All the streetlights but one had been smashed in, and that one was at the far corner. She couldn't tell what color the car was, but she saw the big, ugly bird on the hood. It made perfect sense. The unruly child had himself a muscle car.

He opened the door for her, surprising her with the gesture of courtesy. Resigned, she dropped low into a bucket seat.

"Use the seat belt," he told her, surprising her again.

She buckled herself in, only dimly wondering what would come next. He started the car. Her teeth were chattering and she was shaking violently, whether from fear or cold she wasn't sure. Her hands and feet had gone numb.

He lit a cigarette, and she felt the smoke settling on her, coating them both in its smell. She was keenly aware of having entered Devon McKenna's world, of being cloaked in it, reeking of it. "I'll put the heat on in a minute," he told her. "Engine has to warm up." He shifted into first, and she saw that his jeans were ripped across the thigh in three different places.

He drove past brick warehouses and the town's two factories, past department stores and the bus station, past the projects. Except for the bus station, everything was shut down. They were not driving anywhere near her neighborhood. He was not taking her toward home.

He turned on the radio, and she flinched at the blast of metal. "You don't like that, do you?"

"Not much."

He shrugged, not changing the station or turning it down. "So," he said, "how come a good girl like you doesn't want to go home tonight?"

Cilla's anger returned as the car's heater took the cold from her. "I just don't."

He shrugged again. "That's cool. Hell, I never want to go home. Only drop in to change clothes."

"I thought your family moved upstate."

"What makes you think I live with them?"

Most kids in school still lived with their families. Then again, Devon had never had much use for school. She looked out the window. They were on the outskirts of the city. An auto repair garage, a feed store, a salvage yard for scrap metal flashed by. There were no lights out here. A singer on the radio was wailing about being so far away.

"Where are you going?" she asked.

"You mean, where are *we* going?"

The "we" made her profoundly uneasy. It also made her realize that some part of her liked riding with a good-looking boy in his muscle car. She'd never done anything like this. She had no idea of what "this" actually was.

"I have to make a stop," he told her.

She assumed he meant he had to find a restroom. It didn't occur to her that there was actually a place he meant to go.

"Ain't your momma gonna be mad if you don't come home tonight?" He was taunting her again. "She ain't gonna like it, she discovers you been out all night."

"I don't care if she likes it."

The corners of his mouth turned up. "That's the spirit. Fuck 'em if they can't take a joke."

That's what this was to him, then. A joke. She saw as little humor in it as her mother would.

"I remember your mother," he went on. "Skinny lady, kinda wiry black hair. Had a real mouth on her." He gave her a reckless grin. "Chewed me out a few times. One time, I was sure she was gonna kick my ass. Used to think she was one scary lady."

Cilla tried to remember her mother shouting at Devon and couldn't.

He pushed in the lighter, then held the glowing end against another cigarette. They were on open road now, no cars or buildings in sight. He took a drag on the cigarette and hit the gas. He was doing eighty.

The car lurched as Devon cut across four lanes of highway and veered onto a narrow road. They were well past the outskirts of the city now, heading north toward the mountains that lay beyond. Cilla had no real idea of where they were. She felt as if they'd been riding all night, though she suspected it was more like twenty minutes.

She had not been able to get anything out of Devon as to where they were going or why. He answered all of her questions with smug sarcasm that held no answers at all. She was tired of him and his cigarette smoke, tired of his seesawing between menace and seduction. She was tired. The night stretched out ahead of them like the road, flat and dark and endless.

"We're here," he suddenly announced, slowing the car to about sixty.

She peered through the window. More dark highway. Small, scrubby trees on the edge of the road. There was nothing out there.

"Now what am I going to do with you?" he wondered aloud.

She felt the band of fear around her chest tighten. What *was* he going to do with her? Lurid headlines offered a multiple choice quiz. Would he: a.) rape her? b.) beat her? c.) leave her to freeze to death? Or d.) all of the above?

He downshifted and cut right, skidding across the asphalt and onto a dirt road. The Trans Am jerked down into a trench-deep rut and then up. Cilla braced herself against the dashboard as the car dove into the next furrow, surfaced with a shudder, and pitched forward again.

"This baby could use some new shocks," Devon observed.

*And a new driver*, she added silently. Earlier that night, when she'd left her house, she'd still moved with the assurance that had been with her all her life—that although she would one day die, she had plenty of time before that day arrived. That sense had changed, was changing by the second. Now she knew unarguably that her body could be broken. She shut her eyes as the right front fender missed a thick wooden post by inches. When she opened them again the ruts in the road had become shallower, and the Trans Am was jouncing along past bare-branched trees.

In the distance she saw lights. She could make out two buildings, small wood A-frames, a wooden walkway connecting them, and in the distance another much smaller building.

"Oh no," she said, recognizing it from descriptions she'd heard. "Whatever else happens tonight, you are not getting me arrested. Turn around right now!"

Devon's voice conveyed only mild interest. "You giving me orders, girl?"

Her mother would have called the police by now, she knew. They'd be looking for her. And Devon had driven her straight into what had to top the police hit list of favorite raid sites. "I know what this place is. You get me out of here now!"

"All right." He was bored. "Tell me. What exactly is this place?"

"Deadhead Manor." It sounded silly as soon as she said it, but that was what everyone called the place. No one knew who owned it. Years ago it been a party house, the place where the acid came in and the trips began. Far as it was from the city, the word spread. Kids found their way out here. The Revelers, that's what the acid heads had called themselves. No one knew how many there were, or how many took the trip and never came back. The Revelers found new toys; they played with other drugs. They enshrined a perverse elite, the Lords of the Manor, the ones who'd OD'd there. Connie, a girl who used to baby-sit for Cilla, joined the Lords and died in a hospital emergency room hours later. More recently growers had rented the place. When the police raided it a year ago, they claimed they'd gotten a hydroponic marijuana crop worth half a million.

Eleven people had been arrested, three of them from her school. The place was deserted after that. The owner couldn't sell it, realtors couldn't rent it. But there were still rumors of kids going up there for buys.

"Deadhead Manor," Devon said thoughtfully. "You got any objections to the Dead?"

"You're here for drugs."

"What if I am? You got a problem with that?"

"I don't want to be around when the cops bust you. I want to get out of here now."

"Then you can walk." He pulled into a small clearing, parked, and lit another cigarette. The faint green glow of the dashboard was gone and so were the heat and the blaring music. "No one is going to bust anybody," he told her. "And you can stop acting like I'm about to pump heroin into your veins. Though that could be interesting . . ." He took another drag off the cigarette and offered it to her. She shook her head. "Didn't think so," he said with a low laugh. "Might do you some good, you know. Calm you down. Are you always this jumpy?"

She glared because she didn't want him to know how ashamed she was; feeling helpless against him shamed her. She wished she had the courage to knock him out and take his keys. She knew it would be useless. She didn't know how to drive stick.

"I've got a little business to take care of," he told her. "I'll only be gone a few minutes. Don't go anywhere."

He'd just turned off the car and already the cold was back, filtering down from where the window didn't quite meet the top of the door, cutting straight through her jacket to her bones. She was shivering again. She undid the seat belt so she could wrap her arms around her sides.

"Hey, it's all right," he said softly. He rested a warm hand lightly on the back of her neck. With a sense of dislocation, she realized he was trying to comfort her. "Now be a good girl and stay put," he said, the gentle tone taking the sting out of the order. "I'll be back in ten."

Cold air rushed into the car as he got out. Then the door slammed, and she heard his boots on the frozen ground. He strode toward the houses, disappearing into the trees. In the distance a dog barked.

Cilla didn't know whether to be relieved because he was gone or terrified because she was stranded miles from the city in the middle of Drug Dealer Central. She *could* get out of the car and walk. Outside the wind picked up, keening high in the bare trees. Through the window she saw a thin crescent moon. It was waxing, she remembered; it had been new just a few nights ago. There would be some light. Her eyes would adjust. She knew the roads became a maze of traffic circles and clovers when they neared the city, but she would find her way.

She got out of the car and took a deep gulp of cold air that didn't reek of Devon McKenna's cigarettes. It was better already; she was no longer in his world. She headed for the highway, bent forward into the wind. She could feel the layer of ice coating the ground through the soles of her hightops. She shoved her hands into her pockets, but the wind bit through the jacket and the thin wool gloves. Her fingers ached.

Ahead of her the dirt road forked. She didn't remember that from the ride in. Had they come from the right or the left? The left, she was sure of it.

She walked along the dirt road, relieved as she saw the deep ruts. It was farther than she'd thought to the highway. She refused to think about where she would go when and if she ever made it back to the city. Behind her she heard the dog again. Another thing not to think about. Dogs scared her, and tonight she couldn't afford to be scared by one more thing. Her nose was running; she wiped it on the back of her glove.

Another dark winter night came back to her. Her parents had argued. Her father ended the argument as he'd ended so many others, by finding somewhere else to go. This time he'd gone to buy firewood, and he'd taken Cilla with him. The station wagon had broken down on the way back. Together they'd walked three miles on a highway edged with woods before finding a house where they could call a tow truck. She'd been eleven years old. That was the year something broke between them. That was the year she'd found herself unable to talk to him about anything. She'd seen things in the woods that night—dark shapes watching them, marking them, setting a shadow on her father that he would never shake. And she hadn't said a word.

The sound of something churning brought her back to the present. Electric light slanted through the trees. Cilla could make out a narrow slotted window just beneath the roof of a small rectangular building. She swore under her breath. She'd taken the wrong fork. Instead of going toward the highway, she'd circled behind the Manor to the house farthest from the road. Ahead of her she could see the lights of the two A-frames.

She studied the small back building. This must have been the grower's room. The windows were so high and narrow, no one could see inside. Vehicles surrounded it, splaying out from the building like spokes from a hub. She counted three pickup trucks, a VW van, a Cadillac that looked as if it had done time at a funeral parlor, a Harley chopper, a '50s Chevy missing its left front door, and a pristine white Honda. Car batteries and odd lengths of piping lay scattered on the ground. The churning sound was coming from a tiny washing machine sandwiched between the Harley and the Cadillac. It was hooked up to an outdoor pump, washing away in the middle of the frigid night. Cilla watched it with wonder. She was half-tempted to open it, see if there really were clothes in there, but she didn't dare get so close to the building.

*The road,* she reminded herself, *I've got to get to the road.* She turned back toward the trees and found she couldn't go back. The dark shapes were waiting for her there, she knew it. She couldn't go back that way when there was light here that might keep them at bay. She'd just have to stay clear of the houses. She'd make sure no one saw her.

Her feet were too numb to tiptoe; she couldn't even feel her toes but she walked as carefully as she could, keeping well away from the wooden walkway between the buildings with its wrought-iron lamppost. The lamppost struck her as oddly as the washing machine had; she would have guessed it had been liberated from a street corner except it was too short to have been a real street lamp. It couldn't have been more than six feet high, but it made her feel as if the Manor were really a miniature village, an actual manor, late-twentieth-century-druggie style.

She passed the middle building, the smaller A-frame. White gauze curtains covered its windows. She stood for a minute, watching for Devon's silhouette. He'd been back in her life for maybe three hours but she'd know him anywhere. She felt sick as she realized he'd gotten inside her. A few hours of terror and he was inside her for good. Nothing moved behind the curtains. She walked on.

There were no curtains in the window of the big A-frame. A room had been added onto the side of this one, a kitchen lined with cabinets painted an alarming shade of purple. The upstairs section was dark, but she had a clear view of the main room. A man stood, leaning back against a wood-paneled wall, heavily muscled arms folded across his chest. He was wearing jeans and a faded black T-shirt, and he held a beer can in one hand. He was older than Devon, maybe twenty-five or so, with a day's growth of stubble. Dark blue tattoos wound up his forearms. He was glowering at Devon, who sat relaxed in an armchair covered with red paisley fabric. A girl was perched on his lap. She was the sort of girl Cilla always thought of as a summer girl. Despite it being the middle of February, she was barefoot, wearing cut-off shorts, a lacy camisole that just skimmed her breasts, and a thin silver anklet. She was very tan, with long, straight honey-colored hair, almost the same rich shade as her skin. She had one hand draped around Devon's neck. He had one hand resting on her ass, patting it lightly to the rhythm of the bass that pulsed through the A-frame's walls. Cilla could feel it coming up through the ground. She watched, fascinated and inexplicably hurt.

The man with the tattoos crumpled the empty beer can, threw it down, and strode across the room, disappearing behind a wooden door. The beer can rolled across the wood floor, coming to rest at Devon's feet. Devon gave no sign he'd noticed either. The summer girl had both arms around his neck now, and her head was bent close to his.

Cilla heard it moments before it registered, a low guttural sound and something metallic, like the links on a chain. She turned from the window to see a dog bounding across the frozen ground. It emerged from the shadows, moving steadily, clearly illuminated beneath the light of the lamppost. It had a sleek, powerful body and a chain collar. It was running straight for her.

She bolted for the road, stumbled against the edge of the wooden platform that jutted out from the house, and fell. Stunned, she lay for a moment, staring at the wooden planking, feeling the night wind part her hair, ream her scalp with cold.

The dog was closing on her. She saw its teeth, gleaming wet ivory. She never meant to scream, but the terror rose from her throat with a will of its own.

The door to the large A-frame burst open. Devon and the tattooed man stood silhouetted in bright yellow light.

She heard Devon's voice first, "What the—", then the man calling, "Demon!"

The sound of the jangling metal collar stopped; the dog must have stopped, awaiting its next command. Cilla didn't look. She pulled herself up and ran, away from the houses and the lights, into the darkness.

She heard their boot heels against the wooden steps that fronted the A-frame. Their voices carried clearly, Devon's edged with disgust, "Priscilla! Oh, fucking hell . . ."—the man's with disbelief—"You brought a girl here?"

"I told her to stay in the car."

"And you thought she'd listen."

She was well away from the dirt road now, moving stiffly in the cold, making her way through a tangle of trees and brush. A sharp pain streaked through her rib cage. Just a side stitch, she told herself. She tried to run with a smoother stride so it wouldn't hurt so much and found she couldn't. She could barely see two feet in front of her. Cloud cover had come in; the moon was gone.

The man gave a high-pitched whistle and the dog began running, loping through the darkness, following her as surely as if it were leashed to her. Cilla stumbled, fell again, and blinked back tears as something sharp—a stone, a piece of broken glass, she couldn't even tell—sliced through her pants leg and into her skin. She forced herself to stand, ignoring the blood that streamed down her leg. Her breath was coming in short, hard gasps. Maybe she ought to just give up. She could hear the dog, its metal collar jangling, and behind it Devon and the tattooed man.

"Priscilla." Devon's voice was so close she could almost feel his breath. "I'm not in the mood for this now. Come on, stop playing games." His voice dropped low, became coaxing. "You're not gonna get away, girl. You already know that. So just come on out, and we'll call the dog back. You don't want to get hurt, do you?"

She didn't want to get hurt. She'd never wanted to be hurt, and when she thought of the things she'd agreed to so that she wouldn't be hurt, nausea swept through her so strong it nearly brought her to her knees. When she thought of the things she'd done so she wouldn't get hurt, she knew exactly what had brought this night on. It was inevitable, she realized. This whole night was inevitable. Why was she even trying to run? How was it that she couldn't numb this out like all the rest and simply take whatever came? Somehow, though, she couldn't give herself up, couldn't wait for Devon and the tattooed man and the demon dog to get her. She heard the sound of water running, and vaguely remembered that dogs couldn't trail a scent across water.

She followed the sound of the water the way the dog was undoubtedly following her, instinctively, unerringly. The water was calling her. She shook her head, trying to shake off the distinct but absurd sensation that it was actually speaking, only she couldn't quite make out the words. That didn't matter. All that mattered was she heard it running fast and loud and tantalizingly near.

"Priscilla." Devon's voice was so close, she whirled. There were trees, some sort of evergreen, on all sides; nothing else. "Priscilla." The night was playing tricks with her ears. No, she realized, it was more basic than that. The night was playing tricks with *her*. It had been from the moment the sun went down and she walked into her house to find her mother waiting in her room, waiting to tell her that she'd been thoughtless. She'd forgotten. Didn't she ever think about anything besides herself? Anyone would look at her and think she didn't care. Did she even remember? It had been a year.

She heard the dog moving toward her, heard it panting, then Devon's voice rising from the trees. "You keep on with this game of hide and seek, and you won't have to worry about the goddamn dog. I'll take you apart myself."

She was on the edge of a steep bank. Below she saw water racing fast and white. She screamed as a hand closed on her hair and yanked hard. "You stupid little bitch." His voice was perfectly, frighteningly calm, and the violence that had been in Devon since he was a child, that had always hovered just beneath the surface, was loose. She could feel it as clearly as she could feel the cold. "I told you to stay in the car." He gave another vicious pull, jerking her head down and then up again.

She stood still, forcing herself to meet his eyes, willing herself not to cry. She'd lost count of how many times tonight she'd tried not to cry. A part of her was almost relieved to be caught, to have it over with at last. She couldn't tell anything from his face. It was white and harsh under the night sky, his eyes narrowed to slits. The silver skull swung like a metronome, setting a steady, unbreakable rhythm for the time she had left.

Instinct made her step away from him. Her back foot came down on air. And she slid over the lip of the bank, taking him with her.

She dropped straight into the water, never touched the bank or the countless boulders that lined the streambed. Somewhere in midair, somewhere between the top of the chasm and the stream, Devon let go. She was caught by water deeper than she would have guessed, sent spinning downstream, gliding over moss-covered rocks as if her skin were covered with an otter's pelt. She felt her hair streaming out behind her, her clothes ballooning. She swallowed a lungful of cool, clear water, tried to lift her head above the surface and couldn't. She was too far under. She was whirling. She was going down.

✦✦✦

The stream pushed her up against a large white rock. Cilla found herself with her side curled around the stone, her hand grasping one of the thick tree roots that covered it. It was as if the stream had deposited her there, neatly, without harm.

Grasping onto the roots, she pulled herself out of the water and collapsed onto her knees, choking first, then vomiting water. When the spasms were done she stayed on her knees, arms wrapped round her sides, head touching the rock. She was shaking worse than she had all night. She sent out a brief prayer, not knowing whom she was praying to or even what it was she was praying for beyond a general round of help.

She got to her feet unsteadily, using the trunk of the tree for support. It was a sycamore tree, she saw, its branches silver-white, luminous and alive under the moon. The moon was back, and now there were also stars, brighter than she'd ever known them, blazing so white she could almost sense their fire.

She looked down at the mountain-fed stream racing beneath her feet. She wasn't cold, she realized. The water should have been filled with ice. It should have been cold enough to kill her. And now that she was out of it and soaking wet, she ought to be rapidly dying of exposure. Instead she was warm, as if she'd emerged into a summer night.

She took a deep breath and tried to get her bearings. She was in a chasm of sorts. The bank she'd toppled off of was so high she couldn't see the top. There was no way back to that shore. On her other side she saw a narrow strip of sand bordered by huge granite boulders. Beyond them land rose steep and dark. She tried to remember what she knew about the location of Deadhead Manor; she hadn't thought it was this close to the base of the mountains. Then again, she had no idea of how far she'd drifted.

She decided to get out of the middle of the stream. The strip of sand seemed the most sensible destination. Around her trees grew straight out of the water—cottonwood, willow, and sycamore. They all had leaves, bright green under the February moonlight. The realization made her dizzy as she slowly began to make her way across the stream.

She reached the beach without difficulty, and this, too, surprised her. For so long now everything had been so hard. She sat on the sand, removed the down jacket, which weighed at least fifty pounds wet, wrung it out, folded it, and set it neatly between two of the rocks that edged the beach. Then she removed her hightops and her socks. The sand beneath her feet was soft and cool. And around her the night sky had turned from black to a deep sapphire blue that allowed her to see the green leaves of the trees, the tiny piece of red coral in her ring, the purple violets that grew at the base of the willows. When she was seven her father had taken her to see *Giselle*. She didn't remember much about the ballet itself. What she still remembered was the staging—a deep blue starlit night in which she could see all the colors: the red doors on the village houses; the trees in the woods, dappled green and brown; the dancers' spangled costumes glittering pink and yellow, green and ivory, lavender and blue. There had been no true darkness in that night, and she had wanted desperately to go into it.

This wasn't the same thing. She knew that, as surely as she knew that she would never make it back across the water. At least not here or now. The stream was coursing past her, all swirling white foam, broken only by the trees and rocks. It leapt; it tumbled; it raced to some faraway sea. She felt its sound filling the chasm, echoing through the trees, pulsing through her own blood. It *was* speaking. She could make it out clearly now. "Earth take you," it chanted, "earth take you."

Nervously, she turned away from the stream. Boulders edged the shoreline. Behind them she could see the mountains rising. And lying on his side, fighting for every breath, was Devon McKenna.

He had fared much worse than she. He was gasping, trying to suck the air into his lungs. Blood welled from a cut beneath his left eye. His leather jacket was gone and so were his boots; except for his jeans, he'd been stripped bare. Cilla could see purple bruises on his shoulder and along his ribs. She stood paralyzed, undecided. Now what was she going to do with him?

The choice wasn't hers. As she stood staring at him her vision altered, blurred at the periphery, sharpened at the very center. The rocks, the trees, the deep blue light all vanished. She could see only Devon, as if his figure had been cut out of a photograph and mounted on a piece of black construction paper. Still gasping, he lifted himself from the ground onto his hands and knees and began to pull himself toward the water. He was obviously in pain. Did he really think he could get back across?

He reached the very edge of the stream. Cilla felt a mild ripple of surprise as she realized that although his form was still etched against darkness, she was able to see the stream beside him. No trees or rocks or even sand. But she saw the water running, white foam on black water. It was still chanting, louder than ever. She wondered if he heard it.

"Devon?"

He saw her then and tried to speak but couldn't. She watched a series of emotions flicker through his eyes—hope quickly replaced by contempt and something more powerful in him than either: rage.

"Earth take you, earth take you . . ."

He did hear it. For the first time since she'd known him, Devon McKenna looked scared. Panicked, he tried to stand, but he wasn't fast enough. Beside him the stream kicked up in a wave, the water arcing, then washing over him. It left him coated in a layer of dark red silt. Cilla watched, unable to trust her eyes. It was Devon, there on the edge of the stream, balancing on hands and knees, wet skin and jeans covered in fine red clay, and yet it wasn't. He was changing. He was being molded, shaped—a creature made anew.

The black water gathered and washed over him again, this time rins-

ing the clay from his skin and hair and jeans. And leaving in his place a
buck, his coat a deep red, his eyes longer, narrower than any deer's. Cilla
shut her own eyes briefly and opened them again. Her vision had returned to normal. The boulders and trees and deep blue sky were back.
The stream was no longer black but a deep bottle green. And she was still
staring at a reddish five-point stag who had a deep gash beneath its left
eye. At its feet lay Devon's torn jeans.

The buck was having no trouble breathing. He shook himself, lean
muscles rippling beneath a glossy pelt. Then he swung his head toward
her, the long eyes intent. It was the same look Devon had given her earlier
that night when he'd first seen her in the diner, the look that marked her
as prey. This is crazy, Cilla told herself. Devon McKenna did not just turn
into a deer, and even if he did, deer aren't predators.

For a long, hysterical moment she tried vainly to recall deer lore from
a wildlife documentary she'd seen. The only fact that came back to her
was that deer shed their antlers for winter and began to grow new ones—
were "in velvet"—in the spring. It was the middle of February. This buck
couldn't have antlers. Then again, Devon had always broken all the rules.

The buck's ears went back and it uttered a sound that was a cross between a whistle and a snort. It lowered its head, the tines of its antlers
level with Cilla's stomach and chest. It walked forward stiffly. She *did* remember that from the documentary. The lowered antlers and stiff walk
were all unmistakable signs of aggression.

It moved toward her slowly. Equally slowly she backed away. She felt
her back touch stone. She chanced a quick look behind; she was up
against a massive boulder. The buck stopped about fifteen feet away from
her, standing so quietly it seemed to have emerged from the sand beneath
its feet. Cilla watched, amazed and terrified by its stillness. She could
sense its adrenaline rising. The deer was gathering its energy, readying its
muscles, preparing for the charge.

There was no warning. One second the deer was still. The next it ex-
ploded into movement. Cilla watched mesmerized as grains of sand flew
beneath its hooves, caught in the blue air over its antlers and hung there
suspended, tiny bits of mica and quartz sparkling in the moonlight.

The deer was charging full out, and yet everything seemed to slow, to
be spun out of a place where time moved differently—where there was so
much more of it in any given breath. Cilla found time to marvel that she
would die from being gored by a stag. It was not a common death these
days. And she found time to react, not because she thought she could actually save herself, but because it seemed the appropriate thing to do. It
was what one did when confronted by a raging deer. Her hands flew up to
cover her head and she crouched against the base of the rock, drawing her
body as tight and small as she could.

The buck pulled itself it in, stopped inches from her, its sides heaving.
Cilla looked up in confusion, and saw something in Devon's eyes—they
were definitely Devon's eyes—that she couldn't understand. He stepped

backward, glanced behind him, turned, and moved off with perfect animal grace. He stopped at the edge of the water, swerved, and gazed at her again. She noticed that the blood beneath his left eye had dried. He swung his head to the side, once, twice, three times. He seemed to be gesturing inland. And this time Cilla understood. He was letting her go.

The deer stood waiting. Obviously, she was the one who had to move. She glanced around, looking for her jacket and hightops, and wasn't terribly surprised to discover that they had vanished from the beach. The buck snorted impatiently. "All right already!" she told him, and began walking barefoot away from the stream. She felt slightly foolish obeying a deer; but then, arguing with him didn't seem like a good idea.

She gazed around her, wondering where, exactly, she was supposed to go. The last place in the world she wanted to return to was Deadhead Manor, and yet she knew that eventually she would have to find familiar ground. She decided to go upstream. She would keep well away from the water. She no longer had any idea of what was real or unreal, but she wasn't about to risk the stream again. It spooked her. It was still chanting.

She climbed one of the boulders. From the top she saw woods spreading out across a wide apron of a slope. She took one last look behind her. The buck still stood by the edge of the stream, its flanks trembling with what she was sure was fury. It watched her with unblinking eyes, and she allowed herself a moment of sympathy for the boy who had become a deer. Then she dropped down to the other side of the rock.

She landed on soft, damp earth. In front of her the land rose steeply, the base of some mountain, covered with fragrant evergreens. The trees did not darken the land. She could see perfectly well in the clear blue light. Above her the crescent moon still shone bright; she couldn't tell whether or not it had moved through the sky.

Something darted in front of her, a thin black cat. For a moment she was sure it was the same cat she'd seen earlier in the city with Devon, but she dismissed that notion as impossible. The cat trotted deeper into the woods; it seemed sure of its destination. Cilla shrugged inwardly; she didn't know where she was or which way she ought to go; following a cat made as much sense as anything else.

She followed the cat.

The cat was not a reliable guide. When it was in sight, it led her upward, away from the stream, deeper into the mountains. Mostly, it took great pleasure in disappearing behind rocks and under brush. It circled round behind her only to suddenly dart out in front of her again. It chased a bird. It stopped for what seemed a very long time to wash its toes. Cilla began to think that following a cat was an exceedingly dumb idea.

At one point both she and the cat turned at the sound of something behind them. She saw a five-point stag leaping, soaring through the air as if it had never touched earth. She couldn't be sure it was Devon but if it was, she felt better; there were worse fates than turning into a deer. She waited to see if the deer was following, but it bounded into a stand of pines and vanished from sight.

When she turned back again the cat had scaled a tree, and there was music floating down from some point higher on the mountain—flute and tambourine and guitar.

She didn't question who might be playing or why. That someone, or several someones, were playing instruments in the middle of a forest seemed no stranger than anything else that had happened that night. She decided she would find the source of the music. It seemed immeasurably saner than following a cat.

She climbed higher, trying to move in rhythm with the music and failing; it played too fast and free. And yet she could feel it inside her. It was stirring things, calling up energies she couldn't even name. It pushed her upward, making her walk so fast and hard she was winded, and yet she felt as if she'd never want to slow. The trees grew taller as the mountain rose. Occasionally, she saw an oak or birch but mostly she was in the midst of evergreens—piñon and Scotch pine and thick blue spruce. And there were fireflies. Everywhere she looked in the deep blue night there were fireflies.

The music changed. Its tempo quickened, its sound became even lighter, as if it were a wind meant to coax the leaves from the trees. Something lived in that music, was carried by it, she was sure.

Boulders appeared on the side of the mountain, as big and white as the ones by the stream. More than once Cilla found herself passing between them. Each time it felt as if they might close on her at any second, as if she were being allowed through.

The music became louder and so did another sound, as light and lilting as the flute's. At first Cilla took it for laughter. It was running water, she soon realized, and unlike the music, it had words. She was too far to make them out clearly, but she had no doubts as to what they said. She started as something bounded by her ankles. The cat rubbed against a juniper tree, looking extremely pleased with itself.

Ahead of her were two white boulders, larger than any that had come before. They were taller than the tallest trees and so wide she could barely see their ends. Between them was a narrow opening, maybe two feet wide. She could go around them, she knew. And yet the music was strongest here, and she knew that if she passed between the rocks, she would find its source. The boulders were the gate to the music.

Cilla stepped between them. Smooth white walls of granite rose on either side of her. She put her hands out, feeling her way along the cool stone, feeling the power it held. It was not her imagination that the boulders could crush her. They were as alive as the black cat that trotted neatly in front of her. And they were letting her through.

The music drew her through the passage between the two rocks. Her hands slid from the cool, white stone as she stepped from them. The music stopped. Before her the mountain leveled off for a ways, temporarily halting its steep ascent. The ground was still wooded and covered with soft pine needles, but the trees were thinner here, as if someone had taken care to plant them a good distance apart. The fireflies were everywhere, gold light chasing gold light through a sky that was still a deep, luminous blue. The cat was nowhere to be seen.

Although the music had stopped, the sound of the water remained, lighter than it had been at the stream, but chanting nonetheless, its message unchanged. Cilla decided she was getting used to it.

She moved toward the sound, toward a level wooded area bordered by towering rocks, these a dark slate gray. From above them and through them water fell. It pooled in a huge stone basin, swirling there a while before making its way farther down the mountain. Cilla knelt by the basin, noting that here the chanting water was not the dark bottle green of the stream below, but a green like light jade gone transparent.

The music began again—the flute playing solo behind her. Cilla turned and saw a man wearing a purple vest and harlequin trousers, their diamond pattern purple and green. He sat beneath an oak tree, legs crossed, intent on his music. He was not wearing whiteface, but his skin was so pale that the harlequin pattern and the vest and even his brown hair seemed garish against his flesh. Another flute player emerged from behind a spruce tree, this one a boy who couldn't have been more than sixteen. He, too, was very pale, with straight black hair that fell to his collar bones and long, narrow eyes that reminded her uncomfortably of Devon. His chest was smooth and hairless and he was dressed in pants of a light, worn suede. He played on a silver flute, quick and sweet, his notes rising above those played by the man, chasing them, melding into them, only to dart away again. Around the musicians the fireflies danced, as if the music were their own. There was a guitarist, too—a black man, sitting on a tree stump. He wore faded blue jeans and his long hair was tightly braided into dozens of rows, each wound through with tiny golden bells. They jingled softly as he bent over the guitar.

Cautiously, Cilla approached them. She didn't want to disturb them, and yet they were the first people she'd seen since Devon turned into a deer, the first she'd seen since the night began who seemed to hold no menace. She walked up to them. When no one looked at her, she planted herself squarely in front of the first flute player, cleared her throat, and said, "Excuse me. Hello? . . . I—I really like your music."

They paid her no mind.

She heard the tambourine next. A woman's hand bedecked with rings reached out from behind a spruce tree, shook a tambourine, then disappeared. Seconds later the tambourine emerged again, this time inches from Cilla's face. No hand held it. It hovered in the air of its own will, keeping the loose, easy rhythm of the music. Cilla felt her jaw drop as the hand covered with rings reappeared, this time connected to a woman draped in layers of long, gossamer scarves. Blue and green shot through with gold, the scarves were woven of a fine translucent stuff the likes of which Cilla had never seen. Threads of opal, maybe. The woman kept playing, dancing lightly all the while, and watching Cilla from slanted, kohl-lined eyes.

"That's enough," Cilla said loudly, as much to herself as to the woman and the three musicians. As if making mockery of her words, the music picked up tempo, and dancers began to whirl out from beneath the trees. For a brief moment Cilla was back at the ballet again, only this time she'd mistakenly wandered onto the stage and was surrounded by dancers who had traded in the elegant, classical form of the nineteenth century for— she had no name for it. A boy with blond dreadlocks wearing a silk top hat and tuxedo jacket over a day-glo lime muscle shirt and frayed jams danced with his hands on his hips, his eyes closed. A girl in turquoise overalls and hair so short it looked as if it had been shaved whirled slowly, arms outstretched, head thrown back, throat exposed, as if offering herself to the mountain. A thin, angular man wearing a vermilion shirt beneath a baggy black-and-white checked suit took small, high-kneed steps, only to suddenly dive into a handspring then right himself, high-stepping again, never missing a beat. There were others clad in skins of gold lamé, in capes sewn with sequins, in long flowered skirts and blouses of lace, in simple white gowns that looked as if they'd been lifted from a Greek frieze.

For want of a better response, Cilla began to count the dancers. There were twenty, maybe thirty . . . Were there really twins in velvet harem pants or was it just one dancer, spinning so fast she seemed to inhabit two spaces at once? Every time Cilla thought she had them all accounted for, someone new would whirl out from beneath the trees and someone else would vanish between the boulders. They kept coming. They kept disappearing. There was no end to them. Cilla found it all positively dizzying.

They danced in lines and circles, often in concentric rings. Like the music, the dancers were as fluid as water. They were all barefoot and all exceedingly pale. Except for the woman with the kohl-lined eyes, none of them paid any notice to Cilla. Their eyes were only for one another.

And then Cilla saw a face she recognized—only when she'd seen it last the girl's face had been rounder, framed by straight silky blond hair, and she'd worn short, straight skirts and neatly pressed cotton blouses. Now her hair flowed in long waves, and she wore an ankle-length patchwork skirt and no blouse at all. Necklaces draped her high, round breasts: strands of turquoise and silver and shell, a chain of braided gold, beads of amethyst, moonstone, and tourmaline. Cilla looked at her face, met serene gray eyes, and a strangled cry rose from her throat.

At her cry the girl hovered for a moment on the balls of her feet, still swaying to the music, as if trying to resist its call. Then her heels met the earth, and she stood perfectly still. She held a hand out to Cilla and walked toward her.

"No." Cilla stepped back, edging toward the chanting water. It seemed far less unsettling than what she now faced. "You can't be—"

The music stopped. The other dancers gathered round. The young flute player who reminded Cilla of Devon came to stand behind the girl with the necklaces, his eyes mocking.

"It's Cilla," the girl said softly. "Cilla Biehler. I used to baby-sit her when she was a little kid."

Cilla backed away from Connie's ghost and stumbled over the cat. She knew what she was looking at. These were the Revelers, the Lords of the Manor, although she knew that didn't begin to explain it. There hadn't been that many who overdosed; they hadn't all died. But sure as the crescent moon still lit the night sky, she knew she was no longer among the living.

"What *is* she wearing?" asked the man in the baggy black-and-white checked suit, his voice an aristocrat's blend of horror and disdain.

"It's that haircut," declared a dispassionate harlequin. "She's hiding behind it. She's hiding behind being plain."

"She has no eye," opined a man dressed in lavender toga. "Look at the way that shirt just hangs."

"Not to mention those cords," muttered another who wore a robe of scarlet. "Please!"

What is this? Cilla wondered. Drag Queens of the Dead?

"She has no beauty," stated the boy with Devon's eyes.

Cilla pictured the summer girl and then glanced down at her own flat chest. The boy's simple declaration seemed the whole truth of her existence. In a red haze of embarrassment she bit down on the insides of her mouth to keep it from trembling. It was as if she'd suddenly been hurled straight back into the child she'd been: hurt and shamed because once again she'd been found wanting. Exactly what it was that was wanted, she'd never quite figured out, but she suspected that whatever it was, had she possessed it, it would have been some sort of magic key to acceptance—to being wanted. She'd ached for that key. And long ago she'd given up on finding it, had understood that she'd go through life without it. She'd put up careful walls; she hadn't thought rejection could take her down again. Yet here she stood, surrounded by ghosts—and they, too, found her inadequate. The hurt was as fresh as it'd ever been. It had never gone away.

Connie stepped directly in front of Cilla, shielding her from the others. "Stop it," she said softly. "It's because she was shut down." Cilla flinched; somehow that understanding cut into her, hurt worse than the insults.

Connie turned to face Cilla again, one pale arm reaching for her. "It's all right," she went on in a soothing tone. "Cilla's going to take a bath now. Just like she did when she was little. Gonna rinse her clear. Take off your clothes now, honey, and get into the water."

The shriek was out before Cilla knew it, ragged and hysterical, "No!"

A woman in a dress covered with silver stars shook her head and murmured, "And that voice . . ."

Not daring to take her eyes off the ghosts, Cilla edged backward. Connie followed, her necklaces brushing the tips of her breasts. She moved so lightly Cilla wondered if her feet touched ground.

"Go on, hon," Connie said. "It's time you went in." The others gathered behind her and the music began again, a mandolin playing descant to the chanting water. "Earth take you, earth take you, earth take you . . ."

They backed her to where the dark gray rock caught the water of the falls in its basin of stone. Connie reached for her again and Cilla darted out of the way, flinching from the dead girl's touch.

"I was only going to help you take off your shirt," Connie said.

The boy with blond dreadlocks leered at Cilla. "I'll help her."

"No!" Cilla said, and began rapidly weighing her choices. Could she strip in front of them, go into the chanting water? Briefly she saw Devon, kneeling on the shore, the stream washing over him, covering him with the glittering coat of red silt that took his human shape. The earth had taken him. Would it take her as well?

*What will it do with me?* she wondered wildly. *Change me into a doe? A mouse?* She dared a look over her shoulder into the water—it was whirling so fast and deep that worrying about animal transformations suddenly seemed absurd. She was going to drown. That's it, she thought, feeling increasingly sick. I'm not going to turn into a deer. I'm going to die and turn into one of them.

The black man whose hair was braided with bells came to stand beside Connie. He squatted down on his haunches and gazed up at Cilla, his eyes traveling the length of her body. He had very light eyes, she noted, like clear amber. "We can take her in," he said thoughtfully. "It isn't the way it should be done, but we can take her."

"Take me where?" Cilla asked, trying to keep the hysteria out of her voice.

"Into the water," Connie answered.

"What if I just leave? I'll go back through those rocks there. It'll be like I was never here. I won't tell anyone I saw you. I—"

"Take off your clothes, hon," Connie said again. "It's best if you go in on your own."

"Why?" she asked, her voice ragged.

Connie and the black man exchanged an unreadable glance. Unsurprisingly, it was Connie who answered. "It's just what's gotta be. Come on, Cilla. Don't you remember—you and I used to trust each other. You can trust me now."

"You're dead," Cilla said, stating the obvious.

Connie lifted one shoulder in a careless shrug. Her necklaces swayed, covering one breast, baring the other. "Don't make no difference."

What *does?* Cilla wondered. And how was it that this crazy night kept offering her bizarre choices in which there was no choice, no way out?

Connie was right. It didn't make a difference. Nothing she could say or do would make a difference. She was surrounded by the dead who were insisting on this "bath." They weren't going to let her go.

The black man stood up and moved toward her with that same light, graceful motion that couldn't possibly be mistaken for walking. He held out a hand to her.

"Give him your shirt," Connie said.

Cilla peeled off the faded green turtleneck, painfully aware of the tattered undershirt she wore underneath. One of the shoulder straps was fraying, and there was a run in the cotton that began on her rib cage and ended over her right nipple in an embarrassingly precise hole.

"That, too," Connie said.

The boy with Devon's eyes was staring at her. They were all staring at her, but somehow he was the worst. He'd judged her, said she had no beauty; she couldn't bear to have him see her naked. "Make him turn around," she said, pointing straight at him. "I don't want him to look."

"You have to be seen," Connie said, her voice even gentler than before. "That's part of it, love. Don't drag this out, now."

The black man inclined his head, the bells ringing faintly.

Cilla squeezed her eyes shut tight and pulled the undershirt over her head, felt the cool night air along her back and breasts. She held the undershirt out and it was taken from her hand. Then she felt for the snap and zipper on her pants and undid them. She had to open her eyes to step out of her pants. She would have fallen if she hadn't. But she kept her eyes on the ground. Saw the black man's hands reach for her pants and fold them carefully. Shut her eyes again as she slid her underpants down over her hips and butt and then down her legs. Opened her eyes for the briefest second to step out of them.

"Turn around, hon," Connie said. "Face the water and open your eyes."

Cilla did as she was told, nearly dying of shame at standing there bare-assed in front of them all. She felt the muscles along her back contracting, trying to pull inside. She stood waiting for the inevitable blow.

She fixed her gaze on the water, saw it rushing down from a point so high she couldn't find the top of the falls, even in the luminous blue night sky. Before her the water swept through the slate-gray rock basin, pale green and chanting. A fiddle and a guitar had joined the mandolin's descant, and the water's chant rising above them seemed to infuse all. It was seeping into the stones and trees, ringing from the ground, vibrating through Cilla's bones and coursing through her veins. It persuaded. It insisted. It demanded. It enchanted.

Cilla forgot about Connie and standing stark naked in front of the Revelers. She forgot about Devon and everything else that had happened since the sun set that day. She even forgot her fear of the water. Its song had entered and become part of her, and it seemed the most natural thing in the world to climb over the edge of the smooth gray rock and slip into the warm swirling currents.

The water took her down at once. Pulled her into its warmth, streamed through her hair and along her body. Cilla didn't try to swim or resist. She caught one last glimpse of the crescent moon and let the green waters cover her head. She let them take her into their depths—felt her body spinning, gliding, floating; felt the chant breathing for her—and carried by the waters found the safe place she'd always sought.

She was lying on the pine-scented ground, her head in Connie's lap, and Connie was running gentle hands through her still-damp hair, comforting her the way she used to when Cilla was little. Cilla stayed still, not wanting to move. It was the first time since her father's death that anyone had touched her that way. Connie was humming "Hush Little Baby," the same song she'd sung to Cilla as a child, only now the mandolin and fiddle picked up the tune and played with its tempo, lightning quick one moment, slow and caressing the next. It was as if the Revelers had reached in for a piece of Cilla's past and reshaped it into a form she didn't quite recognize.

She lifted her head and stared for a moment at the bright colors in Connie's patchwork skirt. She didn't remember anything after going into the water. Her body felt the same and yet not the same; something was lighter or perhaps missing. She sat up slowly and looked down at herself. She was still in the clearing with the Revelers. She was still stark naked. The crescent moon still shone in the blue night sky.

"Am I"—she didn't know how to phrase this—"one of you now?"

"You mean dead?" Connie's voice held a hint of laughter. "No, baby. If you were dead, you wouldn't have to ask. Believe me, hon, you'd know."

Cilla took that in, a faint sensation of relief washing through her. "Where are my clothes?"

Connie nodded at a neatly folded pile beneath a nearby pine tree, but as Cilla reached for them they were snatched away by the man in the baggy checked suit. "No, no, no," he declared in the tone of one greatly offended. "These will never do."

Cilla stared at him, too disoriented to be outraged. She no longer felt humiliated by her nakedness, and yet she felt she ought to to get dressed. Habit, she supposed. "You all have clothes," she pointed out.

She stood up and felt the difference in her limbs. Everything was looser, easier. Something was definitely gone. Fear, she realized. It used to sheathe every muscle and bone in her body. Everything in her had been held so tightly; the fear had held her upright. It was the armor that enclosed her, the staff she'd made of her spine. She'd known that if she ever let it all go, she would fall. She looked down at herself in wonder. The fear was no longer the thing that knit her together. The staff was gone and she was still standing.

"Do you want clothes like ours?" Connie asked, distracting her from her new discoveries.

"Like yours?" Cilla tried to picture herself in a baggy checked suit or harlequin tights.

The boy with Devon's eyes spoke again, his voice accusing. "She gave up all her power. She doesn't even have any colors."

"Mmmm." The black man with the braided hair gave serious consideration to this statement. "She'll have to find her power on her own," he said at last, his tone curiously reassuring. "But we can help her back to her colors."

The boy in the tuxedo jacket and surfer jams sauntered forward and winked at Cilla. He whipped his top hat from his blond dreadlocks and held it out to her with a bow.

Cilla took the hat. Hesitantly, she began to place it on top of her head, only remotely aware of how silly she'd look in a top hat and nothing else.

"No, hon." Connie's amused voice stopped her. "You're not supposed to *wear* his hat. You're supposed to take what's inside it."

Cilla peered into the hat, half-expecting to see a rabbit or a dove. Instead she saw what looked like crumpled fabric. She pulled out a short sleeveless tunic woven of silver-green cloth.

"Put it on," Connie urged her.

Cilla slipped the tunic over her head. It covered her in soft, clinging folds.

The man in the checked suit gave a sigh of profound relief and murmured, "Thank you, Jesus!"

"These are yours, too," Connie said, lifting a strand of beads from her neck.

Cilla stared at the necklace, a pulse in her throat jumping. She hadn't seen Connie wearing it before; she would have recognized it. It was a long strand of glass beads—amber, red, blue, green, and purple—fastened with a small square of brass filigree. The necklace was her mother's. Cilla had loved it as a child, had thought it magic—a gift that could only have come from the fairies. She'd gotten in trouble for taking it from her mother's jewelry box to wear with her nightgown.

Connie's voice was a whisper, "Take it."

Cilla reached out her hand and stopped. The memory of the beating was still with her.

*"Take it."*

"Amazing what a body can do with a little less fear in its bones," observed the black man to no one in particular.

"She only wore it once," Connie reminded her. "It was meant to be yours all along."

Cilla stared at her, wondering how Connie could possibly know that her mother had worn the necklace the day she brought it home and had never put it on again.

"Never understood people willing to go through life without their colors," the black man said. Quietly, he began to sing, *"Alouette, gentille Alouette, Alouette, je te plumerai . . ."*

"Take it." Connie's soft voice was fierce. "Take it and it belongs to you."

"It—it's just costume jewelry," Cilla stammered, unnerved by the ghost's insistence. "It's probably not even worth anything."

The boy who reminded her of Devon raised a skeptical eyebrow, and she knew her own words for a lie.

Again, she reached for the necklace and was surprised to see her hand trembling.

*"Et la tête? Et la tête, Alouette? Alouette . . ."* The gold bells rang in soft accompaniment, and the black man graced Cilla with a smile. He let the song trail off. "Cou-raj," he said. He repeated it, a new chant, and she realized it was just the French pronunciation, *"Courage, courage, courage . . ."*

She took the necklace in her hands, the feel of it familiar and forbidden, the glass beads cool and smooth. They were exactly as she'd remembered—and more. They drew in the light of the crescent moon and glowed with it, their colors deepening. Cilla slipped the necklace over her head so that it lay against the tunic.

The man in the checked suit nodded, as if she'd finally gotten it right. The black man went on humming in French, and Connie said, "There you go, baby."

Cilla's fingers closed on the string of glass beads.

"Looks right on you," Connie said. "Sometimes you gotta get what you've always wanted."

"And then what?" Cilla asked.

As if in answer to her question, the music picked up, the flutes leading, merry and wild. The dancers began to whirl again.

Cilla stood waiting for the miraculous change. If this were a fairy tale, she'd put on the necklace and she'd be able to travel miles on a wish, draw gemstones from a well, defeat the wicked witch. She'd stripped in front of a bunch of clothes-conscious ghosts, immersed herself in a talking whirlpool, and now taken her mother's necklace. Something *ought* to change. She waited to become the beautiful princess she'd always secretly been. She waited for magic to streak through her hands. She waited to become other than she was.

The black man turned his left palm up, and a ring of fireflies hovered above it, a perfect golden circle.

Cilla turned her left palm up and held only blue night air.

"Ah, but she's actually holding it," said the black man with an approving nod.

And she was. She could feel the texture of the night—all that was light and dark in it; currents of new things being born and all things dying, of life being sent out of the earth and being taken back in. She could sense the land breathing into the sky and the sky arcing down around her, circling her with stars. Fine strands of energies wove through it all: hunger and comfort, fear and grief, joy and anger, humor and bewilderment, and to her surprise, love. It all flowed through the night sky, and for the first time she held it all, and understood that it had been holding her all along.

The black man picked up his guitar. The music quickened as he began to play, and more dancers spun from the beneath the trees. Without another glance at Cilla, Connie joined them, leaving Cilla feeling curiously abandoned.

There was no end to the Revelers. They came wearing silks and suedes, taffeta and lace, satin and tulle. They danced as if they were dance itself, and there was no other way for a spirit to move in the world.

Cilla felt the music calling to her. She had never danced, except a little in the privacy of her room, quietly so no one would hear her. She'd always been too self-conscious to move that way in front of others. But something *had* changed, and she now knew the music would *dance her* if she let it. She opened her arms, felt the energy surging up from the ground—and then quite suddenly she forgot about dancing, forgot about the music. Later she would swear her heart stopped.

She'd thought that after watching Devon change into a deer, nothing would ever truly take her by surprise again. But trailing the woman dressed in gossamer scarves was a middle-aged dancer—short and balding, with muscular, slightly bowed legs; and as he'd been when she'd seen him last, he was wearing a hospital gown.

It had been a year. Exactly one year.

Cilla found herself on her knees, arms wrapped around her ribs, rocking and keening, unable to believe she'd gotten what she wanted most, and it was sending her back into a grief she didn't think could come twice. Could be survived twice.

More than anything she had wanted him to come back. Maybe not for good—he'd been hurting so much at the end. But she'd wanted to see her father one last time. And now . . . he wasn't quite as she'd seen him last, she realized. The white hospital gown had been stained yellow and brown—IV fluids, mucus, blood. Now it was clean and she could see that it had never been white. It was, in fact, a print—tiny pastel palm trees, each rising from a tiny green island on a sea of blue waves. Her father had always dreamed of going to a tropical island. That last day was the last time she'd ever believed that things would get better. He'd talked about leaving her mother, about taking Cilla with him and moving to an island in the sun. She'd known he was dying, but it had been impossible not to dream with him, not to believe that beyond the hospital walls the island lay waiting for them.

Now he danced on the outer edge of an endless ring of dancers. He was paler than he'd been, even that last day, but his body was no longer emaciated, his stomach no longer swollen with tumors. And he was happy. There was no denying it. She hadn't seen her father this happy since she was a little girl.

She called out to him, and no sound came from her mouth.

I have to tell him, she thought wildly. She'd just been given a second chance. To tell him that she saw the dark shapes the night they marked him. That for five years she knew they rode him and would take him. That it was out of fear that she'd never said anything. That she'd never wanted him to die.

She got up, started toward him, and he disappeared behind a blue spruce. Moments later he reappeared in the clearing between two pines, his arms raised above his head as if he were about to break into a High-land Fling. She never knew he could dance.

"Wait!" she cried, her voice finally unfrozen. "I have to tell you something. Daddy, please, I have to talk to you!"

She rushed toward him, but Connie stepped out of the dance, caught her by the shoulders, and swung her around. "No, love. That's not what this is about. You don't get to rewrite the past. The only things that can be changed are what's coming up."

Cilla tried to wrench herself free but the ghost held her, lightly, inexorably.

"Please." Cilla was sobbing. "He's here because I've got to talk to him. Just for a moment. You said I could change what's coming—how else am I going to do that?"

Connie took her in her arms and held her while she cried. "You see him with us," she answered. "He's a Reveler, hon. Nothing can hurt him now. You need to know that and take it with you. And that's gotta be enough."

"It's not," Cilla said. "I miss him."

"You'll always miss him," Connie told her. "But even that's gonna ease and when it does, you let him go. It's not a betrayal, you understand?" Connie stepped back and released her. "He's not missing you, hon, not anymore."

Cilla turned, searching for where she'd seen her father last, between the pines. But the two pine trees no longer stood next to each other. In their place was a quaking aspen, its golden crown dancing in the moonlight, casting shadows over a sapling that grew beside it. The line of Revelers snaked in and out of the trees. She caught one last glimpse of her father, his bright hospital gown bobbing merrily. Then he was out of sight. She'd never even know if he'd seen her.

"Cilla, babe . . ." She felt Connie's hands resting lightly on her shoulders and turned back to face the ghost.

"We gotta be going now, Cilla." Connie ran a hand through her hair, brushing it back from her face the way she used to, still wanting to see what was in Cilla's eyes. "Yeah," Connie said softly. "I saw what was going on there. Even if no else, including your daddy, wanted to. But I got caught up"—she gave a nod to the dancers—"in other things. Sometimes you just get caught up."

"Really." Cilla fell back into the streak of familiar cynicism that still lingered. "And you're very sorry."

"No, hon, that wouldn't do me much good now, would it?"

"I don't know." The cynicism was gone, leaving her emptied. "I don't know anything anymore."

Connie gave her the faintest smile. "You'll see. You know a lot of what you need. And the rest, it'll come." She glanced up at the deep blue sky. "Gotta go now, hon."

Cilla followed Connie's gaze. The crescent moon had moved through the sky. Perhaps, she thought, it had even traveled west like a normal moon. It was definitely lower, its crescent tilting slightly down so that it appeared to arc over the aspen.

"That moon likes the trees," Connie said. "Always has."

Cilla nodded. It made sense to her, more than most of what had gone on that night.

The dancers were still dancing and the musicians playing, but the music was fainter now, and the line of dancers was slipping deeper into the forest, a whirl of colors against the blue night sky.

Connie leaned forward and kissed Cilla's forehead. Then she took Cilla's hands in hers and began to swing her arms in time to the music, the way she used to when Cilla was little. Connie used to bring her own records and play them on Cilla's parents' stereo, laughing when Cilla warned her that if her mother ever found out, she'd "get it." Then she'd take Cilla's hands and dance with her, dance until Cilla couldn't keep up, till she fell to the floor laughing.

Connie's body swayed, her long hair flowing loose, nearly liquid, in the moonlight. Cilla let her own arms swing, felt the music call to her and the glass bead necklace glide across her chest. Her feet began to move, keeping time to the fiddle. At the core of her body an invisible swing rocked her, sent her soaring, carried her faster and higher than she'd ever gone before. Her hands in Connie's, she whirled. She felt the earth spinning beneath her and the blue night spinning through her. She was alive as she'd never been before—wholly, joyously unafraid.

Beneath the patchwork skirt, Connie's feet quickened in a rhythm Cilla couldn't possibly match. Cilla tried anyway, knowing how ridiculous it was, how silly she must look. At last she fell to the ground, laughing.

Connie stood over her, still grasping Cilla's warm hands in her own cool ones. "Gotta go, love." The old laughter was still in her voice. "The night's drawing us on."

And it was. Cilla could feel it pulling Connie's hands from hers, drawing all of the Revelers through the trees, drawing them deep into the mountain. She watched as Connie left her, her necklaces gleaming silver and gold, spinning into the night, her long hair white beneath the moon.

The last notes of the flute faded and Cilla was alone in the clearing. There was a familiar ache her in chest, and she realized that it was not her father's disappearance but Connie's that left her bereft.

Cautiously, Cilla reached her hand out and ran it down the front of her body. She was still wearing the tunic and the necklace; they, at least, hadn't vanished. And the pale green water was still rushing down from its source, chanting its song.

Around her were trees, rocks, the mountain, the water. Not knowing what else to do, she walked back through the white boulders, trusting them to let her through.

Again she felt the white granite walls rising on either side of her. She walked between them, pressing her hands along the smooth rock, feeling its power. She stepped through into thicker, darker woods. Behind her the boulders slid closed.

Her mother was waiting there for her. Her hair was black, as it had been years ago before it went gray. Except for a slash of red lipstick, she was pale, her skin sallow against a burnt-orange shirtwaist. In her hand was the strap.

Cilla stared at her, unable to move.

Her mother pointed at the ground where the pile of Cilla's neatly folded clothes now lay. "Put on your own clothes, Priscilla."

"No." Cilla's voice was a rasp.

"Where did you get my necklace?"

"Connie gave it to me. No," Cilla corrected herself quickly, "I took it from Connie."

Her mother's eyes were dark and flat, giving away nothing, and yet Cilla could feel her anger, so thick and dense it was nearly a solid object. She didn't remember who Connie was, and she didn't care. She wasn't going to be defied. She raised the strap. "I told you not to touch my things."

Cilla had never fought her mother. She didn't want to now. And yet, though she couldn't have said why it was so important, she knew she wasn't going to put on her old clothes. And she wasn't going to give up the necklace. "Take it and it's yours," Connie had said.

"It's mine," she told her mother.

"Turn around, Priscilla."

Mute with terror, Cilla shook her head.

"Now!"

"I'm not going to do what you tell me." She hadn't meant to say that, and for a second she wondered who it was that had spoken.

"Are you smart-mouthing me?" The strap cracked hard across Cilla's bare arms. "I'll teach you," her mother promised. The strap came down again, leaving a welt of red pain across Cilla's left breast.

Cilla bit down on her gums to keep from crying out. How long would it go on before her mother's anger was spent? How much could she take this time?

Her mother's arm dropped suddenly, letting the strap hang loose. Her eyes gazed past Cilla, curious. "Will you look at this . . ."

Cilla looked and saw that the two granite boulders had melded into a seamless wall of rock. In front of it stood the five-point stag with Devon's eyes. He was even bigger than she remembered, muscles rippling beneath the sleek red pelt. His antlers, silver-white beneath the moon, were stained with blood. He's killed, she thought without surprise.

The buck's long, narrow eyes rested briefly on Cilla. Was there a flicker of recognition there? He moved toward her mother, slowly, smoothly, deliberately. His head wasn't lowered, and yet he was stalking her as surely as Cilla was standing there shaking.

She didn't know what she wanted. She wanted Devon to stop her mother, to attack her, to gut her as she'd been gutting others for so many years. There was a part of Cilla that would have gladly paid to watch. And a part of her that couldn't.

Her mother inched back slowly, brandishing the strap at the stag. The stag showed no fear. He went perfectly still, his eyes measuring her.

"Leave her alone," Cilla said to the deer. "She'll hurt you."

Her mother rounded on her. "You want to talk about hurt? You were supposed to go to the cemetery with me today. I waited for you all day. It's been a year, and you didn't even remember."

The accusation was typical and yet it stunned her. "You really think I forgot?"

"You're a selfish girl. All you think about is yourself. You didn't show up for your own father's funeral and—"

"I couldn't," Cilla said. "I couldn't bury him."

"You couldn't bury him," her mother echoed. As always her voice was honed with contempt, but this night its edge was brighter, sharp enough to slice flesh. "I suppose you were too *sensitive* for that."

"It just . . . it hurt so much," Cilla said, knowing as she said it that the words didn't begin to describe how she'd felt on the morning they were to bury her father.

"You think you were hurting a year ago?" Her mother's voice was quiet now; she'd gone beyond her usual anger into pure, white rage. "I'll give you hurt. You need a beating, Priscilla. Then you'll know what hurt is."

Cilla felt the terror in her rise as strong as ever, tightening a band across her chest, cloaking her like a shroud.

And she realized. It *had* cloaked her like a shroud. The clothes she'd always worn—plain, shapeless, designed to hide her body—they were somehow connected to her mother, chosen in fear so she wouldn't call attention to herself, so she wouldn't bring down more anger. She'd dressed in fear, walked in fear, worn it and breathed it every day of her life. Tonight, dressed in the silver-green tunic, was the first time she was wearing something other than the clothes of her mother's house.

The stag walked between them, cool and easy; if it knew what was going on, it wasn't frightened.

Her mother brought the strap down on the animal's flank, screaming, "Get out of here!"

Like any animal that's been struck, it should have bolted. It should have fled deep into the trees. Instead the stag whirled, facing its attacker. It stood still, its sides heaving, and in the long, tawny eyes, Cilla read a fury to match her mother's.

"No!" Cilla pleaded, not sure whether it was the deer or her mother she was petitioning.

The stag lowered its head and charged. Her mother sidestepped and raised the strap again.

Without thinking, Cilla ran to her mother's side and grabbed the arm that held the leather belt. "Stop hurting him!" she screamed.

Her mother slammed her across the face with her free hand. Cilla's head snapped back and she let go of her mother's arm, stumbling against a birch tree. Dazed, she watched as her mother struck at the charging buck. The strap missed its target, striking instead a large gray rock.

And the dark shapes that had hounded her father rose into the blue night air. They hovered for a second, then gathered, forming a cloak over the red stag.

"Dev," she screamed, "run!"

This time the stag ran, bounding over the rock, darting between trees, soaring across the forest floor as if it owned the wind. The dark shapes swarmed after the deer. Cilla knew what would happen. They'd ride him, hunt him till he dropped, then tear him to shreds. She wouldn't watch it a second time.

She turned to confront her mother. "What are they?"

Her mother's eyes held no emotion. "Some things don't have a name."

"They're like . . . angry spirits or energies . . . the dark things you call to you when rage and fear take over . . . they're always going to make someone hurt, they're . . ." Cilla struggled to identify them. Somehow it seemed important. "The dark gods," she said at last, for want of a better term. "And they're yours. You set them on him. Just like you called them down on Daddy. You're the one who set them loose."

"I never asked for them," her mother replied impatiently. "You know I didn't want to lose your father."

"But you draw them down on the people around you. Your rage, it draws them. And then they have to feed on something."

"Your father had cancer, Priscilla. That's what killed him."

"No, they rode him. And I was too scared to stop them," she added.

"Well, be scared of them now. And be grateful they're willing to take that deer instead of you or me."

"Call them back," Cilla ordered.

Her mother shook her head, stretched the strap between her hands, then doubled it. "You're getting entirely too big for your britches, young lady. You ought to know better than to speak to me in that tone."

For the first time it occurred to Cilla that she could kill her mother. She could rip the strap from her hands, snap her neck, and never have a second's regret. The knowledge was heady, dizzying. It must be Devon's rage gone straight into me, she thought. For a long breath she let herself feel that energy and all the strength it carried. And she knew at once that it was a very different sort of power than she'd had when she'd held the night in her hand. Rage was the energy that fueled her mother and, to a lesser degree, Devon; that was the energy that released the dark gods. It was not the power she wanted for her own.

She backed up as her mother advanced on her with the belt. In her mind she heard the black man's voice, "Amazing what a body can do with a little less fear in its bones."

Cilla looked past the strap and saw the deep blue of the night, the green of the trees, the jewel colors of the glass beads against the silver-green tunic. She felt the earth beneath her bare feet, soft and cool, covered with pine needles. She felt her own body, slim and strong and lovely.

And once again time seemed to slow. Her mother stood, the belt raised but the attack halted. She stood long enough for Cilla to see that although she had the strength of her rage, she had little else. She saw no beauty, had no lightness. Nothing in her would ever dance.

But her father . . . even when he lay dying, he'd had that island in-side—all the colors of sea and sky—he gave it up only with his last breath. No, she realized, he'd never given it up. That was why he was a Reveler. He'd never given it up at all.

She studied her mother, a body arrested in attack. She seemed smaller, reduced to fury, cut off from the most basic truths. And no longer frightening.

"Put the strap down," Cilla told her mother. "You aren't going to beat me again."

"Goddamn you, you little—"

The strap lashed out. Cilla caught it, pulled it from her mother's hands, and tossed it away. "Go home," she said. She nodded in the direction that the deer had gone. "I'm going to try to call them back," she said. "You don't want to be here when I do."

Uncomprehending, her mother walked toward the belt. Cilla stepped in front of her. "Don't," she said. "Just go home."

Her mother reached for the necklace.

"No." Cilla's hand closed over her mother's. "It was never yours, anyway. You never really saw it for what it was."

"Priscilla," her mother's voice was ragged, "you're my daughter."

Cilla shook her head. "You gave birth to me and raised me. But I'm not yours, either. All you gave me was fear. You have your house. Go back to it."

Something changed in her mother's eyes. There was a flicker of recognition replaced by a deliberate distancing. Her mother was looking at her as though she were a stranger, alien and distasteful.

That's alright, Cilla told herself. We've always been strangers to each other. She wasn't surprised when her mother turned and walked away through the trees.

Now came the hard part. She didn't know if Devon was even still alive, but she had to try to call back the dark gods. She'd seen them the minute they'd found her father. She'd let them take him. She'd sacrificed him to them because she'd been terrified they'd come for her instead. She couldn't do that a second time.

Slowly she moved in a circle, looking carefully around her, as if seeing the magic night for the last time. Its colors were so clear she could feel them entering her with each breath. She knew with certainty that she couldn't stay on this mountain, that it belonged to another realm, but she loved it for all it had allowed her to see.

She knelt before the gray rock and opened herself to the earth beneath her and the night around her. Fingers running over the glass beads as if they were a rosary, she summoned the dark gods. "Leave Devon alone," she pleaded. "You can take me this time."

She waited. She waited for the dark shapes to come rushing back through the blue night air. She waited for them to feast on her, to end her life.

Nothing happened. She knelt on the mountain, aware of the scents of the forest, of the stars still blazing through the sky.

She tried again, offering her body and soul if they would just let the deer live. "Please," she prayed, "don't destroy him, too. I'm not afraid this time. You can have me."

After a while, she began to feel slightly silly offering herself as some sort of ritual sacrifice to beings that didn't even have the decency to respond.

At last she stood up. Is Devon still alive? she wondered. She hadn't saved him. If he'd kept his human shape, she wasn't even sure she would have tried. But as a deer, one who had stood with her against her mother, he'd cast his lot with hers. It was an alliance that had to be honored. And though he might be as dangerous a stag as he was a human, Cilla found it easy to have compassion for him in his animal form. When she thought of the dark gods riding the deer as they'd ridden her father—hunting him till they'd ripped the breath from his lungs and the life from his bones—she wanted desperately to shield him. She imagined herself an invincible wall between the deer and the dark gods. She saw herself crouched over him, protecting him from all harm. She stopped, stunned by her own assumptions. Was she trying to mother a deer? The truth was both Devon and the dark gods seemed to have gone from the woods. There was no one to fight. There was no one to protect.

*What now?* she asked herself. She supposed there was still the matter of returning home, but she didn't see how she could go back to her mother's house. And truthfully, she didn't have the first idea of how to get off this mountain or out of this endless night. The night itself had become a country, and she had no clue to where its borders lay, or whether it had borders at all.

There must be a geography to this place, she reasoned. When she'd gone inland from the stream, she'd gone up the mountain. It was logical that she should now go down. She began wandering through the trees, finding that the forest floor was, in fact, quite level.

She walked for a long time, searching for the way she'd come, becoming increasingly sure that she hadn't come this way at all. She saw no familiar landmarks, nothing on the mountain with which she could orient herself. She couldn't retrace her steps. She wasn't going to find a trail out of the woods. She would wander solitarily for as long as the night would last. It made her nostalgic for the time when she'd had an unreliable cat for a guide. It made her feel very much alone.

The forest floor suddenly rose again, and on the chance that it would lead her to the water, Cilla chose to take the slope down. The descent was steeper than she'd guessed. She had to hold onto branches and roots as she followed the land down. After what seemed hours of looking downward so as not to lose her footing, Cilla looked up and saw that the crescent moon was low in the blue night sky, its curve couched in the soft, green leaves of a sycamore tree. Seeing the moon at rest, she realized she'd been awake for a very long time. For the first time she let herself feel the effects of the night and all she'd come through. Exhaustion took her at once and she curled up on the ground. Sheltered by the roots of an oak tree, she fell asleep.

Cilla woke to a lavender sky. The stars were faint, glittering bits of amethyst light. The crescent moon was a white shadow glimpsed low between the trees. She was no longer on the slope of the mountain, but lying on the white sand beach that edged the stream. It was definitely the same stream; there was no mistaking its song. And she was no longer curled up along the roots of an oak tree, but curled around a large, warm body covered with a slightly coarse pelt of thick red fur.

Cilla blinked and sat up slowly, not wanting to startle the deer. The deer slept on, its flanks rising and falling in deep, even breaths.

Carefully, Cilla counted the five points on each of its antlers, noted the narrow white scar beneath its left eye.

"Dev? Is that you? Are you all right?"

A long eye opened, gave her a lazy, indulgent glance, then closed again, clearly preferring sleep.

Tentatively, Cilla reached out a hand and ran it along the animal's cheekbone, tracing the subtle curve beneath the eye, feeling the strong pulse beneath the skin. The bone was so fine, so much a thing of the wild, that a part of her ached as she touched it. The stag was almost unbearably beautiful. That it let her come so close took her heart.

"What are we going to do?" she asked the sleeping deer. "Do we go on together? Do I go back across the water and leave you here? Visit you on weekends and feed you Crackerjacks?"

"Cilla." The voice was soft, coming from the woods.

Cilla turned her head to see Connie, slipping out from between two of the rocks that edged the sand, her patchwork skirt faded to pastels, her skin even paler in the lavender light.

"It's been a long night, hasn't it, hon?" the ghost said. "Cilla, they sent me to tell you, you used your colors well. Just the way you were meant to use 'em. You've got a choice now."

Over the water's chanting Cilla heard the faintest strains of the Revelers' music playing somewhere up the mountain.

The ghost nodded to the other side of the stream. "You won't ever have to go back there. Do you want to come with us?"

The music was faint but Cilla didn't need it to be loud. She knew its rhythms and melodies, how it lilted and rocked and soared. Once again, it was calling her. She could join the Revelers. She knew what it was to dance with them. And there was nothing she wanted more, except . . . Cilla felt the buck stir beneath her hand. He lifted his head and looked warily at Connie. Slowly, he got to his feet, his eyes fixed on the ghost.

"If I go with you," Cilla said, "does that mean I die?"

"It means you never go back to the place you came from. You won't ever have to face that house again."

"What about him?" Cilla asked, nodding toward the deer.

Connie regarded the stag. "What about him?"

"He wasn't always like this," Cilla said. "He was a boy, my age. Will he get his own form back?"

"He's no different than he ever was," Connie told her. "That one's always been wild, always looking for a fight, always running six inches ahead of death and loving it. Boy or buck, don't matter much."

"It does," Cilla insisted. "I didn't like him when he was human, but that's what he is."

Connie gave her a sad smile. "Would you turn him back if you could? Think, babe, it might not be so pleasant."

"I know," Cilla said. "But he tried to help me before. So I've got to do the same for him."

The ghost looked tired. "Cilla, hon, life isn't some giant set of scales you always got to be balancing."

"I know that, too," Cilla answered. "But I can't leave him here like this. I just can't."

"Up to you, babe," Connie said, her voice regretful. "I guess this isn't your time to join us." She turned back toward the woods, a gentle blur of long skirts and shining necklaces.

"Connie, wait!"

The ghost turned expectantly.

"Thank you. For everything." Cilla touched the necklace of glass beads. "Especially these."

Connie smiled, her gray eyes warm in the morning light. "They were yours all along, hon. Don't you let 'em go again."

Cilla shook her head and watched the ghost move off, skimming over the wooded land, light as mist.

Behind her the stag snorted impatiently and the stream sang. In the lavender light the water was still a deep bottle green, its surface covered with racing white foam.

Connie's words came back to her, "Would you turn him back if you could?"

Could she? Was changing a stag into a teenage boy the sort of thing she could now do? The idea seemed preposterous and yet worth trying. "The question is," she explained to the deer, "how?"

The deer nibbled on something green growing out of the sand, oblivious to her question, making her wonder how much of human speech he understood.

"The stream washed over you and the earth took you," Cilla reasoned aloud. "I think that if you want your human form back, you probably have to go back into the water."

The deer raised its head and gave her an indignant look that clearly said, "Are you out of your fucking mind?"

She bit back a grin. "So you do understand." She looked at the stream again. The water was higher and the current faster than she'd remembered. A heart-shaped cottonwood leaf spun by on the swirling white foam and slipped from sight at frightening speed. The water's chant rippled through the trees, filled the air. "Dev," she went on, "it may be the only way."

He began to rub his antlers against the bark of a sycamore tree, and it occurred to her that maybe he liked being a deer. Who was she to insist he change back?

"Well, then at least tell me—" she said, "if you had a choice, would you want your human form back?"

The stag stopped rubbing his antlers against the tree. Slowly, he walked toward her, his red fur glistening in the soft light. Devon McKenna had been beautiful, but no human would ever be beautiful the way the stag was. No human would ever walk with the forest shining out of his eyes, or the strength to soar like the wind itself waiting easy in his limbs. No human held all that was wild in every bone.

The buck stopped a few feet from her, the long eyes grave, considering. She fully expected him to turn and vanish among the trees as Connie had. Instead, his ears pricked forward, listening to something she couldn't hear. Then, without hesitation, he came to stand beside her.

She took it for an answer. "I'll do what I can," she promised.

She gazed again at the rushing water, sure that it held power over his being. And hers as well. She left the deer and knelt by the side of the stream, put her hand into the water, and felt it pulled downstream as if pulled by a lover—his hands cool, almost impossible to resist.

"Earth take you. Earth take you."

She thought of the water farther up the mountain beneath the waterfall. That water was lighter in color and had been warm. The stream and the waterfall, they both sang the same song and yet they were different. One had given her back her life. One had taken some of her fear and opened her to a different sense of what it was to walk on earth. Maybe it was time she gave something back.

She didn't have much to give. So she gave what she knew to be her own magic. She slipped the glass bead necklace over her head and gave it to the water.

The stream took it at once. The necklace floated for a just a second, its colors gleaming deeper than ever, looking as if the glass were spun from the water itself. Then it sank beneath the white foam.

The stag gave a snort of alarm and bounded past her, into the stream.

"Devon, no! You don't have to—"

But she was too late. White foam splashed over the stag's flanks and chest. She saw him struggle against the current, delicate hooves just breaking the surface. She saw the powerful body swept relentlessly downstream at an unnatural angle.

He must have touched bottom because he suddenly arched out of the water and into the air, a final, desperate leap. The water caught him, of course. And took him. He vanished, bone white antlers disappearing beneath rime white foam.

"Earth take you. Earth take you."

She was so stupid. From the first the water had told her what it would do. Now it had done it.

And she'd given up her magic and the closest thing she had to a friend.

She sat on the shore, empty. The air had gone gray. There were no colors for her anymore.

"I thought she told you to hold onto these," said a familiar, annoyed voice.

Cilla looked up, nearly blind with grief.

A good ways downstream Devon McKenna was wading out of the water, soaking wet, stark naked, and holding out the necklace of glass beads.

She didn't even try to answer. She was caught between soul-shaking relief that he was alive and unspeakable embarrassment that he was naked. Before her the glass beads gleamed amber and red, blue and green and purple.

"Well?" he demanded. "Aren't you going to take them?"

She reached out and took them.

"What was she?" he asked.

Cilla fixed her eyes on the dark green water. "My dead baby-sitter. I mean, the ghost of this girl who used to—"

Devon gave a low laugh. "Yeah," he said, "it's been that kind of night." Cilla was aware of him sitting down on the bank a short distance away from her. "Cilla." His voice was so low she barely heard it above the water. "Look at me," he said. "Please."

The "please" startled her into turning her head. She studied the long narrow eyes above sharp cheekbones, the red hair dark with stream water, the straight line of his mouth. The scar remained, a thin white line beneath his eye. And the silver skull was back, hanging from his left ear.

"All of me," he insisted.

He was leaning back on his elbows, legs stretched out in front of him, perfectly, disturbingly at ease—as comfortable in his body as the stag had been. She let herself look first at his neck, then at his chest and arms. Everything in him was long and lean and muscled. Hesitantly, she looked lower at the thick reddish hair over his crotch, at his cock resting on a long, muscled thigh. She stopped staring at his cock, trying instead to see the whole of him. Even leaning back, lazy and relaxed, there was something restless in him, something that would never belong to the world they'd come out of. He was still half wild.

"Am I so awful?" he asked, his tone curious.

She shook her head and shifted her gaze to a tree.

"I'm not going to rape you or anything," he said with an obvious attempt at patience. "I swear. Look, if I had something to cover myself with, I would. But you don't have to die of embarrassment in the meantime. Christ, you didn't have any problems looking at me—*or sleeping with me*—when I was a deer, and I wasn't wearing any more than I am now."

Cilla blushed straight through to the roots of her hair, and watched him out of the corner of her eye.

He raised his hand to his ear, felt the silver skull hanging there. "Looks like I'm wearing more now. . . ." His voice became thoughtful with a faint overtone of disbelief. "You've never seen a man naked before, have you?"

Cilla stared pointedly at a stand of wild grass.

"It's just a body," Devon told her. "We all have 'em. Get used to it." He shot her a wicked grin. "Maybe it'd be easier if you took your clothes off, too. Then we—"

She gave him a panicked look and he sat up and raised his hands. "Only kidding. . . . Here." She watched amazed as he ripped out a handful of wild grass and arranged it artlessly over his crotch. "Better?"

"No," she said, trying not giggle. "I'll get used to you."

"Good."

A silence fell between them, and in the silence she found she could look at him without embarrassment or shame, found she *liked* looking at him. He was looking at her, too, his eyes as tawny as the stag's, the color of topaz. Had they always been that color?

"Where'd you get the dress?" he asked suddenly. "Looks good on you."

"Connie—the one who was here—and some other ghosts."

"They didn't happen to give you a pack of cigarettes while they were at it, did they?"

Cilla smiled. "No, I don't think they work that way."

He blew out a short breath. "It figures."

There were things she needed to know, questions she wanted to ask, but she didn't know yet if what had happened between them would permit that. Were they friends now? Would he talk to her? She might as well try.

"Devon," she began, his name a newfound and uncertain intimacy, "what do you think happened tonight?"

He shrugged and leaned back again. "Near as I can tell . . . we became what we've always been. It's what she said. I was always kind of wild . . . always running with death after my ass, scared shitless but kind of digging it, too."

"I never thought of you as scared," Cilla said.

"That's 'cause until tonight you weren't in on the secret," he said with a trace of self-mockery. "Anger's just the flip side of fear. If you got one, you got the other in there, too."

Cilla saw herself standing by the boulders, perfectly willing to kill her mother. It hadn't been Devon's rage at all.

"And you," he went on, "you were what you've always been."

Now the self-mockery was hers: "Terrified?"

"Well, that, too, but I meant brave."

"I'm not brave."

"Yeah, you are. You stood up to your mother. And you tried to save me."

"I had to," Cilla said, her voice flat. "I didn't save my father. Those things that went after you—they tore him apart, and I never even tried to stop them or protect him. It was like I gave him over to them." She had never told this to *anyone,* and here she was about to make her confession to a naked Devon McKenna. Was she expecting him to grant her absolution? She went ahead with it, anyway. "There was a night when I was eleven. I saw them—they marked him. He began to die after that. And I was so scared, I let them take him so they wouldn't take me instead."

"You've been carrying that around for six years?" Devon asked, his voice nearly breaking. If he was playing priest, she'd never seen one so outraged. "Cilla," he said slowly, "he wasn't yours to protect. You couldn't have given him to them. Or stopped them. His life wasn't in your hands." He stood up and walked to the edge of the stream, where he stood staring into the chanting water. "Jesus, what a thing to carry."

It was as close to absolution as she would come, and it left her lighter, light-headed, nearly dizzy with wonder at the unexpected forms grace could take. From the back Devon reminded her of a young tree; he held himself light and supple and looked as right standing there on the bank as anything that grew out of it. It was as if there'd always been a naked boy with long red hair standing on the white sand.

"You got to let that go," he said, still facing the water. "Besides, what makes you think you've got any kind of power over the things that took him?"

"I don't," she admitted. "I tried to call them back when they went after you. It was like trying to sprout wings."

"That's because they weren't yours to call. Those things really don't have a whole lot to do with you. They belonged to your mother." Something entered his voice that might have been pain. "And to me. You know, you're not the only one who's seen them before. The thing is, when I've seen them its always *me* they've been after."

"I didn't think anything could escape them."

"Yeah, well, I'm sort of one of their own."

"And that's a protection?"

"Protection, my ass, they eat their young. But whatever it is they are, and whatever it is I am, we're still pretty evenly matched."

"I think you're more than they are," Cilla said.

"Do you?" His hair swept across his shoulders as he turned his head to glance at her. Something of the stag glinted in his eyes, an unending wariness, and she knew in that instant that he'd never trusted anyone.

"Your rage, that's what brings them on," she told him. "But there's other stuff in you, too."

"Like what?" he asked bitterly.

"Like whatever made you go into the stream for my necklace."

"Insanity."

"Maybe," she agreed, but she was smiling at him, and this time, he was the one who couldn't meet her eyes.

He gave a careless shrug. "They'll be back. They'll get me one day."

Cilla saw that the pronouncement carried a studied disregard for fear and an acknowledged liaison with danger. Maybe that was the key, the shield against the dark gods. "How'd you get away?"

"I was a buck," he answered. "I did what a buck does when it's in the hunt. I ran. I ran them to the goddamn ground. And here's the sick part—even though I knew what would happen if they caught me, I loved every fucking minute of it. It's like, *that's what I was made for.*"

She had to know. "Are you sorry you changed back?"

He gazed into the woods, longingly she thought, and there was a silence so drawn out she thought he'd forgotten her question. "I got charged by another deer," he said at last. This time she was sure; something in Devon's voice ached. "He was younger than me, I think. . . . How many points did I have?"

Cilla stared at him blankly.

"On my antlers."

"Oh. Five."

"He *was* younger. He only had three. He came charging at me out of nowhere, and then we were going at it. And that felt good, too, fighting full out. Stags . . . they don't hold anything back." Something slid closed behind the tawny eyes. "I mean, I always *knew* that one day I'd kill. Seemed inevitable. And I always thought it'd be this incredible rush. But he just lay there, bleeding from the mouth, and I stood over him, panting like a son of a bitch, watching the life go out of his eyes. It . . . it wasn't what I thought it'd be."

"Nothing tonight has been what I thought it'd be," Cilla said.

He hunched down, his arms resting on his knees, his gaze on the rushing stream. He was seeing the death again, she could feel it. She knew that they would both carry this night with them for the rest of their lives. Always there would be a part of her that would hold the gifts of the Revelers. And always in Devon there would be a place where he would watch a young stag die and know that he had taken its life. As for what had happened between them . . . she still wasn't sure.

"When you were first changed," she said hesitantly, "and you went after me, why'd you stop?"

Now Devon looked embarrassed. He stood up, ran a hand through his hair, and searched the lavender sky. "'Cause you were cowering—the way you used to when you were little and your mother used to go after you." He gave her a sardonic look. "I figured it was bad enough I'd turned into a fucking deer, I wasn't going to turn into *her.* That's a hell of a mother you've got there."

"I know."

"She still beats you."

"Not this last year. She hasn't touched me at all."

"She just tears you apart."

Cilla tried to imitate his careless shrug. "She's no worse than a lot of others. I know kids whose homes make mine look like a TV sitcom."

"That *doesn't* make it okay," he said fiercely. "Don't you get it? What happened to you is not all right. The second you say it is, then you're in it with her, on her side. It's soul murder, what she does. She made you hide so deep, *you* didn't even know you were still in there. But you got out tonight. That's what counts. *You got out.*"

The stream was going down, Cilla saw. Its chant had grown softer, and here and there, she could see the top of a rock breaking through the white foam. They had been traveling all along, away from the moon and stars and into other skies. The blue night was gone, and now its lavender dawn was fading. Her own world would be waiting with the day.

"*You got out,*" Devon repeated, as if he knew that some part of her was wavering, fragile again, unsure of its new center.

Her eyes went back to the boy who had been a stag. "What if I go back in?"

"You won't," he said, and then asked abruptly, "When did you get your ears pierced?"

She'd forgotten that she had. "Sixth grade," she answered, thinking back. "Me and Greta Kreske sneaked out to the mall and had it done. I got in trouble for it, and—"

"And you never wore earrings again," he finished.

"I wore them when I was alone in my room."

"In your room." He came to kneel beside her, took the silver skull from his ear, and slipped it into hers. "This isn't for your goddamn room." He grinned at her and there was a warmth in his eyes that made her senses reel. "Now you look tough. Which, by the way, you are. That's to remind you."

"We're going to have to go back, aren't we?"

He nodded. "I don't think we can stay here, not without dying or something." He gazed across the stream. "It's still going to be winter over there. We're gonna freeze our asses off." His eyes slid over her body appreciatively. "Guess we'll have to keep each other warm."

She ignored the flirting, thinking only of what awaited her. "How can I go back there? How can I ever go back into that house?" A new possibility occurred to her. "Maybe I won't go home. I could run away, and—"

"Uh, Cilla, don't take this wrong. I think you're real brave and all, but I don't think you're cut out for life on the streets. I mean, I've been in shelters. You'd . . . have a rough time of it."

She nodded. She couldn't really picture herself on the streets, either. Her eyes went to a cluster of wild violets growing by the edge of the water, delicate purple flowers above spring-green stems, vibrating slightly in the warm dawn. She'd have to go back into winter streets where the ground was frozen hard and the air itself had given in to a sheath of iron gray. She'd go back to a house where she'd always been in pain.

"Then this was all for nothing," she said, her voice hollow. "What happened tonight was like dreamtime. I'll go home and my mother won't know what happened here. She'll be just like she always was and worse— she'll be ready to skin me for staying out all night. Nothing will have changed."

"*You've* changed," Devon said. "You're not in her power any more. You got your own back. You made it through this crazy night. You can survive that house or a find a way out." His voice became wry. "A way that doesn't involve hanging out in all-night diners, waiting for some jerk to hit on you."

"How?"

His hand closed over her hand, the hand that still held the glass bead necklace. "You take this back with you. Maybe you let her see it, maybe you don't, but you hold onto it. And when it gets scary and hard, you remember this night. You remember what you were given and what you chose for your own—how you got back the things she took from you. You remember *what you are,* and you know that you're going to make it through, that no one is ever going to shut you down again."

She listened. She also read between the lines. "I'm not going to see you again, am I?"

He gave one of his overly casual shrugs. "Don't know." His voice became softer. "Probably not. You don't want to hang out with me. You *know* what kind of stuff I call up."

"At least you see it. A lot of people call those things up and don't even know it."

"Yeah, well"—now the pain was naked in his eyes—"seeing's never been my problem. But the things I see . . ."

"There's more to you than them," she insisted.

"You're so sure."

She nodded. "You—you helped me tonight. I mean, *after* you nearly scared me to death."

"It was mutual," he told her. "We looked out for each other."

She echoed his unspoken thought, "But it was just for this one night, right?"

"I don't know." He turned restlessly toward the water, and she stood up and followed him to its edge. When he spoke again his voice had an odd timbre to it, and Cilla realized she'd never heard uncertainty in him before. "What happened to us tonight—it doesn't happen to too many people. Not the ones I know, anyway. And to tell you the truth, that makes me a little nervous."

She tried to keep her voice light, to keep the hurt out. "You could pretend tonight never happened. I won't tell. I'll pretend—"

"Cilla." He grasped her wrist gently. "No pretending. We didn't go through all this so we could bullshit each other." He released her wrist. "I think," he said slowly, "that what's happened between you and me is, we've seen each other. We each know who the other is. A lot of it, anyway. More than most people get to know. With you"—his voice went from uncertainty to rueful disbelief—"I've got nothing left to hide."

"And that scares you?"

"Let's just say, I'm not exactly used to it."

Cilla saw herself stripping in front of the Revelers, excruciatingly exposed, and heard Connie's voice saying, "You have to be seen. That's part of it, love."

"I'm not used to it, either," she told Devon. "The only ones who've ever known me for what I am are dead. It's . . . hard to suddenly be transparent. To be seen that way."

"Doesn't look like we have much choice." The tawny eyes studied her, flickered with barely concealed laughter. "Of course, *I'm* still waiting to see *you* with your clothes off."

She threw a twig at him and he grinned, dodging it effortlessly.

"So we know each other," he said, his voice serious again. Morning light glinted off his hair, deep copper one moment, wildfire the next. "I don't know what comes next. Maybe we keep looking out for each other. If we can. I can't make you any promises. I . . . I move around a lot."

He was telling her he'd never really trust, never lose the part of him that still ran with the stag. As if she didn't know.

"I don't need promises," she said, then struggled toward something else, an idea that only a few minutes earlier she'd have never dared propose. "Knowing each other like we do . . . that's something we've got to hold for each other, something precious. I'm not saying it'll always work this way. I know we're basically on our own. But if I start to shut down again, I *want* you to show up at my door and tell me I don't have to. And when you see the dark gods coming after you, you can come to me and I'll tell you what else I see, what else is there."

He nodded solemnly, the tawny eyes sealing their pact as clearly as if he and Cilla had signed in blood, sealed it with their souls.

Their eyes lifted at the sound of a hawk's cry. The hawk perched above them, at the top of a pine, surveying the shores below. It gave another loud cry, spread its wings, and soared across the stream. The green water was lower now and a line of rocks broke the surface, their tops flat: stepping stones. A short distance from where the farthest one met the opposite shore, a narrow path wound up the steep bank.

"I think we just got our ticket back," Devon said. His eyes went to the necklace that was still in her hand. "Can I see that?"

She gave it to him.

He opened the filigree clasp, held the necklace up in the morning light, and she knew that the glass had been spun from the stream, the beads still gleaming with all the colors of the night. "Turn around," he said softly.

She did as he asked and saw his hands come around in front her, gently placing the necklace around her neck, then fastening the clasp behind her. "There," he said.

She started to step away but he pulled her to him and held her close, his arms warm around her, his head just touching hers. She let herself lean back against him and marveled that twice now she'd entered the place where she was truly safe, marveled that Devon was there with her.

She turned in his arms, her cheek pressed against his chest. She felt the beat of his heart, memorized the rhythm of life that pulsed through him. It seemed to her then that knowing another person's heartbeat was the ultimate intimacy. She stayed there folded in his arms, listening, knowing they'd journeyed the whole night to reach this.

The hawk's cry sounded again and they broke apart. The water's chant was quieter now, so soft it could barely be heard, a teasing reminder of all that had been, a quiet prayer to echo through them for the days to come. Cilla knew they had to cross the stream while its song still lasted, while the magic still held.

"Let's go."

She held out her hand to him. His hand closed around hers. Together they made their way back across the water.

# A Matter of Seeing

### ◆   Ellen Steiber   ◆

*Little brother took his little sister by the hand and said: "Since our
mother died we have had no happiness; our stepmother beats us
every day, and if we come near her she kicks us away. . . . Our
meals are the hard crusts of bread that are left over. . . . Come, we
will go forth together into the wide world.*\*

So begins the Grimm's tale "Brother and Sister," on which I very loosely
based "In the Night Country." When I began writing the story I knew I
wanted to write a journey taken by a teenage girl and boy into the other
realm. What I could not have possibly envisioned at the time was how
much of the story I'd have to find; that at every stage, no matter how
much I had worked out beforehand, there would still be a great deal I
didn't know and would have to uncover. In retrospect, the first thing that
was not really clear was why I was so determined to use this particular folk
tale as my jumping-off point, especially since I didn't particularly care for
its second half. Then again, I'd wanted to write about an enchanted journey and the story that came late one night was set in a sleazy diner. It was

---

\*All story excerpts were taken from *The Complete Grimm's Fairy Tales*, copyright © 1944 by
Pantheon Books Inc., renewed 1972 by Random House, Inc., New York. The story "Brother
and Sister" appears on pp. 67–73.

only fifteen pages later that I understood they were, in fact, the same story, and by that time I'd made a silent agreement with the Muse that I'd do my best to surrender to whatever it was the story itself wanted. For reasons unknown it wanted "Brother and Sister" as its base. There was something in the imagery of the old tale that needed to be explored.

At the risk of capsulizing a story that deserves to be read in full, I'd like to briefly go through the original and then talk about some of the things it revealed to me, the rich metaphors that deal with abuse and transformation and offer a key to how we go about setting ourselves free.

In the Grimms' story the brother and sister leave home and enter the forest. Hot and weary and thirsty, they soon find themselves searching for water. But as the story tells us:

> . . . the wicked stepmother was a witch, and had seen how the two children had gone away, and had crept after them secretly, as witches creep, and had bewitched all the brooks in the forest.

They come to a brook, but as the brother is about to drink the sister hears the water say: "Who drinks of me will be a tiger. Who drinks of me will be a tiger." The sister begs her brother not to drink, telling him that if does, he will become a "wild beast" and tear her to pieces.

They walk on and find a second brook. This time as the brother is about to drink the sister hears the stream warn that who drinks of it will be a wolf. Again she begs her brother not to drink, telling him he'll devour her, and again they walk on.

They come to a third stream, for like so many European folk tales this story works in patterns of three. The third brook warns that who drinks of it will be a roebuck. Again the sister pleads with her brother not to drink, telling him that if he does, he'll run away from her.

> But the brother had knelt down at once by the brook, and had bent down and drunk some of the water, and as soon as the first drops touched his lips he lay there in the form of a young roebuck.

He does not, however, abandon his sister. The two weep for a bit, and then the sister ties her golden garter around the roe's neck, and weaves a cord of rushes which she ties to the garter. In this manner she leads him deeper into the forest to one of those wonderfully convenient, empty little cottages found in so many fairy tales. (Would that we all found housing so easily in times of need.) There they set up housekeeping. The sister gathers roots and berries for herself and brings the roebuck tender grass, and he "played round about her . . . And if only the brother had had his human form it would have been a delightful life."

Their peace is shattered when the king brings his hunt to that part of the forest.

*Then the blasts of the horns, the barking of dogs, and the merry*
*shouts of the huntsmen rang through the trees, and the roebuck*
*heard all, and was only too anxious to be there. "Oh," said he to his*
*sister, "let me be off to the hunt, I cannot bear it any longer"; and*
*he begged so much that at last she agreed.*

Since the deer has obviously not lost the power of human speech, and the
girl is afraid of opening the door to the rough huntsmen, they agree that
when the deer returns to the cottage, he'll knock and ask her to let him in.

The roe survives the first day of the hunt but is wounded on the second. He makes it back to the cottage, is much improved the next morning,
and despite his wound insists on running again the third day, telling his
sister that if she does not let him out,

*"Then you will have me die of grief . . . when I hear the bugle-horns*
*I feel as if I must jump out of my skin."*

Meanwhile, one of the king's huntsmen has seen the wounded deer
enter the cottage and has related the story to the king. On the third day of
the hunt the king gives orders that the deer is to be chased but not
harmed. That night the king stands outside the cottage door and utters
the deer's password. Thinking it is her brother calling, the sister opens the
door. The king enters and finds "a maiden more lovely than any he had
ever seen."

In the way of fairy tales, the king asks the maiden to marry him on the
spot, assuring her that the roebuck shall stay with her as long as she lives
"and shall want nothing." She agrees and the three of them go off in great
style.

That's the first half of the tale, and until I was writing the very last
scene of "In the Night Country," it was the only part I thought I had any
use for. I wasn't much interested in what happened once the sister wed
the king and settled into married life at the palace. But the images of the
early part of the story haunted me with a strange and urgent resonance: I
wanted to work with a girl and boy who journey together into the forest;
with a magical stream that transforms the boy into a thing of the wild, and
what it means to go into that animal inside us; with a buck who cannot
resist the call of the hunt; with his risking the hunt, and that being critical
to the ultimate lifting of the curse.

Obviously, I took my story in a different direction from the Grimms'
tale. Cilla and Devon are not literally brother and sister; they don't start
out as allies. In fact, in the beginning there's every chance that Devon will
turn out to be worse than what she's running from. For my purposes it
was not the witch whose magic enchanted the stream but another sort of
magic altogether. And by the time I got my characters to the first stream,
it was clear to me that this was a one-stream story and its action was going

to occur during the course of a single night. Further, as a feminist, I had no interest in the images of the rescuer king and his palace and what seemed an awfully convenient marriage that got them all niftily out of the woods. I simply couldn't use it. More to the point, that was not what Cilla and Devon could use; they had other needs.

From early on in the writing process, I knew where things were going. I knew that Devon would turn into a stag, that Cilla would meet the Revelers and the ghosts of Connie and her father. I also knew that she would confront her mother and Devon would be there with her, but until I actually wrote that scene I had no idea of how she would come through the confrontation. I found out very slowly. When I finally reached the point where Cilla wakes up on the shore curled around the deer, I was sure the real work was done. During the months in which I'd been working on the story, I'd already written the last line and most of the dialogue for the final scene. The rest would be easy. I'd simply order what I had and add a few transition phrases. Like Devon and Cilla, I was to find that things weren't what I expected.

Seventeen drafts later the final scene still wasn't anywhere near "right." All that dialogue I'd been writing for months sounded wrong, as if I were putting it in my characters' mouths rather than letting them speak for themselves. And Devon, in particular, was too ornery to let me use him for my own purposes; any time I tried to give him words that weren't his own, he made them sound completely absurd—which was the case with most of the dialogue I'd written for him.

The end was in sight and I was stuck. I was also desperate to finish the thing. And so I went back to my source, and to my amazement found things in the second half of the Grimm's story that I hadn't seen the first five times I read it. It was, like "In the Night Country," a ghost story of sorts. And it had a good deal more to say as a metaphor for abuse.

To return to the tale: Back at his palace the king holds a grand wedding and makes the sister his queen.

> *. . . and they lived for a long time happily together; the roebuck was tended and cherished, and ran about in the palace-garden.*
>
> *But the wicked stepmother, because of whom the children had gone out into the world, had never thought but that the sister had been torn to pieces by the wild beasts in the wood, and that the brother had been shot for a roebuck by the huntsmen. Now when she heard that . . . they were so well off, envy and jealousy rose in her heart . . . and she thought of nothing but how she could bring them again to misfortune. Her own daughter, who was ugly as night, and had only one eye, reproached her and said: "A Queen! That ought to have been my luck." "Just be quiet," answered the old woman . . . "when the time comes I shall be ready."*

There were a few things in that brought me up short. The first was an acknowledgment: "the wicked stepmother, because of whom the children had gone out into the world." Abusive backgrounds often drive the children out of the family and into the world. If you are lucky enough to survive, being driven out into the world can be a very good thing. Clearly, one reason the brother and sister were living in the palace was because they'd been driven out into the world. It is worth recognizing that however lethal she may be, the stepmother is an agent of change. This is not to condone the role of the abuser, but to see the act of "getting out" not only as escape, but as entry into the fullness of life.

The second thing that struck me about the passage was that the stepmother's own daughter, the one who stayed home and didn't get out, only had one eye. *She was half-blind.*

One of the subtler effects of growing up in an abusive household is that it distorts your vision. Sometimes the distortion sets in because you can't bear to see what's going on. Sometimes blinders are deliberately put on you. Sometimes you become astigmatic by osmosis—a result of growing up in a household where everyone around you has unconsciously agreed to see only part of the picture. In any case, you compromise the ability to see clearly, and many things, including the ability to distinguish between those who will help you and those who will devour you, become confused. When you get yourself physically out of the household and yet continue to live with your vision shut down, the abuse has become internalized and self-perpetuating. When you are surrounded by others whose vision is similarly distorted, you get buried. This is very much what happens in the second half of "Brother and Sister."

Time goes on in the palace. The queen gives birth to a little boy while the king is out hunting. With the queen still weak from childbirth, the old witch takes the form of the chambermaid and convinces the queen that what she needs to restore her is a bath. (It is no accident that the witch is able to assume the shape of a helper and "the weakly queen" is unable to tell the difference.) Then the witch and her daughter carry the queen into the bath, shut the door, and run away.

> . . . But in the bath-room they had made a fire of such hellish heat that the beautiful young Queen was soon suffocated.
>
> When this was done the old woman took her daughter . . . and laid her in bed in place of the Queen. She gave her too the shape and the look of the Queen, only she could not make good the lost eye. But in order that the King might not see it, she was to lie on the side on which she had no eye.
>
> In the evening . . . he came home . . . and was going to the bed of his dear wife to see how she was. But the old woman quickly called out: "For your life leave the curtains closed; the Queen ought not to

*see the light yet, and must have rest." The King went away, and did not find out that a false Queen was lying in the bed.*

Again the story stopped me, this time with the image of the witch's half-blind daughter taking the place of the true queen. If you've been shut down, it is often a half-blind impostor self that goes through the world in your stead—the "good" girl or boy, carefully designed not to bring down wrath; the "clown," an equally careful design, bent on defusing all tension with humor; the "bad" boy or girl, the ones who get their own by going farther into rage and danger than anyone else in the household. The list goes on. There are endless roles and combinations thereof that we take on when our own being is not welcome, when we have to become someone else in order to survive. Cilla had chosen the role of the "good" girl, and in doing so had denied her own beauty, vision, and sexuality. She'd given all her power away. When the story opens she is living the life of the half-blind impostor.

Folk tales, coming as they do out of the ancient myths, are deep ground. They lend themselves to many interpretations, and so there's a danger of turning any one of them into too personal a metaphor. There was a part of me wary of reading too much into "Brother and Sister." And then I came to the witch's instructions to the king, and chills went through me, so closely do they describe the devil's bargain made in nearly every abusive home: *"For your life leave the curtains closed; the Queen ought not to see the light . . ."* Abusive households breed a conspiracy of silence and lies in which no one is allowed to see the light, in which everyone consents to blindness "for their lives" rather than risk the consequences of seeing the truth. This is the syndrome of the battered child who takes the stand in court and swears, possibly believing it herself, that her parents never hurt her. This is the belief that what goes on in an abusive household is "normal" and loving when, in fact, it's eating its young alive. This is a metaphor for all the lies and denials that perpetuate destructive environments—the line that says someone is always to blame, or that the child in question is worthless or evil or deserving of cruelty.

There's another level to being shut down, an aesthetic one if you will. What we also stop seeing, beyond the harsh truth, is beauty, and this loss is even more critical. We stop seeing the splendor in the natural world because the beauty has been leached from our lives; instead we see a reflection of what it is that has surrounded us. We stop seeing love, seeing instead fear or treachery. We lock ourselves into narrow parameters that have been set for us by others. Limited, and finding comfort in the familiarity of those limits, we stop seeing the possibilities for growth and joy. We stop seeing the colors. We abandon our dreams. We live half-lives.

But back to the story which, like many fairy tales, is a guide for getting through the forest and past the witch. Although the true queen has been suffocated, she returns silently at midnight to suckle the babe and pet the roebuck who sleeps in a corner of the nursery. The only one who sees her is the nurse. (I do not think it a coincidence that the one who sees her is the one who gives sustenance.) In the morning the nurse asks the palace guards whether anyone came into the palace during the night. Like true co-dependents they answer, "No, we have seen no one."

For quite some time the queen continues to return to suckle the babe and visit the roe. The nurse who, although she sees, is also caught in fear, dares not tell anyone. Until at last the queen speaks during one of her midnight visits:

> *"How fares my child, how fares my roe?*
> *Twice shall I come, then never more."*

Clearly, this situation cannot go on forever; you cannot continue to have a half-blind impostor in your place. It can go on so long and then there's true death.

The nurse doesn't answer the queen but she does tell the king what she's seen, and he comes to watch for himself. Again, the queen makes her midnight visit, this time warning that she can only return one more time. Like the nurse before him, the king "dared not speak to her," but on the next night he watches again. This time she says:

> *"How fares my child, how fares my roe?*
> *This time I come, then never more."*

> *Then the King could not restrain himself; he sprang towards her, and said: "You can be none other than my dear wife." She answered: "Yes, I am your dear wife," and at the same moment she received life again, and by God's grace became fresh, rosy, and full of health.*

The corollary to not seeing is, of course, not being seen, and that is an equally dangerous state of existence. When you grow up hiding who you truly are so that you can survive, it becomes increasingly hard for anyone to see past the construct. We set the impostor in our place and the impostor is what the world reflects back to us. If this goes on long enough, there comes a point when even we can't see the difference, when even we don't know who—if anyone—is inside. Perhaps most tragically, if we don't see the sickness in this extended separation from and denial of true self, we go on to perpetuate the cycle in the next generation.

There's one more bit to the folk tale in which the queen tells the king what happened, and the witch and her daughter are brought to trial. The daughter is then taken into the forest and torn apart by wild beasts, the fate that the witch had planned for the queen, and the witch herself is "miserably burnt."

*And as soon as she was burnt to ashes, the roebuck changed his shape, and received his human form again, so the sister and brother lived happily together all their lives.*

According to the fairy tale, the curse is only broken when its source is destroyed (encompassed in that, the half-blind impostor must be "torn to pieces"). Being repulsed by capital punishment in all forms, even metaphoric ones, I never considered having Cilla's mother killed. It wasn't necessary. Cilla simply had to take back the power she'd given up—a process that, in fact, is not simple at all.

But then Cilla, like so many kids today, has to deal with something that the queen in her palace will never have to worry about. Cilla has to go back home. Abuse takes many forms, and Cilla isn't facing anything as shattering as sexual abuse or beatings that leave broken bones. She will probably never have a social worker or a neighbor intervene. Her home is not so life-threatening that the street is a better alternative. The sort of abuse she deals with is subtler, insidious, more a destruction of the spirit than the body (whereas the more brutal forms of abuse destroy both). Like so many kids in dysfunctional families, until she's older she's going to have to live in that house. And so it seemed the most honest thing I could do was offer her the tools with which to survive that place.

Once you've been shut down, once you've constructed the armor and gone into hiding, how do you open up again? If you're lucky, you cross paths with someone who hands you a key. Despite the fact that we live in an age where a popular "truth" insists "you create your own reality," another truth is that sometimes you can't get out alone. Sometimes you need help, especially if you're working with partial vision. For me, the form that help often took was that by the grace of the gods, I was given true friends—those who saw me not as I saw myself (an image that came from a house in which I hid), but saw inside to what I truly was and welcomed that being, allowed me to finally see my own essence and bring it into the world. Being truly seen is a gift whose value cannot be overestimated. In the fairy tale, being recognized brings nothing less than resurrection.

Fairy tales are journey stories. They deal with initiation and transformation, with going into the forest where one's deepest fears and most powerful dreams are realized. Many of them offer a map for getting through to the other side. Out of curiosity I went back to the patterns of three in the tale, since the very rhythms of repetition set them off and give them importance. There are three brooks, three days of the hunt, and three times that the queen's ghost speaks. Each of these patterns presents challenge and transformation; they are the places of power in the story, the points where true magic occurs. In the first the brother is thirsty; he needs nourishment and finally gets it, a difficult metamorphosis being the price. In the second he must either follow his own nature or "die of grief"; at great risk he runs with the hunt, and that act takes both brother and sister farther along on the path they must travel to a new state of being.

(It's worth noting that in the fairy tales one can rarely remain in the forest—one takes what was found there and brings it back into the world.) In the third challenge, the king must recognize the queen, an act that will restore her to life and lead to a redress of wrongs, a final ending of the curse, a coming into balance. As abuse takes many forms, so does salvation. Here are three of many acts that can get you through: nourishing yourself, following your heart even at great risk, and being seen for what you are.

Vision is one of the five senses, a gift that's easy to take for granted. It comes to us so easily. We simply open our eyes and "see." And yet there are levels of seeing. As the fairy tale tells us, when we constrict or confuse our vision we are primed for betrayal and destruction; we are in the hold of the witch. To free ourselves we must both try to see clearly and allow ourselves to be seen. These are acts of courage and of power. If we can go beyond that and see compassionately, we may even partake in acts of grace.

I'd like to claim that "In the Night Country" was written for everyone who's ever been shut down. The truth is it was written for me. There were things in it I had to find, and writing, like any of the arts, is a way of perceiving, of coming to know the heart of a thing. The things that Devon and Cilla came to know were things I needed to make my own; I suspect I needed those lessons even more than they. The story was part of my way through. And so it is dedicated in gratitude to the "seers," the ones who see us for what we are and send back that reflection in love. And finally, it is sent out in the hope that for all of us who've been shut down, *for our lives,* we'll open the curtains and see the light.

# AFTERWORD:
# Surviving Childhood
### ◆ Terri Windling ◆

*Hard by a great forest dwelt a woodcutter and his wife who had two children, Hansel and Gretel. They were very poor, and one night the woodcutter said to his wife, "Wife, what is to become of us? How are we to feed our children when we've barely enough to feed ourselves?" The woman answered, "I'll tell you what we must do. Tomorrow we will go into the forest. There we will light a fire for the children and give them one more piece of bread, and then we will go about our work and leave them there. They will not find their way home again, and we will be rid of them."*

*—"Hansel and Gretel"*

A man who identified himself as my mother's boyfriend called me the day the police found her unconscious body on her living-room floor with a suicide note beside her, and I caught the next plane from Boston south to the steel towns where I'd grown up. My eldest half-brother met me at our mother's house, on the outskirts of a small industrial city no different from half a dozen other towns through which my family had moved like gypsies over the years.

I'd never been to this house before, but its three small rooms looked identical to the succession of sagging rental houses and trailers we'd grown up in, with their fake wood-paneled walls and gold shag carpets, decorated with my mother's ceramics and figurines. The couch covered in scratchy plaid synthetic fabric and the painstakingly hand-sewn orange flowered curtains were as familiar as my mother's voice on the phone machine and the curlicue script of her handwriting. I hadn't been invited here and I felt like an intruder in the house, although I poured instant coffee into the same cups I had drunk from as a child.

My mother was recovering from her suicide attempt in the mental ward of the county hospital. My brother and I had been informed that we would not be allowed to see her until the following morning. We drank black coffee and waited out the evening, ignoring the calls coming in on the machine. They were all from collection agencies trying to collect on my mother's many debts, which was another childhood familiarity. I had grown up thinking all families had a constant stream of threatening men on the phone; and indeed, in the towns of our childhood, where the mills, the factories, the steel works were all closing down, one after the other, many families undoubtedly did.

As the evening passed we talked about those towns, for I hadn't seen my brother in years, and we no longer had anything else in common. At twenty-four, the boy I remembered was hidden behind a half-grown beard, a heavy-metal shirt and a beer-barrel belly. He flatly refused to believe me when I told him he'd been an attractive child. I went in search of the family photo album and carried it back to the kitchen. Sweating in the July heat, our thighs sticking to the plastic kitchen chairs, we leaned together over the old album with its faded '60s day-glo cover.

Tucked inside the back page was a handful of loose photographs we'd never seen before: small yellowing prints of my mother as a skinny, serious child, and a formal photograph of my grandmother's wedding, when my mother was already a grown girl of fourteen. There was a snapshot of my mother as a teenager in 1959, wearing saddle shoes and white bobby socks and holding me, a drooling infant, for the camera. There were black-and-white, scallop-edged '60s photos of me as a fatherless, scabby-kneed, grinning girl living in my grandmother's house with my mother and her sisters. The final picture was of my mother's own wedding when she was pregnant with my half-brother. She wore a short blue dress and her hair under the stiff veil was cut like Jackie Kennedy's. I stood behind her and my new stepfather, six years old and no longer grinning, as if I'd had a premonition of what was to come.

These photographs had belonged to my grandmother, not my mother; they were labeled in my grandmother's spidery script. Dog-eared and creased, they were thrust haphazardly into an envelope and tucked away like a guilty secret. Mother's own photographs were carefully pasted into the family album. The collection began with a formal marriage portrait and professional photos of her two infant sons; it contained no pictures of me. My brother flipped silently through the pages and then looked up at me strangely.

"Can I ask you a weird question?"

I nodded, a little wary, wondering what shape the past took in his memory.

"Did you ever live with us, when we were kids?"

I was startled by the question. I had diapered him, fed him, toilet-trained him, read him stories at night while my mother worked and my stepfather sat drinking in the neighborhood bars. I had walked the two boys to school, helped them with their homework, and dried their tears at night. "Well, yeah," I said. "I lived with other relatives sometimes, but often I was with you. You must have been nine or ten when I left for good. Don't you remember?"

"Nah," he said. "But that's all right. I don't remember a lot of things. And what I do remember don't always fit together."

He frowned down at the photos: the two boys, the dogs, the years of Christmas trees and birthday cakes. Just as my mother edited her photo album, pasting onto its pages only those parts of family life she considered wholesome and acceptable, she had edited and reconstructed her life story. Dropping out of high school and giving birth to me was one of the chapters she did not care to include, and so my awkward existence was explained away with a variety of excuses, and sometimes edited out altogether. Christmas cards would come to our house addressed to my parents and their sons by well-meaning friends who didn't know a daughter lived there too. It was from our mother that my brother had learned to ignore, then forget, all that was too painful to remember. Our other brother, the youngest, had found his own way to bury the past: he had simply disappeared.

My brother was fascinated now by the old pictures. He could not stop looking at the apple-cheeked child he used to be. He looked at the photos and I looked at him, wondering how the bright-eyed boys who had mugged for the camera, who had cuddled in my lap and begged for one more bedtime story, had grown into the men they became: the eldest, the bright one, working in a factory now; the youngest, the charmer, running from the past and an illegitimate daughter of his own.

But I was asking the wrong question. My brothers grew into the men their environment demanded they become, no different from our neighbors, no different from other undereducated, underemployed steel-town boys. The real question was: how had I escaped? Why do some of us survive our childhoods, while others, raised beside us, lie pinned and helpless beneath its weight?

*Weary and cold, Liza lay down on the hard ground to sleep.*
*And in her dreams a voice said to her, "You can save your*

*brothers. Have you courage and patience? Here's what must be done. In this wood grow many nettles. They burn and sting like fire if you touch them. You must pick every last one, pick them and crush them with your bare hands and spin them into thread. Then knit seven coats. The moment you put the coats on your brothers, they'll be free from your stepmother's spell. The hardest part is this: from start to finish, you must work without speaking. If you say one word, it will be like plunging a knife into your brothers' hearts. Remember!"*

—*"The Seven Swans"*

That night we sat on the front porch above a spare and dusty little lawn. Small houses crowded the street, weather-beaten structures covered with tar-paper shingles or the shiny Kool-Aid colors of aluminum siding. Through open windows we could hear the blare of television laughter, top-forty radio hits, arguments, and children shrieking. I was hot and grimy in a shin-length dress that had looked lovely when I put it on that morning in Boston and looked ridiculous here, like a child dressing up in adult clothes, a steel-town girl putting on airs. Despite all the years and miles between me and the factories, I suddenly felt like I had never left.

I began to talk about Boston to make it real again: about my art studio in the historic North End, and the fairy-tale illustrations I was in the middle of painting. My brother's eyes glazed over. I might have been describing the daily habits of an obscure and uninteresting tribe of Mongolians. His attention wandered down the street and returned only when I brought the conversation back to our family and local terrain.

This is a thing I've never completely understood, why it is that my family of inveterate gossips shows no apparent interest in, or even simple curiosity about, what's become of me in the years since I left home, as though my current life were a distasteful subject that must be discreetly ignored. Other friends who have made the uncomfortable journey from working-class origins to white-collar or creative-arts professions have described similar experiences. One friend, a civil liberties attorney, carefully loses his grammar and education when he goes home for holidays; otherwise his parents snub him for "getting above himself." Another friend, an art historian, married for fifteen years to a celebrated painter, has a mother who cannot remember her husband's name and persists in introducing her to single men with good paper-mill jobs. I had sent my mother inscribed copies of all the books that I had published; looking around her house, I saw none of them on the shelves. Face to face with such indifference I become silent, like the girls bespelled in fairy tales. Silence was a lesson I learned well as a child. There were so many things of which we dared not speak. *Remember. Not one word! Or it will be as a knife in your brothers' hearts.*

Now I turned to my brother. "Can I ask *you* a weird question? Why on earth did you stay here? You've never been happy here. Why didn't you just leave?"

"Leave?" My brother looked at me queerly, but did not deny his unhappiness. "I dunno. You're the one that got to leave."

" 'Got to'? You say that as if someone gave me permission. As though only one of us kids was allowed to go."

"Well, it feels that way. Besides, it was different for you. You were different."

"I don't remember being any different. We grew up in the same houses, ate the same food, wore the same kind of clothes, watched the same TV shows. I always thought you and I were a lot alike."

"So then what happened?"

"You tell me."

This is a question that haunts me. It seems so arbitrary. My brothers were bright, loving, creative children, as most children are; they were healthy white males in a society in which this alone is a license to succeed. If I can't understand how they got trapped repeating our parents' lives, I'll never understand how I've avoided it, or believe I am yet safe. I have a recurring dream in which Someone Up There notices I have sidestepped my appointed fate; I am plucked from my life and sent back to the steel towns, to a trailer park and a drunken husband and six whiny kids fathered by six different men. For years after I left I was still looking over my shoulder, unable to quite believe I'd made good my escape.

"You know," I said to my brother, "I often wondered what happened to you boys after I ran away. You have no idea how terrible I felt about leaving you behind."

My brother scowled. "That's weird that you felt bad about leaving when I don't even remember you being there in the first place. Damn it, I wish I could remember. It makes me feel like I'm crazy that I can't."

"It's actually very common," I said, forcing the words past the injunction of silence and marveling that they sounded so casual, "for abused children not to remember much about their childhoods."

He snorted. "Abused? Us?"

"Well, that's what it's called," I said defensively. "I know it's hard to think of one's own parents that way. Child abuse. Alcoholism. The words are either melodramatic or clichéd. But you know, it doesn't change what happened to avoid the words."

Yet to speak them aloud within my family gave them a sudden chilling reality. I shivered despite the sticky heat, and I saw my brother do the same.

"Alcoholism," he repeated. "I never thought of it that way. Hell, everybody drinks."

Yes, I thought, a lot of people drink, and we all know plenty of decent people who drink a bit more than they ought. But not everyone drinks from morning till night. Not everyone drinks till they're crazy and mean.

Not everybody drinks himself into an early death from liver failure, like my brother's father, or suicide attempts, like our mother.

"Alcoholism," I insisted.

"Well, I do remember Dad drunk a lot," said my brother. "Hell, I'm not sure I remember him ever sober. . . ."

"Mom too. You used to help me pick her up off the floor and put her to bed at night, remember?"

He laughed without humor. "Yeah, I remember that all right. Sometimes she'd be so shitfaced she'd lose control and, you know, pee all over. . . . I hated cleaning that up. It was like a game, coming home from school and trying to find where she'd hid the bottle that day. I used to pour it down the drain, but then she'd just buy another so after a while I stopped bothering. I never touched Dad's beer, though. . . ."

My brother's voice grew soft as a child's, as though someone might hear him.

He said, "I was so a-scared of him. He'd sleep on the couch, drunk. And I'd try hard to be quiet because if he woke up, he'd get you. I remember his hands always coming at my face. I was so a-scared of his hands."

My brother's voice was trembling. Despite his size and his years I could see the small boy I'd once known again. I remembered all the times I'd put myself in the path of my stepfather's endless rage because the two boys were so small, and so breakable.

"But that's not really child abuse," my brother was saying, his voice firmer, adult again. He tossed his long hair back over his shoulder, as though he could toss off the memory as well. "I mean, a lot of kids get smacked when they're punished."

"Hey," I said, reaching over impulsively and taking my brother's big hand in my own, "he broke bones when he hit. I still limp sometimes. You still have that scar on your arm from the time you went through the glass door. You were only, what, four or five? What could you have done bad enough to deserve that?"

He looked down at the long, fishhook-shaped scar where the doctors had sutured his arm back together. "Mom said I fell."

"Yeah, right. Mom has a very convenient way of remembering things sometimes. I've never known whether she was protecting him, or protecting her idea of what a family should be by pretending everything was okay."

"She wasn't very good at protecting *us*, though, was she?" my brother said rather bitterly. "Hell, maybe she was just a-scared of him too. There was this time he was going after her bad, beating her head against the wall. Hard, like he was going to kill her. He was screaming that he was going to. There was blood all over her face, and . . ."

He turned to me suddenly, his face white. "It wasn't Mom, it was you. That was *you*. I can remember all the blood . . . and that stain we never got out of the rug . . . but how come I didn't remember you? How come I've been remembering it as Mom? Where the hell was Mom? I was hiding at the top of the stairs, watching. Crying. And I didn't even try to stop him."

"You were just a little boy," I reminded him gently. "What could you have done?"

"Oh fuck," he said, and the tears came down his face in the raw, awkward way of a person unused to crying. He held my hand so hard that it hurt and the kids playing in the dusky street stole glances at us curiously. I felt cruel, asking my brother to remember, needing him to corroborate my own memories. Yet forgetting it all was no solution. My mother drank to forget, and look where it had gotten her.

It was a lifetime habit to lie for our parents, to go along with my mother's sanitized version of events, to protect the family from public scrutiny, to take the blame both parents avoided, accept the shame they passed on down. When we saw my mother's doctors at the mental hospital in the morning I intended to tell them the truth, and I wanted to warn my brother of what was coming.

We spent the night talking together, sorting through the rubble of our past. Yet I came no closer to the answer to my private question: why I had escaped and my brother had not. Even he did not count himself among childhood's survivors. His dream had been to join the Peace Corps or the Forest Service; instead he had dropped out of high school and settled for a janitorial job. He had wanted to marry and raise children of his own, but he had shied away from close relationships, afraid of his own drinking problem and the rage that drink brought out in him. My stepfather was dead now (one brother refused to go to the funeral; the other went only to spit on his grave), but my brother was still frightened of the father that lived on inside of him. I urged him to get counselling or go to AA, but he listened to this advice with a resigned passivity that saddened me and made me certain he would not follow it. Late that night we finally went to bed, exhausted by the memory of shared terror.

My brother insisted I take my mother's bedroom while he bedded down on the uncomfortable couch. I closed the door and stripped down to my slip, catching my reflection in the big dresser mirror. I have my mother's small build, but my face and coloring come from the soldier boy who'd gotten my teenage mother pregnant, and so even physically I'd never fit into my family, pale and blond beside my dark brothers. Yet I had been there, whether they remembered me or not; whether my mother chose to acknowledge it or not. I remembered these cigarette burns on my mother's dresser, and this scarred place on the corner where I'd once been thrown and hit my head. This bed was the one my young mother and her handsome new husband had shared when I was a child. I looked down now at my mother's bed and found myself shaking. I couldn't possibly sleep there. I didn't even like being in the same room with it.

I went back into the living room, but my brother had already fallen asleep, and what would I say if I wakened him? That a grown woman was frightened of a bed? There were parts of our childhood I still hadn't spoken of, that he still didn't remember or perhaps never knew. I returned to my mother's room, pulled the comforter off the bed, and lay down on the floor to sleep.

> *One day the Queen fell ill and all the doctors in the kingdom couldn't cure her. She said to the King, "I have one last request. Promise me you will not remarry until you find a wife better and fairer than I." The King promised solemnly. And the Queen died happy in the knowledge that there was none to be found as beautiful as she.*
>
> *Time passed and the King wished to remarry. He remembered his vow and bid his councillors find him the most beautiful maid in the kingdom. But as portrait after portrait was brought for his inspection, not one girl could compare with the King's late wife.*
>
> *Now the King had a daughter who was just as beautiful as her dead mother, with the same white skin and the same golden hair. The King looked at her one day and saw that in every way she was like her mother, and suddenly he felt a violent love for her. Then he spoke to his councillors: "I will marry my daughter, since she alone meets the conditions of my promise." The girl begged and begged him to forget this idea. But he would not change his mind.*
>
> *—"Donkeyskin"*

In the morning we drove to the county hospital, a drab concrete building of broken elevators and peeling paint. This was where the police had brought my mother to revive her. They said she cried when she woke up, distraught to find herself still alive. The police insisted the hospital keep her until they were certain she wouldn't simply try to die again.

The mental health ward took up two long floors. My mother was not in the ward for the violent patients, and yet there were locks upon the ward's door and we had to ring for an orderly to let us in. I spotted her immediately, at the far end of the hallway. Cigarettes, matches, and sharp objects were not permitted in the patients' rooms and so my mother, a chain smoker, was pacing the hallway, catching the ashes of her cigarette in a Styrofoam cup. She seemed smaller than I'd remembered her, pale and thin, hunched in on herself. She wore blue jeans, hospital-issue slippers, and a bright pink shirt with a picture of cartoon rabbits hugging gaily under the words: *Some Bunny Loves You.* She had attacked her hair with scissors in one of her late-night drunken fits and it stood up now in uneven tufts all around her head. She saw me and anger clouded her face; then the expression passed and she greeted us as casually as though we'd just bumped into each other on the street.

"Why hello," she said cheerily. "What are you two doing here? This is all such a silly mistake! I had a bit too much to drink, I suppose. I was awfully tired. I took some pills to sleep. I didn't realize what I was doing. Now they seem to think I tried to kill myself—isn't that the most ridiculous thing?"

Her suicide note had been three pages long, addressed to me, and included detailed instructions on how I was to dispose of her body.

"Now this doctor," she said, "he's Chinese, he barely speaks English and he doesn't understand anything I say. I told him I had no intention of killing myself, and do you know that he called me a liar? He said they can hold me here against my will for ninety days." She gave an exasperated laugh. "They say they'll take me to court to do it if I won't stay voluntarily. None of them seem to understand that I have to go to work in the morning."

My mother said this in such a reasonable voice, with such lucidity and sincerity, that despite her surroundings, despite the hacked hair and the suicide note, I was half-convinced it was indeed a ridiculous mistake. Here was a pleasant, soft-spoken, and intelligent woman, well-liked by all her co-workers and friends. What was she doing locked up in this place, surrounded by people who were sick and incapacitated? How could she be the same woman my brother and I had spoken of just the evening before? Growing up, we'd believed in and trusted her, even when that meant disbelieving what we saw with our own eyes, distrusting our own selves and our own memories. Either our parents were crazy, or we were. And it was easier to believe it of ourselves, for what child can face the knowledge that his parents, his protection against the mysterious and dangerous adult world, are themselves a danger?

My mother then began to instruct us on what to say to the doctors, the lies that would corroborate her own story. We had a close-knit and happy family. My mother's drinking was a recent thing, and certainly not out of control. My brother slumped against the wall, tense and silent. Last night we had made a pledge to each other: from now on we will tell the truth about our past. We will not lie, or pretend it never happened.

"Mom," I said, "you have to tell the truth this time. We can't go on like this."

"The truth? Which truth?" she said, perplexed. My brother looked at me and rolled his eyes. For my mother there were many truths to choose from; she changed reality like some people changed hats.

I reminded her gently of our family history, and the hoarded guilt which filled the pages of her suicide note. She tapped ashes into her cup and would not look me in the eye. She did not deny the violence; she simply felt this was no concern of the doctors, or of anyone else but us.

"You have to tell them this," I insisted, "because if you don't, I will."

"You wouldn't do that," she said calmly.

"We have to," my brother told her sadly.

She looked at the two of us speculatively, and lit another cigarette with a hand that shook.

She drew in the smoke slowly, and let it out in a long stream. I looked at her hands on the cigarette, at the orangey-red paint on her nails, and wondered if she'd painted them before or after the idea of ending her life had taken root. I thought about what it must be like to live with pain so great that death seems preferable. Yet a part of her soul had died long ago, poisoned in her own troubled youth. Mother to daughter, father to son, neglect and casual cruelty were an inheritance passed through the generations. I thought of the fatherless, unwanted girl my mother had been, the skinny girl in the photos, another of childhood's fatalities.

"Please don't tell," she said to us now in a small voice as shaky as her hands, like a child avoiding punishment. "I don't want to talk about your father. I'm afraid."

"What are you afraid of now?" my brother asked her. "Dad's dead."

"I'm afraid . . ." She paused, considering. "They'll think I'm a bad mother," she finally answered honestly.

One voice in my mind said: You are. I stifled that voice, appalled by it. She was the only mother I had, and I loved her. "They won't think any such thing," I reassured her. "They're professionals. They're here to help you. But if they don't know what's wrong, they won't know how to help."

"I suppose you're right. I suppose we'll have to tell them." She sagged against the concrete wall, deflated. Her lies, her evasions, her brave, false smiles were the gears and joints that kept the machinery of her life in operation. Could she function without them? Was there ever a time when she had tried?

We waited together in the hallway until a doctor finally called for us. The Asian psychiatrist in charge of her case did indeed speak little English and he would not spare the time to meet with us. The ward therapist would see us instead, and we were led into a windowless office decorated with posters of wide-eyed puppies and kittens. The therapist, a tired-looking woman in her mid-forties, my mother's age, flipped through a file and turned to my brother—the youngest in the room, but the only man.

"We've decided your mother did not genuinely want to end her life. This incident was probably a reaction to the stress of coping with her aunt's death—so Doctor has prescribed drugs to help her through the immediate crisis. We also recommend she look into AA; we don't want this drinking to develop into a real problem."

I found myself overwhelmed once again by the sense of vertigo that was as common as breathing in childhood, the ground shifting under my feet as my mother's stories collided with reality. The aunt in question was still very much alive.

My brother looked to me to say something, and then blurted it out himself. "Mom's aunt isn't dead! And she's had a drinking problem for years—did she tell you that? She promised the police she would go to AA the last time she cracked up the car, but she only went a few times and quit." He turned to my mother and looked at her imploringly. She was silent, sitting primly and smoking her cigarette.

"Mom," I prompted her, "we agreed we'd tell the truth now, right?"

"The truth? About what?" my mother asked, looking puzzled.

"About the problems in our family. About Dad and all that . . ."

"What problems are those?" the therapist asked my mother.

"I don't know," she said. "I don't know what they're talking about."

"What we just talked about," my brother said miserably, "out in the hallway."

My mother looked perplexed, and the look was perfectly genuine. No more than fifteen minutes had passed, but she'd already erased the memory of our entire conversation. I'd had this experience of instant amnesia with my mother before, listening to tearful late-night confessions that were forgotten again by the light of morning, but clearly my brother had not. He looked as though he'd been struck.

I turned back to the therapist and took a deep breath. I felt my mother's eyes on me. Her gaze could turn me to stone where I sat. In the past it had done so; I'd been silent as stone. Now I began to speak, laying open the family secrets at long last, and my mother looked as startled as though a statue had come to life. My brother and I spoke of my mother's persistent alcohol problem, and her marriage to an alcoholic man whose violence had been the daily terror of three young lives.

"He threatened your mother?" the therapist asked, continuing to direct the questions to my brother.

"Yes," I answered her anyway, "but mostly he beat my brothers and me."

"She means spankings and the like," the woman said to my brother.

"No," I answered defensively, "I mean beatings. Hard enough to break bones." My joints still ache from multiple breaks—doctors had to rebreak and set one badly mended bone—yet there was a dismissive cast to the therapist's expression as she wrote something down in her file. I suspect, in that place, she heard worse every day; in those towns, violence was expected and unremarkable.

"And," I said nervously, glancing at my brother where he sat with his hands white knuckled on the edge of the chair, "my stepfather sexually abused me."

Sexual abuse. At the time I'd been afraid to use those words because I feared no one would believe it could happen. Now I find I am afraid to use them because Sexual Abuse is yesterday's news, a lurid Movie of the Week, a Phil Donahue Show topic. The great triumph of my life, to escape that house, that town, that man, is reduced to a tired soap opera plot. Sexual abuse. It's such a clinical phrase, a tidy label to distance us from the hard reality of an adult penis forcing its way into a tiny, terrified child.

The therapist pressed her lips together in a thin line. My mother looked blank, as though we were talking in Swahili.

"You believe this happened when you were what age?"

Believe it happened? My body still carried the scars. "Well, six when it started. And then until I ran away, at fifteen."

"Is this true?" the woman asked my mother.

"Is what true?" my mother asked.

"Did you ever suspect your daughter of being 'sexually abused' by your husband?"

*Suspect your daughter.* Not *suspect your husband,* but *suspect your daughter.* My heart sank and I knew my family would get no help in this place.

"Of course I didn't know any such thing," my mother said. "She should have told me."

"But you were there," I reminded her miserably. She'd urge me to keep quiet, stay out of his way, to sleep over at relatives' and neighbors' houses as often as I could.

The therapist put down her pencil. "Well, that's all in the past now. You've grown up to be a fine young girl," she said briskly to me, as though she were speaking to an adolescent and not a grown woman, "so it seems no real harm was done after all. I think it's best for your mother not to dwell too much on the past. It's best to concentrate on the future."

My brother rose from his seat, his face red. "Best for who? Forgetting is the way Mom's always dealt with that shit—only the booze won't let her. And look where it's gotten her."

The therapist closed the file and stood. "I don't think it's wise to dig too deeply into these old, painful matters. You two obviously survived. What's done is done. Your mother must put that behind her now. Take life 'one day at a time,' as they say. Doctor has given her a prescription; she'll be right as rain in no time. Now I'm afraid your time is up."

My mother looked relieved, the therapist looked uncomfortable, and I found myself as inarticulate as I'd been as a child while we were ushered from the office and led to the ward's locked door. My brother was silent also, his face white and haunted. We'd broken the spell, we'd spoken the truth. I'd been tensed for the thunderbolt that would strike for doing it, the blow to the head, the knife in the heart. None of these things had happened; the truth had not been disbelieved, precisely. Instead it had been dismissed as unimportant. I began to wonder if it was, and found myself rigid with embarrassment for having ever brought it up.

My mother embraced us each stiffly as we left. I ached to leave her in that place, and yet I left her with relief as well, knowing that in ninety days at least they'd dry her out.

"Don't get your hopes up," my brother warned me as we drove back to my mother's house. His hands were tense on the steering wheel and the radio was dialed to a heavy metal station full of static. "She's been through detox before. It never lasts."

"But maybe she really *wants* help this time. They say attempted suicide is often a cry for help, don't they?"

He slowed the car and pulled onto my mother's street, steering around neighborhood kids shouting at each other in the middle of the road. One girl had a bruise down the side of her face and I wondered if she'd fallen or been hit. My brother said, "Why didn't we ask for help? You know, back then."

"Who was listening?" I asked him. There are a thousand ways a child asks for help. But even the most direct require that someone be there to hear.

My brother and I got out of the car, still watching the neighborhood children. *Ring around the rosy, a pocket full of posy.* I didn't know kids still used that rhyme. They probably didn't know what a posy was; I hadn't when I was their age. It was hard to believe I'd ever been as young as this. Or that anyone would hurt children as small as this. I wondered how big our other brother's daughter was now, and where he was, and if he ever saw his child. My brother saw where I was looking and put his hand on my shoulder.

One brother lost and one brother found. *Ashes to ashes, we all fall down.*

When the miller came home with the bag of gold, his wife said, "Tell me, from whence comes this sudden wealth?" He answered, "It comes from a stranger who met me in the forest. In return I have promised him what stands behind the mill." "Ah husband," said the wife, "you have met the Devil himself, for our daughter is standing behind the mill sweeping the yard!"

Now when the Devil came to fetch the girl, he found that she was a fair maiden, tidy and clean. Angrily he said to the miller, "Take all water away from her, or I shall have no power over her!" The miller was afraid and did so, but when the Devil came again, he found the girl had wept on her hands and washed herself clean with her tears.

"Cut off her hands," said the Devil to the miller, "or I shall have no power over her!" The miller cried, "How can I cut off my own child's hands?" The Devil said, "If you do not, I will take YOU instead!" So the miller went to the girl and said, "My child, if I do not cut off both your hands, the Devil will carry ME away. What am I to do?"

She replied, "Dear father, you must do as you will." Thereupon she laid down both her hands and the miller cut them off. The Devil came a third time, but she had wept so long and so much that after all she was still quite clean, and this time he lost all right to her.

At this the miller and his wife rejoiced and said, "Now we can all live together in splendor." But the girl said, "No father. You would have given me to the Devil himself, so here I will not stay. Bind my hands and I shall go forth and make my own way in the world."

—*The Girl with Silver Hands*

The psychiatrist didn't want us to see our mother again during her hospitalization; he said we would simply upset her. We attempted to tidy up my mother's affairs; I put off the collection agencies, giving them as much money as I could afford. I scoured the bookstores for a copy of *The Courage to Heal*, finally found one, and left it on my mother's bookshelf along with a copy of my own latest book, inscribed to my mother with love. Several days later I said good-bye to my brother and returned north to New England.

It was evening when I took the subway from the airport to downtown Boston and climbed the steep cobbled streets of Beacon Hill. Gas lamps lit the neighborhood's nineteenth-century houses; recent rain puddled on the windowbox flowers and deepened the colors of ivy and brick. The night was foggy and carried a hint of the sea. It felt like more than just miles and a few state lines between me and the steel towns. It felt like another planet altogether.

I ducked through an alley between two buildings to my garden and apartment tucked in the back, hidden away from the city streets. As the key rattled in the door my kitten came running to greet me, climbing up my skirt and nestling close to my cheek, purring fiercely. I'd found him half-starved in the alley one day, lost or abandoned, or a runaway like me.

I have a friend who claims that jet lag is caused by the body waiting for the spirit to catch up with it; the two travel at different speeds. That night my body returned to Boston, but my spirit was still stuck in the past, still wandering steel-town streets. I walked around my apartment picking things up and putting them down, touching objects like magic talismans: the books on the shelves and piled in heaps on every table; the Morris fabric I'd brought back from England; the fairy-tale images of Pre-Raphaelite paintings. As if touch alone could assure me that this life I'd created was real, and not just a wistful daydream conjured by a teenage steel town girl. I listened to the messages on the phone machine and let the voices of my friends bring me back into the present with reminders of meetings and figure-drawing sessions, book production deadlines, dinner invitations and love-life angst—the friendships and connections of my Boston life that would break the steel town spell.

It is not easy to mix the girl I have been with the grown woman I have become. The two worlds mix together uneasily, like oil and vinegar, giving a distinctive flavor to my life. Just as I cannot speak of my current life when I am back with my family, it is equally difficult to speak of that world in the one I inhabit now. My family sounds preposterous to publishing colleagues who grew up in tidy suburbs, whose parents were lawyers and executives and doctors who employed people like my relatives to do their laundry, wash their floors, and pump their gas. I cross the border between the two worlds as warily as an immigrant without a green card; I take on the local accent; I can pass, more or less. That determined, street-toughened steel town girl is a vital part of the woman I am now; and yet, like my mother, I am all too skilled at editing her out of existence, pretending she doesn't exist.

I don't do so out of shame, or a desire to conceal the truth, but because I, a wordsmith, cannot find language that does not smack of soap-opera tawdriness to portray a family history that seems utterly peculiar in one world, and is utterly commonplace in the other. What words do I use to talk about my biological father, that teenage soldier boy whose amorous adventures resulted in my undesired birth, when even the word *father* rings false to describe a man I never met till I was grown? My 'father,' a man I shall call Max, is a truck driver, ex-con, and tent revival preacher in the back woods of the Appalachian Mountains. Any fairy-tale fantasies I may have harbored about my true patrimony were swept away like the dust devils they were during my first visit south to meet him.

Max has four other children by two different wives. One is in the army, one is in prison, the youngest has run away and the eldest has disappeared leaving two small children of his own behind. I sat in Max's kitchen, one of three rooms in a mountainside shack, surrounded by strangers with the same face and coloring as mine. Two neglected dogs were tethered in the front yard where dismantled cars were set up on blocks. A television set was a constant background drone of Californian fantasies paraded as Real Life.

I listened to Max's version of my history, as mutable and contradictory as my mother's. In one story he'd married my mother when she became pregnant with me. In another version he'd barely known her and heard about my birth years after the fact. The only detail that didn't change from story to story was the insistence that, whatever had happened, he was not to blame. I wasn't looking for anyone to blame; I was only looking to find the truth. It was there somewhere, mixed in with the lies and fantasies. I left still wondering what the truth might be, and if anyone gave a damn but me.

I haven't visited Max in a long time now. I can handle the poverty, the illiteracy of the mountains, the dangerous belief that in his own household a man is King—for it is just the rural equivalent of the steel town world I grew up in. What I can't handle is watching the children, knowing myself helpless to save them. When Max took his eldest son's kids away from him, the two toddlers were in a sorry state: filthy, malnourished, flinching at every sound. Neither child speaks of whatever happened to them during their early years, yet their actions speak for them: the little boy cannot bear the smell of alcohol; the mere sound of a beer can's flip-top opening sends him scurrying fearfully for the nearest closet to hide in. The little girl wakes from nightmares, shrieking, and complains about mysterious pains between her legs.

They are safe now with Max and his latest wife, or at least safer than they'd been with their own parents; as are a two-year-old cousin taken away by the state when she was treated for V.D., or the bruised twin boys removed from my uncle's heavy-handed custody. The body heals, the mind forgets. But somewhere deep inside the soul retains the memory. Which of these children will survive their childhood? And which will pass their sad inheritance to the next child on down the line?

> *. . . Each night I am nailed into place*
> *And I forget who I am.*
> *Daddy?*
> *That's another kind of prison.*
> *It's not the prince at all,*
> *but my father*
> *drunkenly bent over my bed,*
> *circling the abyss like a shark . . .*
> *—from "Briar Rose (Sleeping Beauty)"*
> *by Anne Sexton*

The next morning I woke sweating from the recurrent nightmare I have had since I was a child, the violence that pursues me still in my dreams. I showered the dream away and dressed, letting the kitten out into the garden to play. Then I walked through the narrow brick streets toward Boston's harbor and the North End.

I passed through the open-air Haymarket with its farmers' stalls of dusty vegetables and shiny fruits, and fresh-caught fish dripping water on the sidewalks. I passed bakeries smelling of fresh baked bread and cafés where men drank espresso and argued in Italian. *"Bella, bella!"* an old man said to me as I stopped to buy a cup of coffee. "Leave the young girls alone, Papa," an old woman scolded, winking at me.

I picked up my mail from my landlord in the tuxedo shop on the ground floor of the building where I rented loft space. Built in the 1890s, it was a factory building that had once housed sweat shops for Boston's garment industry, and now housed artists looking for cheap space and light. The hallways smelled of painters' turpentine and printmakers' inks, of sawdust from the furniture maker, and the salt sea wind off the harbor. As I unlocked the door of my top-floor loft, I was struck by the irony— that I had run so far only to come full circle, had left the steel town factories behind to end up in a factory transformed by art and paint.

My industrial-size windows looked out over the rooftops. I sat at my drawing table savoring the taste of strong Italian coffee, watching the sun turn the cityscape pink, listening to a violin concerto leaking through the walls of the next studio . . . feeling all my senses coming back to life. I had closed them down in that bleak steel town. Now, one by one, they opened.

I wish this was a thing I could explain to my brother, that surviving a childhood like ours means more than just getting through it alive. It means staying open to all life has to offer—for to cut off memories and numb yourself to pain or fear is to cut yourself off from joy as well; from color and texture and sound and scent; from the beauty of the world as well as the fearsome dark. I hesitate to speak of good that comes out of years of pain, for there is no good that is good *enough* to justify a child's terror. But now, as adults, we find that pain can be transformed, like the fairy-tale maid who spins straw into gold. The coin I have minted from the straw of childhood is a daily, childlike sense of wonder that the world is so much brighter than the world I left behind. How precious adulthood is when you've wondered if you'd survive to see it; how miraculous life seems, and art, and friendship, when they are so hard won.

When my brother and I sat on our mother's porch, we pledged each other to tell the truth; we would not lie or pretend or forget. As I looked around at the drawings pinned to the walls of my studio, I saw that I had been telling the truth all along, in the metaphoric language of fairy tales, in its age-old symbols. Here were the poisoned apples, the coat of nettles, the girl whose hands were cut off and replaced with silver. Here was the princess Donkeyskin, who fled from her father and her father's bed. Sleeping Beauty was an image I returned to again and again: the sleeping girl, innocent, vulnerable and yet protected from harm by a wall of thorns as sharp as knives. Fairy tales were a kind of magic that protected me as a child. Not my body, bruised and battered; they protected my spirit and kept it alive.

"Of course lonely or misfit people are attracted to fantasy," a patronizing book editor once told me, who did not count herself among that class. "They want to escape into Never-Never Land where magic will solve all their problems." Her description seems more applicable to television than fairy tales: those jolly family sitcoms were utter fantasy to my brothers and me, and the solving of problems in thirty-minute installments was a more instantaneous magic than any enchanted ring. Fairy tales were not my escape from reality as a child; rather, they *were* my reality—for mine was a world in which good and evil were not abstract concepts, and like fairy-tale heroines, no magic would save me unless I had the wit and heart and courage to use it wisely.

"Just as a child is born with a literal hole in his head," writes Jane Yolen, a modern maker of fairy tales, "where the bones slowly close underneath the fragile shield of skin, so the child is born with a figurative hole in his heart. Slowly this, too, is filled up. What slips in before it anneals shapes the men or women into which that child will grow. Story is one of the most serious intruders into the heart."

I was fortunate indeed that the tales I knew came from a book with old translations of classic German, French, and Russian stories, not the watered-down, anemic versions of the stories as popularized by Walt Disney films, which lie to children by glossing over the darker aspects or cutting them out altogether. In the flawed but interesting book *The Uses of Enchantment*, child psychologist Bruno Bettelheim wrote: "The fairy tale is a verification of the inner life of a child." I needed that verification. I needed to know about stepmothers so cruel they would order a child's heart cut out and boiled and salted and served for dinner. I needed to know about the heroine who climbed seven mountains and wore out seven pairs of iron shoes before she found her true love. I needed to know that fairy godmothers sometimes come in unlikely disguises, or that a fair face could hide a black and wicked heart. I needed to know that with honor and steadfastness and pluck I could survive.

Danish poet Tove Ditlevsen, writing of her working-class upbringing, has this startling image: "Childhood is long and narrow, like a coffin, and we don't get out of it without help." There was no one proffering help to my brothers and me in those steel towns we moved through, one after the other, like gypsies in the night. And I may never really know why I survived, why I finally fled that household or where I found the courage to make that journey. But I do know that fairy tales set me on my road, and gave me companions, and provided a map. They told me that the only way to reach the lands of Happily Ever After was to gather my wits about me and set off through the Unknown Woods.

I wanted to find a way to say this to my brother, for I remembered him saying, "You're the one that got to leave," as if I had won some lottery or reprieve. Yet it was still hard to speak with him. Our lives had become so different that we struggled to find a common language. I telephoned him later in the day, but his first words made me forget these reflections.

"They've let Mom out," he told me angrily. "Do you believe that? They said they'd keep her in treatment for ninety days. It's only been a week!"

"Are you sure? Did you talk to her? Where is she?"

"She's gone back to work already. She gave them the story about the dead aunt to cover her time away. When I called her up there, her boss gave me his condolences. What the hell could I say? I sure hope her aunt doesn't hear she's supposed to be dead," he added dryly.

I laughed, but I felt curiously numb. So it had all been for nothing, I thought. Going down there. Speaking to the doctors. Nothing really changes, except my mother's stories. And at all cost appearances are preserved.

"She's supposed to go back for counselling," my brother was saying, "but you know how long that will last. She's already got half a dozen excuses why she can't go to AA." He sighed. "She sounded drunk when I talked to her. I can't understand why they didn't at least put her through detox before they let her out. They've seen the suicide note. And her drunk driving record. They can see what kind of shape she's in. What if she just tries to overdose again?"

I had no answers to give him. She had talked her way out, as she always did. I was angry when I hung up the phone, but I wasn't surprised that the doctors had decided to trust her, to believe her assurance that there was nothing deeply wrong. The same assurances she'd given doctors in years past, when her children ended up in hospital emergency rooms. My mother's stories are so effective because she herself sincerely believes them. And perhaps they are effective because it's easiest for others to believe them too. It's hard to look truth in the face. To look beneath the polished surface of things. Instead we live the Walt Disney version of life in which the scary bits are toned down, the dark corners are not peered into, the unpalatable is explained away. The Talmud tells us, "To look away from evil: is this not the sin of all 'good' people?"

It is for this reason I had to set pen to paper, to record the story of a steel town girl without the wall of thorns, the metaphors of fantasy, to separate the teller from the tale. It is a tale that should be told, for my brother's sake, for my other scattered half-brothers and sister, for the sake of their children, and their children's children; although it didn't happen Once Upon a Time, but thirty years ago, and ten, and yesterday, and tomorrow.

It is a dark story, and far too often ends as sadly as the ones told by Hans Christian Andersen, the ones where the matchgirls die at the end, frozen by the breath of winter. Yet for some of us, who persevere, who find our fairy godmothers or a magic sword to slay the dragon of fear, there can be a transformative end to the tale: a Happily Ever After earned by a mix of faith, courage, stubbornness, and luck.

Words and paint have been my magic, and like all powerful magic, they are ones that require the wielder use them responsibly. Adrienne Rich once wrote that "When a woman tells the truth, she makes room for more truth around her." I will keep my promise to my brother and continue to tell the truth indirectly in the poetic language of fairy tales, in their rich and potent symbols; and directly, though the telling be ugly and raw and uncomfortable to listen to.

These are stories for the Hansels and Gretels still imprisoned in the witch's cottage. And for the lucky ones, the brave ones, who have found their way out of that terrible wood.

—T.W.

We end with one last story, based on a lovely piece of folklore from our own shores: the Native American "dream catcher". The grandmother in the story (and the granddaughter who follows in her footsteps) demonstrates the same magical traits of heroism that lead to the transformational conclusion of old fairy tales: *perception* (to acknowledge a problem), *courage* (to confront it), *persistence* (to make meaningful change), and the most important of all, *compassion*.

It is rare indeed that one survives an abusive childhood without help. This is a story about such help. May it remind us to extend our own helping hands, wherever they may be needed.

# Dream Catcher
♦ Will Shetterly ♦

ear John Marshall,
My name is Crosses Water Safely. At school, I was called my white name, Janine Skunk. I didn't know my real name then. You always held your nose and waved your hand in front of your face when you saw me, and everyone laughed. Grandmother says skunks are beautiful and smart. She says anyone who can trick Rabbit is smart, and Rabbit knows to leave Skunk alone.

Grandmother dreamed my real name. She saw me in a storm in the front of a canoe. Many people were in the canoe, and they were all scared. But I was not scared. The people stopped being scared when they saw I was not scared. And then the storm went away.

Grandmother lives on a reservation up north. Father said she is a bush Indian. And he laughed like you always did at school, John Marshall. My mother looked down and did not say anything. I want to be a bush Indian when I grow up.

Grandmother came to stay with us last fall. She came because Father told her I was having bad dreams. He laughed when she showed up at our door. He said she was a bad dream herself, and where would she sleep? She said she would sleep on the floor of my room if she had to. She came because she had made something for me. A dream catcher.

Grandmother said all dream catchers look like spider webs. It doesn't matter what they're made of. She made the frame of mine with basswood twine and birch branches. The colored string came from a Hudson Bay store. You hang the dream catcher in your window. Bad dreams get caught in it, but good dreams pass right through.

When we hung the dream catcher in my room, Grandmother asked if I remembered the bad dreams. She looked at me very hard and said it was important. I said not really. She asked if I remembered anything about them. I said maybe. She asked what I remembered. I said red eyes. She asked what else. I just shook my head and laughed like the dreams were silly.

I didn't have any bad dreams that night. In the morning, Grandmother looked at the dream catcher and looked at me and smiled. I smiled at her, too. I wanted her to stay with us forever.

That was the day I took the dream catcher to Show and Tell and told how Grandmother made it for me. Our teacher said it was a good report. But in the hall, you grabbed the dream catcher and said a skunk should be able to scare away bad dreams with its stink. When you threw it down the hall, I was glad it didn't break.

That night, Father asked Grandmother if she wasn't tired of sleeping on my floor. She said she didn't mind. I didn't have any bad dreams that night, either. In the morning, I looked hard at the dream catcher, but I couldn't see any dreams. Grandmother said I didn't know how to look. But someday I would see everything better.

That day, you asked if my grandmother had made me a brain catcher, 'cause I could sure use one. Also, Father asked me to go to the park and play softball with him. I said I was tired. Mother said I was always tired and always in my room and I should go.

When we came back, Father said he needed a shower. Mother said he sure did. Father said I should shower too. I said I was okay. He laughed like I was very funny and said to come on, don't waste water. Then he saw Grandmother looking, and he said oh, forget it.

After dinner, he brought home a brand-new living room couch that folded out into a bed. He said Grandmother should sleep comfortably, since she wanted to stay with us forever. Grandmother said he did not have to do that. He said it was done, and he wanted her to be comfortable. He took a big drink of beer and he didn't say anything else. Grandmother looked at me and didn't say anything, either.

At bedtime, she said if I needed her, I should just call. I could not answer. I laughed like it was okay and went into my room and put on the nightlight and got into bed.

I lay there for a long time, trying to go to sleep. I told myself it was okay with Grandmother in the next room. But it wasn't okay with Mother in the next room.

Then I heard him standing outside the door. I smelled him there. I prayed for him to go away, and I told God I was sorry for whatever I had done. Then he opened the door and whispered my white name. I tried not to hear. When he got into the bed, I tried not to look. He turned my face so I had to look. He said he loved me. His eyes were all bloodshot.

When the door opened, he jumped up and pointed at me and said, "She wanted—" and "You don't think I was going to—" and "I was drunk, I didn't know—"

Grandmother came straight to me and hugged me. She wrapped my blanket around me real tight. She said, "We're going."

Father said, "It's not what you're thinking! You can't believe—"

Grandmother led me to the dream catcher and took it down from the window.

"She's my daughter!" Father yelled. "You're not taking her—"

Grandmother held up the dream catcher and said, "Look."

He looked at it, and then at her, and then at me. I looked at the dream catcher. Grandmother handed it to me. I hugged it. Father screamed and ran out.

Mother was in the hallway. She did not say anything as we went out. Father was in the living room, curled up in a ball and gasping. Grandmother did not slow down.

I am living on the reservation now. I have two best friends, Adam Mishenene and Martha Kwandibens. I have a dog, Socks. He walks funny because he was hit by a car, but he will fetch anything. I have to talk to a counselor every week who thinks if I say everything that happened, it will be better. Mother and Father have to see a counselor too. Maybe we will be a family again this summer. I said I would give it a try, anyway, and everyone cried.

I wrote to my old teacher, asking how everyone was. She said you had been taken away, John Marshall. When I saw that, I was happy. Then she said your parents had been doing something bad to you for a long time. That is why I am sending you what's with this letter. You hang it in the window, and only the good dreams come through.

Your friend,

Crosses Water Safely (Janine Skunk)

# About the Contributors

**Lynda Barry** is an artist and writer who lives in Washington State. She is internationally known for her cartoons, which have appeared in many magazines and newspapers. She is also the author of the play *The Good Times Are Killing Me*.

**Emma Bull** lives in Minneapolis, where she is a member of the musical duo The Flash Girls. Her novels include *War for the Oaks*, *Finder*, and a forthcoming book retelling the English fairy tale *Katie Crackernuts*.

**Johnny Clewell** is an English poet currently living in France, where she has organized "safe houses" for battered women and children. Her poem is reprinted from *The Writing on the Wall*, a journal from Ladies Night Press in the U.K.

**Kara Dalkey** lives in Colorado, where she writes magical novels and stories. Her novels include *Euryale*, a Roman historical fantasy, and *The Nightingale*, an adult retelling of the Hans Christian Andersen story, set in old Japan.

**Charles de Lint** has written many books that bring fairy tales into modern life, including *Moonheart* and *Memory and Dream*. He and his wife live in Ottawa, Canada, where they are both members of the Celtic folk band, Jump at the Sun.

**Nancy Etchemendy** is a graphic designer in California. She has written several books for young people, including *The Crystal City* and *Figgy's Wings*, as well as adult fiction and poetry published in the U.S. and Europe.

**Jane Gardam**'s retelling of "The Little Mermaid," a pointed response to Hans Christian Andersen's original story, was originally printed in the British anthology *Close Companies: Stories of Mothers and Daughters* (Hamish Hamilton).

**Louise Gluck**, who hails from New York City, has won many awards for her poetry, as well as a Guggenheim fellowship. Her collections of poems include *House on the Marshlands*, *The Descending Figure*, and *Firstborn*.

**Steven Gould** is the author of *Jumper*, a "coming of age" novel that touches on the theme of family dysfunction; he is at work on his second novel. He lives in New York City with his wife Laura J. Mixon, also a writer, and their daughter.

**Annita Harlan** is a botanist working with the University of Arizona. She has written a number of works of science fiction and fantasy, and is currently at work on a novel.

**Sonia Keizs** was raised in Jamaica and London and now lives in rural England, where she is a practioner of homeopathic medicine. Her poetry and autobiographical writing often explores her ancestral Jamaican roots.

**Tappan King** is a writer of fiction and nonfiction, and the grandson of utopian novelist Austin Tappan Wright. He is the author of the children's novel *Downtown* and many works of short fiction. He lives in Tucson, Arizona.

**Ellen Kushner** lives in the Boston area, where she is a radio host for WGBH. She has published short fiction and books for both children and adults. Her novels are *Thomas the Rhymer*, which won the World Fantasy Award, and *Swordspoint*.

**Tanith Lee** is a writer and artist living in Kent, England. Her many novels and stories include works strongly influenced by fairy tale themes, including *Red as Blood: Or Tales from the Sisters Grimmer* and *Forests of the Night*.

**Patricia A. McKillip** is a writer and musician living in the Catskill Mountains of New York State. Her many magical books include *The Forgotten Beasts of Eld* (winner of the World Fantasy Award), *Stepping from the Shadows*, and *Fool's Run*.

**Lisel Mueller** is a poet who often works with fairy tale imagery. The poems reprinted here were first published in *The New Yorker* magazine and Mueller's collection *Waving From the Shore* (L.S.U. Press). Mueller lives in Illinois.

**Sharon Olds**'s work has appeared in *The New Yorker*, *The Paris Review*, *The Nation*, and other magazines. The poems reprinted here come from her collection *The Gold Cell* (Knopf), which contains many biting works about family relationships.

**Susan Palwick** is a feminist scholar currently working on her Ph.D. at Yale. She has published short fiction, poetry, and the novel *Flying in Place*. This unforgettable first novel about child abuse won the William Crawford Award.

**Mark Richards** is a writer who divides his time between New York City and Virginia. The story reprinted here comes from his short fiction collection *The Ice at the Bottom of the World* (Knopf).

**Kristine Kathryn Rusch** is the editor of *The Magazine of Fantasy and Science Fiction*. She is also a fiction writer whose work often explores the themes of childhood and family relationships. She lives in Eugene, Oregon.

**Joanna Russ** is the award-winning author of *The Female Man, The Two of Them, Extraordinary People*, and other works of fiction; her critical nonfiction includes *How to Suppress Women's Writing*. She lives in Tucson, Arizona.

**Anne Sexton** often used fairy tale themes and imagery to speak of the realities of women's lives. The poem here is reprinted from *Transformations* (Houghton Mifflin), her collection of poems based on traditional tales.

**Delia Sherman** is a writer and editor; she also teaches at Boston University. Her fiction includes *Through a Brazen Mirror* and *The Porcelain Dove*, two novels which make use of fairy tale themes. She lives in Cambridge, Massachusetts.

**Will Shetterly** is a writer and creative jack-of-all-trades, whose family ran a trading post near remote Native Canadian tribal land when he was a child. He now lives in Minneapolis; his novels include *Elsewhere* and *Nevernever*.

**Munro Sickafoose** has written poetry, makes limited edition handcrafted art books, and is at work on a novel set in the American Southwest. He is also a Zen Shiatsu practitioner in Tucson, Arizona, where he lives and is raising a son.

**Silvana Siddali** grew up in Austria and now lives in Cambridge, Massachusetts, where she is a writer and historian, working on her Ph.D. at Harvard. She also creates costumes for ballet companies and is a flamenco dancer.

**Midori Snyder** has published short fiction and several novels including *Hannah's Garden* and *The Flight of Michael McBride*. The daughter of

French poet Emile Snyder, she grew up in Africa and the United States, and now lives in Milan, Italy.

**Ellen Steiber** has written many books for children, including *Shadow of the Fox*, based on a Japanese fairy tale. Her first adult novel is forthcoming from Tor Books. She winters in Tuscon, Arizona, and spends summers traveling.

**Caroline Stevermer** works for a daily newspaper in Minneapolis. She is the author of several books for children and adults, including *A College of Magicks*, *The Serpent's Egg*, *River Rats*, and *Sorcery and Cecelia* (with Patricia Wrede).

**Peter Straub** is an award-winning writer of horror and dark fantasy fiction. He has published many short stories; his novels include *The Juniper Tree*, *Ghost Story*, and *The Talisman* (with Stephen King). He lives in New York City.

**Gwen Strauss** is a poet living in western Massachusetts. The poem reprinted here comes from *Trail of Stones*, Strauss's collection of fairy tale-inspired poetry, illustrated by Anthony Browne (Knopf).

**Guy Summertree Veryzer** is an artist and writer living in New York City. His photo collages have been widely exhibited and collected in the United States and Europe. He is the author of the poetry collection *The Male Whore's Song*.

**Terri Windling** works with fairy tale imagery as an editor, writer, and artist. She has published over a dozen anthologies; recent fiction includes *The Wood Wife* and *The Changeling*. She lives in Devon, England, and Tucson, Arizona.

**Jane Yolen** has been called "the modern Hans Christian Andersen" for her fairy tales, novels (such as *Briar Rose*), picture books, and poetry—over one hundred books in all. She has homes in western Massachusetts and Scotland.

# A Short List of Recommended Reading

**Fiction:**

*Bastard Out of Carolina*, Dorothy Allison
*The Robber Bride*, Margaret Atwood
*The Bloody Chamber*, Angela Carter
*Dreams Underfoot*, Charles de Lint
*The Ivory and the Horn*, Charles de Lint
*Like Water for Chocolate*, Laura Esquivel
*Ellen Foster*, Kay Gibbons
*The Bean Trees*, Barbara Kingsolver
*Red as Blood*, Tanith Lee
*The Changeover*, Margaret Mahy
*Mary Reilly*, Valerie Martin
*Deerskin*, Robin McKinley
*Flying in Place*, Susan Palwick
*Kindergarten*, Peter Rushford
*Was*, Geoff Ryman
*More Than Human*, Theodore Sturgeon
The detective fiction of Andrew Vachss
*Briar Rose*, Jane Yolen
*Tales of Wonder*, Jane Yolen

(* *Particularly recommended*)

**Poetry:**

*The Women Who Hate Me*, Dorothy Allison
*Beginning With O*, Olga Broumas
*The Golden Cell*, Sharon Olds
*Disenchantments: An Anthology of Fairy Tale Poetry*, edited by
    Wolfgang Mieder

*The Private Life*, Lisel Mueller
*Waving From the Shore*, Lisel Mueller
*Transformations*, Anne Sexton
*Trail of Stones*, Gwen Strauss

## Fairy Tale Collections:

*The Old Wives' Book of Fairy Tales*, edited by Angela Carter
*The Oxford Book of Modern Fairy Tales*, edited by Alison Lurie
*World Tales*, edited by Idries Shah
*Favorite Folktales From Around the World*, edited by Jane Yolen
*Spells of Enchantment*, edited by Jack Zipes
*Don't Bet on the Prince: Contemporary Feminist Fairy Tales*, edited
   by Jack Zipes

## Nonfiction:

*The Courage to Heal*, Ellen Bass and Laura Davis
*Ways of Seeing*, John Berger
*The Uses of Enchantment*, Bruno Bettelheim
*The Power of Myth*, Joseph Campbell
*Images of Childhood*, Peter Covoney
*Resolving Sexual Abuse*, Yvonne M. Dolan
*Women Who Run With the Wolves*, Clarissa Pinkola Estés
*Writing a Woman's Life*, Carolyn G. Heilbrun
*Cold Blue Fire*, James Hillman
*For Your Own Good: The Roots of Violence in Child-Rearing*,
   Alice Miller
*The Drama of the Gifted Child*, Alice Miller
*Here All Dwell Free: Stories to Heal the Wounded Feminine*,
   Gertrude Mueller Nelson
*The Feminine in Fairy Tales*, Maria-Louise von Franz
*Touch Magic*, Jane Yolen